MW00883514

2013

For Carol
Enjoy, Best, PL Byrd

LOVE
in the Fourth Dimension
A RESTAURANT TALE

PL Byrd

ACKNOWLEDGMENTS

Love and gratitude to my first draft readers for being gentle and avid supporters, Jim Wright and Denise Colby for the early editing attention, Leigh Somerville and Warren Cullen for their sharp eyes on the proof, Jennifer Boose for the savvy abbreviation as well as for the constant ascension reminders, Brad Zabel for firing me, and Maudy Benz for tying my thought balloons to the banister (and for the Jeanette Winterson comparison).

Jamie Cheshire, because of your unending patience, insistent professionalism, kitchen dancing breaks and 24/7/365 support, sainthood awaits. You are my beloved companion.

To musicians and waitrons everywhere, please accept my heartfelt respect and deep abiding appreciation. May all your gigs pay north of scale and your tips be plenty generous. Remember: the customer is always right unless they're wrong.

LI4D:ART

To angels and poets, tricksters and hipsters, innocents, addicts and lovers.

In other words, to Us.

"If you say you're gonna go, then be careful
and watch how you treat every living soul."

– Band of Horses

PROLOGUE

Some people are drawn to fire. It isn't always a conscious choice; rather, it comes with the territory of being a natural phenomenon, like lightning.

Sparks kindle easily in the dry season of a human heart. Always have, always will. Take Mimi Lewis, for example. She's a most brilliant fire-starter. I speak with authority because I've been with Mimi since the beginning, and although she can't see me anymore with her physical eyeballs, she knows I'm around. My job is to guard her, but let me tell you right now – and you can quote me on this – guarding her is next to impossible because she second-guesses me, even when the outcome of certain scenarios were spelled out to her years ago, back when she could see me, back when she remembered more than she had forgotten.

For example, when Mimi was three and going through a bout of stress-induced insomnia, six of us surrounded her bed, all dressed up in our finest silk and tapestry. (It's not that we're opposed to white, but given the opportunity, we'll make a fashion statement that'll leave you breathless.) And, just so you know, we're not little like your scary Christian childhood prayer makes us out to be. Don't buy into everything you're taught in Sunday school, either, like this silly myth: angels take sins away.

We don't. We try to help you avert the biggest of them, but hey, you're only human. Enjoy the experience. Just know it'll be a better ride if you listen to us.

For the love of God, you hard-headed people wear us out.

Anyway, the advice we gave the baby Mimi was sound and practical. Did she listen? Yes, attentively. Did she follow? Not exactly. To be fair, she gave it righteous and tortured thought, and although she charted a tougher course for herself than we charted for her, it all works out in the end, but not without her paying a price and me losing more than a few feathers. Really. We have them.

Although you, kind reader, may deem this story as nothing more than a series of bold-faced lies, that's only half-true. What's written on these pages is part fact and part wild imagination. Some chapters will sound like pure metaphysical woo-woo, and they may be the truest of all, but you sort it out to suit yourself. Sorting is not my job.

Net-net, nobody knows Mimi's story like I do, and as my friends guard the other people involved, take it from us: keeping Mimi and company out of harm's way is more challenging than playing charades with Helen Keller.

This is the way it goes down.

RELATIONSHIPS

Whether close or remote, relationships stem from a compatible source of energy. Without concise communication, even the best ones generate friction and grind to a halt...again…and again...and again.

Mimi meets the man who will soon be her husband the day after she resigns from a large advertising agency with no plan for future employment. Carefree, but not irresponsible, Mimi is the cat who, regardless of the height from which she is thrown, always lands on her feet. Nine years of the corporate environment have served her well. She has money in the bank, a closet full of designer clothes, and a reputation, as in 'Stop smiling so much. It intimidates your co-workers.' The gig is up after her boss expressed that strange sentiment in yesterday's evaluation. Mimi decides to always work for people who appreciate a sincere smile.

It's early spring. The sun is pale and thin, but the air is warm. Mimi is comfortably dressed in paddock boots, worn breeches and a dark green jacket, her long brown hair pulled back from a naturally attractive, minimally made up face. She has just spent the first morning of unemployment mudding around in wet pastures, playing with a herd of easy mares and skipping, long-legged foals. To Mimi, the scent of all things horse is divine. Earthy, sensuous. No need to rush home for a shower before meeting a friend for lunch. Mimi believes that what she likes, everyone likes. She overflows with confidence, regardless of how often she's been judged for her lack of decorum. Mimi is sophisticated in a wacky sort of way; organically chi-chi, athletically sexy.

The wine flows freely on the first warm patio day at

Steeles, a tiny bistro known for large pours. Mimi quaffs the house chardonnay, smokes Spirits and listens to Jessie, a new acquaintance who talks without breathing, weaving one topic to another without needle and thread. Mimi doesn't care. She's on leave from high anxiety, peacefully out of her mind. She leans back in her chair, turns her face toward the skinny rays of sun, and closes her eyes.

"Wake up Mimi, damn it! Did you hear me?" Jessie is animated. "Check him out," she says, jerking her head north toward the front door. "There's the man you need to meet, right there."

Mimi pushes a loose strand of hair from her face, yawns, and sits up in her chair. "Where?" She follows Jessie's glance and smiles. "Oh, yeah. Look at those calves. He's got legs. You know him?"

"I've known him for years," says Jessie, "but we've only spoken a few times. Sam Killian. He owns this restaurant. He dated a friend of mine briefly, but they broke up a few months ago. I haven't seen him for awhile; wonder where he's been...do you want to meet him? Let's call him over."

Sam leans against the wall, smokes a cigar, and watches the smoke trail make dust in the sun. Mimi thinks his rugged face looks like a craggy mountain. Great hair, she thinks. I could build a nest in there. "Is he smart?" Mimi asks, and sits a little straighter in her chair.

"Go to the bathroom and check your teeth," says Jessie. "I see spinach. When you get back, he'll be at our table."

"No way," says Mimi, repulsed and drawn by the very idea of a setup.

Jesse leans in closer. "Why not, Mimi? Look, you'll meet a new friend and we'll probably get free wine."

Mimi studies Sam behind her Dollar Store sunglasses. "Oh, as if that makes good sense. You're inviting him over so I can impress him with my barn smell, and then pick his pockets?" Mimi is already out of her seat and on her way to the bathroom. She grins at Jessie. "Work your spell, Witch."

Mimi isn't looking for a husband when she meets Sam, but they go up each other's nose and cloud the part of the brain responsible for thinking. Sam reaches across the table and plucks a piece of yellow straw from Mimi's hair. He smells like butterscotch and tobacco with a hint of honest man sweat, and Mimi has a vision of burying her head in his armpit for a few hours.

Honest man sweat is hard to find. Mimi's last husband covered his own nectar with layers of antiperspirant, heavy with ingredients that hurt her feelings. If a man doesn't like his natural smell, Mimi discovered, how can a woman fall in love with him?

Sam lifts the straw to his nose. "Be right back," he said. Two minutes later he places a glass of Duckhorn Sauvignon Blanc on the table in front of her. "You smell like this wine – sunshine, straw, new spring grass." Had he smelled her boots, his choice would have been red.

Two months later they are married, and Mimi becomes a restaurateur.

...

Mastodon bones are buried under ice so hard that permafrost would be a welcome respite. Little feisty flowers bloom in permafrost, but an archaeologist can't dig deep enough to find loose, fertile ground in a cold-hearted woman.

Case in point: Dr. Jacob Reston and Nurse Julie Masencup bond through a more conventional and time-tested location – the emergency department of Eastern General Hospital, also known as the War Room. Death, drug overdoses, bullet wounds, car wrecks, abused children; the sadness of it all is overwhelming regardless of professional training. Doom, gloom and tears. Julie and Jake work side by side in Hell. They build a safety net for themselves, first through gallows humor, then through drinks after a rough day, then through sex. Anywhere. Everywhere.

But Jake is engaged to Anne, a pharmacist who works at a nearby lab, and Anne has a gut feeling. She knows before she's tipped off that Jake has his eye on another prize. Julie is a petite bottle-blond with size C add-ons and perfect capped white teeth. She's her own toothpaste commercial. Anne hears the gossip; her fiancé displays bad form in a small incestuous pit, a snake pit filled with viperous women who remember Jake's previous girl friend – the hospital chaplain's daughter – with fondness. Now he's leapfrogging from Anne's back to Julie's. Poor Anne. She's on her way to the dump.

From the first time Julie spies Jake, she knows. She whispers to a co-worker, "See that doctor over there, the one with his hands inside that man's chest? I'm going to marry him." Julie's pronouncement causes her confidante to snort. "Dr. Reston? Jake? Get in line, Julie. We all want to marry him. But, he's engaged."

"Not for long," Julie whispers.

Jake's hands are famous for seamlessly ripping the heart out of his former fiancé and implanting it straight into Julie's size C chest. They are married one year later.

...

There are many good, bad, and dangerous men before Sam. Look through Mimi's photo albums and you'll see pictures of them all. Mimi knows heartbreak up close, recognizes fragments of hearts she's broken intermingled with jagged slivers of her own. Mimi keeps the shards in a box with hope of returning them to their rightful owners some day, but she buries the box the night after she meets Sam. Goodbye, Tom, Dick and Harry. Rest in pieces.

Mimi and Sam have good intentions, and love the thought of patiently warming to each other. But karma or immaturity – judge if you must – barges in without knocking and takes over their brief courtship.

"Look, Mimi," Sam says after their third date. "I'm falling in love with you."

"Sam, let's test-drive this car," Mimi says. Her eyes twinkle, the glow emanating from a white-hot coal. "What say we keep the physical on hold and explore the intellectual? We've only known each other a few days. Something's happening here, but let's get it right this time. You in?"

Sam takes a shallow breath and says, "Your mama would appreciate that." Mimi laughs and says, "You tell her I'm a good girl when you meet her." But Sam and Mimi fill that car with gas the very next night and drive the wheels off. By seven a.m., her mama knows Mimi's impetuous nature is intact, unfazed by time, trials, and a multitude of tribulations

Under a hazy summer sky, on a muggy August morning smack in the middle of a lush pasture, witnessed by impatient mares with awkward weanlings, two friends and a mail-order preacher, Mimi skirts piles of horse manure dotted with rose petals toward her perceived final destination, a hot-wired junction box without an off-switch.

"Hey June," says Sam. "Hey Johnny," says Mimi. "We

got married in a fever, hotter'n a pepper sprout..."

. . .

On that same hot August day, Jake and Julie celebrate their tenth anniversary by strategically placing Hallmark cards in each other's offices – a mutual guarantee of minimum contact. Their marriage is in the freezer.

AWARENESS

Separateness is just an illusion; nothing to get twisted and shouted about, regardless of how confusing and tragic it may seem at the time (so sayeth the wily Universe).

When God talks, you better listen. Convinced their marriage is preordained, Sam and Mimi hear God speak from the top of parking decks during conversations regarding architecturally significant buildings, and how the perspectives change when viewed from above. They find God on the grocery store bread aisle while discussing the merits of white bread and its relationship to homegrown tomatoes. They urge God to bless their union every night after watching *Harold and Maude* for the twenty-seventh time, collectively.

God leaves it up to Sam to tell Mimi about his alcohol addiction. (Mimi wishes I would have punched her in the shoulder, insisting she pay closer attention during that conversation.) "Mimi, you have to know this up front," Sam says seriously. "I just went through a thirty-day stint at the farm." Sam pauses. "And it wasn't the first time." Mimi looks at Sam quizzically. "What's the farm?"

"Rehab, Mimi."

"What kind of rehab?" Mimi is dense when it suits her.

"Alcohol," says Sam, never taking his eyes off her.

"So, what's that mean?" Mimi needs a schematic.

"It means I am a recovering alcoholic," Sam says slowly, so Mimi can absorb every word of this short sentence, syllable by syllable.

"I get that part," Mimi says, "but what does that have to do with us?"

"Everything, Mimi. I feel so good right now. I've been

sober sixty days." Sam paces and runs his hand through his curly hair, then turns back to Mimi. "I have a plan and it includes you. But you have to know there will be challenges."

Mimi pointblank fires her answer – shooting from the hip, as usual – and cocks her head. "So, yeah, there's always a challenge. But is there a problem?"

"I don't think so," says Sam, pausing. "But we're forewarned about the dangers of making big life changes in the first year of recovery. We're encouraged to do nothing more than buy a plant and keep it alive."

Mimi smiles. "Yeah, I've seen that in a movie somewhere," she says. Sam's eyes lock on Mimi. He will not be the first to break contact. He takes a deep breath, and forges on. "I feel strong," he says, "and ready. It's over, this drinking binge. I want to move confidently toward my goals. Are you with me?"

"All the way, baby," says Mimi as she moves in for a hug.

"Then strap yourself in, woman. We're going for a ride." Sam emits an audible sigh as he wraps his heavy arms around Mimi's strong body.

Ah, Sam. Mimi thinks you're beautiful and strong and confident and vulnerable and honest, and she finds that sexy. She sings a song of blessings out loud, but Sam, you don't recognize the tune.

...

Dr. Jake Reston – emergency room physician and serial heartbreaker – is famous for his compassion, for his ability to comfort families of the dying, and for throwing a scalpel straight into the bull's eye of the dartboard on his office wall from five paces. He throws from the hall through his open office door into the red ring - the cherry

– with 80 percent accuracy. Jake's day job forces him to engage spiritually while disengaging emotionally, while trying in vain to distance himself from the death and sorrow that surround him.

He fails.

Jake cries at least once a day. He sobs behind his office door to release the grief he soaks up like a sponge, gushing an ocean of high-tide tears before his next round of darts.

Jake knows he must maintain some balance between humor and grief. It's not unusual to witness this type of interaction from the VIP seats, also known as the Nurse's Station: *Code Blue, Code Blue. Paging Doctor Reston, Dr. Reston to the emergency room, please.* And Jake, after throwing dead center, might say to his dart buddy, "Gotta run, Bill. Another cold one on the board. Don't touch my scalpel."

Old women love Jake. He looks them in the eye and connects with their spirits. He sees them exactly as they were before enemas, before loneliness, and taps straight into their juice with the finesse of a Vermonter tapping into a maple tree for virgin syrup. Although Jake's patients are only his during their stint in the emergency room, anyone who Jake has touched remembers him. Jake is a lady's man of the most extraordinary kind. See, plenty of men are better looking and better built than he is, but few have his compassionate demeanor. Few cry as well or as often as Jake. He cries behind that closed office door, but doesn't hide his grief behind muted sobs. No, Jake bellows in his sadness, bellows loud enough to wake the almost dead.

A critical patient, grogged out on drugs, asks, "Where am I?"

"The emergency room," a kind anesthetist answers.

"What's that noise?"

"That's Dr. Reston. He's crying."

"Can you turn him down? He hurts my head."

But Jake does his best emoting behind a piano. On most Friday afternoons, he leaves work and heads to The Dragon, a local club, to set up his keyboard before heading home. Julie rarely accompanies him anymore. Straight ahead jazz bores her – it all sounds the same regardless of how far out Jake drives *Caravan*.

Julie is no longer just a nurse. She is Head Nurse, Ground Control, after recently earning her MBA and accepting a promotion to Director of Administrative Services, Eastern General Hospital. Her office is two floors above and one wing to the right of Jake's. Julie's interests lie far beyond any chord Jake strikes on a mere keyboard. She's turned on by a different kind of power.

Poor Jake. He loves his gloriously vain wife and misses her companionship. He's had only two short-lived affairs in ten years, both of which Julie sniffed out, but chose to ignore. Oh, yeah, and the masturbation episode, but that was on the road and they didn't touch each other, only watched each other. That doesn't count, does it?

Julie has been unavailable emotionally for the last year, due in large part to her work overload, Jake imagines. He was patient and supportive while Julie was in Grad school, believing her need to succeed was admirable and good for her morale. Jake is drawn to strong women. Professional women with Barbie doll bodies, small feet, and big brains. Petite women dressed in designer suits and high heels. Julie was a highly proficient woman with a double major in nursing and social work when they met. Within a few years, Jake learns that Julie wants a title other than Mrs. Reston.

Yes, Julie is driven, but her drive requires an interstate and Jake is a blue highway. Will she lift her foot off the pedal? Doubtful. Julie is a full throttle woman looking for a navigator who will feed her something other than a steady diet of *Romantic Warrior*-type fusion. Julie needs a *ZZ Top* kind of groove. Don't turn the beat around on Julie. Give her time she can count.

Jake and Julie live in a beautifully restored, 1930's Dutch Colonial that could be featured in *Architectural Digest*, in a neighborhood filled with well-tended homes. The neighborhood bustles with lively children and blooms with lush landscaping – although no lively little feet patter around the Reston interior and the flowerbeds are, well, disheveled; Julie doesn't like to get her hands dirty.

The decor is richly comfortable, filled with heavy antiques, luxurious leather, stone fireplaces, and thick, expensive rugs. Then there's the art. Something about the art belies original, perhaps because the hangings are mundane reproductions that represent muted taste rather than tasteful restraint. Everything is in order – even the big stack of unopened mail on the foyer banquet is arranged by size. The home's natural charm is dulled by lack of imagination.

Jake advances to home plate, opens the heavy oak and wrought iron front door, and is met by a thick wall of stale quiet. "Julie? I'm home...Jules?" No answer; typical. Jake's voice rises along with his blood pressure. "Julie!"

"For the love of God, Jake, I'm in the living room," Julie shouts back, not giving an inch toward him as he walks to her. "Hi honey, how was your day?" Jake tries, he really does. "Good." Julie says this with the passion of a dust mite, but Jake continues his effort to engage. "What are you reading?"

Julie places the book in her lap, looks at her husband, sighs loudly, and says, "The same book I was reading yesterday." Jake takes off his coat and sits beside her. "Is it getting any better?"

"Mm-hmm." Julie's eyes return to the page.

"Do you want to get something quick to eat?"

"Not now, Jake. I'm really into this book. There's leftover spaghetti in the refrigerator. Nuke it." Julie's eyes momentarily rise and cut to Jake's quick. "But clean up your mess. And feed Molly, too, please."

Jake feels like a stranger in his house. But, he tries again. "Do you want to go to the club with me tonight?"

"No thanks," Julie says, looking down again, this time for good. A chill wind works its way through Jake's stomach and he subconsciously looks at his jacket. "Will you be awake when I get home?"

"Jake, please," Julie shouts, "let me read!" Third strike, you're out. Somebody moved home base. Jake turns for the kitchen, muttering to himself. "Okay, Julie. Okay. Excuse me for disturbing you. Don't mind me, your husband. Remember me? The man you married? Damn."

A dejected Jake walks slowly to the bland, dark-paneled kitchen, looks in the almond Frigidaire side-by-side, and grabs a designer beer. He opens the double-dutch back door – the best kitchen feature – and invites Molly, his nine year old Golden Retriever, in for dinner. The good dog was meant as a first anniversary present for Julie, but the fair wife has never taken an interest in anything alive other than herself. Jake chugs half his beer, then walks upstairs for a pre-gig shower. He shuts the bathroom door, peels off his dirty clothes, and places them in a neat pile. He washes his hands, urinates, and then washes his hands again.

Glancing in the mirror, he strikes a pose and slaps his flaccid penis against his leg for laughs and sensation. Jake considers pleasuring himself, but he has a gig tonight. He needs to transfer all that energy to the keyboard. "Hands off!" Jake says out loud.

Jake's light shines brightest at night; the darkness of his black clothes cannot hide his beacon. He beams a broad swath across the smoky club, playing for the injured and dead, for the grieving and newly widowed, for the palpable loss of his wife, Julie. But if one relaxes one's eyes and looks softly through the smoke, one can see not one, but a covey, a village, a world, nurturing Jake. He is but one creative part of a connected whole, the whole being one.

ONE

All souls are merely cells of the same body. There is no need for anyone to struggle or compete. So let's ute, ute, ute for the home team!

Sam used to start each morning with a pick-me-up cocktail, but the days of fresh squeezed grapefruit juice and vodka are over. Never, ever again will he allow himself to be controlled by the bottle. Mimi's dowry includes an Acme juicer and some Diamond Brand Kosher Salt. Downright divine; he marries a woman with the good sense to keep kosher salt in her larder. Sam is trying hard to develop a taste for carrot juice and exercise. If he fakes it long enough, perhaps a healthy lifestyle will feel more natural.

There's nothing natural about exercise to Sam. It's counterproductive to his slouch time – sacred time to dry-drunk Sam. Walk, or watch lesbian drill sergeants grapple for position on an x-rated screen? Hike, or visit porn sites that would make even Mimi's open mind shut down like a dangerous Ferris wheel? Mimi is fit and loose and can walk and talk at the same time – for miles, for hours – without gasping for air. She gives Sam reason to believe in the process. Mimi is Sam's G-rated rock hard cockamamie doodle all the day.

Where will they live? Sam's rented guesthouse is too small. Mimi's studio apartment is even smaller. They visit each other's digs, dig each other's digs, and Mimi overlooks Sam's dirty dishes, dirty sheets, dirty laundry, dirty dirt. He's a bachelor, Mimi says to herself. When she opens a drawer looking for a pencil and finds dirty Kleenex balls instead, she isn't disturbed. Mimi is a committed autopilot; she's earning her black belt in denial, starting at eleventh Kyu white.

Not to worry, Sam says, we'll find just the right house. And they do – a tidy brick Craftsman cottage with a yard suited for a picket fence and an English garden. Sam wishes for a drink, but steadies himself by painting the walls pastel, and hanging pastel art on pastel walls. He has an eye for the dead-on center of things.

Mimi's nice little nest egg frees her to seek knowledge rather than a big paycheck, at least for now. She devotes many hours to learning Sam's business, to becoming familiar with the order and chaos of the food service industry. Mimi is a natural restaurateur; her dominant right brain bends all drama toward the humorous and abstract.

So when she's offered a position cooking for a man who is allergic to the world, who hides behind drawn shades, who rarely escapes the confines of his stifling home, and who loves loud music, Mimi accepts. Just another road to wisdom, Mimi thinks. She arrives at his door precisely at 9 a.m. daily to begin The Inspection.

Each grain of long brown rice must be thoroughly examined through a magnifying glass for signs of mold. Each grain! Zen and the Art of Cooking for the Schizophrenic, Mimi calls it. All greens must be free of bug holes and yellow spots, dirt, and natural pesticide residue. Everything must be rinsed in filtered water – never tap or mineral water – then dried with religious fervor, then soaked for twenty minutes – no longer – in purified holy water with baking soda added, then prayerfully dried, then one more holy anointment, then dried one last time with sanitized towels, each handled with rubber gloves to avoid skin contamination. At High Noon, Janis Joplin – always Janis Joplin – is cranked to the max. Nothing like a high volume *Piece of My Heart* serenade to get the adrenaline flowing.

After a wild banshee dance party, the question and answer session begins. Tim asks, "What are we eating today, Mimi?" Patiently, Mimi replies, "Brown rice, fully inspected, and kale. Also, peeled and sliced organic tomatoes. Sound good?"

When Tim scowls and wrings his hands, he looks like a furrow-browed mole. "Did you wash and dry them well? It's important, you know. I could die if you miss anything; any little thing might kill me." Tim raises his tiny hands to deflect pity. "I know you know that, but please take me seriously. My life depends on it." Tim is a freak.

"But of course, mon ami," Mimi gently answers.

"Did you find the habaneras in the freezer?"

"Yes, and I made a paste for you."

"What's in it?"

Mimi is wicked. "Snail shit and dirt," she answers. Tim is shocked into silence.

"Mimi..." Tim's weakened voice is muffled by the refrigerator's moan. He wonders if she's kidding. Mimi puts her hands on her hips and shakes her leg a little."Tim..."

"That's not funny," Tim says, cracking a smile that morphs into an awkward cackle.

"Then why are you laughing?" Mimi reaches out and hugs Tim, and his small world is colorful for the moment. He is emboldened to ask a favor.

"Will you fry me some okra this week? You know it's my favorite," Tim says.

"I know dear, but it takes four fucking hours to fry your okra," Mimi says, sighing. Tim begs, but does not whine. This works in his favor. Plea bargaining is part of the routine.

"But if you cook enough rice and kale today, you'll only have to cook okra, and it will be ready at one o'clock. If it's a little late, I can wait. It's the only thing you'll have to do that day because I can eat leftovers from today! Can we have okra on Friday, please? I promise I won't ask again for two weeks." Tim breaks a sweat from the marathon effort of making a solid request, and Mimi rewards him with a win.

"Okay, Weirdo, okra on Friday. Now, get out of my way and go work on your latest conspiracy theory. I'll call you when lunch is ready." Mimi's compassion for her employer is distinctive.

Mimi also learns the fine art of cooking for the masses. She helps Sam cook Sunday brunch at Steeles; omelets are her specialty. Always, Mimi chooses organic Granny Smith apples, brie, and happy pig bacon (or no) as one of the two omelets du jour. The other is typically filled with leftovers from Saturday night's pantry. Sam teaches her the value of food cost and the necessity of keeping it low, prepping her for the day when they leave Sam's business partners and venture forth on their own.

Sam's staff loves Mimi. She is helpful and kind, and provides soft contrast to Sam's sharp edges. When Mimi isn't busy in the kitchen, she polishes silverware and makes coffee and backs up the tattooed dishwasher without being asked to do so; she checks the toilet paper supply in the bathrooms and answers the phone, but never takes reservations. That territory belongs to Meg, the front-of-house maven who was Sam's lover before she gave up the booze and left him alone in the haze years ago. Even uptight Meg lightens up when Mimi is around, a mood shift difficult for a die-hard pessimist.

After a polite and somewhat formal hello, Meg always asks, "Everything okay with Sam?" Her tone is conspiratorial, serious. Mimi always smiles and says, "So far, so good, Meg. Are you worried about him?" This exchange becomes their daily mantra. Meg cautiously smiles back, afraid her face might break if she expresses happiness, or pleasure. "Not as long as you're around."

"He's steady on his course, Meg."

Meg almost relaxes. "I can see that. He looks healthy. You're a great influence on him; keep it up."

Mimi brushes corn meal from the front of Meg's apron, an intimate move that Meg accepts. It took Meg awhile to feel comfortable with Mimi's touchy-feeliness, and nobody else better try it. "Meg, we're good together. Are you alright with that?" Meg and Mimi are non-combative, but totally upfront, mutually respectful of the tightrope they hold for one another. Meg tries hard to smile. "See this ring on my left hand? What do you think?"

Mimi grins and says, "I think that man is lucky to have found you."

Meg cautiously chuckles, and finds it suits her. "Well, I like my cats better, but he doesn't know that yet."

Silver spoons dance with forks, and napkins fold themselves into a spiral pattern as laughter fills the pantry. Outside, the bluebird of happiness chokes on a berry, providing easy breakfast for a trolling feral cat.

. . .

Sam and Mimi have a plan. Every Sunday afternoon they pack a bag and hit the road, looking for that rough, affordable gem of a restaurant to purchase and polish. It's an extended honeymoon, Mimi says. With a picnic basket full of sparkling apple cider, caviar, and four-star leftovers, they cruise the highways and byways across

Virginia, logging three thousand miles in Sam's 1971 Bathtub Porsche in two months. They stay in extended honeymoon motels, make extended honeymoon love, and eat extended honeymoon breakfast in bed.

Mimi's scrapbook is filled with Polaroids featuring southern landscaping techniques. Her exuberance keeps Sam balanced on a thin thread; he's becoming a master at shape-shifting. "Sam, look, it's another wooden granny butt," Mimi yells over the road noise.

"For the love of God, don't waste anymore film," Sam growls back.

"Sam, slow down! She's watering the gnomes."

"We already have pictures of gnomes." Sam steps on the accelerator.

"I know, but we don't have a picture of a wooden granny butt watering gnomes." Mimi focuses as Sam, huffing his failed revolution through an elegant, buttoned-down nose, slows down. "Geezus, Mimi. What's with you and all this fucked up southern shit? There are only so many ways to plant a rubber tire in front of a mobile home."

Mimi drops the camera into her lap, silently waiting for her brain to catch up with her instinct. The acronym finally appears in her mind. "Sam, that's it! That's the name of our restaurant!"

Sam shakes his shaggy head. Her mother's right; Sam looks like a citified version of the dead but still famous (at least as far as Mimi's mother is concerned) country music legend, Conway Twitty. "Bad luck, sister. Can't name it before we own it." Mimi rolls her green eyes at Sam. "Oh, give me a break," she says, turning back to her subject.

"What is it then? Granny's Big Butt Stop?" Sam looks more like Jackie Gleason to Mimi, but she never was a Conway Twitty fan.

"No Fuss Bistro. F-U-S-S. Get it?" Sam lets out a gut roar and pulls the car off the road. He laughs until his eyes squeak. "Pard, that's a keeper. Do we spell it out for our customers?" He wipes his wet face and pats Mimi's head.

"Not a chance," Mimi responds.

"Is our logo a granny's butt?" Sam is in the moment, a place he rarely visits.

"Not even a smidgeon of a chance," Mimi says as she snaps the picture. "Hello, Darlin'," she whispers.

...

Julie Reston is a workaholic. She works in her sleep and dreams about work in between chronic bouts of insomnia. She awakens at five a.m., fifteen minutes before the alarm signals, every morning like clockwork. Julie isn't fearful of waking Jake. She hugs the right side of the king-sized bed, leaving a yard of cool, unwrinkled 1200-count Egyptian cotton sheet between them. Surrounded by king-sized pillows as if sequestered in her own private turreted fort, Julie always sleeps in her underwear in case of fire, lipstick on the nightstand within arm's reach.

Julie's feet hit the floor with purpose; she has exactly two hours fifteen minutes to prepare for work, and is extremely methodical in her approach. Simple basic needs are taken care of first, including plugging in the hot rollers, before the real show begins at precisely 5:20 a.m.

She takes a twenty-minute shower, then pat dries every square inch of her body before applying Yves Saint Laurent Paris oil, then powder – but powder only to the places that don't show. Never deodorant. Julie is one cool customer. She smokes a cigarette and reads *Vanity Fair* while allowing the oil to soak into her evenly tanned skin, giving the oil time to seep beneath the surface before putting on her mid-knee length Chanel suit. Julie is not an Armani girl. Too hip. She prefers the classic look of Coco. Today's suit is Power Red with black trim and gold buttons, accompanied by a complete set of gold and onyx jewelry, sheer natural hose, and black three-inch patent leather heels, increasing her diminutive height to a more noticeable five feet five inches. Julie unwinds the turban from her shoulder-length dyed blonde hair and methodically brushes her mane fifty times. Adept from years of managing the same classic hairstyle, it takes her less than three minutes to place eighteen hot rollers in their designated spots. Her hair has been trained to fall into place without resistance, to suck it up and take the heat, much like little Christian soldiers marching off to war.

Julie uses a steel gray Halliburton briefcase with custom inserts as her makeup kit. Although a natural beauty, Julie prefers a heavy mask. She frowns at her reflection in the mirror while paying special attention to the raccoon-like dark circles under her eyes. Concealer first, Julie thinks, lots of concealer. With a dancer's concentration and rhythm, Julie pat-pat-pats until she is confidently concealed, and then she pulls the natural tan liquid base from its compartment – without looking down. The base coat begins at the top of her throat and is applied with easy strokes of the sponge over her chin and upward, ever upward, smooth and steady like a veteran Ringling Brothers clown. Now, a dusting of powder to remove shine and set the base – a very rapid, yet gentle procedure, much like powdering a baby's behind. Now, blush. Julie moves surgically, but without an assistant to hand her the proper tools. She prefers working alone. Two tones here, one to enhance her cheekbones, the other to provide the illusion of shadow in the hollows underneath. She pauses. My eyes, she ponders; must not draw attention to my eyes, as they look as tired as they feel. She chooses charcoal and paints a very thin line from the outside in, stopping just short of her eye's iris on both top and bottom. Her palette of shadows gives her pause as well. She chooses light beige for the inside corners, barely gray for her lids, and Confederate gray above. Julie pauses once again. She plucks two stray eyebrows invisible to the normal naked eye, but Julie is a scrutinizer; has been since birth.

Mascara mascara mascara mascara and careful and rhythmic and stroking and four coats. Now, the coup de grace: Long Lasting Lip Liner by Lancôme, blood red, followed by blood red long lasting lipstick applied with a brush. Blot, reapply. Blot, reapply. Blot, done.

Of course, blood red fingernails.

Julie opens the bathroom window, removes the cold rollers, reaches for the large aerosol ozone-layer-be-damned can, flips her hair upside down, and sprays with the power of a fire hose. She stands up, pats the rebellious strands in their proper place, closes the window and leaves the bathroom at exactly 7:10 a.m. without a second glance. As she walks into the kitchen, Jake looks up from the newspaper and greets his beautiful, albeit stiff wife. "Good morning, Love," he says. "Sleep well?"

"No Jake, I never sleep well." Julie opens the pantry door, grabs an energy bar, and slams it shut.

"What about the Ambien? Isn't it helping?" Jake drops the paper on the counter and pats Julie on the ass as she stalks past him.

Julie snorts and pushes his hand away. "Ambien, schmambien. It gives me bad dreams. I'd rather stay awake." She stacks the scattered newspaper into a neat pile, and tucks in her blouse. Jake reaches for a mug. "Coffee? It's half-caff, the way you like it." Julie wrinkles her nose. "No thanks. I'll get some at work."

Jake, a born optimist, makes easy morning conversation. "Have you seen the Business Report?" Julie abruptly returns his simple question with a snarl. "Jake, where have I been?"

"Putting on your game face," he answers, remaining calm.

"Cute." Julie smirks.

"Yes you are," Jake says as he looks above his reading glasses at Julie, who is looking at herself in the kitchen mirror, checking for flaws and finding only perfection. "Tell me about it in thirty seconds or less," she demands.

"Somebody bought the club." Now he has her attention. She checks her profile, finds it acceptable, then turns from her reflection. "Who?"

"Sam and Mimi Killian. They're from here, it says. Newlyweds." Jake ponders the change of ownership for a moment, tilting his head in thought.

"Save the article for me. I'll read it tonight when I get home." Julie flips her hair one more time, then purposefully feels for AWOL members escaping the helmet. Not finding a hair out of place, she picks up her black patent and gold-trimmed purse and strides her exit, heels typing sixteen quick, short goodbyes across the parquet floor.

"I hope they like jazz," Jake wishes out loud. Hand on the door, Julie stops, turns to Jake, and answers, "I hope they turn it into a beach music shag club and get some decent bartenders in there. Jazz is dead, Jake. I need some sand under my feet."

"Bite your tongue, woman!" Jake jumps off the bar stool, catching Julie around the waist as she opens the door. "A kiss, perhaps, before leaving?"

Julie frowns and says, "Just don't mess up my lipstick." He brushes her made-up cheekbone as she turns her face from him.

"How about meeting me for lunch? I'll order from Thorn Thai and bring it to your office," Jake says.

"I don't know. I'll call you."

"Oh, come on, Jules."

"I have meetings all day, Jake. I said I'll call you," Julie snips, and closes the front door without a sound.

She never does.

Jake slides his orange plastic tray down the gray steel cafeteria line, smiling and joking with the service staff. He calls each woman by name, and they beam brilliant smiles directly into his eyes, so bright they blind his vision. All of them, regardless of age, are in love with Jake, but not because he's the best looking man walking through their territory; no, no. They love him because he looks inside. He feels their fear and frustration, their toothaches, their family difficulties, yet never probes for details or gossip. These women are mothers who offer Jake a big collective bosom full of warmth and adoration.

Jake's vegetable plate is filled to overflowing. Mashed potatoes with gravy slop into his turnip greens which slop into his pintos. The extra-large corner piece of crusty cornbread from the fresh batch goes to Jake, along with a secret stash of homemade chow-chow. Pity the next man in line who receives only half as much food for the same price. He couldn't give these women as much as Jake does even if he writes them a personal check for one hundred dollars and *lawd*, don't let him ask for any of that chow-chow. Jake's women watch him walk the line. "I swear that Dr. Reston, he's one fine man. Umm-hmmm, I could sop him up with a biscuit."

"Forget your biscuit. Your ass is a biscuit."

"He likes molasses, I can tell."

"Yeah he does, but not like you sayin'. That Dr. Reston, now, he's a true child of God."

"Well, I'll sing in his holy choir anytime he asks me to. Here, take him some of this cobbler. Put some ice cream on it."

Jake eats another nutritious and delicious hospital meal alone, at least to the naked eye. But be very still. If you're quiet enough, you might tune out the cacophony of loud voices magnified by bad acoustics and hear the heavenly music that surrounds him. Jake is never alone. He is cradled by a holy choir of invisible angels. He rocks in the cradle of love.

THOUGHT

Those who wish to energize need only direct their thoughts toward the desired target. Think about it.

Sam Killian is restless and extremely tired of road trips. His is the type of restlessness requiring a couch, television and remote control. Mimi's enthusiasm is his only motivating factor. Sam makes the mistake of whining one time, really winding out a high-pitched and childish whine, and within minutes Mimi appears wearing a "No Whining Please" button on her baseball cap. Enough said.

It's Sunday – road trip day. Only this day, Mimi has a surprise for Sam. They are heading to the mountains for romance and relaxation, sans touring, sans Polaroid. Mimi has booked a suite at the intimate Emerald Cove Resort and Spa. She's in total control while driving, and glides through the serpentines of Skyline Drive as if piloting a jet. Sam's nauseous; he doesn't like to fly.

The Emerald's owner, Robere, isn't French, but drops the "t" in favor of the "e" as homage to a childhood fantasy, adding a touch of flair to his naturally Gay Paris spirit. Robere welcomes Sam and Mimi, and offers them a personally guided tour of his paradise. The fourteen suites are galleries of jewel-toned velvet quilts, original oils, and expensive pottery. Each has a private courtyard connecting to a garden path. "A most incredible milieu for creative meditation, non?" says Sam in his best French designer impression. Not one room has a television, but all are wired for exquisite sound. "I don't believe in pabulum for the masses," says Robere.

Robere encourages Sam and Mimi to join the other

guests for drinks at five p.m. Making no firm commitment, they are free to conjoin instead under a ceiling of amethyst, in the realm of pure energy, and breathe in perfect rhythm and keep perfect timeless time, although Sam always closes his eyes in a thwarted effort to dispel psychic interlopers.

Morning comes too soon. "Hello, lovebirds," Robere chirps as Mimi opens the door. "I assume all is well here? You look rested and ready for breakfast." He hands Mimi a basket filled with warm croissants as he carries a pot of coffee to the side table.

"Amazing anyone in the inn is rested, considering Mimi's excitement over your CD collection," Sam says, grimacing.

Mimi declines coffee; Robere pours two large mugs and hands one to Sam. He pirouettes slightly, turns to Mimi and asks, "What did you discover that suits you, Mimi?"

"Your entire collection, but especially Al Dimeola's Elegant Gypsy," says Mimi. "It's one of my all-time favorites."

"She danced for a solid hour, Robere," says Sam, with just a touch of whine in his voice. "I hope our neighbors didn't complain."

"No worries, Sam. The rooms are soundproof," assures Robere.

"Well! See, Sam? I can dime the volume!"

"Not without splitting my head in two. Robere, do you sell earplugs?"

"I'll dance naked tonight," Mimi laughs. "You won't hear a thing."

"Sounds like you two will need a nap this afternoon," says Robere, winking. "Do you have plans for today?"

"I don't want to be a pest," says Sam slowly, "but may

I see your kitchen?"

"Sure, Sam, "says Robere, "but the guys are in the middle of prepping lunch. I'm sure it's a mess."

"He's a pro, Robere," says Mimi. "He'll stay out of harm's way."

Robere claps his hands together. "Really, Sam? Are you a chef? We're in need of a chef."

"Mostly just an owner now," says Sam, "but I've worked around."

"Don't be so humble, Sam," Mimi says. "You're incredible."

"Well." Robere gestures toward the door. "Shall we go right now?"

"Sure," says Sam, grabbing a croissant. "May I come, too?" asks Mimi, already following them out the door. She's not waiting for permission.

Robere clips along the garden path, and through a hidden private gate leading to the kitchen patio and back door. "May I ask what restaurant?"

"It's a little eighty-four seater called Steeles," says Sam.

"I know that place!" Status-conscious Robere becomes more attentive; Sam's value is now clear. "One of my guys worked there back in the mid-eighties, I think."

"Before my time," Sam says. "I was working in New York then."

Mimi examines the huge herb pots outside the kitchen door; she rubs her hands across a bush of thyme to freshen the air, and closes her eyes. Sam frowns and whispers, "Mimi, don't touch that. It's not yours."

"It's okay, Sam, I'm not hurting anything," Mimi whispers back, smiling. But, she feels awkward; maybe Sam's right, she thinks. I'll keep my hands to myself.

"Oh no, you'll recognize him," Robere says, politely ignoring Mimi's embarrassment. "He's been everywhere.

Has an ancient tie to the business. I can't tell if he's forty, or eighty, or somewhere in between." Robere leads the way through the back door and into a large kitchen; natural light bathes the prep mess in sunny gold. "Look to your right, Sam. Recognize him?" Robere hands Mimi a cup of fresh-squeezed orange juice from the cooler and pours Sam a fresh cup of coffee.

"I'll be damned. It's the hippie dude. Last I heard he was following The Dead," says Sam, surprised by the sight of the old sous chef. "He got busted for selling bean burritos out of the back of his van," Robere says, watching the hippie dude slowly sharpen a knife.

"At least that's the story he tells you," Sam replies.

"Oh, he's quite harmless. And very mellow," says Robere.

"He ought to be mellow after eating mushrooms everyday for twenty years," says Sam. Mimi shoots Sam a look of consternation. "It's the truth!" says Sam. "This guy's so fried he can't remember his own name. Watch." Sam approaches the hippie. "Harry, how you doing? Remember me? Sam Killian." The hippie turns around, takes a slow look at Sam, and says dryly, "My name's Henry."

Mimi spews orange juice and Robere chokes on his coffee as they turn and run for the back door, collapsing against each other in a fit of hysterical laughter. "What's the hippie's name?" Mimi asks between gasps of breath. "I thought it was David," says Robere, barely able to speak. They laugh hard enough to cry a rainbow, cementing the friendship through a joint bout of uncontrollable banshee shrieking. By the time Sam joins them on the patio, Robere has made a gut decision. Over fresh berries and more croissants, Robere, Sam and Mimi come to an agreement. Mimi will manage the front of the house; Sam will rule as Chef and Kitchen Manager. Included in the package are monthly commissions, health insurance, and a lovely cottage within walking distance to The Emerald.

Sam sells his percentage of Steeles to his partner the very next week. Mimi coordinates the move, and helps traumatized Tim hire someone patient enough to spend two hours inspecting brown rice with a magnifying glass; however, Mimi's replacement Jenny refuses to touch okra, much less cook it. "Tim honey," Jenny says, "I have the perfect okra recipe. Want to hear it?"

"But I like it fried," Tim pleads. Jenny looks hard at Tim and says, "I know, but this one is better for you." Speaking over Tim's meek attempt at interruption, she recites, "Plunge four pounds of fresh okra pods into boiling salt water. Cook for twenty minutes. Flush down the toilet. How's that work for you?"

"Once a month?" Tim's not giving up.

"Only if you cook it yourself." Jenny will not budge.

"I'll pay more on okra days!"

"I'll play hooky on okra days. There will be no okra days, Tim." Tim struggles, and asks the deal-breaking question. "Do you like Janis Joplin?"

"I love her like a sister, Tim," Jenny answers. She opens her purse and pulls out a small bag of hot peppers. Tim's eyes grow round. "Oh, and by the way, Janis didn't like okra."

"How do you know that?"

"I just know," says Jenny. And that's the end of that.

. . .

Sam is a suspicious man by birth, but he's learning to let go and flow, to dance with the Universe instead of fighting so hard to remain seated. Mimi tells him the Emerald Inn stint will be a short-term test of their ability to maintain love and respect under intense working conditions. "Better to find out now, Sam, before we buy something." She says they will succeed. Sam knows Mimi's right, knows that his itch for a shot of vodka – right now – will pass. In less than six months, Sam has married, moved twice, and changed jobs, all in the name of Love. He is the walking example of textbook AA no-no's. Uh-oh. God grant him.

Sam and Mimi are headline news in Emerald Cove. The entire town dresses in church clothes and turns out for The Emerald's inaugural Sunday brunch. In less than two hours, Sam, the hippie and Warren, a young apprentice with high aspirations, whip out seventy-five stellar orders of Eggs Benedict, forty perfect brie and apple omelets, and fifteen orders of mountain trout stuffed with lump crabmeat. Robere wisely stays in his private quarters, drinking champagne and talking anxiously on the telephone, until brunch is over. Mimi tries to disguise the wait staff's lack of fine dining experience, but she can't turn chicken shit into chicken salad overnight.

"Sweet or unsweet?" they smack, approaching a table with two plastic pitchers filled with tea. Against all odds, these people can chew gum and walk at the same time. "Want more butter? Hey, let her borrow your butter," they say, reaching across three customers for the bowl. "Her bread's gettin' cold and you know how hard this real stuff is to spread. I like margarine better for its spreadin' properties." To the unfortunate customer harboring a visible golf ball sized goiter on his neck, a server gives this medical advice: "Sir, you better get that lump checked out. My mama had one just like that, only bigger. Turned out to be a boil. You wouldn't believe the pus that came outta that thing – woulda filled your coffee cup. Smell alone about knocked me over. By the time we got her to the hospital, she had red streaks runnin' down her neck." Look at that. The nice man left her a dollar.

Warren, a local community school student earning his GED, works as a dishwasher during the week, but had been recruited for table service this Sunday; Mimi summons him to the kitchen. "Ma'am? What'd I do wrong, Miz Killian?"

"Spit your gum into this napkin, Warren," orders Mimi. "And see that sink over there? Wash your hands right this minute." Mimi snaps, overwhelmed by the smell of chicken shit. Warren's gum tried and failed to disguise the smell of a morning forty-ounce. The kid wants to be sober. He wants to impress. A little direction and nurturing might carry him down the right road, Mimi thinks as she studies Warren's elegant face. There's a vulnerability exuding from Warren; even jaded Sam has taken a liking to him.

"Mary Lu, wipe that sauce off your face. Never eat leftovers from anyone's plate. You don't know what kind of contagious disease they might have. Keep moving, people. It's a new day! What's the matter, Jane?" Mimi needs oxygen.

"I cain't do this, Miz Killian."

Mimi puts her hands on Jane's shoulders and gives her a little shake. "Yes you can, Jane. The customers love you. Stop crying now. Please, honey, you're doing great – better than anyone else!" Mimi attempts to comfort Jane with a couple of coos, but it sounds more like she's choking on a lie.

"No, I cain't do it. I'm worse than anybody. I gotta go I just gotta go I gotta go right now, okay? I gotta go I gotta go Lord. I gotta go. I cain't do this one more minute I swear I cain't." Jane is beyond hope.

"Oh Jane, please, Jane please, no Jane, please, just another hour and it will be over. Hang in there Jane. I'll give you an extra twenty bucks if you just stay."

Sam turns from the hot stove and yells, "Mimi, get her the hell out of my kitchen! Keep them all away from me, dammit, or I swear this knife is going up somebody's ass!" Jane throws Mimi her apron and runs for the door.

"Chill, Sam, they're doing the best they can," Mimi sighs. Covered in invisible chicken shit that, thankfully, only she can smell, she heads back into the make-shift dining room where customers are cleaning their plates. Back of House, one; Front of House, zero. But who's keeping score?

Robere can't stand it anymore. High on too much champagne and an overdose of anxiety, he enters the din of activity, crow-hops to the edge of a black baby grand piano, and awkwardly sprawls across it. People everywhere! Who are these heathens? They eat from card tables in The Emerald's sitting room, spill coffee on his antique Turkish rugs, leave sticky fingerprints on his matched pair of flawless 18th century French mirrors. He shrinks under the weight of his hair-trigger madness. Despite his experience in the service industry – or because of it – Robere hates people. Unwrapping his pretty package reveals a messy interior.

Mimi glides to him and gently, as if calming a stray, tames him back into his cage – a palatial suite at the far end of a well-appointed first floor hall. Thank God, no stairs, thinks Mimi. Robere hates Mimi at that moment. She has rearranged all of his furniture to accommodate the brunch crowd, and her seating chart works. "This is beginner's luck," snips Robere loudly as Mimi guides him down the hall. "You know nothing about this business, Mimi." He jerks away from her arm, staggers across the threshold and, behind the slammed door, screeches, "I want these people out of my house immediately."

"Robere, calm down. It's almost over, and you'll see how successful this day has been when we run the numbers for you. Just rest now. Sam will call you in an hour or so." No response. "Robere, are you alright in there? I'm leaving." Robere yanks the door open, lunges at Mimi, and grabs her shoulders. His hands are ice on her bare skin. "Meet me in the library in fifteen minutes." He is suddenly stone cold sober. "And be prepared to go home. You have destroyed my reputation in this community with your amateurish style!" Robere is overwrought with bantam aggression. Mimi backs toward the center of the hall. "Are you sure this can't wait until tomorrow?" she asks.

Robere wipes spittle from the corner of his mouth, lowers his eyes, and twists the kinks from his neck; only thing missing from this fighting cock are the spurs. " No, Mimi, fifteen minutes. And do something with your hair. You look like a witch." Mimi takes a deep breath, backs up another step and quietly says, "Robere, it appears you've had a bit too much champagne. Let's wait until tomorrow when we're on a more even keel. Sam needs me to help him clean up, and we still have customers. Excuse me." As Mimi turns her back on him, Robere yells, "Where are you going? Turn around and look at me, you little bitch!" She hears his door slam again as she rounds the corner toward the kitchen.

Mimi utters prayers under her breath as she scurries through the kitchen door. "Sam! I need you." He hears the urgency in her voice, and is immediately beside her. One look at her face and he's worried. "What the hell,

Mimi? What's going on?"

"Listen. Robere's drunk and confrontational. He wants to ream me a new one in the library – I have fifteen minutes until showdown, and we have three customers in the sitting room that won't budge. They've paid, but they're hanging. What do I do?"

Sam readjusts his apron. "Don't worry about the customers. I'll ask Warren to give them a tour of the garden." He takes Mimi's hand and says, "Just remember this – you cannot argue with a drunk. I'll finish up, and then I'll sit by the door and be your wingman. Just center yourself and be calm." The hippie, who speaks in two-word sentences, says, "Good luck." Mimi nods her head, feeling like a boxer going in for round two. "Remember to breathe," Sam says. "You can handle him." Mimi looks for something to do – a plate to scrape, a server to kick into gear, but finds everything under control. "We're in good shape, honey," Sam says. "Go on out there. You can do this, I know you can. Atta girl, we have your back." Mimi hears the bell signaling the beginning of the next round and takes a step toward the hall. Sam puts his hand on Mimi's head and gently turns her toward him. He looks her square in the eye and says, "Mimi, remember: you cannot argue with a drunk. Got it?"

She sits in the red tapestry wingback chair facing the hall entrance. Robere glowers as he enters the library; she has unwittingly taken his power seat, so he stands and begins his verbal assault. The first punch strikes close to the target. "You know nothing, Mimi. Admit it. You know absolutely nothing about the restaurant business. You are ruining my house with your crazy ideas. The only reason I hired you is because of Sam. You're bad for business. Do you agree?"

I cannot argue with a drunk, but I will stand my

ground, Mimi thinks. She takes a deep breath and looks calmly at Robere. "No, Robere, I do not agree."

"Say it, Mimi. Say you're bad for my business."

"I won't say that."

"You're in way over your head, little girl. Say you agree. Say it, Mimi!"

"No, Robere, I won't say that."

"The way you flirt with the customers – it's shameful. You are bad for my business. I want you to leave. Sam gets to stay. Will you agree to that?"

"No, Robere. I will not agree to that. Sam and I are a team." Mimi successfully deflects Robere's best shots. She stands and looks at him, unscathed. As she walks to the door, Robere flops into the red chair, his strong façade crumbling. "Oh, Mimi. Oh Mimi, Mimi darling. You really are a friend. You really are." He begins to sniffle. "Only my best friends in the world will take this crap from me. Oh, Mimi, you really are a friend." Robere is now weeping.

"Robere, I'm going home now. We'll talk tomorrow."

"Okay, Mimi. But will you help me get to my room? I need to lie down." Sam, standing outside the door, intercepts Robere and eases him down the hall. Mimi floats like a butterfly to the kitchen, bums a cigarette from the hippie dude, walks out the kitchen door and collapses into a cold hard chair.

. . .

It's midnight, and Mimi can't get warm. She wakes up shivering, and gets out of bed for a blanket. With her first step, she falls to the floor and crawls the distance on her hands and knees, shaking with seizure-like intensity. Mimi is living in Siberia. Her bones have turned to ice. She thinks Robere has sucked all the warmth from her body and replaced it with numbing cold. And yes, she is right; Robere has cast a spell. He writes her name on paper, crumples the paper until it's the size of a sleet pellet, drenches the pellet in water, and places it in the freezer. Robere puts Mimi on ice.

. . .

Robere's marketing strategy entices small groups to book The Emerald for employee training sessions and personal growth seminars. Mimi's primary responsibility is to sell sell *sell* all-inclusive packages to bankers, trainers, and spiritual gurus. A sunlit conference room with lush carpet and the latest high-tech gadgetry motivates even the most conservative human resources director to sign Mimi's contracts. She is an able and compelling negotiator with a flair for developing instant rapport with her clients, and Robere is smart enough to recognize her talent. The Emerald's traffic increases dramatically within two months; but Robere creates road blocks that Mimi cannot dismantle.

The in-house phone rings. Mimi, hands full of fresh-cut flowers, quickly places them in a large cut-crystal vase and answers on the third ring. "Hi, this is Mimi, how can I help you?" Robere strides into the vestibule and rearranges the flowers to suit him, cutting his eyes at Mimi.

"Mimi, this is Sandra Holman with Southern National. We have a problem."

"I'm sorry, Ms. Holman. What's wrong?" Robere listens intently.

"We're scheduled for breakfast in fifteen minutes. Our meeting starts in one hour, and we're out of hot water down here. Only eight of us have had showers." Robere, chest cocked out, motions for the receiver.

"One moment. Robere's right here. I'll put him on."

Robere grabs the telephone from Mimi's hand and rolls his ice-blue eyes. "Good morning, Sandra," he says coldly.

"Robere, there's something wrong with the water heaters down here, or maybe a pipe's burst. We're out of hot water for showers."

"How many people are in your group?" Mimi eavesdrops as she moves the flowers to a small antique table by the door.

"Twenty-four."

"Well, there's the problem. You need to stagger your showers."

"Excuse me?" Mimi hears Sandra's sharp voice although the phone is several feet from her.

"It's very simple," Robere answers. "Eight take showers in the morning, eight take showers in the afternoon, and eight take showers at night. Then everyone will have a hot shower. Problem solved."

There is a pause, and then Sandra's incredulous voice fills the front room. "Wait a minute, Robere. Southern is paying you over sixty-thousand dollars this year, according to our contract. We have no hot water. Most of us haven't had showers. And you're telling me problem solved?"

"I'm telling you there is no problem if you stagger your showers, Sandra. Otherwise, you have created a problem for yourself." Robere looks at Mimi and winks. He really does.

Robere hangs up the phone, walks to the antique table, picks up the vase of flowers, moves them back to the desk, and begins to rearrange them again. Less than a minute later, Sandra marches into the main house lobby wearing her bathrobe, a towel wrapped around her head. Her lips are blue and she's shivering mad. Mimi looks at Sandra's wide-eyed glare and sees a storm brewing, a strong storm of three-shot espresso magnitude. "How much money have I paid you to date, Robere?"

"Ten thousand dollars, Sandra, as well as a five-thousand dollar deposit for your next session." Robere continues to play with his flowers, and turns his back on the unhappy Sandra. "Let me clarify," he chirps. "A non-refundable deposit, according to our contract."

Sandra doesn't yield. "Here's the deal, you little dipshit. You send that five thousand dollars back to my company immediately, or I will be on the phone today – and I mean today – calling every event planner I know."

Robere turns to Sandra and puffs out his little chest. "Oh hell, you go ahead, Sandra, if it'll make you feel better. You are small potatoes. You have no idea who my real clients are. That money is non-refundable and you know it." Mimi stands stock-still. She is the sole member of what would surely be a riveted audience, if only tickets were available to this drama.

"Listen closely, Robere," Sandra says, composing herself. "We are coming for breakfast in a few minutes – the whole angry mob of us. After that, we will spend the rest of the morning in our meeting because we're set up for that. Then, we are leaving. And we won't be back in this lifetime; I can assure you of that."

Robere shoots back. "What do you want to do about the lunch you've ordered? I'm charging you for that. It's not free, you know, so you might as well eat it."

Composure, be damned. "I want you to shove it up your ass! The check better be in the mail, Robere, or our attorney will be in touch." She grabs a handful of flowers

41

on her way out the door and throws them at Robere's retreating back as he flares down the hall to his suite for a morning pick-me-up from his bedside bar.

As Sandra Holman and her motley crew of bank execs march to The Emerald for breakfast, they must sidestep a smelly path paved with what looks like melting Snickers Bars. The septic tank has blown and the entire upper yard is covered in feces. The bank's money is direct-deposited into Robere's instant karma account.

MAGIC

To create change, all you have to do is disrupt something; whether the disruption is good or bad is of no concern. We are both victims and masters of magic. Presto Chango!

Three months and three days after the move to Emerald Cove, Robere fires Sam and Mimi for not showing up to work. Robere forgets that Sam and Mimi resigned, effective immediately, the day before. The couple makes one last trip to The Emerald and Sam gathers his knives while Mimi, just to leave her mark, changes the hall flowers one last time. Warren is devastated by the departure of his mentor. "Sam, man, take me with you. Please don't leave me here."

"Son, when I get a place of my own, you'll be the first man I call," assures Sam. "You have the potential to be a fucking fine chef. Just stay off the juice." Tears fill Warren's eyes as he hugs Sam around the neck. Sam embraces Warren in a bear hug, lifts him off the floor and kisses him on the cheek. "I love you, boy," Sam says gruffly. "Now get the hell off me."

Sweet goodbyes are exchanged with the hippie. "Goodbye, Mimi. Goodbye, Sam. Safe travels," the hippie says. "Goodbye, Henry," says Mimi. "Name's Harry," says the hippie, and winks. The Emerald hippie survives although the stone is loose in its setting.

Mimi exercises one of her many options by turning the wheel northeast and heading toward home by the highway. "Our little house is empty," she tells Sam. "We'll move back to our nest, fluff our feathers for a few days, and continue our search. We'll be fine," she tells Sam. "No worries, we're on a fun adventure!"

Sam, remembering the rehab counselor's warning to protect himself from this very lifestyle, is experiencing change at a rapid pace. Is he opening to it, or is he shutting down? He can't tell for sure. He knows two things: he's anxious for home and routine, and Mimi's driving too damn fast. "Why the hell did you wave to that cop? Are you begging for a speeding ticket? Geez, Mimi! You're fourteen miles over the speed limit in a fucking sports car. Slow your ass down!" The greatest progress comes through change, Sam repeats out loud, over and over again, for his own benefit. The greatest progress comes through change. Mimi turns the music up louder.

Four days of calm. Four days of no change. Four days before the phone rings with news of a restaurant for sale just forty-five minutes from Emerald City. Even Sam gets excited! "Mimi, listen to this: the aging owners are retiring and moving to Hawaii! The business is seasonal, so there's time for vacations! A lovely apartment is included in the deal, and twenty-four raised bed organic gardens, and two acres of prime bottomland!" Mimi dances as she packs her road bag. "Hurry, Mimi. We can be there in two hours. This is our place, I feel it."

The Fabrezios are gracious hosts and proud of their business. A tour of the property leaves Mimi breathless and Sam on a cloud. "You two are a perfect fit for this community," the Fabrezios say. After an afternoon's discussion, the cards are on the table. "Perhaps you would like to buy the building as well. Because we like newlyweds – we remember how that feels, don't we, Connie – we'll let you have everything, including the pizza oven, for two hundred fifty thousand dollars," Tante Fabrezio says.

"Where do we sign?" asks Mimi. Sam cuts her a sharp look and responds, "Let us go home and think about it.

We'll put together a business plan and call you on Wednesday. We have to make sure this is financially feasible for us. But it sounds like a dream come true." Mimi is ecstatic. She floats to the car after much hugging with the Fabrezios and sits in silence through the curves through town.

"Pull in here, Sam. Here, the Bank of America."

"Why, Mimi?"

"Just pull in," Mimi says impatiently. "I'm going to set up an appointment for Thursday."

Sam makes a quick left-hand turn and cruises through the bank parking lot. "Why don't we go to our bank at home?"

"Because the business is here. It'll only take a minute."

He circles the building. "Woman, you're wasting your time. Nobody in there knows you, or wants to talk to you. Easy does it."

"Dammit, Sam, I know what I'm doing. Just park the car, please. It'll only take a minute." Typical Mimi; flying without a net.

"Well, shit." Sam pulls into a space right in front. "Go ahead then. Just make it quick. I'm leaving the car running."

"Turn it off, Sam. We're not here to rob them, okay?" Mimi puts on fresh lipstick, brushes her hair, smoothes the wrinkles from her jeans, throws a black jacket over her fitted white blouse and squeezes out a short prayer for help. She blows open the bank's front door and lights up the lobby. She's on fire, and the receptionist warms to her energy. "Hi, I'm Mimi Killian. May I see your president for a moment?"

"Let me see if Mr. Marshall is available. Do you mind having a seat while I check?" Within seconds, the receptionist returns. "He's on a long distance call, Ms.

Killian. But he asks that you wait. He won't be long." Mimi takes a deep breath and plays with her lower lip – a relaxation technique that works wonders on horses, and usually children, and sometimes adults. Thank God nobody's watching, except for that large man in the red power tie coming out of a corner office and heading her way. He smiles. "Hi, I'm Tom Marshall. Won't you come in?" He extends a catcher's mitt-sized paw, but grips gently. He must have a very old mother, Mimi thinks.

"Mr. Marshall, thank you for seeing me on such short notice. Mimi Killian – it's so nice to meet you. What a beautiful office! I don't want to take up too much of your time today, as I really want to make an appointment with you for Thursday, if you're available."

Mr. Marshall lifts one eyebrow. "What's this about?"

"Are you familiar with a restaurant called Poppies?" Mimi asks.

Tom's warm chuckle puts Mimi at ease. "I know it well. Tante and Connie Fabrezio are dear friends of mine. My wife and I eat at Poppies at least once a week. Did you see the gardens? They grow most of the vegetables for the restaurant out back."

"My husband Sam and I just met with them. We're interested in buying Poppies, and the Fabrezios are interested in selling to us."

Tom leans forward. "I know they're ready to retire," he says. "They have grandchildren in Hawaii and want to move there. Can't blame them; mine spoil me rotten." He reaches to the credenza behind his desk for a church photograph of his extended family. Mimi studies it for the prerequisite thirty seconds, smiles, and hands it back. Tom leans in closer. "How much are they asking?"

"Two hundred fifty thousand dollars, turn-key, and that price includes the real estate." Tom sits straight up in his chair, takes a deep breath, and slowly releases it. He sounds like a balloon, Mimi thinks. "That's an incredibly low number," Tom says, frowning. "How did you talk them into that?"

"We didn't," Mimi answers. "That's the number they quoted us. I think they're looking for the right couple to fill their shoes. Sam and I feel solid about this opportunity. My question to you is this: will you consider making a loan to us? Our credit is impeccable."

Tom doesn't hesitate. "Oh, most definitely."

"For how much?"

"For the entire amount, if everything checks out, and I don't think you'd be here right now if there were problems." Tom looks at his calendar. "Can you be here at eleven a.m. on Thursday morning? I'm stacked up in the afternoon."

Mimi stands up. "Mr. Marshall, thank you so much. I'll bring a copy of our business plan for you. We'll be here at eleven Thursday morning." Tom places his gentle hand on Mimi's back and escorts her to the office door; the entire interview lasts less than five minutes. But, Sam waits a lifetime. He's like a dog that way.

"Damn Mimi, that was a long damn minute," barks Sam as Mimi opens the car door.

"Sam, listen to this. Bank of America will loan us the entire asking price."

"You gotta be kidding me. Did you show him your tits?"

"Sam, really. Mr. Marshall, the president of the bank, is friends with the Fabrezios and says we're getting an incredible deal on Poppies. He thinks they've underpriced the place – he as much as said so. Anyway, we have a meeting with him at eleven a.m. on Thursday. We need to formulate a business plan pronto because I told him we'd bring one with us." Mimi puts on her shades, kicks off her boots, pops in a Sly and the Family Stone CD, and settles in for the ride home. Sam turns off the music, disengages the clutch, slams the brakes and pulls over. "Geezus, Mimi. How do we get a business plan together in three days? That's nuts. We can't do that. We'll look like idiots. I knew I shouldn't have stopped. Good God." There's a touch of whine in Sam's voice, but Mimi ignores it.

"Sure we can, Sam," cajoles Mimi. Sam's head is in his hands, and his hands are on his knees. He's trying to kiss his ass goodbye. Mimi grabs a handful of hair and pulls him back to a sitting position. "Listen to me. We've been working on a plan since I met you. You can sit back and whine about this, or you can help me work it out. Have a little faith, Sam." She flashes Sam a brilliant smile, and lifts her blouse and bra above her bosoms. Front row at the titty show! "What was I thinking?" says Sam, grinning. Everybody is a star.

A helpful retired volunteer at the Small Business Center gives an A+++ to Sam and Mimi's business plan. Oh, the imagination and goal-setting; oh, the menu and food cost; and oh, your projected growth! You have left nothing out and I'm so happy to have helped and good luck! Oh, and by the way, schmucks, write three business plans. Present the bank with the best-case scenario, the current owners with the worst-case scenario, and keep the real deal to yourselves. But, these words are never spoken. The expert leaves this part out.

The Thursday meeting progresses with solid forward movement. No stalls, no balks – clear fences for everyone. Mr. Marshall loves the business plan; his enthusiasm is infectious. Even Sam is optimistic. Sam and Mimi leave the bank for Poppies, run through the plan with Tante and Connie, and can tell they are surprised and impressed by the effort. "We are moving confidently toward our goal," Sam tells them. "We'll talk soon," says Tante. "You are just what this restaurant needs," gushes Connie. "We couldn't have found a better couple to take over! Next week, we'll sign the papers and get the ball rolling. Sound good?" Sam says, "Sounds good. It's a go." Handshakes and hugs all around, goodbye for now, ciao ciao. "They love us," shouts Mimi to Sam as they drive down the mountain toward home. Connie and Tante Fabrezio are in conference with bank president Tom Marshall before Sam and Mimi cross the county line.

. . .

If houses could smile, the Killian pad would wear a perpetual grin. Sam and Mimi walk through the welcoming, arched doorway, kick off their shoes, race down the shiny wood hallway, and slide into the bedroom – a ritual that brings out Mimi's competitive nature; she always wins. Quickly they change into pajamas – sweats for Sam, long tee-shirt for Mimi – then hunker down like rabbits in a warm hutch. Reflecting on the weeks' rapidly escalating events, they sit shoulder to shoulder in the red overstuffed double chair that fills a corner of their colorful and softly glowing den. Double doses of comfort are imperative in the Killian household. They eat pimento cheese sandwiches and double-fried, crispy potato chips, not too mindful of the crumbs.

Sam hits the mute button on the TV's remote control as the phone rings in the kitchen, and clumsily arises with Mimi's push from behind. He looks at Mimi with wide eyes and whispers, "It's Tante, Mimi. Get on the other line." Mimi, plate in hand, hurries to the bedroom. "Hold on, Tante. Mimi's picking up the extension."

Mimi absentmindedly rubs her lower lip. "Tante, hi! We didn't expect to hear from you tonight." She covers the receiver as she bites into her sandwich. "Sam, Mimi, Connie and I have looked over your plan again. It's brilliant! Can you meet with us tomorrow? We realize it's short notice, but we are very excited. We'd like to suggest some options that may actually work out better for all of us. We can sign the papers next week after we reach a solid agreement."

Sam walks into the bedroom, hand over the receiver. "What the hell?" he whispers. "Should we?" whispers Mimi. Sam nods and holds up ten fingers. "We'll be there by ten, Tante."

Tante laughs. "Good, good. We'll have coffee and a sweet surprise waiting for you, so come with an appetite."

"Until tomorrow, then," Sam responds. "Bella notte." They hang up and meet in the den. "What's that all about?" Mimi asks. Sam pauses. "I'm not sure, but have your game face on," Sam advises, and pops a fistful of potato chips into his gaping mouth.

Sleep is a distant cousin; Mimi and Sam wiggle and squirm and run through a barrage of questions. Finally, Sam's breathing becomes irregular and the snoring begins. Mimi gets out of the quilt-covered bed, throws on her full-length terry cloth bathrobe, pads to the spacious kitchen in her bare feet – room for a dance party there – and puts the kettle on. She brews a cup of Sleepy Time tea, grabs some gingersnaps from the pantry, and picking up a copy of the business plan, settles into the kitchen's brightly striped oversized chair. What options? What do they see that we don't? Morning comes too soon, and the mountain road is shrouded in dense fog – an omen, thinks Sam, but he doesn't mention his intuition to Mimi;

she is mysteriously quiet, for once, and he likes the silence.

"Coffee?" Connie asks, shaking slightly as she pours thick dark espresso from an ancient pot. "Please, have some panettone. It's not Christmas, I know, but we make our own and love it any time of the year." Connie piddles with the exquisite cake while Tante watches. Tension building, he abruptly instructs everyone to take a seat at the table, and softly begins to speak. "We have looked at your business plan," he states. "It's truly brilliant. Only thing is, Connie and I have decided to stay here another year or two. But, we want you to come to work for us. Then, in two years, we will sell the business to you. You can start paying us now as part of the agreement. We project that two hundred fifty thousand dollars will be much too low in two years and have been advised to increase the asking price to four hundred ninety-five thousand." He takes a sip of espresso, waves his hand in the air, and continues. "See, by agreeing to this plan, you can move forward with your loan and be very ahead of the game by the time we transfer ownership. What do you think?" He looks from Sam to Mimi. Connie drops her head.

Deal breaker.

Thirty seething minutes and halfway down the mountain later, Mimi comes to life. "Pull over, Sam," she orders. "Why?" Sam asks without taking his eyes off the road. Lingering fog and the dense logic of the meeting turn this ride into a chore, not a pleasure. Sam's bird-dogging for home.

"Just pull into this parking lot!" Mimi yells. "If I don't get out this car right now my brain will explode and I'll take the floorboard with me!"

"Good idea," Sam says as he makes a sharp right into

an empty, littered parking lot. "I need to throw some rocks anyway." God grant me the serenity, Sam recites silently as he pitches rocks into the side of an abandoned gas station. Mimi is a tornado of motion and emotion – beautifully, almost violently out of control. After a twenty-five minute rage, the storm passes. Mimi sleeps all the way home. Sam drives very carefully so not to wake her. He's not in the mood for discussion.

For Sam, there is no peace in the valley. As he washes his face, he looks in the mirror and questions his worth, his desire for another restaurant. Mimi, standing beside him brushing her teeth before bed, is steadfast in her belief in options – they will always have options. Giving up on their biggest collective goal isn't one of them.

"But I don't want to do this anymore, Mimi. It's been a good run and all, but it's over. Nothing we look at works for us. Let's cut our losses while we still have a roof over our heads." Sam dries his face and turns to the door, but Mimi, toothbrush in hand, blocks his path. She sticks the wet weapon in his wide chest and looks him dead in the eye. "Sam Killian, you are the best at what you do. You are at the top of your game. You've forgotten more about the restaurant business than most chefs in this town – no, in this world – will ever know. Think about that before you give up. You are the best! Nobody can touch you. And your customers, Sam, think about them. We have a built-in clientele just waiting for you to make a move. It's your time, sweet darlin'. I can feel it!"

"Yeah, well maybe it's time to renew my contractor's license and get back into the construction business. I can make a really good living with half the headaches. We can renovate this little house for starters. Wouldn't you like that?" Sam is deflated.

As usual, Mimi has an answer. "Tell you what. Will you go away for a few days to study with some people I know?"

Sam sneers. "I'm not going back to school. What do you mean, studying with people? Do I know these people? People, people! I fucking hate people."

"No, you don't know them."

"Why the hell would you think I'd want to do that?"

"Because I spent a year there one week; because it's hard in all the right ways." Mimi's toothbrush is as animated as a conductor's baton. "It changed my attitude about my own capabilities, just like that." Sam snorts, but pays attention. "If you come back and say you want to be a rocket scientist, we'll move to Houston. If you decide you want to be a ski lift operator, we'll move to Colorado. If you want to change your career, I'll back you up and help you make it happen. But, I bet you'll come back renewed and ready to find the little restaurant that's waiting on your particular brand of genius."

"How much is this gonna cost us?"

"Nothing, Sam. They owe me a free class."

"Geezus, Mimi. How can this make sense? It makes no sense."

"Trust the process. All will be known in due time. I'm calling tomorrow."

. . .

Sam ships out on Thursday for Sedona. He breaks boards and learns Japanese business techniques and writes love letters to Mimi; he gains enthusiasm and wishes for a drink and sings God Bless America at the top of his lungs in front of ninety-five strangers while standing in the middle of the desert in his chef whites.

Before Sam and Mimi return home from the airport, George Landis calls and leaves a message. He hears through the grapevine that Sam is looking for a restaurant. George is looking for a buyer. His hip little joint is located seven miles from Sam and Mimi's front door. Yeah. Just like that. Just like that, the Universe grants Sam passage.

. . .

Jake Reston celebrates his fortieth birthday on the same night Sam returns from Sedona. Julie invites the neighbors over for a cookout in Jake's honor. Look at my beautiful wife, Jake thinks. Look at my beautiful house with my beautiful dog in my beautiful yard. Julie kisses Jake, stands with her arm around his waist, and exudes warmth. She is one happy woman, Jake fantasizes. Listen to her beautiful laughter. She loves me truly and deeply, seven times deeper than the ocean, or I wouldn't feel as good as I do right here right now, regardless of the number of tokes I've taken.

Right Now Jake and Not Now Julie move upstairs to the bedroom after the neighbors stumble home. Julie couples with the same amount of passion it takes to pull a car into the service station. Beige, Julie thinks, while looking at the bedroom wall; I think I'll paint it beige. Her sex drive is an old worn out joke.

Jake is natural in his grace and movement, his rhythm impeccable. Julie is uneasy; she envies Jake's loose sense of style and is beginning to despise it. Conventional Julie, progressive Jake. Why can't Jake be more like the man I fell in love with, Julie asks? Uh-oh. Who's changed? Is it Jake? Wait a minute, Julie thinks. Wait a doggone minute... I fell in love with a doctor, not a musician. Do I still love Jake? I don't know! I love the house and the vacations. I love my car. But Jake bores me. Oh my God! I'm so on the verge of losing my mind. Jake, oh God. Shit! How does he stand me? I am hateful. I need help.

Julie paces, paces. She paces up and down the cream-carpeted steps six times, just to feel her feet moving. She thinks maybe if she falls, she'll feel something loosen deep inside her. But her brain won't let her body go. She climbs the steps one more time, turns the corner, and throws her body on the bedroom floor. Feeling overly-dramatic and unsatisfied with this unnatural reaction – she can't even squeeze out a crocodile tear – Julie stands, emits a small sigh, tucks her tailored pink and lime green, button-down blouse neatly into her size two Calvins, walks into the bathroom, and puts a little lipstick on. Then she calls her best friend, her oldest friend in the world, who happens to be her next door neighbor. "Betsy, it's Julie."

"What's up, Little Pokey?" Betsy asks. Julie is bothered by the pet name, but it's well-deserved, as everyone knows that in a road race, the tortoise beats Julie to the finish line every time. Julie once was cited for driving too slow, but only Betsy knows this. "Dammit, Betsy, I hate it when you call me that."

"Too bad, you earned it. You're the original slow-moving front. What's up? Walk over for a glass of wine. I'm sitting on the deck in my mu-mu enjoying a nice breeze up the skirt. Come keep me company."

Julie drops the bomb. "Betsy, I need the name of a marriage counselor." Betsy almost drops her glass. "Whoa. What happened? Are you okay?"

"No, I'm not okay. My marriage sucks." Julie tries to sniffle, but there's nothing to sniffle. She wants to cry, but she's dry.

"Is Jake running around again?"

"No."

"Are you?"

"Hell, no, but I'm thinking about it. Listen, you know I treat Jake like a dog. You've seen it. I never cook dinner; I never go to his gigs. I hate sleeping with him. I'm the worst kind of wife a man like Jake could possibly have." Julie pauses, and reaching for a tissue, wipes her still-dry eye.

Betsy says, "I'm listening."

Julie continues. "I don't know if I love him, Betsy. I don't support him, he bores me to tears, and right now I hate every little thing about my life with him. I have to get out of this before I kill myself, or die trying."

"Easy, Pokey; I'm coming over right now." Betsy hangs up the phone, grabs her glass of cheap merlot and bolts down the back steps. She's at Julie's door in fifteen seconds flat. "Julie? JULIE!" Betsy's deep voice is familiar to Molly, who wags a hello, but doesn't move from the cool spot on the floor. Betsy rubs Molly with her flip-flopped foot as she steps over her, pausing just long enough to drain her glass.

"I'm in the kitchen," Julie yells back. "Wine or coffee?"

"Wine, red if you have it," says Betsy as she bursts around the corner and makes a quick landing. "White'll work, though. What do you mean you don't love Jake anymore?" Betsy pulls two slims from Julie's pack, lights them both, and hands one to Julie.

"I didn't say I don't love him. I said I don't know." Julie draws deeply and looks at Betsy, shrugging her shoulders. She turns on the stove vent and pulls up a stool. She studies Betsy's broad face, and finds no judgment there.

"When's the last time you talked, I mean really talked, to Jake?" Betsy asks. "Heart to heart?"

"The day we got married," Julie says as she pours two glasses of even cheaper merlot into expensive crystal glasses. Julie dresses up the swill in party clothes because plastic is a buzz-kill. Betsy ignores Julie's cynicism. "I just saw you guys last weekend. You were wrapped up in each other. You looked happy."

"Looks are deceiving. Didn't mean a thing, at least not to me."

"Does he know how you feel?"

"How could he not? I'm rude to him!"

"But, why, Julie? Has he done something bad?"

"I honestly don't know. I can't stand the fucking sight of him or the thought of fucking him. What's that about?" They look at each other and giggle, but it's short-lived; Julie's face drops, and darkens into hollow undertones. For the first time, Betsy sees Julie's pain. She pauses before speaking her mind. "Julie, you're walking a thin line here. You have affair written all over you."

"Believe me, Betsy, I know." They take a deep united breath, and chase it with a long pull. Betsy straightens her mu-mu. "Okay, here's what you do: forget we ever had this conversation. I'll go on home and let you figure this out." She smiles at Julie. "Oh, by the way, did I mention that Ben is playing golf in Charleston this weekend and Megan is spending the night with a friend? And that I'm yours for as long as you need me?"

Julie looks up. "Betsy, I love you." She says the words she cannot speak to Jake, and they ring true. "Thank you so much." Betsy reaches for Julie's hand, and Julie, utterly devoid of affection on most given days, allows and embraces her kind touch. Betsy squeezes Julie's hand three times, drops it, and says, "I love you too, Little

Pokey. Now, dive into the deep end. I'll be your lifeguard. But first, pour a little more of that juicy juice, willya? And I need a snack, too."

Julie passes the bottle to Betsy and opens the refrigerator. "How about cream cheese and olives on rye? It's left over from Jake's party. Should be good, right?"

"This wine's not picky," Betsy says, reaching for two paper towels.

Julie sits across from Betsy, sipping and dipping, sorting the olives out of the cream cheese, searching for a clue. "How long have you known me, Betsy?"

"Let's see...you and Jake moved here when Megan was four and she's twelve now. Eight years."

"Have I changed?" Julie's sniffles are productive this time.

"Well, I've never seen you cry before. That's a change. That's good! Here, blow your nose." Betsy hands Julie her paper towel.

"I didn't know I was crying. God. That feels different." Julie dries her eyes. "What else?"

"Let me think for a minute. Okay, here it is – I never see you outside anymore. Jake always walks Molly." Betsy chooses her next words carefully. "Now, don't get mad at me. You seem to be more focused on your manicure than your flowerbed, know what I mean?"

"Maybe I need to get more dirt under my fingernails."

"Would that bring you closer to Jake?"

"Jake washes his hands before taking a shower. He hates dirt."

Betsy stands up and walks to the refrigerator. Nothing's left but a jar of pickles. She moves to the pantry and finds a bag of pita chips. "Okay, there's your problem," she says. "Y'all need to turn on the sprinkler and roll naked in the mud one time."

"Are you out of your mind? No way."

"Come on, Jules. You think linearly when you need to think spatially. Too far gone to recognize a good metaphor when you hear one?" Julie rolls her eyes at Betsy and pours more wine. "Here you go with the philosophical bullshit. Are you going to suggest meditation next? Have a talk with God? Keep a secret journal?" Julie pounds her fist on the counter. "Solid, Betsy. I need solid. Give me some direct answers, please. Hold the New Agey crap. Geezus."

"Listen to me, now. Are you listening? Because this is important. It seems to me as if you've lost your heart connection with Jake, and probably with most of what you hold dear. Here's a question for you: when you were a kid, how did you spend your time?"

"What is this, some kind of test? Because if you're trying to prove I had a rotten childhood, I didn't. My problems are adult problems."

"Stick with me here. What did you like to do when you were a kid, Julie? It's not a trick question. There's no wrong answer."

"Alright. I read all the time."

"What else?"

"I spent almost every weekend at my grandparent's farm."

"Doing what?"

Julie smiles. "Making vanilla pudding from scratch, and plucking chickens, and riding Granddaddy's old mule double bareback with my cousin Amy. And playing the piano and painting in my room." Julie shakes her head and grins. "I used to see faces in the pine paneling and paint them. I had an extended family of wood people. Kind of weird, now that I think about it."

Betsy laughs. "It's not weird to me. I had a poster of

Del Monte canned peas on my bedroom wall. Each pea had a face, a name, and a personality."

"What kind of drugs were you on?"

"None! I was in between experiences. Now, of all those activities, what did you enjoy most?

Julie doesn't hesitate. "I enjoyed everything but plucking chickens."

"And which of those activities do you enjoy at present?"

"What are you, Betsy, an attorney? Where are you coming up with this stuff? Reading. That's it. I don't have time for anything else."

Betsy makes her case. "See, Julie, that's fucked up. Do you and Jake ever play piano together?"

"No, he used to ask me to, but I never did. He finally stopped asking. I haven't been in his studio in over a year. All he does is play the same weird stuff over and over and over. Fusion, he calls it. I call it a mistake. It gives me a headache." Julie stabs one cigarette to death and lights another.

"No, it's your chain-smoking that gives you a headache, dummy." Betsy fires one up, takes a drag, and blows three perfect smoke rings. Julie sticks a finger in all of them, breaking up the circles. "This is the way I see it," Betsy says. "You are so busy succeeding with your head that your heart is failing. You are on the verge of a nervous breakdown and the only way to prevent one is to engage your heart immediately. Get some brushes and paint some faces. Put down the book and make some pudding. Hit the studio and play piano with Jake. Do something to reconnect with your spirit, and you'll reconnect with Jake's. Does that make sense?"

"What if I just smoke some pot instead? Is that an option?"

"Whatever moves you, but you should always remember to share with your girlfriends." Betsy and Julie eye each other.

"Betsy, tell me if I'm crazy, but I have an overwhelming need to look at Jake. Let's smoke a joint and go to the club. It'll tip him over. He won't believe it when he sees us. It'll totally flip him out!"

Betsy looks at her watch, and drains her glass on her way to the door. "It's 9:15. I'll take a quick shower, and be ready to walk out the door at ten."

"I'll drive," says Julie.

"No way, Pokey. I'm driving. Be on the porch at ten sharp!"

"Betsy, you're wasting your time as an accountant. Why aren't you a counselor?"

"Because there's more money in accounting," Betsy says. "And, I can think linearly and spatially at the same time; not everyone can do that, you know." She looks at Julie, and bestows a silent, calming blessing upon her angst-ridden soul. "I'm outta here," shouts Betsy. "Get your game face on."

. . .

Jake and the band are taking a twenty-minute break between the second and third set of a typical high-energy gig, the usual Friday night scene at the Firedrake and the Dragon. *Return of the Brecker Brothers* revs up the bartenders and increases the volume on conversation from front to back, from up to down, from all around. Above it all, Mimi can hear the ching-ching of the register from her seat on the patio, can feel the vibe of the register as it slams shut. Or, maybe it's the righteous groove of track two, "King of the Lobby," that makes her want to dance.

A competent Amazon-sized red-headed cocktail waitress with a no-nonsense attitude takes their order of two ice waters without flinching and delivers within five minutes. Sam tips her five dollars. The waitress doesn't know who they are and won't until next Wednesday, but Sam and Mimi agree she's a keeper. Sam is counting covers and watching the dollar exchange with sharp, slow motion vision. "I think bluegrass will do well here," Sam says. "I think anything will do well here," Mimi responds. "Jazz certainly does."

"Did you look upstairs?" Sam hasn't left his seat, but Mimi is a wanderer.

"Briefly, when I went to the ladies room. It smells stuffy up there. And hot. Pretty grungy-looking, too. Whole place needs a good scrubbing. It looks like a roach motel."

Sam grunts. "We won't think about that until Monday, Mimi. And we clean on Tuesday."

"Did you make dinner reservations for tomorrow night?" Mimi asks.

"No, let's just show up at seven and see what happens."

"What time do we meet George on Sunday?"

"Eleven a.m., upstairs. We bring pastry, he makes coffee."

"Decaf, too?" Mimi needs no extra palpitation. She throbs all by herself.

"Yep, I told him." Sam looks at Mimi for the first time during this exchange. She smiles at him and touches his face gently. "Let's hit the road, Jack. I'm feeling a fade coming on."

. . .

Julie spies Jake standing outside by the fence

surrounded by his fellow band mates and a few groupies. A mass of humanity stands between Jake and Julie, but Jake feels her; he turns and draws a bead into his wife's eyes from twenty paces. He makes his way to her and they kiss solidly on the mouth before he moves onto the stage to prepare for the next set. "I'll be awake when you get home," Julie whispers. Julie's 500 watt light is on, really on for the first time in months and Jake, fired up, feeds off her energy boost. The rest of the band is coming in the door. The bartender looks at her watch; right on time. "I love these guys," she says aloud.

Julie and Betsy sit outside at the table recently vacated by Sam and Mimi. Jake can see Julie from his piano bench. He can't take his eyes off her, but when he does, she disappears.

If she sits very still with both feet on the ground and closes her eyes, Julie can feel Jake's heartbeat through the concrete patio floor, feel the deep bass notes of his heartbeat laying down the bottom line and stretching the groove so far out that it echoes and Julie feels it in her pulse from the distance of twelve traffic lights. Jake's beat carries her home.

VIBRATION

Dullness draws energy, decreasing vibration; radiance releases energy, increasing vibration. Think positive, receive lovely parting gifts!

Jake declines bartender Dee's offer of the usual post-gig free beer. "Not tonight, dear," says Jake, twinkling as he sashays to the bathroom. "I have a date with my beautiful wife." Thank you, Jesus, for a weekend gig, he thinks, as he washes his face and hands. Jake strides straight to his car after bidding a quick goodnight to his surprised band mates. The usual after-closing, Jake-centered conversation is on hold until tomorrow. The band starts the jive before Jake's out the door. "His woman came out tonight, all sweet and tightened up. He's gonna dip in the honey pot when he gets home. That's the only reason he'd leave us." Dee rips off a line guaranteed to keep the topic of Jake's early exit hot. "How he could choose his wife over you bunch of hairy derelicts is beyond my comprehension, honey pot or no honey pot."

"Hey, Dee, Jake just lives in that house. He's really married to us," Melvin Witherspoon, the trumpet player says. He grins and points to Jake's keyboard. "See that Roland over there? That's his real wife. He makes love to her every night. Watch his face when he plays and you'll know what I mean." Melvin pours himself a cup of old coffee, and lowers his voice. "What's going on with the club?"

"The new owners are coming in next week," Dee answers as she loads the dishwasher. She has the complete attention of Melvin and the band, all of whom are ready for a second round – compliments of the house.

Dee sets them up, although nobody asks – they don't have to – and turns back to her closing routine. "George really sold the place." Melvin shakes his head, and his expression is dismal. "I can't believe it. Have you met them?"

"No," Dee answers, "but George says we'll like them." Dee is a doe-eyed Pollyanna with more heartbreak stories than a *True Confessions* magazine. She hasn't had a serious date in six years, nor is she looking.

"Do they like jazz?"

"I don't know, Melvin. Really, I swear, I know nothing about them. We all have interviews next Wednesday, though. I'll call you after it's over and give you the low-down."

"You mean you might not have a job?" Melvin and the boys are incredulous. "That's not right. I mean, how can they come in here and rip everything apart? Damn, man." Dee gathers empties from the bar counter and dumps them in the trash. "That's the deal, y'all. They don't have to keep any of us if they don't want to." The register clicks out a yard of receipt, and Dee looks at the bottom line. Not bad for a Friday, she muses. "I think about it this way," she says, looking at the dejected faces across the bar. "You guys like me, the customers like me, George likes me, and these people – whoever they are – will like me, too." Dee's feet hurt. She's ready to go home, and the tone of her voice would send a stranger out the door. But the boys in the band are hip to the drill and know Dee has a good forty-five minutes of work in her. There's time for at least two more free beers each, and if they clear the tables for her, it could be three. The party's just getting started for everyone but Dee.

Melvin folds his bar-nap, and tears it to shreds. "I'm not diggin' what I'm feelin' right now," he says. "Why did

George sell this place? It's perfect just the way it is. He doesn't need the money. Hell, I should have asked him to sell it to me for a dollar."

"I don't know why he sold it, Melvin, but he did," retorts Dee. She opens the dishwasher and removes a rack of clean wine glasses. She examines each glass for long-lasting lipstick smudges, violently wipes the offenders, and stretches on tiptoe as she hangs them in the overhead rack. Dee's compressed back begins to loosen, and her nightly headache subsides. "Here's my theory," she says. "George has better things to do. He travels constantly, stays gone for weeks at a time. I think it's business-related, you know, big business, not small restaurant potatoes."

Dee picks up a clean bar towel and wipes the back bar. "It's better for George to get out if he can't keep his finger on the pulse. Those two morons running the show are worthless." Melvin laughs and nods his head. "That's a fact."

"You know he's never here anymore unless it's to impress his latest date. When's the last time you saw him?"

Melvin shakes his head. "I think it's over, Dee. The salad days are over for The Dragon. What's gonna happen upstairs? Are those kids out on the street, too?" Melvin sings the blues, day in and day out. He looks for reasons to sing the blues. He makes up the blues just to say he has them. And he's on his way to making Dee blue, too – a hard thing to do. "We'll know soon enough, won't we?" she says, shrugging and throwing the bar towel on the floor. She cleans a slick spot with her foot, lifts the towel with her toe, and flings it into the dirty linen bag. "All I know is tomorrow night after we close this place down, we're gonna mix up a batch of Hairy

Buffalo and have a wake." She turns to Melvin. "See this liquor? The new owners can't serve anything that's open. All this Remy, and all this Jack, and all this Johnny will be poured down the drain unless it's consumed by the time we lock the doors after Saturday night's run. I consider it community service to make sure every drop finds a proper home."

Melvin doubles over in laughter. "Damn, Dee, don't tell the band that until late. Let us get through the gig first. I have enough trouble keeping Thomas sober through the second set."

"Our little secret," smiles Dee. She's done. "Hey, guys! We're locking up. You don't have to go home, but you can't stay here."

"Yeah, yeah," says Thomas, the guitarist. "Can we all come to your house?" The band loves Dee like a little sister; there's something about her end-of-night demeanor that lets them know they're all special. "Sure, if you stop by the store for tampons, bacon, and eggs, Thomas. And be willing to listen to me whine about menstrual cramps, cook my breakfast, wash my dishes, clean my bathroom, and rub my feet until I fall asleep."

"Guess we'll go on home, then," chuckles Thomas.

"Yeah, I thought the foot massage might discourage you." Dee hugs them all goodnight, turns off the lights, and sets the alarm. Melvin escorts her to her car; in blissful silence, she drives the back road home.

...

Mimi loves flying under the radar. She loves the element of a good surprise, especially one with staying power – and most especially when she's on the giving end. Mimi and Sam invite a friend's teenage son to join them for dinner at The Firedrake and The Dragon. Eighteen year old Mark has heard of the place; one of his schoolmates washed dishes at The Firedrake last summer. He's been inside the restaurant once, but never in the bar. His parents draw the line there, although his dad thinks the calzone is pretty good and worth the price. They always go before things get, uh, too diverse. But, downstairs? Jazz? No way. Mark hears it's pretty cool, though. That it's easy to steal beer. Ha! Sam says. That will stop.

Mimi plays Eye Spy. As soon as they pull in, Mimi spies trash in the gravel parking lot and three kitchen employees smoking something behind the dumpster and a well-dressed couple walking toward the front door and a cat stalking something in the tall grass and an aluminum gutter in the tall grass and pallets – lots of pallets – in the tall grass. A dead body could be hidden in that grass, Mimi thinks.

The upstairs patio is open for dining, but one has to be cold-natured to enjoy the thick Southern humidity on this hot August evening. Mimi follows Sam and Mark through the curtained front door, but not before noting an absence of movement outside; stillness in the trees, stillness in the dark, hollow eyes of a solitary waitress who reluctantly awaits the arrival of her first table. The music isn't right in here, Mimi thinks, as Led Zeppelin's *Heartbreaker* screams through fuzzy speakers. The front dining room is empty of people, but full of static. An unsmiling, deeply tanned young man wearing a starched canary yellow Ralph Lauren shirt, black suspenders, and pressed blue jeans walks toward them. He detours and yells at the dishwasher in an obnoxious show of power. His curly blond hair is slicked back from his forehead and forced into a short ponytail that ends at the base of his upturned collar. "Three? Follow me." A perfunctory welcome at best. He leads them to the back room, to a table in the corner; Mimi chooses the chair against the wall. "Thank you," says Mimi, to no reply.

Eye Spy: Mimi spies crumbs in chairs, flowers decomposing in dirty vases, and chunks of something that looks like cheesecake on the floor. A waitress, her high cleavage wrestling a low-cut Firedrake tee shirt, chews gum in the wait station behind the wall to Mimi's left. Her boyfriend – Mimi hopes he's a familiar – walks through the front door of The Firedrake without pausing, strides into the wait station, grabs a squeeze of booby cake and a Foster from the cooler, and turns and walks downstairs. Does he work here, or just steal from here, Mimi wonders? Sam and Mark discuss the menu. No cheeseburgers, Mark. Sorry to disappoint you.

It's a funky old building with ghosts in the corners, Mimi muses. Feels like a cheap breakfast diner – greasy with fingerprints, but no working hands. Matchbooks steady the uneven tables, or is it the floor that's out of plumb? The décor is cheap, tired. Even the napkins smell used. But something must be right. It's early, and the place is rocking.

The waitress with the empty eyes approaches their table emitting a subtle sigh. Her posture is suggestive of a window-dressed mannequin. "Hi, my name is Jenny and I'll be your server tonight. What can I bring you to drink?" Sam takes the lead. "A glass of Pinot Grigio for my bride, a coke for my assistant here, and I'd like a non-alcoholic beer. What are my choices?"

"I'll check. Our special appetizer tonight is New Zealand mussels in a light, spicy tomato comfit served with crusty French bread for dipping."

"Bring one of those, please, and your crab dip."

"Yes, sir. I'll be right back with your drinks." Unsmiling, she turns away.

"She seems competent enough, Mimi, don't you think?"

"Sure, but short-term."

"Why do you say that? She seems okay to me."

"She's totally burnt out. I bet she won't show up on Wednesday. Shh, here she comes." Mimi looks at her and smiles. Jenny's eyes are on Sam. "Sir, I'm sorry, but we ran out of non-alcoholic beer last night."

"That's okay; I'll have iced tea, please." The tired waitron disappears, only this time there's a trace of recognition in her weak smile. She knows Bill, Sam thinks, as he scans the room." What about that one over there, Mimi? I bet she makes big tits – I mean tips – sorry, Mark." Mark's totally engrossed by the wrestling match. He's betting on the cleavage.

"She's cute, but very loud. A little too much for upstairs. Maybe she'll fit as a cocktail waitress in the club, though. I don't know. Check out that waiter," Mimi says with a nod to the right.

"Who? The Fabio-looking dude?"

"Yeah, he's got it going on. He connected with the man first. That's one smart player. He's the business and psychology combo platter." Jenny winds her way through traffic, easily balancing their steaming appetizers. The joint is tight and getting tighter. "Mussels here, and crab dip. What else can I bring you?"

"We're set," says Sam, flashing a big smile at Jenny. "Smells good, thank you." Jenny turns her attention to Mimi. "How are you on time? I can take your entrée order if you're ready."

"We're in no hurry."

"Fine, then. I'll check on you in a bit. Enjoy."

Sam digs in. "Here, Mark, try a mussel."

"No way, man. Those things look weird. What's a mussel, anyway?"

"It's a bivalve, like an oyster. Do you like oysters?"

Mark snorts. "Yeah, right. Do you like snot?"

Sam grins. "Just taste it. Mussels are sweeter and a bit firmer than oysters. These critters are one of New Zealand's claims to fame – maybe the only one I know of."

Mimi chews a small bite of bread dipped in the tomato comfit, and swoons. She wipes her mouth and adds her tiny New Zealand factoid to the conversation. "It's famous for its horses, too. Remember that little black mare in the Olympics a few years ago? Mark Todd rode her to a medal. What a beauty!"

Sam and Mark look at her blankly. "What's your point?" Sam asks. "We were talking about mussels." "Well, you said you didn't know but one thing...never mind. How about passing that bowl over here?" Mimi bites into a perfectly cooked mussel and feels something hard in her mouth. She works it to her lips and carefully spits a small orb into her hand. "What the heck is this? Look, Sam, a pearl! I can't believe I didn't swallow it."

Sam shakes his head. "It can't be a pearl. It's probably a rock. Let me see." Mimi rolls the little gemstone into his hand. "Sure looks like a pearl." Mark, intrigued by anything that could cause pain, reaches out his hand. "Let me hold it, Sam. Wow, Mimi. This thing's hard. You're lucky you didn't break a tooth." He looks at her. "Can I keep it?"

Mimi grins at Mark. "Sure. You keep it in a special place, but you have to take it out from time to time and make three wishes: one for you, one for me, and one for Sam. Deal?" Mark carefully places it in his shirt pocket, but forgets to remove it before throwing the shirt in the dirty clothes later that night. To a small pearl carrying a big wish, washing machines are vast oceans.

"How's that crab dip, Mark?"

"Great. Here, taste it."

"Thought you'd never ask." Mimi takes a bite and frowns.

"You don't like it?"

"It's bland. Needs capers. Too much cream cheese. And imitation crab. I hate that stuff. It's slimy in my mouth." She turns to Mark. "Have you ever heard of truth in advertising?"

"What's that have to do with crab dip, Mimi? Leave the boy alone." Sam's picking through the mussels like a monkey picking nits. Mimi ignores Sam and continues. "They lied about this crab dip."

Mark stuffs a wad of dip in his mouth before Mimi ruins it for him. "What do you mean?" Mark asks, swallowing without chewing as he reaches for another bite.

"If a restaurant uses imitation crab meat, the menu should state that. Then I'd know not to buy it."

"Arghhhhh." Sam's groan is a welcome diversion for Mark. He's tired of the lecture, and couldn't care less whether his food is real, as long as it tastes good and goes down whole. Sam is simultaneously mouth breathing and gagging.

"This mussel's bad." Sam turns around and with a hackkkk, spits the putrid lump into his napkin.

Mark's excited. "Are you gonna puke? I knew I didn't want to eat one of those things. What's it taste like?"

Sam drains his tea and reaches for Mimi's water. "It tastes like road-kill left in the sun too long smells. Hand me a piece of that bread, please." Sam takes a bite of two day old French bread to clear his palate and becomes even more agitated. "God, what's this shit they're serving? This ain't bread, it's rat food. Good, here comes our waitress."

"Oh, no, are you alright?" Jenny says this like she means it.

"Please tell your chef that there are bad mussels mixed in with the good ones."

"I'm so sorry. I'll tell the kitchen right away." She removes Sam's napkin, places it in the juice-laden bowl, and straight-arms her way through the crowded dining room. Jenny finally has a mission, a reason to step up her game.

In short order, Jarrod, the round, baby-faced head chef, personally delivers a fresh order of mussels and places them gracefully in front of Sam. "I have picked through them myself, sir, and I promise, they are all fresh," Jarrod says confidently. "Bless you," Sam says to Jarrod. Mark stares in awe as Sam attacks the double order of mussels with gusto. Sam looks at Mark and states, "Always trust an honest chef, son. Always trust an honest chef; maybe not with your sister, maybe not with your mother, but always, always with your food."

Next course: a soggy salad for the table, and another round of stale, dry bread, both waitress mistakes. The entrees, however, are fabulous, and the desserts are made with love – divine, and visually stimulating. All in all, not a total fail, but plenty of room for improvement. Sam crunches numbers, mentally adding and subtracting items from the menu. Mark aches to go downstairs. "Let's go!" he says, fidgeting. "The band's coming on."

Mark hears the warm-up beat, picks up two spoons, and turns the table into a drum kit. Mimi snaps her fingers in time with Mark's moves, and begins to sway.

Sam frowns, puts seventy-five cash on the table, and stands up. He leads, the rhythm section follows. Sam has no interest in the groove.

The first set is underway and the band is playing to an inattentive, but polite crowd. Melvin, center stage with his horn in one hand and a coffee mug in the other, doesn't notice Sam, but he can't miss Mimi and Mark. He catches Mimi's eye and smiles; she smiles back, moving in tandem with Mark. Melvin turns to Jake and grins. "It's gonna be a good night," he says. "There's the sign." There's always a sign that sets the tone for the gig. Melvin doesn't know he just made a connection with the new owner.

Sam looks at the fully stocked bar and silently recites the Serenity Prayer. He says it again. After the third take – his liver is laughing at him – he must go. He must go now, although Mimi has ordered coffee. It sits on the bar, untouched, and Melvin watches his sign make a quick exit. Mimi subtly nods goodbye and politely clears a path for Mark and Sam through the gathering crowd. The Dragon is awake and beginning a long, slow stretch before belching a raging blaze of fire that doesn't burn out until the wee hours of the morning. Melvin's next sign is the one he runs into at three a.m. after doing his part to give Johnny Walker a home.

CO-CREATION

2+2=4; 3x3=9; 4x4=16; 44 to the 10th power=world change; working as a team=graceful ascension to the greater good!

The morning arrives fuzzy and out of focus for Jake Reston. Julie pads downstairs in her white slippers and beige silk pajamas at nine a.m., and finds Jake sleeping in the living room. She kneels on the floor and gently shakes him. "Good morning, darling." Jake moans. She shakes him a little harder. Jake moans louder. "You don't look so good. What time did you get home? I didn't hear you come in. Why didn't you come to bed?"

Jake moves his head slightly and feels a wrecking ball shatter what's left of his brain. "Four or five, I think. Couldn't make it any further." Talking hurts his teeth. "Julie, help me," he whines through clenched lips. "Water. Aspirin. Aww, don't make me sit up. I think I'm blind."

"What's all over your glasses?" She yanks them off his head as Jake whimpers. "Yuck! No wonder you can't see, this is blood!" Julie pushes Jake's head to the right; he thinks about wetting himself, but controls the urge to let go. "Good lord, man, what happened to your ear? Hold still, you big baby. Let me look. Damn it, there's blood all over the sofa!"

Jake tries to sit up, but the effort makes him gag. "Melvin ran into a stop sign on the way home last night after the gig. Then I rear-ended Melvin. I think I hit my head on the driver's side window. It was funny at the time. Then I threw up. I don't remember much after that."

"So I guess I don't have to ask how the wake went last

night, or whatever you called it." Julie is disgusted. "Did anybody die?"

"Not that I know of. What time is it?" Jake asks feebly.

"Nine o'clock. We have to be at my parents' for lunch in two hours."

"No way. I'm sick." Jake's eyes won't focus, but his gag reflex is working just fine. "Please call them and tell them I'm dying."

"Get your ass up, Jake. You're going."

"Look at me, Julie. I can't go anywhere. Tell them I had an emergency at the hospital and we'll be there for dinner instead." Jake rolls off the couch onto the floor, knee-walks to the nearest chair, and drops his head into the seat. "Shit, I can't even stand up."

"If you get blood on that chair I'll kill you, you damn drunken sot." Jake reaches a hand to his head and searches for the pitchfork somebody jammed in his ear. Julie pulls Jake to his feet and leans him against the nearest wall. "Mom has a surprise for us. I think she's giving us the big hall mirror."

Jake's groan reaches its pinnacle of self-pity. "Oh God, Julie, that fun-house-looking piece of shit? It makes me gag just thinking about it." He gags until his eyes bulge. "See? I'm not kidding. Ugh. I need to throw up."

"I love that mirror. It's an antique! It'll look great in the foyer." Jake's gut rumbles like thunder. "You damn wuss. Go on before you vomit in here. Then, you better find the peroxide and start scrubbing this sofa. I'm not doing it." Jake gags. "I mean it, Jake. Get upstairs and take a shower. You'll feel better." Julie turns for the kitchen.

"The only thing that will make me feel better is twenty-four hours." Jake leans against the wall and painfully tracks the corner with his backbone. "And maybe if that mirror shatters into a million pieces before you get it home."

"You'd take seven years of bad luck, just like that?" Julie shakes her head at her pitiful husband.

"I'll chance it. That thing's uglier than the mess I'm gonna make in a minute. It's the ugliest thing I've never wanted."

Jake crawls up the steps, reaches the landing, and pulls himself into an awkward pose; balancing like a toddler, he stumbles into the master suite bathroom, and pauses long enough to look at his ear before falling to his knees and purging his leftover sins. "God, help me!" he cries.

"I'm busy," God answers.

Standing carefully, he shuffles three feet to the sink, and washes his hands. He drops his boxers and, with the posture of an old man, creeps to the shower. He leans over to adjust the temperature and breaks a cold sweat. Jake gags three times, loses his balance, grabs hold of the towel rack and, as he falls, jerks it from the wall.

He's lucky. He lands butt first and skids backwards into the closet door, not fully registering the stinging of the large, nasty carpet burn on his bare ass. He carefully picks himself up and steps into a cloud nearly as thick as the fog surrounding his brain. The hot water drives into his ear, making him wince. Jake bends his knees, grabs the soap, and works lather from top to almost bottom. He cannot lift his feet, so he wisely sits in the bathtub and pulls his feet to him, deliberate movement by deliberate movement.

Fifteen minutes later, Julie experiences a moment of concern when she finds Jake passed out in the tub with shampoo drying in his hair; it quickly passes. "Wake up, you damn idiot," Julie yells as she shakes her husband's limp body. "Come on, stand up."

Jake moans. "Help me, Julie."

Do I slap him, or laugh? Maybe both, she thinks. "Crawl over the side. I've got you. Come on now, you have to help me. I can't pull you out by myself." She grabs his arm and drags him over the side of the tub. "Ow! That hurt. Stop laughing at me." Julie's laughing hard. So hard, her teeth are showing. Only to Jake, they look like fangs. He closes his eyes and sees a three-headed dog at the gates of Hell.

Julie gasps for air. "I wish you could see your ass. It looks like your butt has measles on top of road rash." She steadies herself and notices a new, unwanted hole in the wall which, for Julie, is the equivalent of cold water in the face. "What the hell? What happened to the towel rack? Jesus, Jake!" Disgusted, Julie reaches in the back of the linen closet for a dark-colored towel, a color that blends well with blood. "Here, get the soap out of your hair."

"Just help me to bed. I don't care about soap."

"Want another shot of tequila, Jake? How about a margarita? Stop gagging. Suck it up like a man."

"Julie, please stop talking." Jake is whining now, on the verge of tears.

"I really need a picture of your ass, Jake. This is priceless. I'm getting the camera."

"Too late," Jake mumbles as he falls into bed and pulls the covers over his eyes. "Tell your parents hello. I love you. Tuck me in, will you?"

"Tuck your damn self in. See you later if you're alive." Jake is snoring within thirty seconds. He doesn't hear Julie snickering as she pulls back the bedcovers and snaps a close-up of his dimpled and rug-burned backside. Jake has crossed the border into deep sleep. But, he'd laugh if he saw his bum, too – soft laughter, the kind that tickles a dream and makes it sweet.

. . .

Sam is rarely awake before Mimi, but he needs some quiet time this morning and rises at six, takes a shower, and drives downtown to his favorite parking deck – the one overlooking the city's finest architecture. Downtown is deserted at this hour, providing Sam a peaceful environment in which to clear his troubled mind. Sam leans against the upper deck rail and feels a slight, warm breeze on the back of his neck. A kiss from God, Sam thinks. Maybe AA is working if I'm thinking about God. Sam knows his personal challenge requires hell-bent, steadfast dedication. He is now sober for one year, three months, fourteen days, and two hours. Sam still feels the strong pull of the bottle, his inner struggle against the riptide of self-destruction, as real this morning as it was last night.

Sam walks to the east side of the parking deck roof and says a rising prayer. The sun relaxes his shoulders, soothes his weary spirit. Tears roll one by one down his rugged face. Help me, Sam asks of the sun, and it does. The obliging sun melts Sam's doubts; he is weightless.

Mimi hears the low growl of the old car's engine, then the opening of the front door. Her husband looks refreshed and eager for the day, an unusual morning affect for Sam. She greets him with a smile and a hug. "Hi, Mandarling. Where you been?"

Sam hands Mimi a white bag. "To Hermann's for pastry. I couldn't sleep any longer, but I didn't want to wake you."

Mimi opens the bag and smells the goodness inside. "Yum," she says, delicately lifting out the top pastry. "What's the name of this scrumptious-looking toast? I can't remember."

"Brioche. Orange with toasted almonds. Go ahead, eat

it. There's plenty more."

"I can wait. I just had an apple. But, that'll be my piece since I touched it. Well, maybe just one bite." Mimi is fresh out of the shower; she's a low-maintenance kind of woman. Dry the hair, pull on a pair of jeans, a white tee and sandals, and she's off to the races, the art gallery, or brunch with the Queen. "Fifteen minutes, Sam, and I'll be ready."

"Can I turn the music down, please? You're waking the neighborhood." Usually Sam doesn't ask, but this morning he feels especially accommodating.

Mimi smiles at the gesture. "No, turn it off. Your fishing show's on. Count how many times they say nice fish, purty fish for me, willya? I bet, oh, fifteen times in fifteen minutes, unless it's a really hot hole, then I bet twenty-eight. Oh yeah, and lots of silver. They'll say that seven times. Niiiice fish, purty fish, lots of silver. Maybe you can pick up a new menu item from today's cooking feature."

Sam grins, grabs Mimi's half-eaten brioche from the bag, and turns on the TV. "Get ready, wench. You've just wasted two minutes of precious time making fun of my friend Bill Dance. Go on now; it's show time! Biggest catch of the day, Bill, right here in my living room," he whispers.

. . .

George Landis arrives at The Firedrake fifteen minutes before Mimi and Sam. He pulls up front and doesn't notice the four cars parked in the back lot. George enters through the main door, goes immediately to the alarm keypad, disarms the system, and walks to the wait station to make coffee. As George pours water in the urn, screeching cats and wailing foghorns and yipping coyotes shatter his ears; he throws the pot in the air and spills a quart of water down the front of his shirt.

Then people, maybe they're people, George can't tell for sure, but there's Dee, he thinks it's Dee, and yes, he recognizes the busboy what's his name and they're running up the steps pulling on clothes and they don't know he's here because he's in the back with his hands over his ears and they're yelling what the fuck and then blessed silence.

"What the fuck, Dee?" says Whatshisname.

"I don't know. I didn't set the damn thing last night. Must be a bug."

"Well, it's off now. God, that scared me. Do you think the police will come?"

Dee nods her head. "Oh yeah, probably. We better get everybody out of here. Get everybody out now. Grab the bag of pot off the bar, too. Hurry! I'm calling the police now." The bus boy runs out the unlocked front door, and freezes. Confused, he turns and looks at Dee.

George taps Dee on the back. "Tell them it's a false alarm."

Dee jumps as if shocked by an electric cattle prod. "GEORGE! Oh my God, what are you doing here?"

"I'm meeting the new owners here in fifteen minutes." George looks at Dee sternly, and then averts his eyes. "Button your shirt, please. Who else is here?"

"Jesse and Susan, and I think a couple of guys from the band."

"Get them out of here! And clear off this kitchen bar right now. I don't want them to smell this stinking leftover crab dip." George rubs his forehead and takes a deep breath. His next words feel like a leather belt strap against Dee's heart. "What the hell were you thinking? I should have listened to Todd and never put you in charge of the bar. What's the downstairs look like?" Dee is dumbstruck by George's insult. "Forget it; I'll go see for myself."

"No George, don't do that. I'll take care of it." Dee dejectedly turns for the stairs.

"Well get a move on, sister. Geezus Christ! Look at the chalkboard! Who wrote Mother Fucking Cheesecake under the dessert choices? I hope to hell that wasn't up all night."

"I'll erase it."

"No, I'll do it." Dee watches as George walks toward the board. "Are you waiting for a hug? Get downstairs! I'd fire your ass right now if I still owned this place. Just get a bag and scrape everything into it and leave it out back by the bottom door. Then get the hell out."

Dee tries. "George, I couldn't let them drive home last night. They would have killed somebody. It's my fault."

"No, it's mine. I should have been here. Get your ass in gear and get outta here, or I swear I'll start shooting." George turns around and quickly walks to the wait station, cleans up broken glass, brews a pot of decaf and takes the glass shards to the dish room for disposal. He hears the front door open and Mimi's laughter enters first, but quickly makes room for a gasp, then a question.

George wasn't aware of his storytelling ability until this very moment. "I was washing up a few things from last night, got a cramp in my hand, and sprayed myself good. That dang dish hose has a mind of its own when the pressure builds up," he continues, gaining confidence in his story. "Curled up like a cobra and spit at me." He grins and excuses himself. "I need to run downstairs to, ah, grab some paperwork from the office. Meet you on the patio, help yourself to coffee. It's decaf," George says breathlessly. Lord God in Heaven, I'd make a good politician, he mutters under his breath.

George props open the bar doors, imploring fresh moving air to enter, begging for a strong, cleansing breeze to sweep out the scent of cannabis and stale beer. He checks the bathrooms and finds a bucket of gray chunky mop water in the ladies room, but no puke on the floor. At least they cleaned up the puke, George says, as he rolls the mop bucket outside. The parking lot is empty of bodies, but full of empty liquor bottles. He retraces his steps and heads up the stairs, stops, and turns around. George remembers to pull a file – any file – from the closet his inept manager calls an office. His heart is beating so strongly that he's sure Mimi and Sam will see it pounding through his shirt. He takes a deep breath, composes himself, and calmly walks through the front door. He wonders if they will notice the insistent tic in his left eye.

"You guys, the kitchen staff is coming in tomorrow at ten a.m. to deep clean. I think you'll meet one of our bartenders tomorrow, too. Dee mentioned doing inventory, and that will save you some time. She's as honest as they come; you'll like her." George runs a mental marathon, and the big hills are yet to come. Imploring his mind to pace itself, he reaches for a cheese and spinach scone. After a few minutes of schmoozing, he's ready to tackle the hard part and sprint for the finish. He looks at Sam and Mimi, takes a sip of coffee, and pushes on. "Now, you don't have to do this if you don't want to, but I promised Todd and Matt that I'd run something by you."

Sam and Mimi look at each other, but don't give anything away. "Who are Todd and Matt?" Sam asks.

"My two managers."

"Which one has the slicked back hair and wears suspenders?" Mimi asks.

"That's Todd. Here's the deal: these guys want to make sure you're comfortable with the transition. I told them I'd see how you'd feel about them helping you out."

Sam's immediate response is firm. "No thanks, George. I don't have any use for them." He takes a sip of coffee and watches as George rubs his twitching eye.

"Sam, wait a minute," interjects Mimi. "Let's give them a chance. I bet they can help me."

Sam rears back in his chair. "How, Mimi? Just how can they help you?"

"Well, for starters, with the little things, like showing me how to run the credit card settlement at night, and maybe some shortcuts or something – some insight into their system." Sam shakes his head. "From what I've seen, they don't have a system." George is looking at the sky and extending his right eye with his fingers, trying to stop the twitch. "Don't mind me," he says. "My eye's spazzing a bit, but that's normal. It'll pass."

"Come on, Sam," Mimi says. "Let's at least meet with them. It'll be enlightening."

Sam rolls his eyes and sighs. "George, call them and see if they can come around noon. That'll give me time to meet my crew and get some grease under my nails again. Looks like I'll be jumping in to show these boys how to clean the hell out of a kitchen."

George blinks a couple of times. "There. It's gone." He looks at Mimi and smiles gratefully. "I'll tell you right now, Matt will help you all he can. Todd's gonna be tough. He and Matt thought I'd sell the business to them. They're pretty crossed up about it, so be prepared for some resistance, especially from Todd."

"I'll resist his prissy little ass right out the front door,

George," huffs Sam.

"Oh Sam, lighten up. You haven't even met him yet." Mimi dunks her almond brioche into her coffee; happy flavors tap-dance on her taste buds. "Yeah, but I've worked with his type before. He's a troublemaker."

"We don't have to hire them, honey."

"And we won't."

. . .

Monday morning at nine o'clock sharp, an attorney seals the deal, exactly one year, five days, and two hours after the Killian's first wedding anniversary. Sign here, the attorney says. And here. And here. And here. Last one, sign right here. Congratulations! It's official: Sam and Mimi are the proud new owners of The Firedrake, an unpolished gem of a righteous restaurant, and The Dragon, her nasty little brother of a funktified bar.

Jarrod is the first to show up for kitchen duty on Tuesday morning. He immediately recognizes Sam as the mussels man from Saturday night and steels himself. I'm gonna be fired, Jarrod thinks. Mimi looks up from her notebook and smiles at him. Sam approaches, introduces himself and extends his hand. "How much are you getting paid, son?" This is not what Jarrod expected. Cautiously he responds. "Nineteen thousand a year, sir. But I only work three nights a week. I'm off on Tuesday and Wednesday. Chef Van works those nights."

"Is he any good?"

"Yeah, but he steals. You gotta watch him."

"Can you work Tuesday and Wednesday nights, too?"

Jarrod lights up. "Sure, Mr. Killian!"

"Call me Sam, it's shorter. Let's take him to twenty-six, Mimi. Can we do that?"

"Yes boss man. Effective immediately." Mimi grins at Jarrod, who isn't sure what just happened to him. "I thought you were firing me for sure. Am I dreaming?" He looks at Sam. "Are you kidding? You don't even know me."

"No we don't, Jarrod. But you impress me. If you help us keep this tub afloat, I'll give you two cash bonuses a year, and pay half your health insurance after six months."

"Thank you, Mr. Killian, I mean Sam. I can't fucking believe this." He looks at Mimi and apologizes. Mimi looks up from her notepad. "Hey, Jarrod, don't worry about it. You may hear me say it from time to time; it's one of my favorite words. Who's this coming in the door?"

"That's Rod, our dishwasher. He's not that good, but he really needs the money. He's blind in one eye."

Sam throws his hands in the air. "Now, that's an asset." Rod walks past the table without uttering a sound. "Where's he going?"

"Probably to the bathroom," Jarrod says.

"Can he see us?"

"Oh, yeah, he knows we're here. He doesn't talk in the morning. But, he never complains. We can hand him dog shit on a platter and he'll knock it off in the trashcan, wash the platter and have it back on the counter in a second."

Mimi makes a face. "Have you done that?"

"Only once."

Sam rises and stretches his back, prepping his body for the long day ahead. Jarrod waits for orders from the master. "Before we start cleaning, let's take a tour of dry storage. I peeked in there earlier; looks like we inherited a couple of boxes of Diamond Brand kosher salt and a few cans of tomato sauce, but not much more. I need to know what's in the freezers and the walk-in, too. Lead the way, son."

"There's a lot of alligator meat in the freezer, but not much else. It's been there for months. It was Todd's idea, but we can't give it away. And Sam? We don't have a walk-in, really. It's more of a reach-in."

"It's more of a cold, damp food coffin," Sam says. "You have to be a flippin' midget to stand up or turn around in there."

Sam pounds his fist loudly on the bathroom door. "What the hell you doing in there, Rod? Let's get to it, buddy." Sam hears some shuffling, nothing more. "Answer me damn it, or get the hell out of my restaurant!" Rod cracks open the door and peers out, leading with his good eye. "You paying cash today?" Sam's eyes are tired of rolling, but they can't help themselves. "Yes, I'll pay cash for a job well done, or I'll fire your lazy ass if you're a slacker. The clock starts now. Get moving, son."

Rod crouches in the quarterback position, fades back, and heaves a pass to his receiver, but it's a fake! He cradles air, breaks fast to Sam's right, and dodges imaginary blocks on his way to the dish room. He crosses the threshold, turns and breaks into the chicken struttin' victory dance. A sign hangs above the dish room door. 'Rod's World: A Scrub-Free Zone.' Mimi cracks up. Two hours in, and she's having fun.

Mimi makes notes in preparation for the meeting with Todd and Matt. She is counting on a positive experience, regardless of the outcome, and will gather as much information about The Firedrake and The Dragon as they will divulge. Mimi searches for clues with the focus of a morel hunter. She moves attentively through the restaurant – one step, two steps, pause. Who cleans this place, she wonders? Apparently, nobody. The small, dark blue entrance hall is devoid of personality. No love here, Mimi thinks. No welcome mat. Cheap posters are tacked to the sauce-splattered walls in the front dining room. Mimi's eyes track up; the ceiling fan is covered with soot. That's an easy one to fix, Mimi thinks. We'll take it apart and run it through the dishwasher. This place needs major decontamination, starting with a deep clean and ending with a smudge. I'll ask the wait staff to help me, and we'll see who's made of what.

Mimi inspects each bathroom. There's a buildup of grunge in the corners from months, maybe years, of dirty mop water sloshing and moving dirt around, but not out. A toothbrush will handle this. I'll do the bathrooms myself, Mimi thinks. She glances at the register, but doesn't touch it. Petri dish comes to mind; the keypad is breeding germs of epidemic proportion. Who cares about this place, Mimi wonders? Guess that would be Sam and me, she thinks, and grins.

The back dining room is small, but accommodates at least sixty people. Mimi makes notes on her pad – draw diagrams and seating charts; find a table supplier. Paint! Mimi reaches over to straighten out a cockeyed picture and jumps back as two roaches appear from behind it. She shudders and scrawls "call bug man immediately" on her notepad.

The wait station is in shambles. Mimi takes a quick glance, flips the page, and begins writing. Coffee grounds under espresso machine; bread left in warmer; dirty towels in hand sink; broken glass on floor. Mimi examines the wine glasses, and throws three chipped ones in the trashcan immediately. She holds one up to the light and gets a bright view of soap scum and lip stick. Oh my God! What's the health rating in this place? Did we check?

The more Mimi sees, the less inclined she is to warmly welcome Todd and Matt. Within minutes, she is even less inclined than she is right now. Mimi makes her way downstairs, her feet audibly sticking to each step. She's not smiling, and her brow furrows when she sees Todd behind the bar – bleach-blonde, pinky-sized pony tail, overly-tanned, pouty face, pink polo shirt, and blue jeans tighter than George Michael would be comfortable wearing. Same jerk, different day.

Mimi reaches the bottom step and says loudly, "Excuse me, may I help you?"

He dismisses her with a quick glance. "No, you may not. I know what I'm doing."

"I'm sure you do, but I don't. I'm Mimi Killian. You must be Todd."

"I'll be with you in a sec, Mimi."

"No, you'll be with me right now, Todd. Come on out here. Right now, please." Todd, avoiding eye contact, walks with the speed of a turtle toward Mimi, brushes by her closely in what he considers to be an Alpha move, and stakes out the head seat at a nearby table. Mimi bites her tongue and asks, "Where's Matt?"

"I'm here, Mrs. Killian, in the office getting a few of my personal things out of your way." A chubby, bald-headed youngster wearing a big smile approaches her. "Hi, I'm Matt Sink. Nice to meet you! I really look forward to making this transition work." He's making the effort, but Mimi's not impressed. "Thanks, Matt. Will you be kind enough to run upstairs and introduce yourself to my husband Sam? And ask if we can meet down here, please."

Matt stops his shuck and jive routine, looks at Todd, and frowns. "Yes ma'am. I'll be right back."

Todd tilts his chair back on its legs, looks smugly at Mimi, and begins his game. "So. Mimi. Do you know anything about the restaurant business?"

Oh, this is gonna be fun, Mimi thinks. "A little, Todd. Do you?"

"More than you do, apparently."

Mimi walks behind Todd, pushes his chair into position, and takes a seat directly across from him. "Listen to me, Todd. My husband will be coming down those stairs any minute now. All he has to do is look at my face and you are out of here without another word. I suggest we start this conversation over and find some common ground."

Todd rises deliberately and raises one thin, plucked eyebrow. "Excuse me, Mimi, I'm going to the bathroom. Go ahead and start without me. I doubt I'll miss much."

"Actually Todd, you might miss it all," Mimi responds. Sam and Matt are in serious conversation as they head down the stairs. Mimi takes a deep breath, fiddles with her bottom lip, and heads behind the bar. "Matt, do you drink coffee?"

"No ma'am, but thanks." Matt looks confused. "Where's Todd?"

"He's in the bathroom. He'll be right out. See, here he comes. Todd, would you like coffee?"

"Yeah, Mimi, black for me," he says, noticing that Sam has taken his seat. He adjusts his crotch, repositions himself, and says, "So Sam, what do you know about the restaurant business?" Sam isn't as polite as Mimi, but anticipates an amusing exchange. "Well, Todd, let's see…oh yeah…I earned my first four star rating when you were shitting your diaper. Does that answer your question?"

Todd shakes his head and plays businessman. "Sam,

you're entering a different kind of situation here. Matt and I are prepared to help you in any way we can. It's going to take a long time before you're ready to tackle this restaurant on your own."

"Yeah, Todd? Why is that?" Sam leans forward and adjusts his crotch, and Mimi chokes on her coffee. Todd doesn't notice. Matt stops breathing.

"Simple," Todd replies. "We know a bunch of stuff about this place that you don't. Now, I have a restaurant deal waiting in Martha's Vineyard and Matt's moving to Florida in October. We'll do everything we can to get you up to speed in four weeks. After that, you're on your own." Todd's encouraged by Sam's attention, and Mimi's silence. Matt is turning blue. "I have several years of experience as a restaurant consultant, and I'll be happy to pass along some helpful tidbits to you and your lovely wife here. I'm not cheap, though." Todd cocks the chair onto its back legs; he looks from Sam to Mimi, waiting.

"How much is this service going to cost us, Todd?" Todd makes the unfortunate mistake of thinking Sam's interested. "Matt and I will stick around for four weeks; it'll cost you ten thousand dollars. Without us, you'll lose at least ten thousand the first month anyway. You make the decision."

Sam stands up, and looking at Todd, adjusts his crotch one last time. "Thank you, Todd," Sam says politely as he slaps Todd on the back. "Now, get the hell out of my restaurant." Todd stands, slowly, shakes his head and looks at Matt, who is about to hyperventilate. "Why am I not surprised?" He looks at Mimi and says, "My prediction is you'll fold within six months. Matt, let's go." Todd starts for the door, but Matt's not sure he can walk without help. "Matt, get your ass up. Come on, or I'm leaving you." Matt submissively rises and meekly says,

"Mr. and Mrs. Killian, nice to meet you. Sorry about this. I think you'll do great here."

"Thanks, Matt. Don't worry about it. We understand. Good luck." Mimi watches the duo walk out the door, Todd in the lead. "That went well," Sam and Mimi say, in stereo. Jinx.

Mariachi music blares from the kitchen. Sam feels energized when he steps behind the line. "Who loves the restaurant business?" he yells. "I love the restaurant business," Jarrod yells back, with perfect inflection. Rod grins, fakes right, falls back into the dish room, and launches a bullet to Jarrod. He connects! It's complete! The mariachi band cheers.

Chef Van shows up at one p.m. with a plausible excuse and Sam pushes his intuition aside. He hears the man can stand the heat. No "vaya con Dios, adios mi amigo" for Van today, Sam thinks.

Dee pulls in as Matt, who looks like a deflated doughboy, and a sore, gelded Todd walk to the parking lot. Todd is in her face before she closes her car door. "You better quit while you're ahead," he utters. "These people don't have a clue." Matt stands behind Todd rolling his eyes, signaling Dee with his eyes that it's okay; he gives Dee the high sign. Dee doesn't respond to Todd's negative vibe, doesn't dignify it, and says to Matt, "Call me." Dee and the rest of the staff have called Todd "Toad" for eight months, and she's happy to see him go. Dee enters The Dragon, her grin stretching from dimple to dimple. Mimi welcomes her with open arms and a hug.

. . .

If you are a fly on the wall, you have an eight-day life expectancy. Your sight is magnified through compound eyes, and you're entertained by a most amazing mosaic of color and patterns – quality images that constantly flicker with movement, images that peak at the moment of your timely death. In eight short days, the new lifecycle for The Firedrake and The Dragon has begun its gestation period in earnest. Sam and Mimi are sowing seeds for what promises to be a long and painful pregnancy.

CREDIBILITY

Accept credit for your good deeds; refuse credit for good deeds that are not yours. Let your conscience be your guide.

It takes Mimi one spin around the tiny office to determine that most of the previous Firedrake business records have been purged. The file cabinet is empty, drawers bare except for a couple of sticky pennies and rubber bands. No stacks, no invoices – not even a Rolodex of business contacts remains. Okay, Mimi thinks; we start fresh, design our own roadmap for success.

Three weeks later, Mimi finds two file folders hiding on the very top of a dusty shelf. The "pink slip" file has three complaints about a server who takes leftovers home for her dog. She pitches it into the trash.

The other file is more interesting. Mimi finds a contract with a company called Eat-and-Meet agreeing to a "Buy One, Get One Free of Equal or Lesser Value" food deal. She shows the contract to Sam, who takes one look and dismisses it. "Ignore it, Mimi. We bought the assets of this business, not the liabilities. We're a different corporation, and not bound by law to accept this agreement. We won't honor it."

"I don't get it, Sam. What's Eat-and-Meet? I've never heard of it."

"Here, let me see it again." Sam snorts as he scans to the bottom. "It's a scam of very large magnitude. If one of their reps walks in the door, you come find me immediately." He turns to the last page, and hands it back to Mimi. "Can you read this signature?"

Mimi squints. "It looks like Todd's name, but I can't be sure."

"Shoot, Mimi, Rod could have signed this thing. Give it here." Sam takes a closer look and becomes indignant. "Good God. This is a two-year contract signed in March of this year." Sam rips it up and throws it in the trash. "No fucking way, Mimi! We are not giving away food. We're not a pizza joint." Sam's a pilot light in search of a gas leak.

"Now I see," Mimi slowly says. She cautiously looks at Sam. "We're getting these weird coupons in the paperwork every night. Not many, but people are using them. I've been honoring them thinking maybe George gave some out to his friends as a thank you."

"Damn it, Mimi! How much have you given away?" Sam ignites.

"Close to three hundred dollars. I'm keeping them in an envelope and thought we'd take the final amount off our payment to George next month, or at least ask him to split it with us."

"Why the fuck didn't you tell me this before now?" In an effort to put out his raging fire, Sam fills the bar sink with cold water and dunks his head in it. Mimi hands him a towel and smartly steps back. He comes up smoking. "Put signs on the window and on the doors and in the bathrooms, right now! Let these gomers know the free ride ends today." Sam dries his head with the towel and reaches in the cooler for an O' Doul's, twists off the cap, and swallows half the bottle in one pull. He glares at Mimi. "Water-drinking freeloaders! I don't want those people as my customers. Send them down the road. Let them put our competition out of business, not us," Sam yells. He stomps out the door, leaving Mimi to deal with her scorched ass.

The Eat-and-Meet pitch: if you sign this contract, you'll get free advertising for your company in this four-color, professionally-designed book right here. It will cost you nothing. Watch your business increase. The customers will flock to your door! Aw, no, you don't have to be the owner to sign this. Go ahead. Your boss will be so happy he'll give you a raise.

The Eat-and-Meet Company sells their coupon books to churches, scout troops, and schools for ten dollars each. The groups sell the books for twenty-five dollars each. The buyer has hundreds of dollars worth of coupons good for free meals at local restaurants. Quite a tidy profit for each party. Nice little fund raiser. And how beneficial to a small, independently-owned restaurant. Niiiice fish, purty fish, lots of silver.

The Eat-and-Meet Vice President of Sales won't tell Mimi and Sam how many books have been distributed in their area – classified information, you know. "But, I will tell you this; you can expect approximately three thousand coupons per year to be redeemed at your restaurant."

Sam's eyes are bulging and on the verge of popping out on the table. "You fucking carpetbagger! That's over forty thousand dollars of our blood, sweat, and tears walking out our front door every year!" His head spin puts Linda Blair to shame. "Mimi, call our attorney."

The VP doesn't break a sweat; he's been called in for this kind of meeting countless times. With a glued-on smile, he looks at Sam and politely says, "Oh, but they will be repeat customers, Mr. Killian."

"Are you fucking kidding me? These people will eat free in our restaurant once a year, that's it. They'll put us out of business. There goes our profit. Mimi, call the attorney right now."

"Mr. Killian, look at this contract. Read the fine print. This contract is transferable from owner to owner. In other words, we can and will sue you. Not only that, but you'll have to come to New Jersey for a hearing in our courts."

Sam stands up. "Expect a call from our attorney today. Now get the hell out of my restaurant." The carpetbagger is cool. "Thanks for your time, Mr. Killian. We look forward to doing business with you."

"Kiss my ass, you fucking shyster!"

Mimi and Sam pay their attorney a handsome fee to change the names of The Firedrake and The Dragon. Effective immediately, The Firefly and The Phoenix are open for business. Neither establishment honors Eat-and-Meet coupons. David defeats Goliath.

. . .

Dear Mr. Killian:

My wife and I dined at your restaurant last Friday and were very disappointed. When we arrived at The Firedrake, we were dismayed to find that you no longer accept Eat-and-Meet coupons.

Mrs. Killian made us feel welcome and offered us a glass of free wine if we would stay. My wife enjoyed her white zinfandel very much. Had I looked at the menu before sitting down, I would have left immediately. $13.95 is just too much to pay for chicken and mashed potatoes.

While wishing you all the best, rest assured — we will never return to your establishment.

Sincerely,
A Former Customer

Dear Mrs. Killian:

I am appalled and shocked that The Firedrake no longer accepts Eat-and-Meet coupons. My husband and I are newlyweds and received a coupon book as a wedding gift. I don't care how many free appetizers you offer as a bribe, I will never set foot in your restaurant again. We are struggling to make ends meet and can't afford to go out to eat without help. We feel cheated out of a very valuable gift. You are an embarrassment to non-profit organizations and are greedy and selfish. I hope you rot in Hell.

Signed, Your Enemy

Dear Owner,

Why did you take kalzone off you menue. It was cheep and I like it. I'm coming back next weekend and it beter be back on, or ther will be truble.

Bye,
Chad

Dear Kind Woman Hostess with the Mostess:

Please forgive my napkin stationary. Just wanted to tell you that you are doing a great job, but why did you change the name? It's not that I don't like the new one; I'm from the south and love fireflies.

Anyway, I ate at The Firefly last Saturday night and loved it! The food and service were great and the new décor is funky and fun. I just read your review in today's paper and the critic nailed it: "It's the party everyone wants to be invited to." I love that you renamed the bar The Phoenix. That's good luck.

Keep up the good work! I'll be back.

Sincerely,

? xxooxo ! (an anonymous fan of your husband's tush)

To Whom It May Concern:

I understand you no longer take Eat-and-Meet coupons. Good for you! Although I own one of those books, I prefer to pay full price for my meals. As a matter of fact, your prices are too low for the quality of food coming out of your kitchen. Have you considered raising your prices? I'll support you, and so will my friends.

I'm a little concerned about the downstairs. There's a rumor going around that you are going to stop playing jazz and feature bluegrass instead. While I am a die-hard fan of Ricky Skaggs, I'm sure that most of your clientele don't know who he is. How many black people do you know who like bluegrass? Your crowd is diverse. I hope you keep it that way. It's the only club in town where people of all colors and persuasions mingle so well.

Thank you. Let us know about the music. I look forward to playing in the new and improved Phoenix soon. Do you pay scale?

Sincerely, Al Hampton

Bass player, Al and the Beat

. . .

Sam is on alert. Filet mignon and shrimp are disappearing from the inventory with alarming speed, but he can't catch Van in the act. Sam never asks Jarrod to be a spy – Jarrod provides that service on his own. "We're down on filets, Sam," Jarrod mentions. "We sold twelve last night and should have thirty-six left, according to the prep sheet. I only counted twenty-one. Oh, yeah, and I only found one box of shrimp. Did you toss the other one for some reason?"

Sam's decision to keep Van on has proven to be a poor one. That's what I get for being a softy, Sam thinks. He asks Van to step outside at the end of the shift, after the cleaning is done. Van lights a cigarette and leans casually against the wall. "What's on your mind, Boss Man?" Sam is beyond casual. He's totally relaxed, inhaling a Cohiba and feeling a bit of a tobacco high. He looks at his cigar, then at Van. "I know what you're up to."

Van jumps. "What do you mean, you know what I'm up to?"

Sam blows a large smoke ring without taking his eyes from Van. "You've been busted."

Van laughs and shakes his head. "No, no…that was a

long time ago. Since you and Mimi bought the place, I don't even deal outta the kitchen anymore out of respect for you, man."

"Van, I have two hundred dollars in my pocket. I suggest you take it and go find another job. Just don't tell them you worked here, and I won't have to say I fired you."

"Fire me? What are you talking about, man?" Van is caught totally off-guard. He was expecting a raise. "Think about it, Van." Sam is cooler than Minnesota spring water. He blows another smoke ring, reaches in his pocket, and pulls out his money clip. Van starts begging. "Look man, I'm supporting two kids. I haven't stolen anything from you in two weeks. I swear. My car's been broken down and I can't hide the shit anywhere. I won't steal anything else, I promise. I need this job." Van visibly shakes; his cigarette makes uncontrollable circles in the air.

Sam shakes his head, takes another long hit from his cigar, and scratches his back on the corner of the wall. "Two hundred dollars, Van. You walk away now with two hundred dollars cash in your pocket, or you walk away with nothing; your choice."

Van takes a last draw of his cigarette, drops it to the ground, and angrily crushes it to dust. "Alright, damn. Give me the money. You're one bad mutha fucka, man." He grabs the money from Sam's outstretched hand and stuffs it in his front pocket. "You have a check coming next week. We'll mail it to you. I don't want to see you around here anymore, you understand?"

"Got it, man. Loud and clear." Van starts walking away without purpose, and then doubles back. He looks back at Sam, opens his mouth, and wisely, shuts it.

"Good luck, Van. Don't put that money in the pipe.

Now, get outta here." Sam feels a pang of compassion as Van's shadow disappears down the dark street, but that passes with the fading of his next smoke ring. He walks into the back dining room, where Mimi inventories wine. "Mimi, will you see if you can find Warren's number? It's time to bring a new dog in here and teach him a few old dog tricks, if he's still willing."

Mimi looks up and grins. "It's in the office – black book, left-hand drawer. Tell him he can stay with us for a couple of weeks if you want to. But tell him he can't drink if he does."

Sam ponders a moment. "Maybe he'll go to AA with me. I'll make that part of the deal." Two days later, Sam fills a hole on the line with a new buddy, who, it appears, is quick to reform – a two-legged, easily-trained puppy of a line cook named Warren.

. . .

The applications are stacking up on Mimi's desk downstairs. Everybody wants to work at The Firefly. Mimi and Sam hire several people who fire themselves. The well-groomed transvestite who can't work Saturday because he has a sprained ankle, but who can dance in high heels at a Saturday late-night after-party; the waitress who arrives late, leaves early and refuses to sell wine because it's against her religion; the numbskull who, on his application, lists his first name as Marcus and his last name as Marcus (he's known as Marcus Marcus to the staff, Circus Circus to Sam); Rod's back-up dishwasher, who speaks no English, locks herself in the women's bathroom during a Saturday rush and repeatedly yells 'sheet sheet sheet' until Sam takes the door off the hinges, gives her cab money and sends her home; the prima donna Culinary Institute of America boy who doesn't understand the importance of playing well with others.

Circus Circus, indeed.

The core wait staff at The Firefly and The Phoenix is tight, professional. Underachiever Kyle Shanahan is a tall, sparkling cover boy with an eye for a sucker. He can sell sugar cane to a diabetic, and consistently has the highest ticket average. Greg Sanderson – chronically depressed unemployed actor and unpublished writer – is intellectually disheveled and charmingly brooding. His dark good looks, cynical repartee, and deprecating humor appeal to older customers of both sexes; he's creamy under the crust, like crème brulee. Tom Garland has a Mensa-level IQ and a thimble's worth of common sense. He checks everyone's paperwork for accuracy at the end of a shift, but is the kind of guy who needs help sharpening his pencil. He may show up for work in shorts and cowboy boots, or a kilt and tennis shoes – a bona fide member of the Firefly freak show – but he always gets the job done, and more. Catherine Shiffman, known as Beauty Cat, or simply BC to her co-workers, is small, quiet, and moves with the grace of a panther stalking her prey. Her dancer's body is rock hard, and she can carry twice her weight in dirty dishes. BC, a vapor trail of speed on busy nights, waits on the most people, but has the lowest ticket average. She's a table turner – hers is a quantity game. She'd rather sell ten bottles of Beringer White Zinfandel than one bottle of vintage Caymus Cabernet Sauvignon. Every restaurant needs a Beauty Cat. There's goofy, smooth Jose Covas – so smooth in his goofiness that one doesn't recognize the goofy part unless one works with him. He sings with a voice so deep and rich that it'll make you reach in your pocket and contribute to his American education fund – that is, unless you're bilingual. Then you might understand he's singing about making love to your wife and daughter at the same time, or that you're a cheap bastard who should eat at McDonald's. The restaurant is Jose's stage, the customers his willing audience. Sam would insist Mimi fire his ass if not for the business he brings in. Then, there's Carly Cavanaugh, a buxom, brown-eyed, Irish spitfire. Bronx born and bred, Carly has a work ethic that pleases Sam and Mimi. She comes in early, stays late, bats cleanup when everyone else is too tired to lift another finger, and bosses the boys around like little brothers. Carly would rather tend bar than wait tables, but her edge is a bit too cutting for The Phoenix employees. Dee is Queen of the Downstairs and won't relinquish her rights to the crown, especially to someone who doesn't like grits, who doesn't say y'all, and cusses like a sailor's parrot. Mimi is the only one who can control Carly when her temper flares. Even Sam appreciates Carly's need for perfection, although there is usually a war between the stainless steel when Carly's on the floor. "This dish looks like shit," Carly might say to the sous chef. "Make it over," she demands. "Get my order out now!" she screams. And oh, her customers love her hard-edged honesty.

"Don't order the catfish special," she'll say. "It's tired." Sam asks, "Carly, why didn't you sell any catfish tonight?"

"Because it's tired, Sam," Carly retorts. "My customers deserve better." Sam shrugs his shoulders because he knows she's right.

Tip average is well over one hundred dollars – almost twice that amount on weekends – in part because Sam and his kitchen poets create love on a plate for a packed house every night. But it's also due to The Firefly's small, exclusive wine selection. Mimi makes sure her staff knows the wine list cold and hosts a tasting every Saturday night for staff only, but not until all stations are clean and the last piece of paperwork is completed. To taste a bottle of a fine Italian Super Tuscan – something by Angelo Gaja, perhaps – each person contributes what he or she can afford toward the wholesale price. Mimi always makes up the difference, but gives herself an extra pour. These kids know wine!

Mimi enjoys setting up for these occasions; she chooses her wines carefully, polishes the glasses, makes sure the flowers are refreshed and the tablecloth is clean. She wants her staff to have respect for the ceremony, to honor the sacrificial wine. By candlelight and big moonbeams, Mimi hosts a late-night communion on the upstairs patio. She starts with a bottle of Firesteed Pinot Noir and pours a generous ounce in each glass. They swirl, sniff, taste. "Kyle, how would you describe this wine?"

"Light, refreshing, a perfect summer red or quaffing wine."

"What else, Carly?"

"A nice note of spice rounding out the fruit. Perfect with fish or chicken, but not with heavy dishes. Light, like Kyle said, but there's enough going on to keep it interesting."

"Everybody agree?" Nods all around, and the next bottle is poured.

"Okay, guys. Now taste the Steele Pinot Noir. How does it compare, Jose?"

"Wow! This is a pinot?"

"Yep. Very different, isn't it? You have to be able to explain the difference to a customer since the Steele isn't a glass pour." Jose takes another sip, and ponders. "I would say the Steele drinks more like an old vine zin –

heavy and comparatively full-bodied next to the Firesteed. How would you describe them, Mimi?"

Mimi sips the Steele. "I'd say the Firesteed is a ballerina and the Steele is a football player. Okay, rate 'em. One to five, five being the best. You know the drill. Moving on."

"Can we taste the Chianti next?"

"Sure, Tom. Everybody drink up or dump your glasses. Greg, put that bottle of Steele down. Hand it to me, come on. No bogarting the good stuff. We'll divvy up the leftovers in a minute. Quiet on the set. Everybody have a pour?"

"Yuck."

"Gag."

"Hey, I like it!"

"You like everything, Greg. You have a palate of stone." Greg looks at BC's notes and feels compassion for the little wine that fails. "Dang, Cat. This isn't great, but it's better than a one. What do you think, Mimi?"

"It's bug spray. I agree with Cat. We ain't sellin' it. And now, for our feature presentation: may I present, as our star tonight, the 1989 Bertani Amarone. It's gonna cost you guys forty dollars. Who's in? All six of you? Okay, ante up five dollars each; I pour, and there will be no complaints when I pour the most in my glass. Greg, get your grubby little hands off that bottle before I break your fingers." Mimi looks at the littered table and stops the action. "We need some fresh glasses here. Tom, will you please fetch seven clean glasses and take the used ones to Rod? Thanks. Carly, will you please round up some bread? We need to cleanse our palates for this one."

Sam's in the kitchen putting away his knives when he sees Tom carrying glasses from the patio to the dish room. Carly passes Tom carrying a basket of bread, and then Tom resurfaces with more glasses. Under normal circumstances, Sam ignores this post-service show and tell. However, he has just discovered his protégé, Warren, and his sous chef, Jarrod, chugging a six-pack in the small walk-in cooler. "Fuck, boy, you had me fooled," Sam says to Warren. "Get your ass out of here." Sam is not in good temper.

Mimi's rules of engagement include not arguing with Sam in front of her staff, especially during a training session. She's in church, standing on hallowed ground; she's preaching to the masses, delivering the message of the grape, and Sam rudely interrupts her litany by throwing the weight of his anger at his wife. "Mimi, what the hell are you doing?" He stands three feet from the table, and glares at her. The staff freezes.

Mimi stares at Sam for a long, long second, and slowly says, "We're tasting wine, Sam, as usual. Everything's put to bed inside."

"Damn it, I wish you wouldn't do that. I can use all the open bottles next week in sauces."

"Honey, look in the back. There are five bottles you can use. These aren't glass pours, at least not yet."

"Then you're wasting wine! Put them back, now!"

"No, I'm not." Mimi slightly raises her hand to the wait staff in an effort to assure them; her face is still, calm. She softly says, "Sam, this is part of the educational process. They have to know what they're selling."

"Bullshit! You look like a bunch of damn winos to me. Am I paying for this? By God, Mimi, this is the last time. You waste more money than anyone I know. Why don't you stop playing and start working?" Sam's hands are on his hips and he's mouth-breathing. Mimi excuses herself from the group. "Kyle, everybody, stay right here. I'll be back in a minute." Sam follows her inside, his temper growing with each step. "You're all a bunch of fucking winos," he screams. "I'm surrounded by alcoholics." Sam's a fear-biter, and Mimi backs away slowly. She's confused, confounded by his outburst. "Sam, I don't know why you're acting this way, but now is not the time to discuss it. I'm working as hard and fast as I can, like you. Give me a break. Leave us alone, please. We'll talk about this when we get home." She puts her game face on, turns, and walks back to her safe haven. "You guys ready?"

"What was that all about? Are you all right? You're shaking."

"Don't worry about it. Sam's just cranky and tired." Mimi takes a deep breath, and smiles. "Okay, where were we? Ah, yes, the Bertani Amarone. Carly, will you open it, please?" Standing, Carly takes the proffered bottle from Mimi, uncorks it easily, and hands the cork to Mimi. "Everybody feel this cork. It's malleable and spongy, not dry. Good sign. Now, get a little air in there, and stick your nose in it. How about that bouquet, huh guys? What are you picking up?"

"Earth…"

"Leather…"

"Tobacco…"

"Raisins! Why does it smell like raisins?"

Mimi smiles. "Wow, Greg, you nailed it. The grapes are dried on straw mats in the sun – a process which intensifies the flavor of the wine as well as increases the alcohol content slightly."

"You mean like sundried tomatoes?"

Mimi nods. "Exactly. You're drinking sundried grapes."

"Oh my God, this is a mouth orgasm," shrieks Carly. "How much of this do we have in stock?"

"I just bought two cases. Our supplier has three cases in reserve. Do you think we can sell it?"

"Oh, yeah. I can sell every bottle, no problem," Carly answers. Mimi looks around the table. The staff agrees. "Even at a buck and a quarter a shot? Tell you what. You guys sell this stuff, and I'll treat us to the last bottle. Deal?"

"Yes, ma'am!"

Tom says, "Queen Mimi, you are the wine goddess of my life. I have to know how you would describe this indescribably delicious wine."

Mimi is silent. Her movements are slow and deliberate as she gently swirls, releasing the wine's aromas and catching them with her nose. "Let me see...okay, here it is: this wine is a soft, round passionate opera singer dressed in black velvet and rubies, performing under a full moon while standing barefooted in a richly mulched hayfield."

"Well, damn," says Greg. "How do we describe it to our customers?"

"Just like that, man." Jake Reston stands on the top step of the patio, enthralled by the convocation and Mimi's poetic, visual wordplay. He can't help but join the church. "I'd buy two bottles based on that description alone."

"Well, now, that's the idea," says Mimi as she turns, wondering whose deep and unfamiliar voice just entered the conversation. She extends her hand to a gentleman dressed in black jeans and a black button-down shirt, cuffs rolled to his elbows. His hand feels like part of her body. "Hi, I'm Mimi Killian."

"Jake Reston. I'm the keyboard player in Melvin's band. It's nice to finally meet you. Is it okay if I use the upstairs phone? I can't hear a thing in the bar. You have some frat boys hanging with a bachelorette party. Dee's selling Lemon Drops as fast as she can make them."

Greg jumps out of his chair, followed by Jose, Tom, and Kyle. They playfully make for the stairs. "Is anybody naked?"

"Not yet, but I'll definitely keep my eyes open." Jake winks at Mimi, and they laugh. He realizes he is still holding her hand, gently drops it, and smiles. "Sorry, I didn't mean to intrude."

Mimi blushes, but doesn't know why. "No, you're fine. The door's open – I bet you know where the phone is. But wait; do you like red wine?" Jake nods. "Yeah, I don't know much, but I like it."

"Mimi hands him her glass. "Give me your first reaction."

"Smells like feet," says Jake.

"Doesn't it? We call that barn funk, Jake. Jim's dirty socks, Rover's old collar." He hands the wine back to Mimi, and their eyes lock for just a second. Something subtly clicks into place, easily, like gently-adjusted vertebrae. They both stand a little straighter now.

After evening vespers, the patio is cleared; before the stroke of two a.m., the Killians leave for home. Mimi pauses as she enters the front door. The house is quiet and dark; usually Warren beats them in, takes a shower, and sprawls out on the sofa watching the Comedy Channel. "Where's Warren?" she asks Sam, the first words she's spoken to him in three hours. Sam doesn't answer. Mimi kicks off her shoes, picks them up, and pads toward the bedroom while Sam strips his clothes off at the back door and walks naked to the shower. "Leave the water on, please, I'm right behind you," Mimi says. Sam ignores his wife and purposely turns off the faucet. Mimi ignores Sam, resets the water and steps in. Sam pees, flushes the toilet, and scurries out the door as scalding water hits Mimi's back. Mimi gasps, moves away and waits for the water to even out, robbing Sam of a satisfying yelp. She takes her time, allowing the hot water to penetrate her pores. Sam usually leaves her towel within reach, but not tonight. Mimi grabs one from the linen closet and, as she wipes herself down, reaches in the medicine cabinet, removes Sam's favorite mouthwash, and pours it down the drain. They don't waste more time on passive-aggressive behavior; both prefer a swift, hand's on battle to pussyfooting subterfuge. Sam's in the den arming for battle when Mimi enters; she's wearing red silk pajamas – a walking bull's eye.

.Sam fires the first shot. "I caught Warren drinking tonight, and told him to get the hell away from me." He reloads and, narrowing his eyes, draws a bead on Mimi's chest. "He probably saw you drinking, Mimi, and figured it was all right for him, too." He drops stink bombs in Mimi's path for the next two hours. Although Sam's caustic diatribe shakes her, she holds her ground. They argue until four a.m. – and finally call truce over scrambled eggs and toast. Sam and Mimi never get to the heart of the argument because the stomachs overrule. But, something shifts inside of Sam. Tonight, for the first time, Mimi is the enemy. Alcohol is a cruel temptress and Mimi is her wicked friend.

Warren, heartbroken and full of apologies, stops by early the next morning, but Sam won't speak to him. The whipped puppy tucks his tail and packs his bags. "Sam has made a difference in my life," he tearfully tells Mimi as they stand by the back door. "He's like a father to me." Mimi hugs Warren. "Give him some time. He loves you, but when he saw you drinking, it knocked him off-center." Mimi pauses. "Look, Warren. It's not your

110

responsibility to take care of Sam, okay? That's Sam's job."

"I know Mimi, but I owe him a lot."

"Do you have a place to live?"

"Yes, ma'am, I'm moving in with Jarrod. It'll be good." Warren hugs Mimi one more time. "Tell Sam I'll see him at AA." By brunch-time, Warren fills a hole at Steeles. The kid speeds around the kitchen like Quickdraw McGraw, confidently expediting, garnishing, and making friends. Sam's puppy has found a new home.

. . .

Melvin Witherspoon decides to pay Sam and Mimi a cold call on Wednesday afternoon. The local musicians look to Melvin for news and informally appoint him truth-seeker. It's up to Melvin to discover the musical future of The Phoenix. Mimi welcomes Melvin and motions toward a seat at the bar. She pours him a cup of coffee. "Black, right?"

"Thanks, Mimi. I was in the neighborhood and thought I'd stop by, but I can come back another time if now's not good for you."

"Wednesdays are good; it's a no-stress day for us. We're as caught up as we can be. Sam should be back in a few minutes. He went to the grocery store to pick up a few things." Mimi pulls out a cigarette and looks at Melvin. "Will it bother you if I smoke?"

Melvin doubles over in laughter – his funny bone begins in his head – and says, "Obviously you've been too busy to notice that I smoke and play the horn at the same time," he chuckles, as he fires up one of his own. "I think my lungs are about double the normal size, and I have a theory that all the bad stuff blows out when I play. My doctor doesn't agree, and neither does my wife." Melvin grins. "I'm convinced they're wrong."

Mimi's next words light Melvin up. "I absolutely love your band, Melvin. You guys are total professionals; Dee appreciates not having to round you up for a set, you know? I've noticed the crowd really picks up when you're in the house. Will you consider playing more than once a month?"

Melvin swoons. "Wow! That's not what I expected." He shakes loose all the negative preconceptions he'd carried in the door before he answers. "I'd consider it an honor, Mimi. I might have to pull in different musicians on occasion, but that would be a gas. Melvin Witherspoon Quartet with Special Guest whoever...yeah, I can cook something up."

"I've hired another bartender to back Dee up, have you met him? Mo Bowman. He's a keeper. Loves jazz."

"That big brother? I saw him in action last weekend, saw him step right off the floor and plant a size sixteen foot on the bar, reach out, and grab a guy's collar because he was trying to skate on his tab."

Mimi laughs. "I saw that, too. He was up and over, got the guy's credit card, asked how much tip to add on, rang him up, and thanked him. Never missed a beat. The guy tipped him ten bucks. Beautiful!"

"That guy'll never mess with Mo again and I doubt anyone else will, either. Don't let that big grin of his fool you. So Mo likes jazz, huh?"

"Oh, yeah, Melvin."

"Do you, Mimi?" Melvin's on task now. He stands up, walks to the pot, and helps himself to another cup of coffee.

Mimi takes a deep draw off her cigarette. Transported to another time, she pauses before responding. "I was raised on it. I was smoking candy cigarettes, wearing a black beret, and dancing to Sonny Rollins and Thelonious Monk when I was four years old. I love tenor sax, but I love alto even better, and piano best of all."

"No shit!" Melvin steps back and puts his hand on his heart – a dramatic gesture, but given the nature of the visit, the pronouncement is a godsend.

"Really," Mimi says, smiling. "My mom and dad's best friends had reel-to-reel in their living room. Jazz, all night long, uninterrupted. One flip of the switch, and we had our own little club. The women and children danced upstairs while the men played poker in the basement. Listening to jazz reminds me of all things good in my childhood. It paints pictures in my head...me dancing with my young, hip mother, mom teaching me to do the Camel Walk, you know, the ultimate kid experience."

Melvin nods his head. "See, that fits, now that I think about it. But I heard you and Sam might turn this club into more of a country scene with bluegrass music."

Mimi looks hard at Melvin. "Over my dead body," she snaps. "Jazz works here. If it ain't broke, don't fix it." Sam, hands full of bags, abruptly kicks the door with his foot. Melvin rushes over to open it. "Hey Sam, let me help you."

"No, this is it. I've got it." Sam eyes Melvin suspiciously. "Nothing better to do than hang out in the club when it's closed?" Sam takes in the scene, sets the bags on the bar, and looks at Mimi, unsmiling. The air becomes a little thicker.

"What's up, Sam?" Melvin asks cautiously, feeling the energy in the room shift. "Just thought I'd drop by on the way home from work and see how you two are doing, maybe talk a little music."

Sam grunts. "Melvin, I don't give a shit about music.

I'm in the restaurant business. If you're looking for a raise, you've come to the wrong place."

"No Sam, no man, nothing like that. The guys are worried you and Mimi are gonna change the vibe in here, but Mimi tells me you're doing okay with the jazz and blues scene."

Sam can't let the opportunity pass for a good rant. "Vibe? Let me tell you about vibe, Melvin. If one more of your fucking musicians tries to get free beer from my bartender, I'll lock the doors. I'll close this place down and there will be no vibe. You tell them I said that." Mimi's smile is turned upside down. "Sam, for heaven's sake. That's very rude."

"So what, Mimi? I like bluegrass! You tell the bands, Melvin, I mean all of them, that I'm a bluegrass fan. I don't want them in here. Jazz sounds like a mistake to me. Tell them, Melvin. Tell them all what I said. I'm tired of being taken advantage of. Fucking losers." Sam points toward the door. "Now, excuse yourself. I have work to do. Don't you have anything to do, Mimi?" Sam grabs the groceries from the bar and huffs, puffs, and blows his way upstairs.

Mimi looks at Melvin's downcast face and touches his shoulder. "Good Lord Melvin, please don't take that to heart. Sam's really tired and a bit grouchy right now, that's all. BMI and ASCAP are pushing for money so we can feature live music downstairs as well as play CDs upstairs. We have to pay a royalty of around twelve hundred dollars – copyright infringement or something." Mimi shrugs. "But, hey, if some starving musician somewhere gets to eat because we pay royalties, then money well spent, I say."

"Damn if you don't get it, Mimi."

"Sam gets it, too. He just hides his soft side. Can't be

too vulnerable, you know. Do me a favor, will you? Let's keep what happened today between us. Just tell the musicians that life is good at The Phoenix; that jazz will be favored above all. Sam and Mimi say so – you heard it straight from the source. But, also tell them this: no more free beer. Starting tonight, beers are a dollar."

"Even Beck's?"

"Yep, even Beck's."

Melvin smiles. "That'll make Jake very happy. Thanks, Mimi."

"Anytime, Melvin. You're always welcome here. Stop by more often."

. . .

It's Thursday night and there's a small, but enthusiastic crowd in The Phoenix, most who spend at least thirty-five dollars per head on a splendid, slow food dinner upstairs in the Firefly before heading downstairs for jazz. Tonight's featured performer is Odessa Hargrave, a vocalist of international renown whose two lives are divided by an ocean. Mimi is hopping mad. She's paying Odessa more than she can afford – more than scale – to perform three sets, and she's not getting her money's worth. During the break, Mimi calls Odessa into her office. "Odessa, what's your story? Is your throat sore?"

Odessa is confused. "No, I'm fine. What do you mean?"

"I mean you've sung three songs in two hours. What am I paying you?"

"One hundred dollars."

"So, right now, that's thirty-three dollars and thirty-three cents per song. Does that sound like a bargain to you? No, don't answer that." Mimi's on a roll. "Let's see, Odessa. Let's plug in the numbers here and see what kind of deal I'm getting. Let's say that each song is about four minutes long. You've worked twelve minutes in two hours. Is this what you normally do?"

"No, ma'am. Bobby's the bandleader. I'm just following his lead." Odessa cuts her eyes at Bobby, hoping for some backup, but Bobby drops the safety net. "Wait a minute, Odessa," Bobby retorts. "You're the leader tonight."

"Don't blame it on me, Bobby. I'm here to sing, and that's all."

"Bullshit, Odessa. We talked about this earlier. It's your gig."

Mimi looks at Bobby and Odessa. "I'll tell you who the bandleader is. It's me. And if I don't hear "Song for my Father" followed by about a dozen more tunes in the next two hours, plus some friendly banter with my customers, none of you will ever be asked here again. Do I make myself clear?"

"Wow. Yes, ma'am." Bobby's transparent. "We thought you were a pushover," he says, smiling. But Mimi's not kidding. "Think again, pal. Get a glove, get in the game, or get off my field."

"I'm sorry, Mimi. I didn't mean anything by it."

Mimi's squall is squelched by her sunnier nature. "You're all forgiven, just make it right." Bobby and Odessa tuck tail. "Guess she told us, huh?" Odessa says as they linger by the office door. "Just goes to show you, Odessa," Bobby says, "not everybody's gonna kiss your ass."

"Kiss my ass, Bobby."

"Make it bare, baby. Right here. Bend over and I'll kiss it."

"Don't tempt me brother." Odessa raises one perfectly plucked eyebrow.

Mimi doesn't look up from her paperwork. "I don't pay more for nudity."

Odessa laughs on her way to the stage. "Guess these black drawers will stay on, then."

...

Mimi is a businesswoman who respects value for the dollar. Ask any musician who plays at the Phoenix and they will say Mimi's tough, but she's fair. She knows music. When the customers are gone and the band is packing up and the beers are a dollar and the paperwork is done and the details of the night are being recounted for the eleventh time, Mimi's attention drifts. She removes herself from the intimate scene, steps into her office, cues up Jean Luc Ponty's *Elephants in Love,* dimes the volume and dances with the abandonment of a four-year-old child.

If you soften your eyes and follow her rhythmic sway, you will see that Mimi dances with her mother, with her sisters, with a protective posse of winged gypsies; you will know that love and goodness keep her on the beat, keep her moving along the serpentine for Eternity. Mimi is pure energy.

ETERNAL UNFULFILLMENT

Every single moment is more or less incomplete, and more or less complete. Happy now?

Julie Reston feels refreshed this morning, and begins her beguine with a touch more spring in her step, a bit more lilt of spirit. As she looks in the mirror, she notices her eyes and smiles. The raccoons have moved. Her morning routine never changes; same twenty-minute shower, same oil, same brand of cigarettes, oh yes, a different magazine, same fifty strokes to the hair, same concentration on mascara, mascara, oh yes, different Chanel suit, different shoes, same lipstick, same window up and down. She leaves the bathroom without a second glance at precisely seven ten a. m.

Julie's moving on up – a new job, a big fat office, dust-free silk ferns and a computer programmer at her beck and call. No more standing in line at the copy machine, no more tiny windowless office on the reeking gastrointestinal floor, no more mile trek from the office door to her enclosed parking space. All this and I still get to dress up, too, Julie thinks. Julie is a conservative modern woman with a big paycheck. Her biological clock has never ticked, has never chimed on the hour – ever – until she compares Rolex watches with her new boss, Doctor Tucker Bush. Doctor Bush is separated from his wife of thirty-four years (but not divorced), incestuously wealthy, and twenty-one years older than Julie. He likes eggs. He's a fertility specialist cum geneticist to be exact, with four grown children. On Doctor Bush's office door is an enlarged copy of a Gary Larson cartoon entitled

How the Human Egg is Often Deceived. Squiggly sperm are dressed in baseball caps, vying for entrance into the faceless egg's corpus luteum. 'Excuse me, ma'am. Here to read your meter, ma'am. Phone repairman, may I check your lines? Package for you, ma'am.'

Julie is GeneLife Planning Corporation's new Director of Risk Assessment. She is responsible for gathering detailed family histories and developing methodologies to help practitioners understand a patient's risk for certain genetic conditions, from heart abnormalities to juvenile arthritis, from Acromesomelic Dwarfism to Zollinger-Ellison Syndrome. Julie expands her scientific mind, and although she doesn't wear a white coat – a momentary setback – she is flush with importance. Explaining the meaning of Anorchia and its potential lifetime effect on one unlucky newborn is not Julie's job, however. Julie provides the research, and Doctor Bush is the messenger. "But Doc, he's a boy, ain't he? Where's his little nuts?"

Doctor Bush breaks it to the new dad as gently as possible. "Mr. Smith, they didn't develop during gestation."

"Jestashun?" Mr. Smith is confused.

Doctor Bush smiles sympathetically. "The nine months he spent growing inside your wife's womb."

Mr. Smith's expression changes to recognition as he develops his own scientific theory. "Are they hiding somewhere? Maybe he got cold in there. When I get really cold, mine disappear, too."

Doctor Bush picks up the Smith chart, takes a deep breath, and stifles a yawn. "Mr. Smith, with your permission, I'd like to do a series of tests to determine the proper treatment for your son. Who's your health care provider?"

Mr. Smith reaches for his wallet and extracts a plastic

card. "Grandover Benefit Services," he says, handing the card to Doctor Bush. "Right here it is." Doctor Bush politely looks at the worthless card and hands it back to Mr. Smith. "Why don't you step to the front desk and speak with Anne? She'll get all your paperwork together and then we'll determine how to proceed."

"Will it help if I keep him warm?"

"It certainly won't hurt, Mr. Smith. Good luck, now. We'll be in touch."

. . .

If she were a musician, Julie's band would be called Julie and the Routine. She spends her first three hours of each day researching genetic birth defects, then two hours painstakingly detailing her findings in both medical and layman's terms. After a fifteen minute break for lunch (a Slim Fast and an apple at her desk except on Wednesdays when she meets Betsy out, but never Jake) she spends the afternoon organizing her alphabetized system – she's up to Dancing Eye Syndrome – and updating her computer base. The final hour or so of every day is reserved for a status meeting with Doctor Tucker Bush which may include drinks and dinner, depending on Tucker's social agenda.

Julie loves her new job, finds security in the unending research. She takes her work home every night, camps on the sofa surrounded by books and files, overflows with desire to learn every physical and mental anomaly caused by a faulty or missing link in the human gene pool – and Jake feels her attention to their relationship wane again. Bliss caught a cab to the airport and bought a one-way ticket to Nowheresville when Jake wasn't looking.

Resigned, Jake walks into the living room. "Julie, please put down your book and talk to me for a minute."

Julie sighs loudly. "I'm working, Jake. Can it wait?"

"No, it can't. What's going on with you?"

Unwilling to make eye contact, Julie pretends to read. "What do you mean?"

Jake sits on the sofa beside her, and rubs her leg. "We were soaring, and now we're back to that old familiar nothing. I don't mean to be dense, but damn, where are you?"

Julie moves her leg to the floor. "Come on, Jake, not now. I'm busy." Jake grabs the book from Julie's petite hand and throws it against the wall. Julie barely flinches as she looks at him with contempt. "When's the last time we made love?" he asks. "God, Jake," Julie responds, annoyed. "Yesterday, don't you remember?"

"No, that's not making love, Julie. That's two horny people getting off in ten minutes or less."

Julie moves her body away from Jake and stands up before he can touch her again. "What's your point?"

Jake rubs his head, looks at his irritated wife, and asks a question that stops his heart. "Have you met somebody?"

Julie walks to the fireplace, picks up a small brass urn and inspects it for dust. "I meet people all the time, Jake, just like you do."

"Have you met a man, Julie? Are you falling out of love with me?"

"That's ridiculous," says Julie, retrieving her book from the floor. Finding her place again, she marks it, places it on the coffee table, and waits. Jake slowly rises from the sofa and faces his wife. "Someone told me that you and Tucker Bush had a drink after work the other night. They saw you and Tucker in the hotel bar across the street from the hospital."

"Who told you that?" Julie quickly smothers the blaze

in her eyes, but Jake records her quick defense. "Look, Jake, everything I do is work-related. Doctor Bush and I are busy people and on occasion, we both work late, as you know. We have a drink together once or twice a week and finish up the day. That's it." Julie wills herself to stay loose.

Jake watches Julie's effort to control her breath, but doesn't take advantage of it. He turns his head away from his wife's embarrassment. "Don't you think it'd be a good idea to tell me these things before I hear it through the gossip network?"

"I will from now on since it bothers you so much," Julie snaps. Jake's exasperated. "Wouldn't it bother you?" Julie finds her form again. "No! It wouldn't bother me at all. Tucker and I are business associates, Jake. That's all. Why don't you take that cute little head nurse, what's her name, out for a drink after a hard day at the hospital? It's okay with me, really." Julie smiles coldly. "Yeah…why don't you do that, Jake? It'd be good for you." Julie's face contorts into a smirk.

Jake reaches out and gently takes Julie's hand in his. "No, what would be good for me is to have a wife who loves me. I want to come home after a rough day and be with you, not out having drinks with someone who had a child die in her arms in the ED. We have nothing more to talk about at the end of the day. We need space and light and love from our families when we walk in the door – not another cold body. You seem to have forgotten that." He drops her hand and wraps his arms around her, hoping for simple reciprocity.

Julie flinches in response. "Did you walk Molly?"

Jake backs away. "Julie, did you hear what I just said?"

Julie's nerves, on edge since Jake began this stupid discussion, have short-circuited. The savage cruelty of their marriage surfaces with the speed of a lioness taking down an injured zebra. "Yes I did, Jake, and I want you to listen to me. You knew when you married me that I wanted a career. I'm not Mrs. America and I'm not gonna try. I'm not your personal sex goddess, nor do I want to be. You are looking at the woman you married. I haven't changed. If you want something different, go for it. I don't care."

Jake's ribcage shreds under Julie's claws. "Wait a minute. What happened? Didn't we get back on track a few months ago? Or was that my imagination? Did I imagine being happy?" The prey seeks safety of shelter, and finds only a bare, open landscape as the predator goes for the kill. "Back on track? Jake, we derailed a long time ago. I wanted to take this wedding band off the day after I married you. I just wasn't brave enough." Emasculated by his wife's words, Jake turns and quickly strikes a final connecting blow. Julie screams. "Damn it Jake, not the mirror! Break something of yours, asshole!" The only pain Julie feels is when she removes a glass shard from her pinkie finger.

. . .

Wednesday night is Gospel night at The Phoenix. Upstairs in the restaurant, Sam and Jarrod serve fried catfish, hushpuppies and homemade slaw for $8.95 a heaping plateful. The joint is jumping up and down; God is in the house in the form of a small contingent from the Union Baptist Church choir. They're covering Donnie McClurkin's *That's What I Believe* when Jake walks in the door. The driving bass goes right through Jake and he is off the ground, elevated by the spirit, and he is hungry. He takes a seat at the kitchen bar. Sam greets him, slaps a hot catfish platter in front of him, and pulls a non-alcoholic beer from his private stash. "On the house, my friend," a grinning Sam says, "I'm feeling charitable." Jake feels the beat of the bass through the floor, feels it with every bite, but the goodness in his stomach doesn't ease the pain in his chest. He's thinking about leaving when he feels a hand on his shoulder. "Hey, man! 'Bout time you came around on a Wednesday night. Listen, after you eat, will you spell me on keys while I grab some of this fine fish while the grabbin's good?"

This is the savior Jake needs. He turns to his friend and smiles. "It'll be my pleasure, Tinker."

Tinker leans in closer. "You all right tonight?" He sees the worry in Jake's eyes.

"I am now that I'm here," Jake says. "It's been a rough day. Lost a kid."

"God bless you, man." Tinker shakes his head. "You ever think about becoming a full time musician? It's painful, but in a different way, know what I mean?"

"I think about it every day, man."

"Make it happen, and God will watch over you. You're the most righteous player I've ever met. Tyner has nothing on you, Jake. So, you'll start the next set for me?"

Jake nods. "When's the break over?"

"Fifteen minutes, man. Be on time, or suffer Dee's wrath."

"I'll be down in ten." Jake smiles at Tinker, and catches Mimi's eye as she carries a load of empty plates to the dish room. She disposes of her load and stops for a quick chat. "How you doing, friend? Glad to see you made it out. This is my favorite night of the week – gets everybody in a good mood except the bar staff. They hate making virgin daiquiris and the tips, well, you know how it is."

Jake chuckles. "Tell them it's community service, Mimi. Tell them it adds much good juju to their karmic account." Mimi looks more closely at Jake. "Rough day at the hospital? You look tired."

Jake's face crumbles. "Mimi, I just need a hug."

"That's why God gave us arms, Jake."

"Amen, sister."

Jake leaves five dollars on the bar, thanks Sam, stops by the bathroom, and washes his hands. The face staring back from the mirror shocks him. He sees the grieving father of the dead child. Jake closes his eyes and looks again. He sees the mother of the child, and the grandmother. He feels as if he's falling but he's standing, and he floats to the stage and spreads his lovely hands across the keys and the choir sings *We Fall Down*. Jake cries as he plays; he cries for the family of the dead child and for the heartbroken nurse who held the child in her arms and for the love of his beloved wife, Julie.

But Sam is on another plane, and the engines roar as he grabs Mimi by the arm and takes her outside. "Mimi, do you have to touch everyone who walks into this restaurant? Can't you keep your hands to yourself?" Mimi is flabbergasted as Sam continues his rant. "Some people don't like to be touched. Like that girl with the tag sticking out of the back of her shirt – I doubt she appreciates you fixing it for her."

Mimi is incredulous. "I think she very much appreciated me doing that, Sam. I know I'd appreciate it."

"Yeah, but that's you. One of these days, you're gonna get shot."

"Why? For fixing somebody's tag?"

Sam is belligerent. "For touching the wrong person!" His tone becomes hateful. "Like Jake; why did you hug Jake?"

Mimi is exasperated. "Because he needed a hug, Sam. Sometimes people just need hugs. Don't you feel better when I hug you?"

Sam ignores the question and shrugs. "You're too touchy-feely. It gives people the creeps."

"You're the only person I know who gets the creeps from a touch." Mimi bites her tongue and pauses. "But you're right. I'll tone it down some. I sure don't want to creep anybody out. You've just pointed out a character flaw, one I've never considered. I'll be more aware of touching people. Point taken."

Mimi immediately goes downstairs to The Phoenix and hugs no less than twenty people. They hug her back. She touches their shoulders and their hands. They reach for her. Mimi softens her heart. She reaches into her own chest and touches it; now, she opens her heart's door, and gently, very gently, gathers and releases a bright hot spark from its innermost chamber and sends it through the holy people where it grows and ignites Jake's dull ember. God is asking for a tithe.

Mimi smiles and knows, for tonight at least, nobody plans to shoot her.

MERCY

Forgive all error in yourselves and others; with forgiveness, there can be no error in the world. Forgive someone now, right now.

Sam and Mimi don't agree on much these days, but they resolve to always back up their wait staff and reward them for the difficult job of pleasing a fickle public that includes people who have never worked in a restaurant before. On ugly days, they believe people who haven't worked in the business shouldn't be allowed to eat out, or should be required to take a course in restaurant etiquette taught, of course, by restaurant employees.

. . .

Bob and Mandy are regular customers from back in the old days when nobody cared. They enjoy sitting at the kitchen bar and watching Sam work his magic. At first, Sam and Mimi are smitten because Bob is polite and complimentary. It doesn't take long for a mind shift.

After finishing their usual split entrée, Bob and Mandy ask to see the dessert tray. They choose the homemade chocolate pecan pie, warmed please, they request, an extra big piece. Regular customers get preferential treatment at The Firefly, so Mimi cuts the Mac-daddy slice, loads it with whipped cream, and serves the pie herself. Bob and Mandy lick the plate clean; not a crumb of evidence is left. Waitron Carly knows Mimi personally delivered the pie, but when she asks how they liked their dessert, Bob says, "Dessert? We didn't have any." He pats his tummy for effect. "We have no room," he says. Carly confers with Mimi, who chooses to let it slide. But, that's not all.

Bob and Mandy steal candy from the non-profit honesty box in the lobby; Bob comes in for dinner with last night's leftovers in tow and asks the kitchen staff to reheat them; worse still, he consistently leaves nine percent tips. Nobody wants to wait on the couple, and Mimi understands why. She charges Bob a pain-in-the-ass tax, and states it directly on the bill as such. Bob and Mandy are quickly traded to another team.

. . .

It's cold as Mimi's feet at bedtime and sleeting outside and The Firefly is slammed! Fifteen people stand patiently at the front door, waiting to be listed for a one hour minimum table delay; the phone rings off the knob, the Moore party of four head upstairs from The Phoenix to be seated, and there's total gridlock by the credit card machine. Jose is standing, but his body is curled in the fetal position, mouth wide open and eyeglasses covered with fog. Mimi's not in the weeds – she's in the woods and it's dark in there and she feels the hot breath of a wolf on her neck; she's one step away from total chaos and panic, and loving it! A well-dressed man used to getting his way barges past the waiting crowd and plants himself in the skinny front dining room aisle. He grows roots, crosses his arms, and stares at Mimi with pure malice. Mimi makes eye contact with him. "Sir, come to me, please. Please, sir, come to me," Mimi beckons.

He stands stock still, muscles tense, and waits for Mimi to have a nervous breakdown or a bout of hysteria, neither of which is gonna happen. Strike one. Mimi ignores him, walks customers right past his all-over-the-way ass for a solid three minutes, and still he doesn't move. Regular diners, keenly aware of the standoff, are firmly on Mimi's side and wait, forks poised above pasta, for the showdown. They know the house rules, but the new guy doesn't.

Mimi returns to the front lobby and grabs the incessantly ringing telephone. She tries, once more, for a peaceful resolution. "Please sir, please." Mimi kindly says. "Please, sir, come to me," Mimi gently urges. He thinks he can best Mimi, but he might as well try to kill a buffalo with a Gene Autry cap gun. "Lady," he spews," you have a real control issue going on." Strike two. Mimi's eyes are steel beams as she channels Sam. "Mister, I'm fucking busy up here. Tell me what you want right now, or get the hell out of my way. Now, what's it gonna be?" Pow-pow! goes the cap gun.

The man submits, pinches out a tearful apology, sheepishly puts his name on Mimi's waitlist, and heads downstairs, where he politely waits for dinner, spends sixty-two bucks on wine and appetizers, and leaves a whopping tip for the bartenders. An hour later, he spends ninety more, tips thirty percent, and becomes a regular customer who occasionally brings Sam fine cigars and Mimi beautiful writing tablets. Detente: the game where everybody wins.

. . .

Mimi learns many things from Sam, including the importance of a strong and well-maintained safety net. She never, ever makes light of a situation that might compromise her staff's integrity or character. If there's a shadow of a doubt, Sam and Mimi always stand firmly behind their employees – never dressing down the staff – at least until the customer has moved on. Then, and only then, will they fire an incompetent server on the spot if the situation warrants it. "The bottom line," Sam says, "is building trust and loyalty. Back your staff!"

Sam and Mimi offer the customer great value for the dollar. However, The Firefly is not your typical modern day restaurant with the latest gadgets; in fact, it's fairly primitive in the area of high-tech expertise. Sam and Mimi don't see the sense in spending thousands of dollars on computerized registers when their system works just fine if you hold your mouth right. Passing savings onto the customers and generating profit is the name of their game. Rather than hiring a cashier, the servers carry their own banks, balance nightly checkout sheets, and are held accountable for any discrepancies. Sam and Mimi also protect their ace staff by guaranteeing tips on busy nights. The customer knows this up front; it's not a secret. For parties of six or more, twenty percent is automatically added to the check. If a check must be divided on a busy night, the staff has the option of adding twenty percent to each bill. In a perfect world, Sam would accept only cash – like that burrito joint in Texas with daily lines long enough to circle the Astrodome.

The Firefly's policies are akin to a game of crazy eights, the version with the additional rules of skip a card on the four and switch directions on the seven. Sam and Mimi learn the hard way; they try to please everyone, and fail in the attempt. Their one-check policy draws fire, but customers get antsy when the server divides checks; a customer may have a credit card that's declined, and then all hell breaks loose. The wait person must call a toll-free number, speak with someone who talks very softly with a strong accent, and then suffer through a ten minute hold, or worse yet, get transferred to the black hole. Meanwhile, the customer waits so long for the hopefully completed transaction that he forgets what he had for dinner, or that his service was exceptional; he gets angry and complains about the twenty percent add-on tip; other customers get angry, too, and leave crummy tips because their server is tied up with the frustrating six-way check split for the once happy but now obnoxious table in the corner.

Mimi clearly explains The Firefly's house rules to all customers. She spells them out on the menu, and recites them over the phone. When a customer agrees to the rules up front, then ignores the agreement, all hell can, and usually does, break loose. When a customer ignores Mimi's best-laid plans, it's downright insulting.

. . .

Mimi takes a reservation for a party of ten, Saturday night, eight p.m. sharp. She explains the one check, twenty percent policy over the phone to not one person in the party, but two. The house rules are reluctantly accepted (warning!). A third call comes in. "I'd like to bring a dessert for the table, as three people in our party are celebrating birthdays this week." Mimi closes her eyes and prays for understanding. "Sure," she says. "We'll allow you to bring your own cake, but there will be a two-dollar per person service charge." The caller pauses. "You must be joking. Why would you charge a fee for that? I've never heard of such a thing."

"Well, it's like this: somebody has to cut and serve the cake, someone has to clear the table and wash the dishes, and we lose the opportunity to sell our wonderful desserts to your table," Mimi pauses, and then continues optimistically. "But, the three birthday celebrants will receive dessert on the house anyway. See, that's what we do at The Firefly. So, sure, you can bring your own, but the service charge remains. Does that make sense?"

"Well, I've never heard of such a thing. We just won't

bring it. And, why must we pay with one credit card? Why can't you separate our check five ways?"

Warning, warning! Mimi slowly and politely explains the policy for the third time; she's happy to share this information with as many people as possible to decrease the risk of communication errors. However, her caution flags are flying at full mast. Mimi hopes the group cancels their reservation. The vibe isn't there. She even offers to call a neighboring restaurant for them, but they insist on dining at The Firefly.

The group arrives Saturday night at seven forty-five – fifteen minutes early for the eight p.m. reservation – and is miffed because their table isn't ready. Mimi sends them downstairs to The Phoenix for a quick drink and calls them up at precisely the stroke of eight. Mimi's most experienced and crowd-pleasing server, Carly AKA Potty Mouth, is sent into active duty. "Mimi, these people have already fucking asked me twice about fucking separating this check five fucking ways. I'm not sure what to do, so I'm pretending not to fucking hear them."

"Good," Mimi says. She's in total agreement with Carly's feigned deafness. "Just fucking ignore them for the time being." Fifteen minutes later, Carly reports in. "It's all under control, Mimi. The fucking leader of the pack says that one check is the deal and she's sticking to it. These people are fucking great! They're getting in the groove and having a fucking good time. I'm glad I'm fucking waiting on them." Two hours later, Carly's song changes. "Mimi, come outside for a minute. I have a fucking problem. The party's inspecting the fucking bill with a fine-tooth comb. One man thinks I charged him for an extra glass of Stonestreet chardonnay. I politely disagreed with him, and now he's yelling at me for calling him a fucking liar."

"Well, did you?"

"No fucking way!"

Mimi takes a slow breath and pulls on her lower lip. "Here's what you do. Ease the tension, babe. Give him ten dollars cash, tell him you're sorry, and forget about it. We'll eat it, no sweat. Not on you. Just make a note in your paperwork." As Mimi and Carly reenter the front door, they find a slobbering maniac pitching a class-five, hurricane-force fit in the front dining room, where customers put down forks and turn their attention to the drama. Carly detours wide as the man points at her. "She called me a liar! She called me a liar in front of my friends!" Mimi approaches the rabid beast without a stun gun. "Sir, please calm down. Sir, please. She didn't really call you names, now, did she?"

"I don't care! She made me feel like a liar, and now you are calling me a liar! What kind of shit hole is this?" Mimi sees Sam from the corner of her eye, and motions him away. "Sir!" she snaps sharply. "You are disturbing my customers. You will either calm down, or get your coat and leave immediately, and I mean right now!" Mimi conjures the eye of the storm. The apoplectic, red-faced man glares and snarls and skulks to the backroom corner table where his group anxiously awaits the latest news. They don't see him blow a gasket, but the customers in the front of the house do, and they erupt into mad applause. Bolstered by an unfortunate shot of adrenaline, Mimi approaches the angry table. "I'm really sorry this celebration turned into a bad time for you all," she calmly says. "So am I," says the Alpha bitch. "You wouldn't let us separate this check five ways, nor bring our own dessert, and now you are accusing us of stealing. We've never been treated like this before, and we certainly won't be back."

Mimi tries to take a deep breath, to no avail; she's almost to the point of hyperventilating. "I'm sure you are all lovely people individually, but tonight, as a group, you are a nightmare. I'm asking you to leave before we all say something we'll regret tomorrow." The Alpha bitch stands up, her bulk outweighing Mimi by a good one hundred pounds. "I need to see the owner immediately," she commands loudly.

"You're looking at her," Mimi says calmly. Did you hear that? Was that loud enough for you? Alpha bitch slams Mimi with the full weight of her ego. "Obviously you don't know what you're doing or who you're talking to! You're kicking some very important people out of your restaurant! We are business people, and well-respected in this town. As a matter of fact, one of us has owned a restaurant before and feels your policies are totally unreasonable."

Mimi doesn't hear Sam come up behind her. She feels his hand on her shoulder as he gently moves her behind him. "I don't give a damn who you are, lady, there's the door. Get out!"

"Rest assured, we won't be back, and neither will any of our friends," she shouts as she hurls a fur around her wide body, looking very much like a groundhog.

"Good!" Sam shouts back. "Don't let the door hit you in the ass on your way out!"

Alpha looks scathingly at Sam's dirty apron and makes a wrong appraisal. "Just who the hell do you think you are?"

"The other owner, lady. Now, get out before I call the cops!"

Mimi's bones are shaking. "I should have stayed away from the table," she says later. "I should have never taken the reservation." Shoulda, woulda, coulda...the incident haunts Mimi and Sam for months. The vendetta to hurt The Firefly is strong. The hate mail flows. But, Sam and Mimi weather the storm. Business is better than ever. Customers hear that each meal is served with a couple of acts of grand theatre thrown in at no extra charge, and they come in droves. Carly moves on after this incident, but as a show of deep affection, Mimi and Sam hang her picture in the upstairs men's bathroom. Potty Mouth oversees her domain through the glass of an eight by ten, black and white glossy that hangs on the wall over the toilet.

. . .

It's three o'clock on Friday afternoon. Mimi is scrubbing one of the four bathrooms when the phone rings. It's her ace server, Kyle. "Mimi, I'm going to be late today, and I'm well, this is really gonna push your buttons. It's really bad." He pauses, not sure if he should tell the truth.

"Oh, God, Kyle. Are you okay? Did your dog get run over? Have you been in a wreck? Tell me! Just spit it out!"

"I'm drunk. But I'll be in, I promise."

"Geez, Kyle. Go to sleep for awhile. Call me back around five and let me know if you can make it in. Take some aspirin, okay? We're slammed tonight."

The phone rings at 3:45pm. "Mimi, it's BC. I'm really sick and I can't even walk. I feel like I'm talking underwater and my ears ache. I've been attacked by the crud."

Mimi sighs. "No sweat, little darling. Just take care of yourself. Call me tomorrow and let me know how you're feeling, okay?" Great. Mimi and Sam are heading into a busy Friday night understaffed. Kyle never calls, but shows up at 5:30. He's remorseful, still somewhat buzzed, and looks like a stray cat with mange – putrid gray skin and blood orange eyes. Mimi sends him home without a word of derision. Kyle will beat himself to a mental pulp without any help from me, she thinks. God bless the child.

The Firefly staff includes many alcoholics and drug addicts in various stages of recovery. Mimi and Sam don't battle this dilemma alone. The industry is flush with addiction. This beast known as the restaurant business drags its victims through a dark and slimy grease pit, then burps them up covered in toxic waste. Mimi and Sam wait at the top end, bathe their battered soldiers in tender warmth, wipe their snotty noses and send them back to the front line of the war zone. It's a tough and selfish business.

Statistically, an incredibly high number of chefs suffer from alcohol abuse, compared to other professions. An intense stress level and the proximity to a fully stocked bar signal the death knell for many alcoholics who try and fail to maintain sobriety while working in this environment. But, an active alcoholic can be successful in any business. Just ask Sam.

You may wonder how Mimi doesn't recognize relapsed behavior in her husband. You may think Mimi knows, but chooses to ignore it. You may think that you, with your brilliant expertise and worldly experience, would spot the signs immediately. Well, bully for you.

But, Mimi never sees Sam drunk. As the days get longer and the business gets steadier and the workload gets heavier at The Firefly and The Phoenix, Sam and Mimi spell one another; they break up the hours to provide much-needed relief from the never-ending stress. Some nights, Sam closes and sends Mimi home early. Some nights, Mimi closes without Sam. They spend less and less time together. And, vodka doesn't smell. Everyone suspects that Sam is drinking again. Everyone, that is, but Mimi.

One might ask in a voice overflowing with concern, "Mimi, is Sam drinking again?" Mimi answers, "No, of course not. He's just tired. And when Sam gets tired," she explains, "he slurs his words a little and he staggers a little and he's a little grouchy." She shakes her head. "No, he's not drinking. He goes to AA meetings at least twice a week. He's just stressed out. But thanks for caring," she says, smiling.

. . .

Jake and Julie also live a fractured fairy tale life. Both continue to withdraw, but neither is brave enough to flee or free, to release the bird from the cage. But, who's the bird? Jake doesn't leave because his soundproof studio is downstairs. Julie doesn't leave because she has an investment in the décor. At least, that's what one surmises as one stands on the outside looking at their discontent. Jake and Julie build a comfort zone that is filled with insomnia and night monsters and stomach ulcers and Valium and Xanax and silk flowers and designer pillows. And a good dog.

Julie and Jake play the game well. The neighbors entertain and, arriving arm in arm, they fake cohesiveness; they laugh at each other's jokes. They spend a week at the beach with family and play the traditional partner's charade. Julie takes long walks by herself and Jake swims so far out in the ocean that you can't see him except with binoculars, but this is Julie and this is Jake. This is what they do, year after year after year. Julie sleeps in her underwear, even at the beach. Jake reaches across the three feet of cool, unwrinkled sheet and touches a pillow barrier, even at the beach. He removes the fort that Julie builds around herself, caresses her cheek, smoothes her hair from her face. Julie turns to Jake, pulls him to her, and spends the next ten minutes fantasizing about Doctor Tucker Bush while Jake fills his mind with images from Playboy. Ten minutes after Julie fakes her last orgasm, she springs from the bed and takes a long, hot shower. She twists her hair into a towel, pulls on a pair of white shorts and a navy blue tank top, and walks back into the bedroom. Jake, lying on top of the sheets in his bathing suit, reads last month's *Musician* magazine.

"Jake, I think we need to see a marriage counselor." Jake lowers his magazine, removes his reading glasses, and stares at Julie in disbelief. "We did, Julie, last year, remember? We went to three sessions and you decided not to go back because it was boring."

Julie rolls her eyes. "I know, Jake. You don't have to remind me. We've talked about that fiasco until I'm blue in the face. That woman – I still think she's a fake – droned on and on and said absolutely nothing of value."

Jake drops the magazine and sits up straight. "What about that book she recommended? You know, what's the name of it…"

"*The Five Love Languages.* Interesting book, but it didn't work for us." Julie dismisses the memory with a shake of her tanned arm. "Yeah, I remember a little about it," Jake says. "Wasn't there something about service and gifts and stuff?"

"Well, that's why it didn't work, right there. You couldn't remember to fill up my tank with gas or love or whatever. You let me run on empty, so I let you run on empty, too."

Jake snorts. "That's the way to build trust and repair a marriage, now, isn't it darling?"

"Shut up, Jake." They look at each other, each imploring the other to understand, each willing the other to find solid ground and pull the other to safety. Jake reaches for Julie, but misses as she moves to a corner chair. He says, "I think two people have to love each other for any counseling to work." Jake is tender in his speech, hopeful, and Julie recognizes his need – as well as her own – for honest discourse; no fighting, no pettiness. Julie rises from the chair and takes a seat on the bed beside Jake. "That book works for a lot of people, Jake. You didn't give it a chance." Jake grins at his wife and says, "Yeah, well, it read too much like a Christian Cosmopolitan. You know what I mean." He picks up Julie's hand, kisses it, and places it back in her lap. "So," he asks, "have you picked out the perfect marriage counselor?"

"I think so. Betsy recommends Dr. Catherine Rousseaux."

"You talked to Betsy about our marriage?" Jake is irritated. "God, Julie, she has the biggest mouth in the neighborhood. That was a huge fucking mistake."

"Betsy's my best friend, Jake. She likes you, a lot! Why are you so defensive?"

"Because, Julie, our business is our business. If you'd talk to me instead of your girlfriends, maybe we could work on our problems without interference. And forget Doctor whoever you just said. I'm not going to her. If we're going, let's go to somebody who doesn't know who we are."

"Dr. Rousseaux doesn't know us from Adam's housecat, dummy."

"Yeah, but she knows Betsy, and that's too close."

Julie stands up and stretches. Her interest is waning, on the verge of disappearing forever, and Jake senses it in her next words. "Look, forget I mentioned it," she says, and looks hard at Jake. "But, it's either this or a divorce."

"Or an affair with Tucker Bush, right?"

Julie shrugs. "It's possible, if I make myself available. But, it won't be an affair. It will be a relationship. He's made his feelings known."

Jake walks to the closet and starts packing. "I think you've done a pretty good job of that, Julie."

"Done a pretty good job of what?" Julie unwraps the towel from her head, brushes her hair, and pulls it into a pony tail. She knows the end is near.

"Making yourself available." Jake moves to the chest and empties socks and underwear into his suitcase.

"No, not really. He's going out with an exercise physiologist, just out of college, I think. Probably the same age as his daughter." Julie looks in the mirror, adjusts her tank top, and shakes her pony tail. I'm much better looking than she is, Julie thinks.

"And how does hanging out with a man in the middle of a mid-life crisis make you feel, Julie?"

"Save it for the marriage counselor, Jake." Julie doesn't have to pack her suitcase; she's been packed for three days. She turns to her husband. "Jake, I'll tell you the truth. I thought I would never find anyone in the world who would love me as much as you do. That's worth a lot. And, I loved you when we got married, I really did. I just wasn't in love with you. Don't take this the wrong way, Jake. I thought it would be okay, that we'd grow into each other. But, it didn't work out that way."

"Why do you want to go to a marriage counselor, then?"

"I really don't know. I guess so somebody can tell you that this marriage can't be saved. That it's over." She looks at Jake, expecting anger and hurt. But she sees a calm man, a man who breathes easily when he asks the final question. "Is that what you want?"

"I want out, Jake."

He slaps his suitcase shut, and walks toward the door. "Then we need an attorney, not a marriage counselor."

"What do I tell my family?"

"Tell them anything you want, Julie." He puts the suitcase on the floor, walks back to his wife, and hugs her for the last time. He's surprised when she hugs him back.

. . .

Jake finds a house in the country with a big front porch and good acoustics; he snaps his fingers and there's no slap-back. The large living room is dead rather than live, although the floors are made of heart pine. I can practice a band here, Jake thinks. Now after a sad day at the hospital, he is greeted by a beautiful four-legged red-head who showers him with kisses, who, when he cries, licks the tears from his dimples, who wraps her body around his and touches him with a compassion that Julie could muster only a handful of times in the life of their fourteen-year marriage. Molly is happiest when Jake is happy, and Jake is happiest when his house is filled with music, when his bass player steps up and slaps it, and jazz turns to funk and fusion stew cooks in the kitchen and coyotes dance in his front yard at two a.m. under a waxing gibbous moon.

Jake's co-workers do their level best to help the brother climb out of his perceived blue hole, but he's getting in the groove of flying solo. "Doctor R., come out with us tonight. It's Sandra's birthday and we're all going out for drinks after work."

Jake smiles, but declines. "Thanks, but I can't. Not

tonight."

"Oh, come on. You got something to do?"

"I promised myself I'd run today after work. I need to stick to my plan."

"Listen, Jake. It's been two months since you left Julie. It's time to get your groove on, man. Use it or lose it."

"I didn't leave Julie. She left me."

"Whatever. Look. See that cute nurse with the bunny covers on? Her name's Nan. She's interested in you, we can tell, and she's coming out tonight. Jake, are you listening? Look at her. She's a hotty. Use it or lose it, man."

Jake laughs and shakes his head. "Nah, another time maybe. I need to get home. Molly needs to be fed. But ask me again; just give me a little notice next time."

"What do I tell the bunny chick?"

"Nothing. She's a baby doll, though. You ask her out."

"No, you should ask her out. I know she likes jazz."

"Probably Kenny G."

"Hey, you're right! See man, right up your alley."

Jake turns toward his office and ends the conversation. "Thanks anyway," he says with a wry smile. "Have fun tonight. Gotta run."

Doctor Tucker Bush sleeps on Jake's side of the king-sized bed two nights a week, spends two nights at his apartment with his young squeeze – no sign of Julie there, not even a toothbrush – and spends weekends with his wife at their mountain home. Julie knows about the wife. "We don't sleep together, Julie," he says. "It's just an agreement between the two of us. She doesn't know about you and I prefer to keep it that way, at least for now." The squeeze is never mentioned.

Julie is falling madly in love with Tucker Bush and feels in her heart that he will finalize his divorce and marry her; Julie is used to having her own way. Tucker and his wife have been separated for six years and intend on staying separated, a choice which provides freedom without the complication of a large settlement. Tucker isn't interested in marrying Julie or any of the other women he sleeps with. But, he doesn't tell Julie that. He doesn't tell Julie anything; he lets her believe what she needs to believe.

"Tucker, my diaphragm slipped. I can feel it; hang on, I'll be right back."

"No, lie still. I'll fix it. Put your legs on my shoulders. Ummm…there, that should do it. How's it feel now?"

"Perfect, Doctor."

"Okay, then. Where were we? Oh yeah, you just leave those legs right there, baby. Plumber, ma'am. Here to fix your faucet, ma'am. Mind if I come inside?"

"Don't make me laugh, Tucker. It'll slip again." Julie laughs; the plumber does a backward gainer and soars, soars, soars.

A few weeks later, Julie's not laughing anymore, but glowing nevertheless. She rarely enters Tucker's office during the day, but this day is special. Julie tiptoes behind him, softly throwing her arms over his shoulders and rubs her tender breasts in his hair. Julie whispers in his right ear. "Tucker, I'm pregnant." The kind doctor's reaction, one might imagine, is rather cold. He stiffens against her body. "Is it mine?"

Julie nuzzles his neck. "Of course it's yours, silly. It's ours. We made a baby." Tucker turns to face a smiling Madonna dreaming of a nest. His face and coat are similar shades of pale. "How many weeks?"

Julie smiles. "Probably eight. Maybe nine."

"Have you made an appointment?"

"Ah, sweetie, not yet."

"Let me call my buddy Tom over at Evergreen. He'll get you in right away."

"A little Tucker, can you imagine?" Julie is on the verge of breaking out the blue color palate. Doctor Bush feels a migraine coming on. "No, Julie, I can't imagine. We'll get this taken care of within the next couple of days. Damn, where are my glasses?"

Julie balks. "Taken care of? What are you saying? Are you suggesting I get an abortion, Tucker?"

"No, I'm telling you that you will have an abortion. No suggestion about it. Hush now," he says, motioning to the phone. "Tom? Hi, it's Tucker. Listen, I have a little problem." He pauses. "Exactly," he mutters. "No." He picks up a pen and begins writing. "Friday at nine a.m.?" He looks at Julie's crushed face and feels nothing. "Julie Reston. That's right. She'll be there. Thanks, buddy. See you this weekend on the golf course."

A devastated Julie stands in front of Tucker with her hand on her abdomen. "I want to have this baby, Tucker."

"Are you out of your fucking mind? My wife will hang me from the highest tree if she ever finds out about this. I've already raised my children, Julie; forget it."

Julie is dedicated to her personal agenda. "But, Tucker, you're separated. You're practically living with me!" She shakes her head, trying to ward off an outcome that has no possible happy ending. "Didn't you tell me you love me? Didn't you?" Julie is dumbstruck. "I swear I thought you did. Was I hearing things? Did I make this up?" Tucker grabs Julie's shoulders and gives her a firm shake. The contact focuses her teary eyes on his serious and hardened face. "This isn't about love, Julie." He softens his gaze as he hands her a tissue. "I'm not about to have a child with you, or anyone else." This pronouncement causes Julie to moan. "That didn't come out right," Tucker grumbles. "Look, take the rest of the week off. I have to go out of town on business tonight anyway. Do you know where Evergreen is? You won't be presented with a bill, and they're very discreet. Be there a little before nine on Friday." Tucker shuffles papers, averting his attention from Julie. "Don't worry about a thing. Tom's a professional, and he'll take very good care of you." Tucker looks at his wristwatch in an effort to seem busy. "Listen, I'm late for my lunch meeting. I have to run." On his way out the office door, he looks back at Julie and, in his best doctor to patient voice, says, "Take some time to compose yourself. We'll talk next week. Just take it easy this weekend and you'll be fine. See Ann if you need anything. And don't worry, she can keep a secret." She has before, he says to himself.

"You son-of-a-bitch. You cold-hearted bastard." Julie hisses her words – vapor rises off her tongue. She's a tea kettle screaming on a high-heat burner, and Tucker swears he feels a scalding blister forming on his forehead as she steams past him without looking back. Julie wears the mask of a Zulu warrior, but her movement is robotic. She pulls open the drawer to her alphabetized filing system, the one housing her genetic disorder research – she's up to Nystagmus – and in a fit of rage, she erratically rips each sheet of paper from its file; she mixes and creates new chromosomal mishmashes which are born of humiliation, of regret, of bitterness. Nature has a new recipe book for gene-encoding anomalies.

. . .

If you are a carry-on bag belonging to one Doctor Tucker Bush, you snuggle alongside the exercise physiologist's designer duffle, zipper to zipper in the overhead of a wide body jet on its way to Las Vegas, bound for a three-day seminar featuring the latest technology in the field of genetic research. In your compartment are only three pair of underwear, two ball-gripping bathing suits, and a shaving kit. And one dozen Trojan latex condoms, the gold standard for a man who loves eggs.

GRACE

We may request it, we may seek it, we may beg for it, but we have no right to demand it. Being granted grace is strictly a karmic thing.

Lifestyle of the Rich, but Not Necessarily Famous, and Truly Blessed: Wake up on the sunny side after a solid night's sleep in your well-appointed Italian villa. Practice yoga for one graceful hour followed by twenty minutes of wild dancing. Shower and steam in a native marble double-headed bath. Fresh squeezed orange juice, two perfectly poached eggs, just-plucked asparagus from the garden, a triple decaf skinny latte, homemade hazelnut biscotti and today's schedule of events are delivered to your desk, the one by the window overlooking the mature perennial garden. Dress in your favorite riding breeches, the ones with a hole in the knee – you can't part with them because they fit so well – and head out to the ancient stone and wood barn where Songbird, your happily retired, totally sound, dark bay Grand Prix dressage schoolmaster, is perfectly groomed and tacked in only a bareback pad and halter. He accepts your offering of carrots and nuzzles your hair in appreciation. Ride for thirty minutes, hitting all the letters in perfect balance and harmony. Hug him as you swing from his tall back and hand him to your trusty working student, then hop on Pal, your happy, totally sound, and retired three-day event mahogany bay Thoroughbred, and enjoy a cross-country gallop with flight over short log fences. Walk Pal back through the vineyards, fingers lightly on the buckle. Il Cordellino, the European Goldfinch, flies by your shoulder as your incredibly smart and loyal mountain dog Benito keeps pace. Upon returning to the barn, groom Pal to a shine and turn him out to play with Songbird in the lush pasture by the lake. Head to the gazebo and eat a light lunch of homemade foccacia, olive oil, fresh herbs, and garden tomatoes with your wonderfully attentive and delightful multi-racial, multi-cultural staff. Hit the hammock with journal in hand, write a haiku worthy of Clark Strand's appreciation, and take a catnap with Ciao-Ciao, your favorite feline, curled by your head. Awaken to good news: your latest Super Tuscan release has received ninety-five points from Robert Parker and the calls, oh, the calls roll in. Put on a pair of well-worn leather gloves, stroll to the vineyards, and work alongside Italian wine master Angelo Gaja, who imbues you with his bounteous knowledge. At dusk, hit your office after taking off your boots and return calls to Wine Spectator – the time difference, you know. Take a long, hot shower, dress in cool silk, and entertain one hundred delightful friends and business associates with a five-course dinner and live music by the lake where soft candles float on lily pads. At midnight, retire to your inner sanctum with your significant other, the love of your life. Send up sincere prayers of gratitude to God Goddess Mother Father Divine Spirit, close your eyes, and soul travel for seven straight hours. Wake up, reach for your lover, make sleepy but passionate love and start a brand new day.

. . .

Lifestyle of the Struggling, but Truly Blessed, Independent Restaurateur: Wake up at nine a.m. wondering why the hell you didn't get up earlier, then remember you went to bed at three a.m. Jump out of bed with a nervous heartbeat, grab a quick shower and curse because the drain's still clogged and you forgot for the tenth day in a row to bring home the mercuric acid from the restaurant. Slam some weird-tasting green powder in the blender, reach for the juice, and it's not there, so you mix it with water instead and chug it for much-needed energy. Dress in whatever doesn't smell like bar funk, go to work, make a pot of coffee and let the answering machine catch the calls for thirty minutes until you can speak without croaking like a bullfrog with grasshopper legs stuck sideways in its throat. Accept wine shipments, fish shipments, linen shipments, cold-calling salesmen and solicitors. Then, go to the bathroom. Prep, check and recheck the reservation book, post the endless stream of necessary paperwork, pay bills, and freak out because the health department just showed up and the bar is trashed. Look at the clock: 4:52 p.m! Yell a threat to your staff and rush out, praying the road rage patrol is in another neighborhood. Hit the bank at 4:59 p.m. for change, take the shortcut home, drive fifteen miles over the posted speed limit, quickly pull clothes from the dryer, check for wrinkles (everything's wrinkled), change into the least wrinkled, feed the critters, clean chipmunk guts off the living room floor, call the restaurant for any last-minute dire strait needs and head back to work. Pray out loud the wait staff has completed their set-up and managed to avoid confrontation with the kitchen staff. Get in your car, notice the reserve tank light is on, pray for fumes, coast into the parking lot as the first customer is entering the front door, breathe deeply to expel all negative vibes and plaster a smile on your torqued-out face. Work your ass off upstairs in the dining room until 10:30 p.m., then head downstairs to bar-back. Shout Last Call! at 12:45 a.m. Last Call! Thank you Jesus Last Call! Play the *Theme from Rawhide* four times before the drunks stop line-dancing and fucking get the hint. Pray the toilets aren't stopped up with vomit, and clean up the evening's gooey mess. Say goodnight to all the musicians after a short recap of the day's events, and if luck is a lady, head home at two a.m. No hot meal since last Tuesday and scrambled eggs sound really good but opt for cold two-day old pizza instead because there's nothing much to clean up. Watch BET comedy on the tube until the sandman cometh. Sidestep little gutless furry presents and congratulate the talking cats on their prowess while walking the littered path from the den through the hall to the bedroom. Thank God Goddess Mother Father Divine Spirit for your many blessings, do wine inventory in your sleep, and wake up and do it again!

. . .

It's three p.m. and The Firefly is in shambles from the front door to the wait station, from dry storage to the back bar; every foot is littered with produce boxes, dirty coffee cups and piles of paperwork – the perfect time for a visit from the Health Department. "Oh my God! It's the Health Department!" Mimi runs upstairs yelling. "It's the Health Department, clean something!" She runs to the wait station. "It's the Health Department! Throw out the Chinese takeout in the wine cooler!" Breathe, Mimi, breathe, that's it, suck in air, blow hard, inhale, exhale, ohmmm. "Fuck!" Gotta buy the staff time to find the ice scoop and replace the empty hand soap container and empty the nasty gray mop water and change the burnt out light on the line and calm down, Mimi, she thinks. Brushing her hair from her forehead, she calmly walks back downstairs. With a look of surprise that fools nobody, she extends her hand. "Hi, Conrad! How are you? How's your son? Been to the beach lately? Didn't you tell me you were going to the beach?"

Conrad smiles, and looks up. "Did you know your ceiling is leaking right over the bar there?"

"No, Conrad. Thanks for pointing that out." Mimi walks to the stairs and yells, "GUYS, WE HAVE A LEAK IN THE BAR!" She closes her eyes, and turns to Conrad with a contrite look. "I have to explain this mess, Conrad. See, we're not open down here on Tuesday nights. The bar doubles as our office until tomorrow and we also accept shipments down here and Mo's coming to clean in about an hour."

Conrad keeps on smiling. "You told me all that last time. Don't worry about it. Is Sam upstairs?"

"I think so, but let me check. I'll be right back." Mimi grabs six dirty mugs parked by the register and slowly walks up the stairs, Conrad right behind her. "Sam! Did you hear me yell about the leak?"

"Yes I did, Mimi, and so did the patrons at the art gallery across the street. Hi, Conrad, good to see you." Sam had the foresight to change aprons, and is almost clean.

"Sam, how you doing?"

"Fine, Conrad. Just busy as usual. How was your beach trip? Didn't you say you were going to the Banks? I used to fish down there some when I was a kid. Do you fish? I bet the water is still cold. How's the undertow this time of year?"

Conrad is a true gentleman caller. He knows the ruse, gets the same shuck and jive from owners at every restaurant in town. And he knows as well as they do that a good stall tactic can't buy enough time to replace those worn-out refrigerator gaskets or clean that nasty grease trap or empty the ice cooler or rearrange dry storage on the fly. But, he plays the game so well. Too late, Mimi thinks. Take the hit, pray for a 90.5 rating – still an A – and hope your patrons look at the letter and not the number.

Mimi is no longer Alpha-dominant bitch of her domain. If she dies today, her epitaph will read *She Willingly Kissed the Health Department's Ass.* If Sam dies today, his epitaph will read *Do Not Offer Them Money, You Fool!* And at the wake there will be a lovely photo collage of Sam and Mimi in the chew, lick, tuck, drop, roll, and bend over positions displayed next to a signed copy of their latest health rating, a solid ninety four points – excellent considering the age of their charming, but rickety building. Sam and Mimi breathe a sigh of relief, and smile. They know it's a good day to die.

. . .

Unfortunately, several people at Eastern General Hospital feel the same way. Jake leaves his latest loss and feels a vibration on his hip. "What the hell is this?" he mutters as he looks at the familiar number. "Julie?"

"Jake. How are you?"

He keeps it short. "Good."

"I know you're busy. I'll cut to the chase. I'd like to see you as soon as possible. We need to talk. Can you come over for dinner tonight?"

"Actually, Julie, I have plans."

"No problem. I know it's short notice. How about tomorrow?"

Jake hesitates. "I'm not sure that would be good for me right now."

Julie pauses before jumping in with a nosy question. "Are you involved with somebody?"

Jake looks at Nan's purse sitting on his desk. "Not

really," he answers.

"Are you seeing her tonight?" Jake doesn't respond. Julie thumps away in typical Julie style. "How long have you been seeing her?"

"That's none of your business, Julie."

"Are you in love with her?"

"I have to go now, Julie. Bad day." Jake can't hang up; he wants to, but Julie's voice pulls him through the receiver like an electromagnet.

Julie presses. "Look, Jake we really need to talk. Will you call me? I don't have your home number and I don't want to call you at work. Just call me tomorrow, will you?"

What the hell? Jake thinks. He pauses, and takes a deep breath. "Why don't I come by tomorrow night around seven?"

"Great! Will you stay for dinner?"

"Let's play it by ear, okay?"

"Yep, that's fine. Bring Molly, too. I miss her."

Jake's blood pressure rises; he can feel his heart beat against his ribs. He hasn't heard from Julie in four months. He rode by the house one night by mistake, took the wrong highway to the wrong home after a troubling day at work, his short-term memory taking a vacation less than a week after he moved out, and what did he see? Dr. Tucker Bush's car parked in the driveway. No official separation papers are signed, but Jake knows the gig is up and anticipates a divorce. He's settled about it, but wants Julie to make the first move; let Tucker pay the attorney fees, he thinks.

Jake leaves work, drives to the right house, his house, his haven – his. Nan arrives at seven sharp, kisses Jake, loves on Molly, walks in the kitchen – she loves his kitchen – puts a chicken pie in the oven, sets the table, changes Molly's water bowl, walks to the bathroom, brushes her teeth — she keeps a toothbrush there now, has slept in Jake's bed three times a week for the last two months — and feels comfortable as she marks her territory. Nan is young and cute and talkative; Jake, whose mood swings like a monkey from a banana tree, is charmed, but mostly bored, by Nan's youth and cuteness and conversation. Jake's mind is otherwise engaged. Does Julie want to sell the house? Is that it? Is she moving in with Tucker? She needs me to sign papers, I bet that's it, he thinks. He eats quietly, barely making a dent in his chicken pie.

Nan snaps her fingers from across the table. "Jake, did you hear me?"

"I'm sorry, Nan. I'm a little distracted tonight. What did you say?"

"I said let's take Molly for a walk before the sun goes down."

Jake shakes his head. "I can't right now." He stands up. "Listen, I have some stuff to take care of."

"Let me help you." Nan can't help herself. She's a service provider on and off the clock. "What can I do?"

"Nothing, Nan. I have to get on the phone in a minute and find a bass player for next week's gig." Jake stares out the window looking for answers to a multitude of questions — one being, how do I get rid of Nan?

"I'll clean up," she says, "then I'll walk Molly while you make the call." Nan starts to clear the table, but Jake intercepts her. Removing the plates from her hands, he looks at her kindly and says, "Don't worry about it. Molly's fine, and I'll do the dishes later. Sweet of you to offer, though." His politeness chills Nan; she feels a slight twinge of that old familiar 'getting kicked to the curb' feeling. "Well, I was planning on staying over. Is that okay, or do you want me to leave?" The curve of her mouth turns south.

"No. Yeah, yeah. That would be best." Jake rubs his head and says, "Nan, I'm just low on energy tonight. You're a baby doll, though. I really appreciate dinner. I'm sorry you came all this way just to turn around and go home, but thank you." Jake's ambivalence tips Nan's confidence in a precarious direction. Her vulnerability is painful for Jake to witness, but he's not good at dishing out rejection. Nan reaches down to pat Molly, avoiding Jake's distracted face. "So, can we get together tomorrow instead?"

"Yeah, sure. No, wait, we can't. Julie called today. I have to sign some papers at the house tomorrow night." Nan picks up the plates again and heads to the sink. Jake doesn't stop her this time. He kindly lets her process. "What kind of papers?"

"Probably separation papers," Jake says as he walks to the sink and refills his water glass. Nan is visibly relieved. "So, that's what's bothering you. Now I understand." She wraps her arms around Jake's waist, pulls back from him, and smiles. "We're still going to the beach on Friday, right?"

"Right." Jake doesn't feel like dampening Nan's spirits again. He smiles, and hugs her. That's all Nan needs. She gives Jake a kiss on the cheek, and with a lilt in her step and voice, turns to the door. "Okay, lover, call me later. I'll come back over if you want me to." Jake walks her to the porch and takes a deep breath; the evening air is perfumed with the aroma of new mown hay. Reason number twenty why I live here, thinks Jake. "That's sweet of you, Nan, but let's just say goodnight. It's been a long day. Watch for deer in the driveway. See you tomorrow."

. . .

Jake calls Melvin first. Good news: Melvin's hooked up a bass player. His grandkids are over and their laughter fills the phone; Melvin is merrily distracted, so it's a short powwow. Jake cleans up the kitchen, then sits down at his keys and plays for an hour, but he doesn't find what he's looking for. Molly's damp nose on his leg provides a welcome diversion – good timing because it's a warm, clear night on the farm and the cattle are lowing. After a lilt around the pasture with Molly to clear his head, Jake returns home and turns on the television; he still can't concentrate. The ringing telephone offers no assistance, as Nan's number shows up on caller ID. Jake doesn't answer, but considers his options for a long minute before picking up the phone and calling Julie, who answers on the second ring. "Jake, I'm so glad you called me."

Jake has no time for small talk. "Do you have papers for me to sign? Is that why you want me to come over?"

"Papers? No… what kind of papers?"

"Separation papers, I guess." Jake pauses. "Are you thinking of selling the house?" Julie laughs. "Why would I want to do that? No, it's nothing like that. It's just – look, I want to talk about some things; some personal things."

"Talk, then," Jake says. "I'm right here."

"No, I want to talk in person, Jake. Do you have company?"

"She left a couple of hours ago." Julie's happy to hear that. "Great! Can you come over now?"

"Where's Tucker?" Jake asks.

"We stopped seeing each other a couple of months ago," Julie says. "I don't work for him anymore, either."

Jake digs. "Did he dump you for a younger model?"

"I guess I deserve that."

"No, I'm sorry. That wasn't fair."

"How about it, Jake?" Julie is relentless in her pursuit. "Come on over."

Jake sighs. "Julie, it's ten o'clock. I'm tired. I haven't heard from you in over four months. What's a few more hours? I said I'd come over tomorrow night."

Julie pleads. "Come on, Jake, it's only twelve miles."

Jake shakes his head and ponders his next thought. He grins. "Will it be worth it?"

"Absolutely, at least I hope so."

Jake hesitates, but gives in. "All right, I'm on my way."

"Bring Molly."

Julie and Jake talk until two a.m., talk and cry and laugh and hug and kiss – kiss passionately. Julie tells Jake almost everything. Almost. She doesn't tell him about her trip to St. Petersburg and her visit to Bread and Roses Women's Clinic, about her roundtrip ticket, about flying companion and returning alone. Jake calls the hospital at three a.m. "I'm unavailable until early afternoon," he says. "Please call for backup." Julie sleeps naked with her body pressed against Jake's muscular back, with her arm wrapped around his chest, with her blue-veined hand resting on his steady heart. Julie homes in on her husband.

Jake is happy for the first time in four months, and forgets about Nan – until he sees her crushed face in the hall just outside his office. She spends the better part of the morning finding reasons to spy on his door. "Where did you go after I left last night, Jake?"

Jake blankly stares at Nan. "Nowhere." He's a proficient liar when he feels he has to be. Nan's innocent, but not stupid. "Why didn't you answer the phone, then? I called you four times."

"Nan, look." Jake puts his hand on her heart as if protecting it from his next words. "You're a sweetheart, but I can't see you anymore."

Nan is one part anguished child, two parts distraught woman. "Why?" Nan wants an explanation; her sky is falling. "It just doesn't feel right," Jake says.

"But, what about our beach trip?"

Jake removes his hand, and waves impatiently to a scurrying, eavesdropping nurse. "I'm sorry about that, too. Look, Nan," he says softly, "you're a good girl, and we had fun, but it's over."

"What about my stuff at your house? Can I get my stuff?"

"All you have is a toothbrush, Nan."

Nan's anguished child throws a temper tantrum, right there in the hall, right there in full view of the nurse's station. "That's it? No explanation, just a brush-off? You have a lot of nerve, Jake Reston."

Jake puts a finger to her lips in a feeble attempt to quiet her. "Shhh, Nan. Shhh." He quietly says, "Baby girl, you don't know me." Nan smacks his hand away. "I think I do, Jake. This is about Julie, isn't it? That's where you went last night, isn't it?" Her voice throws itself against the wall and echoes through the ER, making the patients moan.

"Nan, let it go."

"Tell me, dammit!" People notice; curious eyebrows rise. Jake, not daring to take her behind closed doors, grabs a rather beefy little arm and steers her down the hall seeking privacy, but this is prime time entertainment of soap operatic proportion, featuring a favorite daytime star. Not even one wanton gaze is diverted. Jake smells popcorn. "I don't want to see you anymore, Nan. That's it; now, please, just let it go."

Nan shrugs Jake's hand from her arm and plants her feet; the riveted audience emboldens her, and she plays to them, speaking with amplitude and clarity so spying eyes can get their ears full, too. "Well," she slowly says, "you want to know something, Mr. Hot Pants? This is perfect timing. I was about to fall in love with you. What a mistake that would have been, you big fucking shit! I came so close to turning down a pie job just to stay in this miserable little town because of you." Nan dramatically hits herself in the head, and says, "What was I thinking? Those nurses over there were right – you have way too much baggage, and you're really high maintenance. Not my kind of guy at all."

The nurse's station is full of bug-eyed women shaking their heads to disavow ownership of the gossip, but all vying for the front row. Nan's summary is less than poetic, but her delivery receives high marks from the gallery of onlookers. "Go to Hell, moron," she declares with a three-fingered salute. "You're making a big mistake, and you deserve what comes your way. If Julie knows what's good for her, she'll leave your ass hanging out to dry."

Nan takes aim and drives in the last stake. "And by the way, you old fucker, your taste in music sucks." Chin up, she exits stage left to a short burst of quickly stifled mad applause; the nurses would love another act, but the thought of a repeat performance's effect on their critical care patients puts the quietus on.

"Has anybody seen my brain?" Jake asks of no one in particular as he walks past the nurse's station. Grabbing a handful of popcorn, he removes a scalpel from his pocket with his free hand, munches his way down the hall, and, pausing midway to his office door, takes aim; he hits the bulls eye from twenty feet, turns, flashes a luminous grin and bows to thunderous applause which almost, but not quite, smothers the moans coming from critical care. A week later, Jake moves back home to Julie, moves from his lovely country cottage with the big front porch, moves forward so fast that back is front and air is earth and fire is ice and time is motion. Beautiful house, beautiful wife.

If you drive to the country when the summer moon is rising and you detour down the right unmarked dirt road, you might see a lonely cottage; but the cottage is not alone, for in surrounding fields, thousands of fireflies blink a signal of love or a signal of duplicity, or sincerity, or mimicry – a signal solely dependent upon the mating behavior of the signalee.

HONESTY

See things as they are, check your need to alter the truth, and release all fear. There is no advantage in lying – not even about the little things.

Sam and Mimi share a fleeting moment of truth when Warren, gainfully employed by Sam's old partners at Steeles, stops by The Firefly at the end of service just to say hello, he says, but his visit is more than social; he has a mission, and his mission is to find out why Sam hasn't been to an AA meeting in over a month. Warren is direct in his questioning. He hasn't learned the fine art of diplomacy, but bravely takes the offensive against Sam's battering, cynical tongue. Mimi is an innocent bystander who stands in the shadows watching the two trains collide. Much as she'd like to, she can't avert her eyes from the wreckage. "Sam, you're drinking again," Warren states. "Why don't you admit it, and let me help you get back on track?"

"Nooooo, I don't drink, not Sam I Am," he sing-songs in a scathing Dr. Seussical impression. Sam cracks himself up as a breathless Mimi freezes.

"Why are you laughing, Sam?" Warren asks. "Do you think this is funny? What's so funny about lying to your wife, or to me? Or, more importantly, to yourself?" Warren is painfully sincere, and so very, very ineffective.

Sam jabs Warren like an aggressive child might poke a vulnerable kitten with a stick. "Why, I'm laughing at you, boy! Look at you standing there judging me, all rosy and sober and self-righteous. When's the last time you had a drink, yesterday?"

Warren is stirred, but not shaken. "Sam, you're drunk

right now, aren't you? Bet you don't know Mimi's listening. She's over there, watching you act like an ass. Now would be a good time to tell her the truth." Warren points at Mimi's stricken face. "Doesn't she deserve the truth?"

Sam laughs maniacally, and stumbles. "No siree, buddy, I am not drunk. Nope." He leans against the nearest wall and cuts his unfocused eyes toward Mimi, but can't see past his vodka-enhanced ego. "Why don't you go on home now, little boy, and have yourself a cold one?" Jab, jab. "You're about as strong as weak coffee, Warren." Sam swings, but misses. "Damn wimp. I bet you squat to pee."

Warren tires of straying close to the bully's fist and walks dejectedly out the back door, but not before making a deep impression on Mimi. Sam follows Warren up the street, baiting him, mocking him, but degrading only himself as Mimi sadly watches. It makes sense now, she realizes; Sam's confusing behavior makes sense. 'You're working too many hours, Mimi; you're not working enough, Mimi; you're ordering the wrong wine, Mimi; you're spending too much money, Mimi; you're hiring morons, Mimi; stay out of my way, Mimi.' She finally gets it loudly, deeply, clearly. Warren breaks the code to the map, replaces Mimi's broken compass, and helps her find true north, although the path he uncovers is strewn with broken dreams.

The confrontation with Warren leaves Sam bubbly. He's Master of the Universe, and goes about his business very happily for the rest of the night; he's so happy, in fact, that he stumble-dances, paying homage to his favorite celebrity drunks Jackie Gleason and Dean Martin. He's loud and funny in a twisted, obnoxious kind of way – scary funny, which isn't very funny at all. At home, he lies to Mimi multiple times before the indigo-stained sky gives to a blood red morning. "Alright, you win, dammit," he finally admits. A resigned but unsettled Sam sighs heavily. "I'm drinking again, but not much, and only for two months. It's not a big deal," he says, avoiding Mimi's set face.

"Is that why you've been so rude and disrespectful lately?" Mimi seeks answers, answers that make sense. But she can't make sense of Sam's puffed up response – none whatsoever. "No, that's not why I'm so rude, dammit! I don't think you do a good job with the staff. They run all over you." Jab, jab. "That's not why I'm disrespectful! Respect is earned, Mimi. You just piss me off!" Sam turns his head from the window's fitful light, closes his eyes, and within seconds, his thunderous snoring conjures heavy rain; Sam's fury shatters the sky and sends the sun on a two-day hiatus.

. . .

Sam reluctantly agrees that counseling is imperative if the marriage is to be salvaged. Mimi pleads her way into a Sunday afternoon emergency session, and as if taking a cue from the unrelenting downpour, Sam releases the floodgate. Under the watchful gaze of grandmotherly Donese Bradford, MA LPC LMFT, a regular customer and long-time fan of Sam's unique shrimp and grits, Sam admits he's been drinking again for two years. Mimi's reaction is strangely calm for someone seeking shelter in the middle of a maelstrom. Donese directs her attention to Mimi. "You must be shell-shocked about now. What are you thinking?" Mimi looks from Sam to Donese and pauses. "I feel a strange kind of relief, lighter somehow, like I could blow away, but solid at the same time; maybe this is how it feels to drown."

"Remember, Mimi, this is Sam's problem, not yours." Mimi takes a deep breath and looks gratefully at Donese before continuing. "For two years I've been trying to please Sam and couldn't do it. It's been confusing; no, awful, really." She hesitates. "But, tell me, how could I not realize he's been drinking for two years? I feel so naïve and ignorant." Mimi looks intently at Sam. "Am I the only idiot? Does everybody else know, Sam?" Sam's smug answer tips her tenuous balance. "Well, probably not everybody, but Jesse brings me vodka shots when I ask her to."

"Oh, great. Now I have a cocktail waitress who helps my husband get drunk. What a gift! Is that why we gave her a raise last year?" Sam's sarcasm is contagious; Mimi feels a rise in temperature until Donese quickly cuts the thermostat on her anger.

"What's Jesse supposed to do, Mimi, ask you first? Get fired because she's enabling one boss and the other boss finds out? Get in the middle of your crisis?" Donese glances at Sam and continues. "Mimi, Sam's good at drinking. He knows all the secrets, isn't that right, Sam?"

Sam grins and leans back in his chair. "I have more tricks up my sleeve than a Las Vegas pimp has hookers."

"That's really nothing to be proud of." Donese stares at Sam until his face turns red, and when he drops his eyes, she makes her call. "I don't think rehab is the place for you. My suggestion is to immerse yourself in AA, Sam. Go to ninety meetings in ninety days. You make a three-month contract with sobriety. That's where you start, and you start today. Can you do this?" Sam tearfully consents to what sounds like a sentence of hard labor, but with the possibility of parole for good behavior.

"Now, Mimi," states Donese, "your job is to open your heart and stand upon the rock of your original attraction to Sam. Keep the faith. If that requires you to fake it until it feels right again, then you do just that." Donese pauses, and softens toward the hangdog couple. "It appears to me you have way too much to lose by giving up now. Can you two stick together on this?"

Mimi silently implores Sam to speak first. "I can, Donese, if Mimi can," he finally says after two minutes of tension-filled silence. He turns to Mimi and takes her hand in his. "What do you think, Wife? Can you do it?" Mimi puts on her rose-colored glasses. "I can, and I will, Sam." Donese smiles at their vulnerability, and pulls out her appointment book. "Okay, then. I want to see you both back here next Monday, and every Monday for the next three months. If there are emergencies, call me. It doesn't matter what time it is, I'll see you right away. Deal?"

"Deal!" says Sam, moving confidently toward his latest goal.

"What kind of insurance do you have? You might be able to write these sessions off." Sam reaches in his pocket and pulls out a fat wad of wrinkled bills. "Donese, we'll pay cash if you don't mind."

Sam and Mimi keep very quiet about their marital challenges, especially around the business. The last thing they need is gossip, although the topic is old news to The Phoenix and Firefly employees, all of whom have been aware of Sam's drinking for much longer than Mimi has. Sam goes to meetings at least once a day, but attends a new group that doesn't include Warren; he's not ready to make that apology. Mimi trusts the process; she fakes it until it feels right again, but soon trips over reality; her rosy glasses hit the ground and Sam steps on them on day eighty-four when he pardons himself with early parole.

Sam tries outpatient treatment. "I'm too good for

those losers, not nearly as sick as they are." So he quits. Donese suggests another twenty-eight day gig at The Farm. Sam says no. Group therapy, no; meetings, no. Bottle, yes. Niiiice fish, purty fish, lots of silver. Sam makes his choice, and it's not Mimi. Better to be alone than in bad company, Mimi thinks. She moves into Warren's old bedroom and lives like a stranger in their house until she finds a safe haven in the country, a lovely cottage with a big front porch, with a modern kitchen and heart pine floors.

. . .

Diving from high places into a tightly-woven safety net is safer than jumping into a net with holes, but freefall is an altogether different category. Mimi knows the difference firsthand, thanks to Sam. She describes her depression as if it's another person; Mimi knows depression, gives it a name and a personality.

Meet Fatty Patty. Fatty Patty wears muumuus and lives in a rusty house trailer and reclines in a stained, worn out brown corduroy Lazy Boy recliner with squeaky hinges that groan under her weight. A scurfy little mutt sits on her fat lap, scratches its infected ears, and chews its flea-ridden, rodent-like body constantly. Fatty Patty eats bonbons between each cigarette – forty-seven butts form a teepee in the overflowing ashtray, and it's not even bedtime. Fatty Patty's long, stringy hair is greasy because she hasn't taken a shower in three days. She watches game shows in the morning and soap operas in the afternoon, and after that, she watches Court TV. Fatty Patty takes a nap during the local news, awakens and slides a TV dinner in the microwave for a quick appetizer, then drives her old low-riding Buick Electra to

McDonald's – the drive-thru, of course – for two double cheeseburgers, supersized fry, and a jumbo diet coke. The TV tray beside the Lazy Boy is littered with used tissues and National Enquirer magazines.

Mimi allows Fatty Patty VIP entrance into her psyche for three days before she kicks her out; seventy-two solid, miserable hours of abjection are about all Mimi can stand. Then, Mimi stands alone in the dark, fully engaged with the poverty of her spirit; she embraces the darkness until she sees a shadow of light, until she hears music in her head again.

Sam? Sam's not depressed. Depression is for babies, Sam says. He'll never admit he's human that way. Julie? Hell, no. She doesn't have time for depression. Put a little lipstick on and forget about it, that's Julie's answer when dark thoughts sneak in. She dispels depression with an internal vacuum cleaner, sucks those unwelcome thoughts away one, two, three at a time.

Jake describes his depression as a nebulous blob.

Recognizing a kindred spirit in Mimi, Jake watches her closely when he's at the club, sees her going through her paces like a professional. She's unaware of a covert operation, so Jake sees the real thing. He sees Mimi's mask crack when she thinks nobody's looking. He feels the sadness in her eyes from the stage, sees it in her usual late night solitary dance after the club closes. Mimi smokes more and smiles less, but is engaging and kind to the musicians, to her staff. There's a distinct difference in this woman and Jake knows something has changed, but what? What is it, he wonders? He observes Mimi for months, exchanging pleasantries and late night stories and basic weather facts and political opinions and they know each other, but they don't.

Jake gratefully accepts the beer Dee hands him after

the night's gig ends. He takes a big pull and pats the bottle. "Thanks pal," he says to Dee, grinning. "My throat was beginning to feel like scarecrow guts."

"Great gig tonight," Dee responds. "The crowd went crazy over that new blues tune you guys did; I've never heard it before. What's it called?"

"We debuted two new ones tonight, which one?"

"The one you funked out at the end, with the line 'sit, beg, and behave."

"That one's *Cornbread*, and Tommy wrote it. Fine, isn't it?"

"You have to play it every gig from now on. Did you hear the call and response from the crowd? They were barking like dogs."

Jake laughs. "You'll hear it so much you'll get tired of it, I promise. Give it three weeks and you'll be begging for a reprieve." Jake motions Dee closer and lowers his voice. "Hey Dee, I have a question. Tell me if it's none of my business." He stops and looks around, making sure they're alone before venturing into personal territory. "Is Mimi okay? Something's going down with her, but I can't put my finger on it."

Dee shakes her head and looks at Jake. "I'm not supposed to talk about it."

"Well, don't then. It's none of my business." Jake takes another long pull of his beer and looks around the bar again; Dee does the same, and determining their conversation is private, moves in closer to Jake. "Did you know she and Sam split?"

"No! Hadn't heard that, when?"

"Last month." Dee's eyes swing around the bar once more. Mo's entertaining the rest of the band at the far end, so she continues. "Okay, Jake, I'm gonna tell you some things that could get me fired. You promise to keep this between us?"

"Dee, stop. You've said enough."

"No, listen. Somebody around here needs to know. She won't talk to the staff. We've tried, but she shuts us down."

"I get that," Jake says, "you're too close; but I bet she talks to her friends."

Dee shakes her head. "I doubt it. She's in flames. I've watched her shake like a leaf for no apparent reason and have to grab a chair to keep from falling down. You're a doctor, Jake. Maybe she needs medication. I think she's having a nervous breakdown."

Jake ponders before answering. "She's losing weight, that's for sure. And smoking like a piece of burnt toast."

"Sam's drinking again, Jake, and not just a little bit."

Jake looks surprised. "I didn't know he ever stopped."

"Well, he lied to Mimi about it; she was the last to know. They went through marriage counseling and it didn't take, but she tried, Jake. And he did, too, for almost three months. Can you imagine how hard it must be for them, working together like this? Sam's so hateful to her, just awful. It makes me sick. The stress is about to tip her over. I've seen her bite the head off more than one customer lately and that's not like Mimi. At least she doesn't have to go home to his shit anymore."

Jake finishes his beer, bids goodnight to a departing Melvin, returns to the conversation and lets Dee in on a little secret of his own. "You know Julie and I split awhile back, for four months. We tried again too, Dee. But the honeymoon phase of our reconciliation is long gone. Nothing's changed except the silence is louder, the distance is wider, and the sheets are colder." Jake stares at the back wall, thinking about the declaration he's getting ready to make. "We're back together, but not for long.

Please, Dee, don't mention this to anyone. Melvin doesn't even know yet. And although I'm relieved, it pains me like a nagging toothache." He covers his jawbone and chuckles. "I think Julie's yanking out my last bit of wisdom."

"I'm sorry to hear that, Jake."

"Don't be. Julie and I are taking our last dying breath as a couple." He rubs his face and sighs. "We're total opposites."

Dee frowns. "I've always heard opposites attract."

Jake shakes his head. "We've disproven that old theory." He grins at Dee. "A strange notion, isn't it? I mean, think about it: two negatives make a positive, two positives make a positive, but put a negative and positive together, and they do not bond. Like attracts like – it's a scientific fact, baby, hard core undisputed truth."

"Sam and Mimi are opposites, too."

"Yep, saw their picture in the textbook, right by mine and Julie's." Jake and Dee share a hollow laugh; there's nothing funny about dying relationships. "Where's Mimi living, do you know?"

"Somewhere out west of town in the country, at the end of a dirt road. I haven't seen it, but she says she'll invite the staff out soon for lunch. Doubt she will, though; she keeps to herself these days."

Jake focuses in on Dee. "Do you know the road?"

Dee playfully grabs Jake's shirt and pulls him close. "You're not gonna stalk her, are you? I'll have to kill you if you do."

"Okay, this is weird, but I'm getting a feeling…" Jake pauses. "No, it can't be…" He shakes his head as Dee releases her grasp. "I lived in a wonderful house for four months when Julie and I split the first time, a great little pad at the end of Jenkin's Bottom Road."

Dee laughs. "No way, Jake. Mimi lives on that road. How weird is that?"

"Pretty damned weird," says Jake. "Nah, couldn't happen. Too weird."

"Hang on, I'll ask her exactly where she lives." Before Jake can protest, Dee is halfway to Mimi's office door. Sensing Jake's hesitation, Dee turns and offers casual reassurance. "It'll be fine, she'll dig it. She's probably ready for a glass of wine anyway."

Mimi tucks away her furrowed brow, worried eyes and the night's paperwork, takes a deep breath and joins Jake at the bar. "Dee says we may have a shared experience. I live at the end of Jenkin's Bottom Road in a lovely little farmhouse with a big front porch. Sound familiar?"

Jake grins. "Sure does, Mimi. Great sunsets there, very peaceful." Jake shakes his head. "I used to live in your house, can you believe it? Have you heard the coyotes?"

Mimi's tired eyes light up. "I thought they were dogs howling at the gates of Hell; woke me from a dead sleep, Jake, what a sound. Now, I love them; they echo my soul." Mimi takes off her sweater, picks up a menu and fans herself. "Dang, it's hot in here. Dee, do you have a bottle of Atlas Peak Sangiovese or Markham Cab open?" Dee holds up the Atlas Peak. "Great, will you please pour me a glass with water back? And I'd like to buy this man a beer, Beck's I think."

"Yes, ma'am," Dee says, turning around before Mimi sees her wide grin. Dee pours a hefty eight ounces into a sparkling glass and places it on the bar. "Why, thank you Dee! Being an owner certainly has its privileges, now, doesn't it?" Mimi laughs as she walks toward the door. Jake picks up her water and his beer, and follows her. "We'll be right outside if you need anything, Dee."

"I'm good," Dee says. "At least forty-five minutes

before I'm ready to roll." Her boss is visibly relaxed for the first time in weeks, and Dee isn't in the mood to rush.

Jake doesn't mention Sam, and Mimi doesn't mention Julie. They don't talk much at all, but sit quietly instead under the stars and listen to the thirty-two calls of a mockingbird, a songbird with the blues at two a.m.; they count his songs and hoot when the mockingbird mimics the first five notes of *Blues, Greens and Beans.* Jake and Mimi name the bird Gino; he visits The Phoenix regularly, late at night when only songbirds with the blues are awake, when the audience is filled to capacity with only two.

FREEDOM

No one is free until we are all free and are freeing each other. Give each other space to taste sweet freedom; expand your heart and make room for all!

The sun casts golden light across Mimi's closed eyes and wakes her gently, wakes her from a sleep so sweet she can taste the morning. She stretches her muscles until they respond, and rolls onto her stomach; easing her torso sideways across the bed until the mattress's edge supports her trim waist, she slowly reaches downward until her hands feel warm wood. Bending her elbows, she touches her forehead to the floor as blood fills her sleepy brain; she becomes fully awake as axons cross the synapse and shake hands with dendrites, and gray matter greets white matter with a welcome slap on the back. I have my own little church in my head, Mimi thinks. Ten sun salutations add extra length to her back, and after a light breakfast of two soft scrambled eggs, a bowl of chilled Swiss chard, a hunk of raw cheddar, and one piece of crispy brown sunflower toast, she quickly showers, dresses loosely in shorts and tee-shirt, laces up her trusty five-eyed Doc Martin's, pulls a *Life is Good* cap over her long braid, and cheerfully heads for The Firefly.

A few miles away, Sam kicks tangled bedclothes to the floor, medulla shouts at oblongata, and grapefruit juice angrily splashes into a breakfast vodka shot; morning is just the beginning of another long, miserable day for Sam. He takes a quick shower, and tugs on his red hot chili pepper pants, a faded Yankees tee-shirt, and his tomato-stained running shoes. In an effort to dim the day, he reaches for a pair of dark sunglasses and heads to The

Firefly; the last person he needs disturbing his bad mood is Mimi, but he spies her car in the parking lot. He opens the door, and there she is, staked out at the bar drinking coffee and reading the paper like she owns the place. If the heart has a hateful chamber, Sam's opens wide when he sees her. "Mimi, I don't want you here anymore."

"Good morning to you too, Sam," Mimi says politely, never lifting her eyes from the front page news. "I made a pot of coffee." Sam silently walks behind the bar, reaches into a humming beer cooler, and pulls out an ice cold Corona. "Yeah well, enjoy it," he retorts. "Did you hear what I said? I don't want you here anymore. You're dead weight."

Mimi shudders, drops the paper to the bar and looks at her pitiful husband. "Sam, I own half this restaurant, remember? If you want me out, you have to buy me out." Sam's eyes roll like a tight quarter slot. "Yeah, right, like this dump is worth anything." Sam holds the glistening Corona to the light; it looks like liquid sunshine. Sparkles like the Mexican Riviera, Sam thinks, and takes a deep pull.

Mimi shrugs. "Okay, then, I'll buy you out."

Sam thrives on cruelty, especially when he runs low on grapefruit juice in the morning. "I'm the one with restaurant experience, remember? You didn't know shit five years ago. You'll run this place into the ground, six months, guaranteed, if you can find anybody willing to work for you."

"I'll take that chance, Sam; how much?"

Sam shakes his head. "I'm not selling."

"Tell you what," Mimi says, pushing Sam closer to a total meltdown, "let's hire a restaurant consultant to estimate what this place is worth, and we'll get an attorney to draw up the papers."

Sam tilts precariously toward malfunction. "Brilliant!" He howls. "Let's open the books to Joe Schmoe on the street here. Do we tell him about the safe at home? Do we tell him about the cash we take outta here every week? Shit, Mimi, we'll both end up in jail." Sam's Corona takes on the patina and taste of cat urine. He smells the almost-depleted bottle, burps loudly, and pours the dregs in the sink. "You're a fucking pain in the ass; do you know that about yourself? This business is worth nothing, and nothing is what you'll get."

Mimi breathes deeply in a vain attempt to idle her heart. "Sam, please stop it."

Sam jumps. "No Mimi, you stop it! You've done nothing to build this business. It's time for you to go." You can't argue with a drunk, Mimi remembers Sam saying. She sits silently as Sam continues to spin toward his warped version of a big payout. "Ask anybody; the staff hates you now; my old customers have always hated you, did you know that? Everybody talks trash about you when you're not around."

Mimi's core body temperature drops as her heart goes into shock. She shivers as she stands, carefully moves toward the sun, and silently asks the beams to deflect Sam's cold words. "Are you having fun, Sam?"

"Yeah, Mimi, this is fun, isn't it? I'm having fun, are you having fun? If I hear you mention the word fun one more time, I'm gonna puke. Life is just one big fun game to you, isn't it?" Sam's inflamed eyes exit their sockets as his frontal lobe pushes on his last occipital nerve. "Why don't you go on home now and have some fun with Jake?"

Now I get it, Mimi thinks. Gino must have spilled the beans. "What are you talking about, Sam? Jake has nothing to do with this." But for the first time, she knows he does; Mimi sees a crack in Sam's demeanor that leads to a deep fissure, an abyss so deep it would take a two-ton dump truck to haul away the rancid, rushing and painful ooze of his backed-up rage.

Pigs wish they could snort like Sam. "Oh, I've heard, and I've seen, too. You can't keep your hands off him. Everybody's talking about it. You've been having an affair for years, you damn slut. Having fun yet?"

"Sam, calm down. You know that's not true."

"The hell it isn't!" Blame travels boldly when escorted by a lie.

"You're way off base, Sam," Mimi cautions. "Friendly conversation isn't an affair; be careful what you say now."

"I may be stupid Mimi, but you're a big fucking slut. Jake's a married man," Sam yells to an invisible audience; he opens the door and spews his toxic rant to the empty parking lot across the street. "Everybody hear that? My wife's having an affair with a married man!" Turning his attention toward his gray-faced wife, he says, "Now get the hell out of here."

Mimi plants roots in her little piece of ground. "I'm staying, Sam. If you don't want to see me today, you go on home. I have work to do."

"Not for long; it won't be long now, girl. This restaurant is folding, wait and see." Sam loiters by the door and pants with the need for a drink. "People are lining up to help me because they know the shit you've put me through." He catches his breath in preparation for next tirade, his last chance money spin, his big hit. "Go ahead, Mimi, call an attorney; see what happens. We haven't shown a profit in five years. Any businessman worth his salt will think you're crazy if you put a price on this place. You won't get a dime from me; I have friends who'll make damn sure of that. The best money I can spend right now is to take you out for good, and it'll only cost me five thousand dollars. Your head is cheap, Mimi."

"Are you threatening me, Sam?"

"No Mimi, I'm telling you. Get the hell out of here."

And Sam is right. He knows the business better, he cooks better, he steals better, he lies better, he hides better, he cheats better, better, better. Mimi is having no fun, no fun at all. She calls an attorney who makes sure of that.

. . .

Attempting to avoid his vigilante secretary, Jim Morris sneaks through a side door and creeps into his plush penthouse-view law office; he pulls a forbidden well-dressed cheeseburger and fries from a greasy brown bag and, rifling through the bottom left drawer of his Cadillac-sized mahogany desk, finds the new Carl Hiaasen novel given to him by his wife on his fortieth birthday. He swivels his Levenger Huntington executive desk chair into position, props his Fratelli Rossetti leather wingtips on a stack of unopened mail, and turns to page one. Jim queues up a huge bite of his dripping lunch as the phone softly rings. He reaches for the intercom button, mouth full, and impatiently addresses his ancient, pinched secretary as a glop of mustard, chili, slaw, and onions parks in the middle of his pink Aspinal silk tie. "What is it, Sybil?"

"You know better than to eat that cheeseburger, Jim."

"Slaw is in the salad category, Sybil," he says, lifting the tie to his mouth and sucking at the spreading yellow stain.

"It's your blood pressure, do what you want. But don't expect me to cover for you when your wife asks if you're following doctor's orders."

"Well, don't expect me to give you a Christmas bonus

this year, either." Jim grabs a handful of salty French fries and shoves them in his mouth. "Why are you bothering me?"

"I'm putting a client through who comes to you compliments of your father, so you better take this one; she's called three times already. Here she is."

Mimi introduces herself before Jim can object to the unwelcome interruption. "Mr. Morris, this is Mimi Killian. George at your father's office referred me to you. He says you'll be able to draft a contract protecting me from a business liability."

Jim reluctantly puts down his cheeseburger, splays his book spine-up on his messy desk, and, after wiping his slick hands with a crumpled napkin, picks up a Lanier handcrafted pen. "What business, Mrs. Killian?"

"The Firefly and the Phoenix; you've been there, right?"

Jim perks up. "Best shrimp and grits this side of the Mississippi, and the homemade cheesecake's not bad, either. Call me Jim. What can I do for you?"

"I need a contract releasing me from all liability in exchange for giving my partner all the assets of the business. I have a hand-scribbled contract from Sam's attorney, but it looks pretty scary. I'm not about to sign this thing."

"Who's Sam?" Jim takes another bite of his drooling cheeseburger; richly-colored condiments splatter on the canvas of his starched white Burberry shirt.

"Sam's my business partner and soon-to-be ex-husband."

"Why don't you sell your shares to him?"

Mimi sighs. "Jim, that would be ideal, but Sam refuses to pay me anything, based on the fact that we haven't shown a profit in five years."

"That doesn't mean it's not profitable, Mimi. Complete transparency isn't always a plus, believe me; I understand how the restaurant business works." Jim reaches across his wide girth, grunts, and flicks chili from his wingtips. "How much is the business worth?"

"According to an advisor, my half should be worth a minimum of two hundred sixty thousand dollars. I'd love to get at least sixty out of it, based on good will alone."

"What do you mean by good will?"

"It's the steady customer base and the reputation," Mimi explains. "It's the draw. Even potentially great restaurants with world-class chefs won't last long if there's no draw. A built-in customer base, like we have, is worth more than gold." Mimi pauses. "But Sam says that's because of him, not me. I disagree."

"Then, why does Sam figure the business is worth nothing if good will is so important?" Jim swallows the dregs of his stale Pepsi, covers the receiver, and burps loudly; Mimi pretends not to hear.

"Because he knows how hard it is to prove, Jim. He believes in good will as much as I do, but maybe Sam's right. Nobody's gonna pay me sixty thousand dollars for the honor of being Sam's business partner."

Jim bores easily, and wishes this rambling conversation were over. "Sounds like a domestic issue to me," he says, picking up his book. If page one were a crime scene, Jim would be the primary suspect based on fingerprints alone.

"I went to a domestic attorney first, who suggested I contact your father, then your father suggested I speak with George, and George suggest I hire you. Am I on the wrong track here?"

Jim cuts to the chase. "How's your cash flow? The business, I mean."

"It's a cash cow. Most of the restaurant revenue is

generated by credit cards which covers our business expenses. The bar provides most of the cash – an easy two grand a week, after expenses, walking."

"And you're willing to give that up to protect yourself from a perceived liability? You may want to reconsider, Mrs. Killian." Jim flips to page two.

Mimi's patience wears thin. "I don't want to be Sam's business partner anymore, Jim, okay? Do you understand that? We're legally separated, but that doesn't protect me from his bad business decisions. He's a sloppy, delusional alcoholic with a very bad temper." Mimi plays her last card. "He, well, he's offered people money to make me go away."

Now Mimi has Jim's attention. He marks page two with a mustard-stained napkin and places the book on his desk. "What do you mean, take you away?"

"Well, what does it sound like to you?"

"It sounds like a criminal charge waiting to happen." This case may have legs after all, Jim thinks. "Okay, I need a list of everything you want from the restaurant in exchange for releasing all assets, if you're sure that's the route you want to take. What tangible items do you want?"

"Not much, just some artwork that belongs to me, and my old computer. Oh, and some of the wine. We have a few cases that'll never move unless I'm there to sell them." Mimi quickly runs through the inventory in her mind. "Two thousand dollars is a pretty good guesstimate on the value, and the longer it sits, the more valuable it becomes."

Jim whistles. "That's a lot of wine."

"Not really. Maybe three cases wholesale, but it's the hard-to-get really good stuff, and Sam will probably cook with it." Mimi shudders at the thought, and summarizes for the seemingly dense attorney. "Listen, Jim, Sam's been shuffling money from our business account for a long time. I've seen the books and deposit slips – the real ones. And yeah, I can take him down the river, baptize him in the holy water of your religion, tear his little world apart, and give you all my money to feel good about myself. But that's not my deal. Please, all I'm asking is for you to draw up a contract stating, very simply, that Sam Killian gets the business assets in return for releasing Mimi Killian from any and all liability."

"I can do that," Jim replies. "But, it's gonna cost you a little."

Mimi laughs at the little part. "How much is a little?"

"Two-hundred-fifty dollars an hour to start, including this phone call; and the contract work will take five hours, minimum." God, small potatoes after all, Jim thinks; this better be a quick fix.

"Let's do five maximum, Jim. Please, don't stretch this out." Jim makes no promises, but agrees to address the potential criminal offense as a separate issue in exchange for two bottles of vintage wine. "A short, well-worded letter should be all that's needed," he says. Jim schedules an appointment with Mimi for later in the week – an appointment that will take fifteen minutes, but he'll charge a full hour. He hangs up the phone and shakes his head. Lady, you've lost your mind, he thinks. But if you can pay, I'll play. Now, where was I? He plops a well-shod foot on his shiny desk, picks up his novel, and resumes his hard work.

Two days later Mimi organizes her attaché, dresses in her best left-over corporate attire and enters the world of high overhead. Damn, she thinks, studying an opulent flower arrangement that could attract a swarm of killer bees; that ugly thing must have set him back a cool two-fifty, hold the aesthetics. "Nice office, Jim, great view of the city from way up here. Who's your florist?" Jim smiles, but doesn't waste time explaining Sybil's penchant for funeral arrangements. "Did you bring the list?"

Mimi reaches for her attaché. "Yes, and the contract from Sam's attorney." She slides one neatly typed watermarked list and a wrinkled handwritten contract across the table. Jim looks at the contract first and frowns. "Who's Sam's attorney?"

"Drew Wissle, do you know him?"

"Oh yeah." He shakes his head. "This is crap. It doesn't protect you from anything. My advice is to burn it," he says, and passes it back to Mimi before changing his mind. "No, give it back. I'll call Drew tomorrow, let him know I'm representing you, and ask about it."

"Can I sue someone for making me feel stupid?"

Jim takes notice of Mimi for the first time, and looks at her intently. "You're not stupid; if you were, you'd have signed this contract. Nope, my guess is you're one sharp cookie, but somebody's trying to take a big bite out of you." He picks up the precisely-typed inventory list, and frowns again. "There's not much on here; are you sure this is it?"

"I'd like to include my initial investment, if possible. I invested my retirement fund into this venture." Jim shakes his head. "You'll be able to recoup some of that loss when you file your taxes, but most of that money's long gone; have you considered suing for alimony?"

"If we had kids, Jim, I'd do it, but it's just me. I'm not worried about the money right now; I'll land on my feet." Or your ass, Jim thinks, and shrugs. "Okay, your call."

"Once Sam signs this agreement, it's over, right? If he has a wreck in the company car and kills someone, or knocks his vodka bottle onto the gas burner and lights up the place, I'm not liable in any way, shape or form, right?"

Jim looks at his watch and pushes back his chair. "That's right. I'll give you a ring when the contract's ready so you can read it before we send Sam a copy. In the meantime, lay low. Avoid contact, and by all means, stay away from the restaurant."

Oh, Mimi. Where's the fight song? Where's the trainer in your corner – the one who says, look, don't walk away from your business; stand up and fight for your financial rights. It might cost you a body part, but limbs are replaceable. Take him down, girl, sic'em! It sure isn't Jim; he's working hard to finish the second short chapter of his Hiaasen. Jim's a slow reader.

. . .

Laying low isn't easy for a woman like Mimi, especially when five messages to Sam go unanswered; Mimi left something very precious in their house by mistake: six delicate, tulip-shaped, cobalt blue, mouth-blown champagne flutes, circa 1940's, inherited from her Aunt Agnes, and they must be retrieved before their condition changes from mint to flea market. On a whim, she stops by and boldly knocks on the front door, not expecting an answer although Sam's car sits in the driveway. Sam has a more pressing need, a need more enticing than a confrontation with his nemesis. Mimi walks through the gate to the back yard, passes the lovely purple irises she planted three springs ago – they're in full bloom – and notices the back door standing wide open. She tiptoes to the threshold, peeks around the corner, and gets an eyeful; Jesse, the red-headed, enabling cocktail waitress, walks through the kitchen from the direction of the bedroom. A rat built a nest in her hair, Mimi thinks.

Jesse's wearing one of Sam's shirts and nothing else; she doesn't notice Mimi silently gaping. A large bong sits on the coffee table alongside a quart-sized zip lock bag full of what is either catnip or cannabis, and Sam doesn't like cats. Mimi fantasizes for a moment, but revenge is tricky business; she simply wants her champagne flutes. A note will have to do, Mimi thinks; she pulls a tube of lipstick from her pocket, and, using Sam's glass door as her canvas, scrawls "FLUTES" in large, Femme Fatale-colored cursive letters across its center.

Mimi's phone rings two hours later. The voice on the other end is agitated. "Mimi, Jim Morris here. I just received a call from Drew Wissle a minute ago. He says you've been trespassing on Sam's property, is that true?"

"Well dang, Jim," Mimi replies, conjuring her best childhood innocence; she knows the dress-down is coming, and expects nothing less. "All I did was drop by his house on the way to the grocery store this morning to pick up something. His car was in the driveway; it's not like I broke in or anything."

"You shouldn't have painted on the door, Mimi. Drew says it's ruined and will have to be replaced."

"Jim, it's lipstick; tell Drew to pull his head out of his ass." Black beret and candy cigarette notwithstanding, innocence was a strong player in Mimi's formative years; however, the virtuous Hayley Mills act is not in her current repertoire. Pollyanna has a black eye. "I just want my champagne flutes."

Jim sighs. "Sam will put the glasses on the front porch and you can pick them up tomorrow. Drew also said that a No Trespassing sign will be posted on Sam's front door the minute you get them." He pauses. "Is there anything else you want from the house? Because if you do, now's the time."

"Nope, that's it."

"Okay, I'll call Drew." Jim's tone turns from reprimanding to conspiratorial. "Something's very strange about this deal; Drew says he doesn't really represent Sam anymore and refuses to discuss the contract with me. I think he's hedging. But he did say he tried to represent both of you through mediation, is that true?"

Mimi isn't surprised by Jim's skepticism. "You saw the contract; whose side do you think he took in mediation? All I know is Sam told me to go through his attorney for everything, and he says his attorney is Drew Wissle. God, these guys are such liars."

"There's nothing we can do about that unless you think Drew misrepresented you, and then we'll have a real legal battle on our hands. It'll cost a lot of money and take a lot of time. But," Jim says, crossing his fingers, "I'll represent you if you want to go there."

Mimi doesn't hesitate. "Nope, let's get this over with as soon as possible."

"All right," Jim says, once again missing his chance to earn an all-expenses-paid trip to Hawaii. "I'll call Sam directly instead of dealing with Drew. I'll remind him you're not pressing criminal charges against him for threatening to have you taken away." Whatever that means, Jim thinks. "Oh, but Drew did mention that Sam is afraid you'll call the IRS and report him for tax fraud."

"Good!" Mimi exclaims. "I want him to be afraid. Tell Sam he has one week to sign the contract, or I'll make the call."

"That should do it. I'll be back in touch."

Jim Morris calls Mimi ten days after their first meeting. "It's a wrap; Sam has signed the contract," Jim says. "Save that wine," he chuckles. "It might be worth something someday." Mimi laughs. "It already is, Jim," she says. "It's worth the year it will take me to drink it."

Mimi's heart and head play tackle football. Sam teaches Mimi about spite, and the lessons are bitter and tough. She moves painfully forward with the hesitancy of a blind man touching a cold dead animal for the first time; a very deep freeze sets up camp in her chest. Is it human nature to put love on ice? Mimi needs a military issue wool blanket to keep frostbite from permanently damaging her heart.

. . .

Sam dogs Mimi's every step when she returns to The Firefly for the last time. "Just the computer, Mimi, no backup discs. Not that picture, Mimi; that belongs to the restaurant, not you. Not that wine, Mimi; not that book, Mimi; nope, that's mine. It's all mine. Hurry up," Sam sneers and looks at the velvet Elvis clock in the kitchen. "Your twenty minutes are up; now get the hell out or I'll call the police."

Anger and alcohol mix a combustible and toxic blend. Sam opens the telephone book, looks up Jake Reston's number, but doesn't dial. Not tonight, Sam thinks. But he is sure of his right to revenge. He sparkles with spiteful glee, sparkles like a laser-cut Blue Nile diamond under a jeweler's backlit case. His mouth puckers as he bites his tongue until it bleeds and he tastes the bitterness of his own blood; his mouth fills with it until he can't swallow. Sam looks at his reflection in the bedroom mirror and sees a mouth curved like an upside down horse shoe; all the luck runs out, all his good will spills out and dissipates in a blue vapor. Sam personifies bad intention. This will be good, he thinks. Sticks and stones are meaningless; I'll hurt Mimi with words. He tries to right his smile, but it pains him.

. . .

Sleep eludes Mimi, and the howling coyotes can't soothe her; their calls conjure death tonight, conjure the thrill of the kill. She jumps out of bed and into her car, wheeling toward the black horizon in bedroom slippers, pajamas, and a baseball cap. "I'm going trespassing," she says out loud to the wind blowing through her open window. "I'm going to collect sticks and rocks and soil and plants. I might even break a window," she whispers to the wind. "I might even set off the alarm." She smiles, but finds no satisfaction in the act. "Maybe I'll get arrested, then make a scene and become hysterical. Yeah, that's what I'll do." Her fantasy gains speed as her foot guns the accelerator up a long, dark hill. "Maybe the cops will take me to the hospital…the psych ward sounds good. I'll get a big shot of a pharmaceutical cocktail, and they'll put me in the rubber room where I can wear myself out." Mimi laughs at the headwind as it tries in vain to drive her back home. "No, no…I'll just tell them I want to kill somebody, maybe myself; then they'll give me big drugs that'll knock me out for days." Mimi slows at the next corner, thinks about pulling into the golden arches for a double cheeseburger instead, but beats Fatty Patty in a hard-fought wrestling match; if Mimi lets her in tonight, she may never leave. "Fuck you!" Mimi yells, battling with an army of forked-tongue fiery demons. "God, this is stupid; just get to a cool, dark corner and pull the covers over your head for a few days. It's only money, it's only money, it's only money." Mimi slams the brakes one quick time, tries to right her mind with a hard snap; it doesn't work. "You incompetent shit," she scoffs. "I fucking hate myself right now; I'm so incompetent. No, no, dammit, I have to stop this, or Sam wins." She

187

punches the gas again, sticks her head out the window and takes a deep breath. "Go home," her brain orders. "Go for a walk," her legs suggest. "Buy a pack of cigarettes," her hands plead. "Chill in the hammock and read a book," her intellect chimes. "Get shitfaced! Drink a bottle of Bachio Divino for breakfast!" her liver implores. "Calm down, all of you," Mimi instructs. "It's important to calm the hell down before we get in serious trouble. No, I already am in serious trouble; it's important that I not let Sam steal my money. No, fuck the money, let the money go. You've been in need of money before and found a way to survive. What makes this time different? Here I am, no big deal. Breathe, let it go. Let...it...go." And she does, but not before trespassing. Not before gathering rocks and sticks and soil and not before staring into The Firefly's large plate glass window, and not before considering how it might shatter into a million pieces if she stares at it long enough; it never does.

By sunrise, the hammock, eight cigarettes, and a half bottle of Bachio Divino lull Mimi into a dreamless, motionless sleep.

...

Jake hangs up the phone and considers his next move; the enticing offer to accompany Odessa Hargrave on an adventure safari leaves him lighter than a twelve gram dart. He focuses intently on the bull's eye, stands back, and releases; the scalpel stabs the sheetrock wall, marking a point due east. Three times he throws; three times he misses his intended mark. Or does he? It's a sign, he thinks. Full time musicianship requires an immense amount of dedication. Local is good, regional is better, but a three month trip to Europe touring with Odessa

Hargrave may turn my life around. Germany first, Amsterdam after Hamburg, then Barcelona. Weeks of playing gigs, good-paying gigs. This is your break, man, he thinks. Are you strong enough to make the change? Do you want it bad enough? No room for complacency here. He closes his office door, bids a quick goodbye to a bevy of moon-faced nurses, and follows his inner compass west toward a dead-end destination; his most difficult adventure to date is rapidly coming to an end.

Jake finds his wife camped out in her usual spot, book in hand. "Julie, I got an interesting call today."

"Good, honey." Julie doesn't shift her eyes from the page.

"Julie, please," Jake asks, "put the book down for a minute."

"Two more pages then I will. Feed Molly, will you?"

"It's eight o'clock, and you haven't fed Molly? What the fuck, Julie?"

Julie sighs. "She's not gonna die, Jake. Just leave me alone for a minute so I can finish this chapter, then we'll talk, okay?" Patronizing Julie, Pissed Off Jake. Per usual.

Jake walks to the kitchen and fixes a gourmet dinner – complete with cheese and leftover steak – for the only female he trusts. "Molly, come here, girl, here you go." He bends toward his loyal dog's grinning face and accepts a kiss. "I love you too, baby. You're the one I'll miss." Jake has a vision that solidifies his decision. "Wanna go to the country for vacation? I bet I know somebody who will love on you like I do. Yeah…maybe this is meant to be." Jake reaches in the refrigerator, grabs a beer and a chunk of rotisserie chicken, and walks back to Julie's private library. He puts the beer on the coffee table, being careful to place it on a coaster to avoid Julie's nagging. Julie stretches, marks her page, and, turning to Jake, waits for him to speak first. Her face exudes the warmth of a Siberian weasel.

"Odessa paged me at work today; she's looking for a keyboard player to tour with her in Europe for a few months," Jake says, watching his wife's face for a reaction.

"The hospital's not gonna like that, Jake."

Jake shrugs and smiles. "I've given them a three-week notice. Baby docs are ready to take my place today; we're crawling with residents hungry for a job."

"Are you out of your fucking mind? Why don't you take a sabbatical instead? You can't make money as a musician."

"I've been an ED doctor for fifteen grueling years, and I don't want to see anymore dead people; it's not always about the money, darling."

Julie sneers. "You're not cut out for that lifestyle; you'll get eaten alive!"

Jake narrows his eyes. "I'm being eaten alive as we speak, Julie."

Julie crosses her left leg over her right; her dangling foot paddles furiously as her head bobs toward a dangerous thrust. "Let's get this over once and for all, shall we? I'm not interested in your midlife crisis. You go ahead and do what you have to do, and I'll do the same." Julie reaches for her book, but Jake grabs her hand, willing her to make good on her words. "Julie, when I leave this time, it's for keeps."

Julie shakes off her husband's touch and stands up; her hands shake as she lights a cigarette. "So, Mister Bohemian, you're gonna grow your hair long and hang out with star fuckers, is that it? What a proud moment for you." She takes a hard draw and blows a furious trail of smoke toward Jake. "Is Mimi Killian going with you?"

Jake is thrown off balance. "Where'd that come from?"

Julie smirks. "Sam Killian." Ice crystals are forming around her tight, sharp mouth. I kissed the wicked witch and lived to tell, Jake thinks. "I haven't talked to Mimi since she left The Firefly, Julie."

"Well, I've talked to Sam, and he says you and Mimi are having an affair."

Jake is incredulous. "Did he call you?"

"He sure did, Jake, and he asked me out. I might actually go, too."

Jake looks hard at Julie and issues a warning. "Be careful, Julie, that man is sick."

Julie's blue-gray mouth is twisted like a sailor's knot. "Sam wants to sue you, Jake; he says you fucked Mimi in the office one night, but I told him that was highly unlikely since you can't get it up."

Jake looks disgustedly at someone he used to love. "Who are you, and what have you done with my wife?" He picks up his beer, turns his head toward the east window, and prays for a quick end to this dawdling death march. "Look, Julie, I'm leaving in a month; it doesn't make sense for me to move until then, but I will." He rubs his head and slowly turns to his wife. "This is what I suggest we do, if you'll agree. First, I want legal separation papers; I'll give you everything except my equipment, my clothes, my car, my retirement fund, and Molly. You can have the house and everything in it."

Julie laughs and shakes her head. "Bad deal; I want alimony."

Now it's Jake's turn to laugh. "You have more money in your account than I do, Julie; be reasonable."

"I'm not signing a thing, Jake. Is that reasonable enough for you?"

"I'll make the house payments for six months and pay off your car next week, how about that?"

"I can say you abandoned me and get a mean-ass attorney to take you to the cleaners," Julie retorts. "I can make your life hell."

Jake considers throwing his beer on Julie to see if she'll melt, but takes a sip instead. No reason to waste good beer, he thinks. "Go ahead, Julie, show the world your ugly bones." He hesitates, wishing he had a better option. "Look, I need to live in this house until I leave for Germany. I'll move downstairs to the studio, and you won't even know I'm here."

"You'll have to pay rent if you're staying in this house!"

"Hell, Julie, I make the house payments, remember?"

"Well, six months doesn't start until you move out." Julie stands and walks across the pale beige room, studies herself in the nearby mirror, and spies what appears to be a small wart beginning to erupt from the tip of her nose. I need a facial, Julie thinks as she shakes her pony tail. "And just so you know, I'm not keeping Molly when you're gone."

"When I leave, Molly leaves." Jake's heart skips ahead like an excited child catching fireflies on a warm summer night. He drops his head so Julie can't see his smile. "I'll move downstairs tonight; it'll only take a couple of hours." He gathers energy before speaking his next thought. "As far as I'm concerned, we've been separated for six months. Do you agree?"

Julie winds out a caustic sneer. "How do you figure that, asshole?"

"Because, Julie, the last time we made love was six months ago, on my birthday. I'll pay all the court costs if you'll agree."

Julie considers the new offer. "That's a fine idea," Julie replies. "The sooner this sham is over, the better."

"Deal," says a mentally exhausted, but victorious Jake. "Now, can we shake hands and agree to live in peace for the next month?" Julie walks away from her husband's outstretched hand. "Actually, Jake, I don't want to ever touch you again." She turns her back on him, and picking up her book, settles in for a date night with Steven R. Covey; Julie's all about the win-win.

"Can we at least be polite adversaries?"

"The word polite is not in my vocabulary right now, Jake."

"How about neutral, then?"

"How about invisible instead, pal? I'm going to pretend you can't see me anymore, and then maybe you'll go away."

Jake watches as the familiar stranger fades into a dusty blur. "I haven't seen you for a long time, Julie."

"Fuck you, Jake."

"Fuck you right back, Julie." The highly effective habits of a fourteen-year bad marriage close with a whisper and a draw.

. . .

Mimi has twenty-five thousand dollars in her bank account, thanks to home equity; she donates the bulk of her closet, choosing only to keep her favorite clothes, and leaves everything to Sam except one of their four stereos and her thirteen year old Volvo station wagon. She is unfettered and free to roam. Do I buy stock or go to Italy? Neither, she decides; I need to invest in my life. Mimi's conservative realism overrides her vagabond nature; she visits a local estate sale in the grand part of town and purchases a used washer and dryer, an overstuffed down-filled tapestry sofa marred by a well-camouflaged but permanent coffee stain, a garbage bag housing a tattered but salvageable Bella Notte lavender velvet bedspread, and one slightly ratty but vibrant vegetable-dyed Turkish rug. She splurges on a full set of hand thrown stoneware dishes from a potter she admires, and plunks down a few more dead Bengies on a new bed – she can't sleep in the bed she shared with Sam – and now has seventeen thousand dollars left.

Mimi grows beautiful flowers, and her prolific gardens are envied by the few sightseers ambling down her country road on weekends. She takes long walks with her enormous rescued black lab whom she names Ben, but nicknames The Boogieman because he likes to dance; she listens to Coltrane for sensuality and Joni Mitchell for wisdom and Adam Holzman for wild inspiration; but she aches for The Firefly, aches for purpose and company – both of which are in short supply. The ache invites longing to the table, and longing invites suffering. Suffering, Mimi reads, is the short road to spirit. Mimi likes that phrase; it gives her hope that suffering will be a quality guest and leave before the party's over. I'm on a short, but well-defined path, Mimi thinks. It's simple, she thinks; all I need is patience. I'll find a great job in due time; I always land on my feet.

Mimi peruses the classifieds each morning over breakfast and networks with former customers and places a dozen calls each day and determines that nobody, nobody will hire a strong-willed woman with a high profile. Mimi sends out thirty resumes and is rejected thirty times. "You're way overqualified, Ms. Killian; we can't pay you enough, Ms. Killian; are you able to work third shift on weekends and be on-call twenty four seven? Will you dig ditches? Are you certified to operate a forklift? We pay six and a quarter an hour to start, Ms. Killian." Downcast Mimi asks for a little easy with her simple, and Fatty Patty comes to visit for an entire month.

. . .

Jake reads Frommer's Travel Guide until his favorite pages are dog-eared. He pays close attention to the medical sections, as sickness is not part of his travel plan. "Completed the alphabet of Hepatitis vaccines long ago – check; better boost the tetanus and diphtheria just to be safe – check; not going to the woods, so not worried about tick encephalitis – check; will pack plenty of Imodium and Septra – check; insured out the wazoo – check; no prescriptions to fill – check. Check, check. Jake continues through his list with gusto: ask Melvin to store personal belongings until return; get flight itinerary from Odessa; call airlines and figure out equipment regulations; pack light; get haircut; find passport – I think it's in the home safe; go to bank for Traveler's checks; pack Real Book – must remember my Real Book; ask Mimi to keep Molly – I need to do that right away, Jake thinks. He calls The Phoenix before he chickens out. "Dee, it's Jake."

"Jake? It's really loud in here. I can barely hear you!"

Jake hears high pitched rebel yells in the background. "What the hell's going on down there?"

"Bluegrass, Jake. Can you believe it? Sam booked the Red Creek Travelers and people are hopping like frogs."

Jake is confused. "But it's not even dark yet."

Dee covers her left ear with her hand in an effort to block out dueling banjos. "I know, but hopefully they'll wear themselves out and go home soon. I'm sorry, Jake, but I'm slammed. Wish I could talk, but…"

"I need Mimi's number Dee. Do you have it?"

"No, I don't; I think it's upstairs though, but I can't get there right now. Call me back in a couple of hours. Shit!" Dee yells. "Some tall guy just knocked a hole in the ceiling with his head and I see blood. Gotta run!"

. . .

I know this woman, Jake thinks as he loads Molly into the back seat of his secondhand jeep. He rolls down Molly's window, climbs in the driver's side, and, questioning his sanity, heads down the two lane toward Jenkin's Bottom. Mimi won't mind if I stop by without calling first, will she? What if she has company? I'll just drive by and see what's up. Should I take her something? Yeah, I'll take her a plant; I'll get a plant, where do I get a plant? Nah, forget it, he thinks. I'll just stop by for a minute to say hello. What if she doesn't like dogs, Jake wonders? What if she's afraid, or allergic; then what am I gonna do? God, Jake thinks, this is ridiculous – I don't even know if Mimi likes dogs and I'm gonna ask her to keep Molly for a few months. What planet do I live on, Molly? He reaches around, scratches her ears, and slows his racing mind to the slower rhythm of her wagging tail. Must be Uranus, he laughs; that's every dog's favorite planet, right, old girl? Jake slows, travels down a well-maintained gravel driveway, and spies Mimi outside pulling weeds from a lush flowerbed; a huge black dog lies on the ground beside her. Mimi rises from her knees at the sound of Jake's car, and is pleased to see an old friend smiling at her. "How are you?" she says, removing her worn work gloves and extending a hand to Jake. "Come on over here and identify this spider for me, willya? Ben, get your nose out of Jake's crotch." She turns her attention to the car and smiles back at a grinning dog.

"Who's that pretty redhead with you?" she asks, as Molly wiggles her body out of the window, reaching for Mimi's outstretched backscratcher.

"That's my best friend, Molly," Jake says proudly.

"Molly, huh? What a beautiful girl! Can I let her out? Ben's very friendly, I'm sure you've noticed." Mimi doesn't wait for an answer.

Jake and Mimi laugh as Molly and Ben bow to each other in play posture, and, nose to nose, kiss. Mimi looks at Jake. "The Boogieman's lonely, Jake; he needs a four-legged dance partner."

I might be able to help your man out, Jake thinks, but stifles his request until later. Mimi stretches and grimaces slightly. "My back's stiff from working in the garden; you timed this visit well. How about some iced tea?" she asks, rinsing her hands at the nearby spigot. Jake accepts her offer and, following Mimi up the back steps, can't help but notice her tanned and toned legs. She walks like a cougar, Jake thinks. She moves like a cat. His old place looks good – comfortable and cozy, but with a bit of hip thrown in for good measure. Mimi's mishmash taste and eye for quality pull a room together on the cheap to stunning artistic effect. She hands Jake a glass filled with something that looks nothing like the southern iced tea he's expecting. Mimi takes note of his hesitation. "It's Red Zinger, have you ever had it?"

"No," says Jake slowly, swirling his glass. "What's the green stuff floating around in it?"

"Spearmint; did you notice the big stand of weedy-looking stuff in the barrel outside the door? I thought maybe you planted it when you lived here."

"No, when I lived here, nothing bloomed like it does now." Jake leans against the kitchen counter and looks around. "Wow, Mimi, this place sings. It's a happy house." He takes a timid sip of the red elixir, not knowing what to expect, and is surprised by its strength and crisp flavor. "This is really good; what makes a Red Zinger zing?"

"A bunch of herbs, Jake; no caffeine."

"What makes it red?" Jake hopes Mimi doesn't notice him staring at her rosy lips, but she does, and, blushing, turns to the sink. Be careful, Mimi says to herself. Breathe deep, she says; keep it light. "Hibiscus flowers, the favorite nectar of Hummingbirds," she answers. Jake shifts his weight and glances toward the door, suddenly feeling awkward. All this tea talk unnerves him somehow. "Is it okay I stopped by? I didn't mean to interrupt you."

"It's fine," says Mimi, smiling, intuiting Jake's discomfort as hers passes. "I have some really good tomatoes, will you eat a sandwich?"

"Sure," says Jake, never one to turn down a homegrown tomato sandwich. "Are you gonna have one?" Mimi is already prepping, fluidly grabbing provisions from the refrigerator. "Oh, yeah," she says. "Two a day is my minimum when the tomatoes come in, and I'm one short. Do you like a little mayonnaise or a lot of mayonnaise?" Jake relaxes and finds his groove. "Lots, please, all the way to the corners, on both pieces of bread." Just like me, Mimi thinks. "A little pepper or a lot of pepper?"

"Make it black." Mimi hands Jake the pepper mill. "Grind away, and make mine just like yours," she says, reaching for a bag of chips and a couple of crisp carrots. "Do you prefer the porch, or the kitchen?" Jake grins. "Al fresco."

Mimi cuts the sandwiches on the diagonal and piles chips in the middle of the halves. "Grab the plates, please sir, and I'll refill our glasses. I'm right behind you." She follows Jake out the front door to a picnic table dressed in muted yellows and blues; a blue speckled metal milk pitcher holds a bouquet of perfect pink cosmos and purple salvia from the garden out back. Mimi follows Jake's eyes to the pasture pond, and senses his longing as he watches Ben and Molly flush bull frogs from the reeds. "So," she says easily, "are you missing your old house?"

Jake sighs and smiles tenderly at Mimi. "Yeah, I do; I really miss the solitude. But, I only lived here for about four months when I was separated the first time, and then I moved back in with Julie, my wife." Mimi listens, but doesn't interrupt; Jake needs space between notes. "That was a big mistake," he says softly. "We're separated for good now; just made it official yesterday at the ceremonial signing of the papers."

"I'm sorry to hear that, Jake. It's not easy, is it? You feel like a failure, or at least I did, when I left Sam. Blame lies heavy on the soul, doesn't it?"

"Don't be sorry for me," Jake says. "It's been a long time coming." Jake takes a big bite of his sandwich as Mimi grabs a chip. They sit in silence, temporarily revisiting recent history. "Mimi, your situation was totally different," says Jake. He lifts his glass to his lips and searches for his next words; he wants to get it right. "You probably don't know this," he says, "but I witnessed the slow demise of your marriage; that man put you through hell. You might not blame Sam, but I do! He lost the best thing he'll ever have when you left, and I'm not the only one who believes that." Jake takes a huge bite of his messy sandwich and licks a wayward dollop of mayonnaise off his thumb. His words are balm to Mimi's sore heart, and she accepts them graciously, but makes it plain she's not without fault.

"Thanks, Jake, but I'm not the easiest person to get

along with; no, really," she laughs as Jake politely disagrees. "I've had lots of time to think about what happened; I'm sure I put way too much pressure on Sam, and pressure was the last thing he needed. I helped kick him over the edge." Jake turns his gaze back to the pond where Molly and Ben engage in a swimming contest with a group of mad Canadians. He ponders her words before answering. "You're definitely intense, Mimi, I know that from watching you; Sam's energy couldn't match yours. I'm sure it was tough."

"Tough on both of us, Jake," she responds. "I'm as much to blame as Sam is."

Jake doesn't accept that answer. "Blame alcohol, Mimi, not yourself." They reach a quiet understanding, and the inclination to dredge up muck from old tainted wells passes quickly.

Mimi cocks her head at Jake and playfully raises her eyebrows. "Wait a minute. You're here because you want this house back, aren't you?" Jake picks up the mischievous bent of her tone. "I have your eviction papers in my car," he says, grinning as he inhales the last bite of his perfectly gooey sandwich.

"You'll have to haul my cold, dead body off this property, man," say Mimi, feigning indignation. "Shall we set a time for the duel? Ben's my second, and Molly's my third; you haven't a chance."

"I'm not scrapping with an alley cat like you," Jake laughs. "Seriously, Mimi, you and this house are perfect for each other; I hope you stay forever." Mimi frowns at the mere thought of leaving her peaceful cottage; she knows her lack of income may drive her to bigger, but not necessarily greener, pastures sooner than she'd like. "I can't find a job in this town that suits me or my pocketbook, Jake."

"What about opening another club?"

Mimi shrugs. "The investors are calling, and it's an ego stroke. But, I'm not ready; maybe someday, but not now." She changes the subject to avoid more discussion. "Where are you living?"

"In my studio for the next few weeks. Then – you're gonna love this – I'm touring Europe with Odessa for a few months."

Mimi snaps her fingers. "Congratulations, that's huge!"

"Yeah, it's huge logistically right now; you won't believe how much it costs to ship my equipment."

"I bet; but once it's there, it's there!"

"All two hundred fifty pounds of it; I'm not looking forward to schlogging it through airports and hotel lobbies."

"That's why bellhops and baggage handlers were invented, Jake; just keep a big wad of cash on you at all times."

Jake's not sure what to expect when he drops his next bomb, but hopes for understanding. "I'm leaving the hospital, too. No more Doctor Reston, at least for awhile."

"Good for you!" Mimi exclaims. "I don't see how you worked in the emergency room for as long as you did; it depresses me to think about it." Mimi grins and leaning into Jake, pats his shoulder. "How exciting! Abundant new gigs! What are you doing with Molly, can she stay here?" Molly and Ben, still wet and panting from their synchronized, but failed attempt to usurp the pond from the Canada geese, wag their tails in unison, sounding out a rhythmic percussive beat on the wooden porch. Jake stares wide-eyed at Mimi; he's overwhelmed by her offer, by not having to ask her for this favor. "Are you kidding?"

"She's wonderful, Jake. I'm not sure you'll ever get her back without a fight. Look at those two; they're in deep puppy love." Mimi looks at Jake and grins. "Ben's neutered; I promise Molly won't be a teenage mother when you get home."

"Yeah, Molly's spayed; she doesn't even know what sex is. You can't miss what you never had, right?"

"If one hasn't had sex in over a year, doesn't that make one a virgin in some cultures?"

"In the culture of my mind," Jake answers playfully. "I'm over the six month mark myself; my face is breaking out."

"Well, you need to masturbate more often, Doctor. Look at my face – clear as a bell." Jake watches Mimi's face turns from pink to scarlet as her flirtatious remark catches up to her brain. "Not anymore, dear; you're blushing."

Mimi is horrified. "I can't believe I just said that."

"I'm glad you did," says Jake, blushing in return; he's glad to be sitting down. Mimi, red as a German Johnson tomato, excuses herself and walks to the kitchen to pull her foot out of her mouth. She reappears with two pieces of strawberry shortcake, and feeling quite the imbecile, impatiently says, "Can Molly stay here? I've asked you three times, and I won't ask you a fourth."

Jake, understanding her embarrassment, gently says, "Yes, Mimi, Molly can stay here. Thank you so much." Mimi takes a deep breath, exhales the biggest part of her humiliation, and sits. She picks at her luscious dessert, and places an exact amount of strawberry, Grand Marnier-infused whipped cream, and homemade angel food cake on her fork. She takes a bite of summer, and, still feeling like a dork, looks shyly at Jake. "When do you leave?"

"Three weeks from today," Jake says, and crams a heaping tablespoonful of Mimi's best dessert in his mouth. "Damn, woman, you're spoiling me; best meal in a month of Sundays; all this and dog-sitting, too. You are an angel walking." The moment is precious for Jake; he's never seen Mimi quite so human, so feminine, and can't remember the last time he felt this completely nourished.

"And, how long will you be gone, do you think?"

"Probably three months, maybe a little longer; is that okay?"

"Absolutely, Jake. Molly's a gift, and I'd appreciate you leaving her here for as long as you can. When do you want to bring her to me? I know you have lots of prep before you go, so I'll take her anytime between now and then."

"What if I bring her out a few times to visit before I leave? Just to make sure you don't change your mind," he says with a twinkle in his eye.

Jake's easy banter helps Mimi forget her faux pas. "How about dinner tomorrow night? I have a slew of fresh spinach that needs picking; I'll make spinach and garlic pizza, and we'll drink a bottle of Firefly-sponsored red wine; how's that sound?"

"Sounds perfect; I work until four, and I'd love to go for a walk around the farm before dinner." Mimi picks up the plates, and Jake follows her with the glasses. "I see you've painted your mailbox blue; paying homage to Taj Mahal?"

Mimi giggles. "Yeah, moving to the country, you know; I had to do it."

"Wasn't this hanging in The Firefly's back dining room?" Mimi puts the dishes in the sink as Jake gawks appreciatively at the large French marquee poster poised over a heavy, hand-painted block kitchen table. "It hung in my grandmother's kitchen when I was a kid; it's my favorite thing from forever ago, and it's the one thing Sam knew he couldn't fight over." A massive white rooster with bright yellow talons, a large red comb, and beady black eyes glares at Jake through the glass, looking for a fight.

"That's one very funky rooster, Mimi. That bird has the soul of a funkmeister; speaking of which, don't you love the way sound carries through this house?" Mimi gets the hint and directs Jake to her vast CD collection. "Perhaps it's time for a little Sly, Jake. Or, wait a minute, here's one for you; when's the last time you listened to Mother's Finest?" She hands him the case to *Another Mother Further*.

Jake looks at Mimi and shakes his head. "This is spooky," he says. "Go check my car, Mimi; Truth'll Set You Free."

And Jake and Mimi connect, just like that. Just like that. Synchronicity is the blessing Jake and Mimi are given; it's also the curse. All in favor of the blessing rather than the curse raise your hands; raise them high so they can be counted. Raise them in praise of a friendship blessed by dog love, homegrown tomatoes, and the funktified vibe. A simple spark may grow a fire, but we know this: simple is not easy. Fatty Patty tells us so; darkness tells us so, so it is so. And, we know this: suffering is the short road to spirit. The Bible tells us so; the Tarot tells us so. So it is so.

AFFECTION

When hearts are open, affection enters and shines warmth and love upon the world. Affection cannot be manipulated, for its only purpose is to give. Control freaks, give it up.

Jake leaves for Hamburg with 250 pounds of musical equipment, including three synthesizers, assorted cables and wah-wah peddles, and one duffle bag of carefree black and blue clothing. He's nervous about the trip, but not because he's charting unknown territory. Jake is afraid for his equipment like most people are afraid for their children, or animals. He takes a deep breath; out of my hands now, Jake assures himself. He swallows an Ambien, dreams fitfully through dinner and the in-flight movie, then reads, sketches, and writes until landing.

Jake is not a seasoned traveler; a trip to Quebec for the jazz festival, a quick stint in a Jamaican jail during college, and scuba diving off Isla Mujeres are the three marks on his passport. But make no mistake; Jake looks like a veteran as he seeks out and pays for the help he needs. The foreign words playing against Jake's ear are confusing, but money is part of the universal language, and he has plenty.

Odessa books Jake into the Wedina, a lovely eighteenth century town house on Gurlittstrasse, near the lake. All he has to do is check in – the room is paid in advance – and wait for Odessa's call. A shower, a nap, and some food would be nice, he wishes. But, an unexpected complication shatters Jake's revelry, compliments of the front desk. "A minor glitch, Mr. Reston; there has been a slight change in your reservation," says the impeccably dressed and sincerely polite agent. "Unfortunately, your original room is still occupied. The couple preceding you had an emergency and will be with us for another few days. However, we've taken the liberty of moving you to a very nice suite on the third floor."

"That's fine," Jake assures the gentleman. "Where is your elevator?"

"Oh, I'm sorry, sir, we have no elevator at the Wedina."

"No elevator? Do you see my luggage?" Jake looks at the mile-high pile of cases stacked behind him, and grimaces. "A third floor room will not work, not at all. Please, find a room on the first floor."

"Let me check again, Mr. Reston." After a few seconds, the kind man shakes his head and sadly looks at Jake. "Sir, I am very sorry, but only the third floor room is available."

Jake emits a long, low moan. "Can you move the couple in my room to the third floor?"

"It will be impossible. The wife suffered a bad sprain yesterday and cannot negotiate the stairs."

"How many stairs are we talking about here?" The man counts in his head, visualizing the winding path. He knows he can't fix this, but he is determined to make it right somehow. "Forty-five, maybe more." Jake never loses his cool, but he feels beads of warm sweat meet in the middle of his neck and create what feels like a major tributary coursing down his back. "Will you please call Odessa Hargrave?"

"Yes, of course; one moment." The kind man dials, waits, looks at Jake, and, once again, shakes his head. "I'm sorry, but there's no answer."

"Did she by any chance leave a message for Jake Reston?"

The man knows she didn't, but feels compelled to show Jake he's trying. "Let me check. No, nothing is here, sir." Jake rubs his forehead as if conjuring a genie from a magic lamp, but all three wishes are denied, delayed until the genie feels Jake is more deserving of the grant. "I can't drag this equipment up and down forty-five stairs; therefore, I am unable to stay at your wonderful hotel. Where else might you suggest?"

"Mr. Reston, please accept my sincere apology. Please, relax in the lounge while I make new arrangements." Jake is too tired to relax. "No, I'll stay right here," he says, closing his eyes and stretching his tired back. His body absorbs his well-disguised anger, and begins to ache. He paces, but feels like a caged bear; he turns to the window and listens to the conversation at the front desk. "Hello, this is Hans at the Wedina calling. I need a room immediately for a very weary traveler, can you help? Bottom floor, please. Yes, private, eight nights. Yes, please take good care of him; we have caused some trouble for him here. Yes, he will arrive within thirty minutes, and will need help with his luggage." Hans pauses. "American, yes. A musician, I think, and by the look of his baggage a very important person. Thank you, he is on his way." Hans leaves his station, quietly approaches Jake and gently wakes him from a wall nap. "Mr. Reston? I'm sorry to wake you, but you are booked into the Steens on Holzdamm, not ten minutes walk from here. They are expecting you, and I will take you there myself."

Jake sighs, smiles graciously, and extends his hand. "Thank you, Hans; much appreciated." Jake scribbles a quick note to Odessa and gives Hans the folded paper. "Will you please make sure Ms. Hargrave receives this message?"

"Certainly. Shall we go?" Hans asks.

"Yes, we shall certainly go," Jake answers.

. . .

The Steens Hotel is short on style – short on the one thing Jake cares nothing about; Jake has style to spare. He soaks up every last drop of hot water, water hot enough to melt his bones. He takes another Ambien, falls down on the bed and says a prayer. No gig tonight, thank you God, he whispers, and sleeps for seven blissful hours before awakening to Odessa's rap on his door. "Hey baby," she says as Jake pulls her close for a bear hug. "Sorry about the mix-up. Everything make it?"

"Yep, no problem there," he says. "I'm starving; what time is it?"

"Time to eat, Sugar Pie." Odessa takes a chair and wraps her long, ebony legs into an elegant curve. She takes a look at Jake's sparsely appointed yet sleek room and nods. "Nice digs; not as pretty as mine, but nice."

Jake's priorities don't include comparing room décor with Odessa. He moves to the bathroom, splashes cold water on his face, runs a hand through his bed-head, rehydrates his rested but dry blue eyes, and changes into the least wrinkled of his four black shirts. "When do I get to meet the rest of the band?" Jake asks.

"Tomorrow night; they'll meet us at The After Shave for sound check at nine."

"What time's the gig?" Jake asks as he pulls on a black jacket and opens the door for Odessa. "We start at eleven, can you believe it? A normal gig, like New York!" Jake follows her tall curvaceous body out the door. "I could eat the ass-end out of a rag doll about right now," Jake says, and his stomach agrees wholeheartedly. "Come on, then," laughs Odessa, "we'll hop on the Bahn and take a little trip."

"What's the Bahn?"

"The subway, Jake, only it's above ground. U-Bahn for the city, S-Bahn for the suburbs; it's a fast ride. We'll hop off near the Reeperbahn and go to the Old Commercial Room for dinner."

"Okay, what's the Reeperbahn? Ain't related to the Grim, is it?" Jake is goofy from hunger and jet lag, and Odessa loves it; she's never seen this side of Jake. "It's the Saint Pauli's district – the Genital Zone, as it's affectionately called," she says. "You'll see; we'll take a walk on the wild side after dinner. You up for that?" Odessa winks and grins; her pliable lips spread across her animated face, reminding Jake of a Tall Ship in full sail. "I'll tell you after dinner, Odessa," he says. "A lot of dinner."

"Gotta save room for dessert, Jake," she says. "I'll take you to the Erotic Art Museum tonight and you can get pussy on a stick." Jake takes Odessa's arm. "Liking this town already, Odessa."

Jake orders Labskaus, or sailor's hash, a tradition at the Commercial Room. Corned beef and ham, onions, potatoes, leeks, hardtack, and heavenly spices create a luscious stew that warms even the coldest man's heart. Top the bowlful of goodness with a fried egg and, voila! Jake devours a devoted chef's house special filled with love, fat, and enough gas-producing matter to create the ultimate gut bomb. Jake is happy and full, but takes Odessa's advice and saves room for dessert.

The Reeperbahn makes Amsterdam's Red Light District look like Pollyanna's playground. Prostitutes are highly regarded members of the income-tax-paying financial base of Hamburg and are officially sanctioned by city officials; Saint Pauli Girl beer is named in honor of Hamburg's hookers. Hamburg: a good time town! "Geezus, Odessa, where did all these people come from? And why are they all naked?" Jake is gawking. "My God, wouldja look at that thing? What is it?"

Odessa chants her answer. "The freaks come out at night, Ba-Boo; the freaks come out at night."

"Damn, I can do an internal exam on that one from right here on the street! Is that legal what she's doing?"

Odessa takes a closer look before responding. "Honey, I think that's a she male. Everything's legal here except bestiality; no animal sex acts. That's where Hamburg draws the line." She looks at Jake's wide eyes. "It's a city with a conscience, don't you know. Wanna go to the theatre?"

"A movie? I don't think so. I'd probably fall asleep."

Odessa laughs. "No, innocent boy, the erotic theatre."

Jake shudders. "Would I have to touch anything, like a chair, or a handrail?"

"Probably."

"Forget it, then. I'll watch erotic theatre from the comfort of the sidewalk. Makes me want to wash my hands."

"Wow, you are one uptight little white boy, aren't you?"

"My mama raised me to stay clean or she'd beat my ass," says Jake. He smiles wickedly at Odessa. "Now let's go get that pussy on a stick."

Four stories of sex make Jake dizzy. He goes to the gift shop, buys postcards and his sweet pink treat, then begs Odessa to get him back to Steens before he does something stupid like blush in her presence one more time, or erect another tent in his pants; Jake needs privacy. He thanks her for the educational tour, bids farewell after seeing her safely to the Wedina's front door, and, not quite satisfied, hurries back to his quiet ground level room. He washes his hands three times, pulls a virgin bottle of travel-sized Aura Glow from his shaving kit, partakes of his dessert before passing out in a slick sweat, and dreams in flesh-tone.

Jake thrills when he meets the band at sound check. Peter the drummer speaks fluent English as a second language, but Marc the bassist and Franz the sax man rely on vibe rather than words. Jake knows the secret password and enters the sacred world of musician-speak, phraseology of simple facial expressions and body language, a most sought-after territory, this ground, solid and familiar ground for Jake. And oh, the conversation is magic, pure and simple, transporting the most eloquent of linguistics experts, if they are paying attention, to frenzy. It is the language of God that is heard at The After Shave, a language of ascension, of higher and higher elevation. Watch Jake's face; last night's dessert orgy means absolutely nothing, cannot begin to compare to this moment of completion and fulfillment.

Three nights of playing straight-ahead jazz at The Cotton Club, the band tightening up their sound; two nights of standards at Dennis' Swing Club, the band loosening into improvisation and building momentum; two nights at Birdland, the band moving instinctively into fusion. Inspiration! The guys are hot, but when Odessa hits the stage, they move easily back into straight-ahead and standards. Crowd-pleasing standards are Odessa's bread and butter, her highest calling. Jake rarely turns down the sheets before the sun comes up, and sleeps until noon. Then he walks the Aussenalster Lake bridges, watches the old world in silence, feels the beat of Hamburg under his feet. He grooves on his silent day routine because post-gig late-nights take him to Molotow for funk or the Mojo for acid jazz or Grosse Freiheit for smoking, toking, and joking with Peter and the band. Now, the Reeperbahn represents music to Jake; music, not sex. He no longer feels like a tourist. He is home.

Dear Mimi,

How are my farm girls? Fine here, just short on sleep; nobody sleeps. I saw this funk hat and thought of you playing dress-up. Put it on and play your music loud and dance with Molly for me one time. Funk Hat will protect you from the wrath of rabid animals and snooping neighbors. Write back, but don't send as I have no address; will collect mail directly from source upon return, whenever that may be. Headed to North Sea Jazz Fest for three days of gigs...more surprises to come!

Love, Jake

Dear Jake,

I'm playing with my funk hat, learning its many styles. I am a Cajun chef, a sexy tart, a farm marm goofball. I am blinded by the bill or protected by it. I stuff it, roll it, bend it, point it, flatten it, and decorate it; what a lid! The ultimate good juju reality diversion. I fall down, roll around, perform splits, handsprings, and belly flops, burn things, dance like a maniac, skip, laugh, sing loud badly but in perfect pitch, turn circles, and howl at the moon. Funk Hat? It moves with its own mind, but never leaves my head. I wear my funk hat during yoga meditation. I make carrot juice while singing Baby Love in my funk hat. I stalk skunks and am invisible under the bill of the funk hat. You have set my imagination on fire. So much creativity inside the threads of the funk hat. It's the A ticket, Mr. Jake Reston. Molly looks good in it, too, but the Boogieman wears it better than both of us.

Love, Mimi

. . .

Miles played there; so did Ella and Joe Zawinul. The Brecker Brothers, BB King, David Sanborn, and McCoy Tyner are frequent performers at the North Sea Jazz Festival. Tony Bennett and Chick Corea and Herbie Hancock, they're there. The spirits of Dizzy Gillespie and Count Basie are there. Stage upon stage upon hall upon hall; indoors, outdoors, in town and all around, hours and hours of pure sound. Pick a room, any room. Listen and learn, or don't learn, just listen. It doesn't matter if you understand as long as you feel it. Jazz is jazz, and it rules Europe for three days every year; over 70,000 visitors representing most countries on Earth and the outer rings of Saturn are transported by unending notes ranging from the abstract to the sublime and back again. The Hague is Mecca for the jazz masses; it's the industry equivalent of the Super Bowl.

Odessa Hargrave and her ace musicians check into the Dorint Hotel Den Haag, famous for catering to festival musicians. The Dorint pulses with activity, drawing serious listeners and relaxed performers to its lobby. Jake's first gig is there, in the lobby, before the festival officially opens. He looks across the expanse, and damn, he's excited; standing at the bar is Archie Shepp chatting with Freddie Hubbard. Archie recognizes Jake from past gigs in the States and gives him his props. There's McCoy! Jake's on go; no nerves, he's confident. He talks to Peter and Peter talks back and then Marc and Franz join up and all conversation ceases at the bar and the focus is on the band, man, on the conversation between Jake and Peter and Marc and Franz. And here comes Stanley Clarke and he watches Marc coax some serious love out of his bass. Odessa walks to the bar and orders wine because she can't control them, doesn't want to; she's grinning because her boys have taken the lobby – they own it – and Stanley walks toward the band and Marc hands his baby to the master with a deep bow and picks up a set of Peter's sticks and keeps time to *Illegal* which rolls right into *Funk Is Its Own Reward* and nobody, nobody is standing still. And, holy shit. Michael Brecker blows in and all of a sudden it's four a.m. and nobody wants to go home. But, they are Home, and they know it.

Although the festival officially begins at five p.m. and closes with a midnight jam session each night, and although Jake is proud to be part of the various workshops and clinics and performances in Van Gogh Hal, it is the Dorint lobby that provides the most satisfaction; it's the lobby he remembers when he is old and his hands are arthritic and his shoulders are locked, and he is thankful to remember.

KARMA

We all make payment for actions that affect the welfare of oneself or another; it is irrevocable. What goes around comes around.

Life is one big disappointment for Julie Reston. She engages in a multitude of unfulfilling relationships with men who can fix a leaky sink, but can't patch the hole in her heart. Julie camps on a cold mountain too high for any sane man to climb; many attempt to reach the pinnacle of her personal Mount Everest, and freeze during the effort. "Darren, get up." Julie shakes her latest camping mountain climber. "Darren!"

Darren yawns widely, stretches and grins. "What time is it?" He scratches a hairy armpit and a colorful mermaid tattoo on his right bicep begins to undulate wildly; Julie's wide-eyed fascination quickly turns to disgust.

"Time for you to go. Get out of my bed."

"Come on over here, girl." Darren's second brain is wide awake.

"Darren, I mean it; get up. Now!"

"What's the matter?" The tickled mermaid slowly treads water before floating belly-up. "I made a mistake, that's the matter." Julie throws Darren's jeans on the bed and heads for the door.

"Julie, wait a minute. Come back here, baby." Julie stops at the threshold, sighs, and looks blankly at her confused plumber. "Darren, last night was fun…I guess it was fun, I really don't remember much about it. Now get the fuck out of my house."

"Damn, bitch, that's cold," says Darren, reaching for his pants. "Where's my tool belt?"

"It's in the kitchen where you left it. Thanks for fixing

my sink. Will a twenty cover it?"

Julie concentrates on finding success through her work, although she cannot find a job that sustains her in the manner to which she has grown accustomed. She puts the house on the market while Jake's in Europe, but it doesn't matter; Jake has no ties there. The house sells in two days, and Betsy is the only neighbor who cares. "Are you sure you want to leave? I know you can find another job here. It's a big house but you can afford it; I'll even help you with the yard work."

Julie shakes her head. "Money's not the issue, Betsy; the ghosts who live in this house are. I can't afford the emotional upkeep on all the Caspers who keep me awake at night; they inhabit every corner."

Betsy has an answer for everything. "Let's smudge it, then, you know, chase them out. I'll even chant."

Julie laughs and appreciates Betsy's vain attempt. "Darling Betsy, I'll miss you; but, you know I've always wanted to live at the beach, and now you have a reason to take solo mini-vacations. I expect you to visit at least once a month. Now, come on and help me price this mess."

"God, Julie, I hate yard sales."

"Me too, Betsy, but it's time to purge." Julie scans the garage and mentally calculates the worth of her cast-off wares. "Do you think seven hundred is too much to ask for that mirror?"

Betsy gapes. "But you love that mirror! I know it's shattered at the bottom, but the cracks add character," she says, looking at a series of distorted images. "I look like a Multiple Personality Disorder diagnosis," laughs Betsy as she tries to decide which mouth is hers. "Julie, are you sure you want to sell this? I've never seen anything like it."

"Yeah, I'm not carrying seven years of bad luck to the

beach. I'll give it to you if you want it, though."

"Nuh uh," declines Betsy. "Makes me dizzy."

By the end of the week, Julie accepts a social worker position with a minor hospital in a large coastal town and is quickly promoted to Director of Community Affairs; the pay is a far cry from the six figure salary she's used to, but she is happy for the moment; *at least I retained a title and a good parking space*, Julie thinks. *At least I'll have my feet in sand.*

Meanwhile, Sam Killian is busy building a raging fire on the Bible Belt's pearly white doorstep. Sam gains notoriety in the local community by becoming a not so anonymous alcoholic businessman with a loyal, "Members Only" client base dubbed "The Bulletproof" by the press. Sam spends two thousand dollars on a professionally crafted, colorfully lit neon sign advertising discount vodka shots for all active alcoholics between four and six p.m. every afternoon, and with the professional help of renowned attorney Drew Wissle, stands behind his First Amendment right to party. Sam makes national news and is the darling of the media, the darling of a stable of regulars who clamor to collect Sam's specially made "Drunks Are Delushes" medallions which are emblazoned with "It Ain't a Real Drink Unless It Has Vodka In It!" on the tails side. Rolling Stone, Playboy, and Esquire magazines follow his story as the Moral Majority turns up the heat. "Sam Killian, may you burn in Hell!"

Sam is a generous host. "Reverend Williams, come on inside where it's nice and cool. I have a drink made with vodka and cinnamon schnapps; we call it Hell Boy, named after you! If you can drink four shots in four minutes and still touch your nose, we'll give you a coaster with a devil motif as a take-home party gift."

Reverend Williams bows his sweaty forehead. "Brethren, let us pray for this heathen; he has lost his way. Jesus, we pray in your name that you will smite the hand that brings this destruction on our families, on our youth, on our Christian values; in Your Sweet Name, Amen." Sam grins and mugs for the gathering crowd of onlookers. "And if you can kiss your own ass goodbye, Brother Williams, I'll give you the fifth shot free!"

Sam's business is hotter than a California Death Pepper.

PATIENCE

All things have their time and season; patience can't be rushed, or practiced enough. Be patient now; right now!

Mimi – broke, unemployed, and optimistic – has never felt more alive. She is physically fit from running with Molly and Ben; her garden is home to four varieties of basil, a party pack of zinnias, and colorful nonpoisonous writing spiders. Mimi is happy in the moment, and reeling from Jake's latest letter.

Dear Mimi,

Finally, I'm discovering what it takes to play professionally. Musically, I have the right stuff! The only thing missing is that you are there and I am here. When I get home, and if you're willing, let's take our friendship up a notch and see if we have what it takes to mesh our lives together. I'm consumed with my own ego-stroking right now, but the real quality hours are the ones in which I allow myself to be consumed by thoughts of you. I hope you like the compass – all girl scouts need a homing device. I am east northeast of you and separated by a couple of oceans and some good earth. Dial me in and remember: we look at the same moon, only my moon is six hours older than yours.

Love, Jake

Dear Jake,

I am awake and think you are, too, although the moon has gone to bed in your town and is beaming in mine. I walked to the apple orchard today, ran my hands down warm wooden limbs, and an apple tree talked to me; it said you want to make love to me here. So, I climbed the tree and listened closely and, sure enough, the tree spoke again. I am the love apple tree, it said. Climb my branches

219

without worry of falling. The ground under me is soft and even if you fall, it will only hurt for a minute. Then I ran home and ate the chocolate icing off the tops of four brownies for dinner. Trees are talking to me, Jake. I'm on a sugar high. Come home and save me from schizophrenia and insulin shock.

Love, Mimi

Mimi discovers a barn across Jenkin's Creek and through the woods, a barn full of cobwebs, black snakes, and twelve happy horses; David, the crusty old barn owner, is looking for a reliable hand. "Are you sure you want this job? I can't pay you what you're used to making; I can't even come close; eight dollars an hour, no raises. But see that big bay Thoroughbred over there? His owner died four months ago – he needs his own person. Name's Cajun. He's only eight, and he's in good shape, but he's blind in one eye. A little crazy, maybe, and he scares most people, but he's totally harmless, sound as a C-note, and a sweet ride once you gain his trust."

Mimi pulls on the bill of her baseball cap and extends her hand to David. "When do I start?"

. . .

Odessa and her band hop the fast train to Amsterdam's Centraal Station, the main terminal located in the heart of the city. Upon debarking, Jake closes his eyes and makes a slow, complete circle, moving with the grace of a guru meditating to the four corners of the world. Accordion to the East of me; percussion to the North of me; trumpet to the West of me; guitar to the South of me. Jake's prayer ends and he opens his eyes; he's surrounded by the music of street performers, surrounded by the Zen of Dam Square.

The concierge at The American Hotel immediately recognizes Odessa, breezes her through check-in, and upgrades her to a large, elegantly decorated private room. The band shares a huge suite recently occupied by Prince. They know this because the bellboy tells them so, tells them that Prince is a really good tipper. Jake tips the bellboy Dfl 120, over fifty American dollars, and the bellboy grins and tells Jake he is a better tipper than Prince. "If there's anything you need, you ask for Werner," the stocky blonde bellboy says. "I am your man. I am also a sound technician at the Bimhuis and am available to help move your equipment as you have a lot of equipment to move," Werner continues. "I will be your roadie. I know all of the clubs and am affordable." The band adopts Werner as its very own runner and personal assistant. Everyone is very kind to Werner; he is maybe eighteen, certainly no older, and they all remember being eighteen. Even twenty-seven year old Marc feels like a father to Werner.

Jake takes a hot shower while Marc and Peter peruse the gift shop and pick out trinkets for their mothers. Franz orders room service, orders enough food to feed the entire band and a hungry audience. Odessa keeps to herself and writes a love letter to her husband. A couple of hours later Werner knocks on the door and offers a guided tour of the Red Light District, but nobody's interested; they've been on the Reeperbahn. Werner's face drops, but only momentarily. Jake tosses him a bone. "Let's go, young man, just not there. Take me anywhere else."

"Okay, Jake!" Werner's enthusiasm reminds Jake of a happy puppy – he's all but jumping on the furniture. "What would you like to see?"

Jake grabs his water bottle on the way out. "Lead on,

Scout. I will follow you; just take it easy on me. I'm a little tired and don't want to stay out too late. Tomorrow will be fairly intense."

"Do you smoke, Jake?"

Jake pauses. "Smoke what?"

"Hashish."

"I take an occasional toke of high-grade cannabis, but it's been awhile since I've smoked hash." A hint of nostalgia creeps into Jake's voice.

Werner shrugs. "What's the difference?"

Jake's eyes smile. "Oh, about one hundred eighty degrees of buzz." Remembering he's talking to a kid, Jake addresses Werner in his best parental voice. "Are you old enough to legally smoke hash, young man?"

Werner grins. "Yeah, I just don't because it makes me sleepy. Do you want to go to a smoke house? I'll go with you and make sure you get back here safely."

Jake thinks about the negative consequence of taking that action, and finding none, says, "Okay, I'd like to check out that scene. Yeah, yeah, take me to a smoke house, Werner. Peter, you wanna go?"

Peter hunkers down on the sofa, remote in hand. "No way, man. I made the mistake of buying off the street last year and got into some trouble. But, will you bring some back for me?" Peter scootches onto his left side, and, striking an impressive plank-like yoga pose, deftly frees a thick wallet from his right hip pocket. Noticing Jake's hesitation, Peter explains. "You can legally possess up to thirty grams, but you can only buy five grams at a time. Here, Werner," says Peter as he shoves some bills in the boy's hand, "buy whatever's best."

Even Jake knows better than to buy on the street. He's heard about the dubious quality of street hash from other musicians, knows that local authorities frown on drug activity on public sidewalks. Why would Peter take a chance on having a bad experience when he can walk right in, order legally, and smoke as much as he can stand? "Yeah, you're the textbook example of crazy musician," Jake says as he punches Peter on the arm. "Stupidity should be painful, man."

Of the smoking coffee houses, The Bulldog is the most prolific with branches scattered around the city. But Werner takes Jake to Blue Bird, which serves fewer people at night than the others, although it appears as if some of its patrons haven't moved from their overstuffed chairs in several days.

Jake walks into the Blue Bird, and, captivated by the atmosphere, is immediately at ease. Hand painted murals cover the interior walls; the vibe is happy and friendly. Two large menu books displaying samples of each variety of cannabis scream for Jake's attention until he spies "The Book of Dreams." My God, Jake thinks, am I in Wonderland? Slap my fanny and call me Alice. "We Pride Ourselves on Exceptional Hashish at Attractive Prices!" Jake gets a contact high by simply reading that line from the Dreambook out loud, a little drool forming in the corner of his mouth as he studies the twenty varieties of hashish available for purchase. Jake buys black hash, the stickiest, skankiest, and most potent hash on the menu, a five gram bag of soft black hash for around eleven American dollars, and Werner buys five grams for Peter.

Jake loads a water pipe, inhales carefully the first time and deeply the second. "Be careful, Jake; I mean no offense, but you are an old man," warns Werner. Jake chuckles as he leans back in his chair. "And you are an old soul, Werner." Werner orders two coffees and two slices of apple pie with ice cream and observes as Jake melts into an altered state; first, silent relaxation, but within minutes, he's talkative, and hungry for the pie. Mimi appears as a smiling apparition in the pie crust, prompting Jake to close his eyes and croon. "Werner, I have a friend back home who is taking care of my dog. I'm falling in love with her."

"Does she love you back?"

"I don't know…I hope so." Jake opens his eyes and smiles at Werner. "Have you ever been in love?"

"Yes, I have a baby."

"Babies having babies," Jake tenderly says with no judgment. "Are you in love with the mother?"

"No," Werner states, "I'm only in love with the baby. Nika and I never married. She lives next door with her family. We have been friends since we were children; she is like a sister to me." Jake considers this unlikely detail of Werner's life, and thinks he may have underestimated his youthful friend's adult status. "This is enough for you?"

Werner nods emphatically. "More than enough. It works out well – many babysitters! But, I want to hear more about your friend." Jake tries to sit up straight, but finding the effort fruitless, settles back into the people-eating, ancient leather chair. "Ah, Werner, Mimi's beautiful. She has long brown hair and hazel eyes that are expressive of a kind and passionate nature. She's sassy, too."

"How did you meet her?"

"At a club she owned. With her husband."

Werner is shocked. "She is married?"

"No, no, not anymore. We are both separated."

"Do you intend to marry this Mimi person?"

Jake grins with his eyes closed. "I intend to fuck this Mimi person."

"Tell me more, Jake. What does she like?"

"She likes dogs, and spiders. She grows flowers like

Jack grows beanstalks. And she loves music, pure music. As long as it's pure, she says. It doesn't matter if it's jazz or rock or country or classical. She has a great ear and perfect pitch. And she dances; the woman can't stand still; she's intense that way." Jake bobs slightly in his chair; looking rather pale, he stands tenuously. "Where's the bathroom in this joint, Werner? I need to splash some water on my face." Mobility requires coordination and Jake doesn't have any; he feels like a Sit and Spin. "No, just get me back to the hotel. I'd be better off in a room where I can't hurt myself." Jake smiles weakly at Werner, who tries unsuccessfully to cover up his perpetual grin. "Are you going to throw up, Jake? If you throw up, you'll feel better."

"Damn, Werner, and waste that pie? I feel really good, but would prefer to take my shoes off in my own room. Don't want to be the old man in the club, you know," Jake says with a nod to his perceived senior status. Werner offers Jake his arm, and without embarrassment, Jake gloms to it like an old woman clings to a lost son. Werner keeps Jake cognizant by talking about music. "Okay, Jake, you're playing the Bimhuis tomorrow night, right?"

Jake's gait is slow but steady, and he answers in a strong voice. "And for the next three nights. Can I leave my equipment set up there?"

"Oh yes. Nobody will bother your stuff. You will love it – it's very secure. I'll go with you for sound check; will that be good for you?" Jake laughs. "Yes, Werner, that will be good for me. Are we almost home?"

"We're there, Jake. Can you find your room?" Jake slowly spins around the lobby one full rotation. "No, do you know where my room is?'

"I will take you there and you will remember next

time." Werner is a patient young man, and treats Jake gently, as he would treat a child afraid of the dark.

"Werner, you are a good man and you must be an excellent father. Kiss your baby for me. And here, take this," says Jake, reaching for his wallet. "Buy your mother something nice." Werner declines. "Oh no, Jake, no money for tonight," he says. "It was my pleasure. No tip, please; this was as a friend." Werner hands Jake a small package. "Here, give this to Peter. I'll knock at three tomorrow and we'll go to the Bimhuis."

"Godspeed, young man," says Jake; safely in the door, he tosses Peter his five grams before dipping his face into a slick marble bathroom sink; nothing like a cold water revival, thinks Jake, feeling centered once again.

"Come here, dude," says Peter. "I want to show you a trick; if you want to get a little black gold home, do this." Peter reaches for a drinking straw from the room service tray. He unpeels the paper cover, and then packs the hash into the plastic straw. He melts both ends of the straw with his lighter, creating a tight seal. Peter retrieves an unopened tube of toothpaste from his shaving kit and gently plants the hash into the center of the tube. "See? Simple. The straw displaces the areas formerly taken up by the paste, creating a tube that returns to the appearance of being full."

Jake is interested. "And nothing much to clean up," he says.

Dear Mimi,

The items in this package are not a statement regarding your personal hygiene. Ignore the toothpaste — put both tubes in a secret place for now. RE: Belgium chocolate: the Zen truffles will make you crave sex with me — at least that's what I'm told. You can get these treasures at some fancy stores in the US, but why fly to NYC when I can play middleman and save you the trauma of breathing stale air in a stuffy deathtrap with wings? The shopkeeper insisted I pay extra to get these to you within two days or suffer a decrease in quality, but he says that you do not, I repeat, do not, have to eat them all in one sitting. Strange logic...he also insisted that you not refrigerate these chocolates. Upon my return, I will show you a trick I learned in Amsterdam. We will go to the highest pasture and write music together, chart a love song based on the stars and revisit a little café called the Blue Bird, my favorite smoking coffee shop. Great apple pie there!

Love, Jake

Dear Jake,

Why would I crave sex with you when I can rub a Zen truffle on my inner thigh and immediately reach orgasm? The experience is even more gratifying when I suck on a little Zen Orangette. A ménage a trois, Jake, a trifecta! You stay right there and send me a package of Zen every week for the rest of my life. You are a romantic warrior at heart – I know for sure. Love songs and star charts and high pastures. Count me in. Toothpaste's hidden in top right drawer under socks, in case I am attacked by a rabid cow before your return. Until then...

Love, Mimi

Load-in at the Bimhuis is a breeze, thanks to Werner. The staff knows him, loves him, and gives him free rein. Odessa and the guys set up and practice for about two hours, getting in gear for three nights of good gigging. First night, good; second night, better – bigger crowd, more energy. The Bimhuis is a fairly large venue compared to the small clubs Jake's used to, and the buzzing crowd is at capacity. He emits a low whistle. "Wow, Odessa, are you really that well known over here? I know this crowd's never heard of me. Look at all these people, happy people getting ready to dig our music."

"Yeah, Jake, that's it. It's all me!" Odessa grins. "Welcome to Amsterdam. The Bimhuis is always at least half packed regardless of who's here to hear. It's a jazz town, remember?"

"Yeah, Odessa, but this is amazing."

"But they've never heard anybody take it out quite so far as you do, Jake. Look at the faces out there; at least a third of these people were here last night and will be back tomorrow. They'll definitely know who you are when you come back here. They'll call you by name on the street, like they do me." Jake studies his audience and within thirty seconds, makes eye contact with five people, all who acknowledge him with a smile. "It's really gratifying, getting the props and respect we don't even get in our hometown," continues Odessa. "That old adage about jazz being a local scene is bullshit. It's global, Jake. We're riding the rainbow across oceans and landing in cultural pots of gold; now, ain't that great, South'ren boy?"

Jake shakes his head in wonder. "Yes it is." He pauses and takes it all in. "I swear, Odessa, I've never seen anything like it."

"And you never will unless you come back."

"Is that an invitation?"

Odessa smiles her answer. "Next year, Jake, or later this year if I can pull it together. You've made an impression over here. Don't be surprised if you're asked back without me. And you better take them up on it, too."

All is well until load-out on the third night when Jake makes the mistake of talking to the tall blonde woman who leans against the stage and tracks his every move with eagle eyes. "Watch her, Jake," Werner says as he passes behind him. "She is bad news." But Jake is flying high on the love of his new tribe. He doesn't feel her pick his pocket, but knows the timing of it. As he poses for a picture with her, she leans in for a hug, and with one hand on his crotch and another inside his jacket, she lifts Jake's wallet out of its inside secret pocket at the very same time she slips her tongue into his mouth; she's gone before the blush overtakes Jake's face. Werner's hackles are up. "Jake, check your pockets."

"Why, Werner?"

"You just got ripped off."

Jake, laughing, says, "No, I just got sexually molested, but ripped off? No way."

Werner is animated. "Where's your wallet? Where do you keep it?"

"Shit," says Jake, coming up empty. "How did she do that?"

Werner is at a dead run and halfway out the door before Jake can level his jaw and check his pocket one more time. He yells to Werner, "Where are you going?"

"I know her!" Werner returns in twenty minutes with Jake's wallet, but there's nothing in it except Mimi's address; identification, money, business cards – all gone. Werner is confused when Jake shrugs and smiles. The loss is temporary and minimal; Jake's hip to a street scene played out with the same script everywhere. He even packs a small piece on some gigs back home, those late night gigs requiring load-out in dark alleys early in the morning when the addicted cats prowl. Jake's wallet carries nothing of value except Mimi's address, and it's still there. He has more money, more identification at the hotel. Jake just wants to get back to The American and get the woman's scent off his face.

. . .

The band says goodbye to Werner at the train station the next afternoon. Werner hugs each of them warmly and cries when he receives Dfl 1000, almost five hundred dollars American. "Even Prince doesn't tip as well as you do," Werner says. "And he is a good tipper. Hurry back! I miss you already. Goodbye! Good gigging in Barcelona!"

And back at The American, Werner helps another band to their suite. "Prince stayed here right before you," Werner says. "He just left this morning – he's a very good tipper."

. . .

It is 346 miles from Amsterdam to Paris, a rail trip that takes about four hours on the Thalys Direct. Spacious, reclining seats in a first-class compartment soothe Jake into the sleep of the dead. Jake dreams of Molly; she's stalking a skunk in downtown Amsterdam. The skunk waddles into the Blue Bird and Molly follows it inside. A child feeds Molly a treat, but the treat is hash. Molly lies down and turns into a rug. The skunk moves in on Jake and begins to speak, but before Jake can learn skunk language, Odessa yells him out of his dream. "Peter, what the hell are you doing? You can't smoke that in here!"

"Chill, Odessa, we're the only ones on this car, babe."

"We won't be for long; put it up before you get us all busted!"

"Anybody want a hit first?" Peter grins as Odessa thumps his head like she's testing for ripeness. But Odessa's not playing. "Peter, you put that away now or I'll leave your ass on this train! I'm not kidding. Good drummers are cheap in Barcelona. Christ, man, you about got us all busted last year. If I see you doing anything to jeopardize this tour one more time, I'm serious, you're gone."

Peter puts his pocket pipe away. "I'm sorry, Odessa. You're right, I'm sorry." Odessa makes a face at Peter and strikes a match. "Anybody got incense?"

"Only the kind that smells like hash," answers Marc. Odessa can't help herself; she cracks up and the band joins in. "Smart asses, all of you. Just shut up." The momentary tension dissipates with the smoke; all is well on the Thalys.

A three-hour layover in Paris gives the band a comfort zone as they make the transfer between Gare du Nord, their terminus from Amsterdam, and Paris Austerlitz, their destination station for Barcelona. Jake and Peter have eight well-packed pieces of luggage between them, but it's easily distributed to the five band members and survives the transfer without a hitch. Musicians are responsible that way. Fuck the clothes, they can always buy more. But, God forbid a Wah-Wah peddle or a single cable should go missing. Just the mere thought of losing equipment, big or small – size has nothing to do with importance – sends most musicians into the depths of despair for at least three hours and could make a man contemplate suicide if a synthesizer goes missing. "But, that one can't be replaced. Chick Corea touched it before I bought it…oh, man, that cable's been with me since the beginning, man…I can't play shit without my bag of sticks, man; yeah, I can buy more, but they won't sound the same, I guarantee it." Mother hens counting biddies aren't as careful as musicians counting equipment.

The Talgo Night Train is filled with dark travelers – sexy young feminine night hawks who love musicians. Jake and Peter share a compartment with a shower, a sink, and a private toilet. Marc and Franz are next door, Odessa next to them. They dine in the restaurant car and drink in the bar car and play cards until eleven p.m., eventually hibernating until seven a.m.; they don't quite capture the sleep they lost in Amsterdam, but decrease the deficit before hitting Barcelona. Jake, a night owl by nature, is just beginning to feel alive when a lovely raptor moves in on his perch.

"Excuse me," she says, "I can't seem to make my way to the bar. Will you order something for me, please?" She flashes Jake a one-hundred watt smile, a smile that brightly snaps of intelligent smugness and worldly knowledge. Blatantly sexual. Unconsciously sensual. Anima rising. Jake feels it; she captures his spirit quickly, and his lust is begging for a snare. He's as good as dead. She is beautiful, Jake thinks while appraising the hunter. Petite, long blonde hair, tight body. "I'll be glad to. What would you like?"

"How about a B & B, heated?"

"Sure," Jake says casually. "Where can I find you?" What's your name, little girl? Hello, hard-on. Damn, Jake thinks. She's gorgeous. "Oh, I'll stay right here. I'm Lucinda."

"Jake. Nice to meet you, Lucinda; are you from the States, too?"

"New York. You?"

"Virginia. Are you going to Barcelona?"

Lucinda smiles. "Aren't we all? I'm checking out the art museums and working on my Master's thesis, so this trip's part of my research." Lucinda turns toward the window, studies her reflection, and pushes her hair from her face, exposing a perfect profile. "Jake, right? I like that name."

Good morning little schoolgirl. "So keeping your nose in the books, huh?"

"More like keeping my nose on the street. What are you doing here? No wait, let me guess. You're a musician."

Jake is pleased. "How can you tell?"

"You're wearing all black. You're too cool for school. Is this your first time to Barcelona?" Lucinda squeezes her arms together and her high perched bosoms push against her tight white halter top. Jake's south pole is facing due north; he has an almost uncontrollable urge to rub himself on her leg. "Uh-huh." He's reduced to caveman responses. "It's my third," Lucinda replies. "I love B-town. Need a guide?"

"Mmm, now, that's a thought. Here you go, B & B, heated glass." Lucinda flashes big blue eyes at her prey as she reaches into her little black purse. "How much do I owe you?"

"Nothing. I bet you'll buy me a drink before we say goodnight."

"Don't count on it," Lucinda laughs. "I'm a student. Where are you staying?"

"La Terrassa."

"No kidding! Me, too – sharing a room with three other students."

"That sounds like a tough gig."

"It's a financial issue. Not my preferred accommodations, but a hungry student must survive." Lucinda reruns her fingers through her hair and moves closer to Jake. "I bet you have a lot of luggage. I know how you musicians travel because I used to date one. No such thing as packing light unless you're the string or horn man. I bet you play keys."

Now Jake is impressed. "How could you tell that?"

"Other than the vibe, your hands. Look at your hands, they're gorgeous. Show me your spread, Jake." Jake grins. "Not on the first date," he says. Lucinda picks up his right hand and places it just above her cleavage. "Here, right here, on my chest. Spread 'em, Cowboy, let's see what you're made of. See? Your reach is almost as wide as my shoulders. Do you have a gig tomorrow night?"

Jake's tongue wants to touch Lucinda's tonsils, but he plays it cool. This child could be dangerous, he thinks. "No. Night after."

"Do you have plans for tomorrow?"

Jake shakes his head. "Just acclimation, food, and sleep."

"Would you like to hang out and see some really cool architecture, go to the museums, grab a bite to eat, have a drink or something?"

I'll take the or something, Jake thinks. "I'm not much of a planner, Lucinda. Maybe, I don't know." Jake's response sets Lucinda back a bit; she's not used to rejection.

"Tell you what," she says, shifting slightly away from him. "I'll be in the lobby at eleven sharp. I'll wait for five minutes, then I'm leaving. If you're interested in a private tour of the best spots in Barcelona, meet me. If not, it's no big deal. Gotta run! Thanks for the drink." Lucinda is ready to move on to another perch. This bird, Jake thinks, is cute, but lacks spontaneity.

Jake reaches out and gently takes hold of her arm. "Wait a minute; where will you take me?" Lucinda turns her head and looks at Jake. "Ah, you must show up to find out."

"Maybe I'll see you tomorrow," Jake says, suddenly wishing he had said yes.

"No worries. If you're there, you're there. If you're not, you're not." And she flies away, just like that. Jake thinks eleven a.m. is a perfect time for a tour.

. . .

Dear Mimi,

Paris flyby; I see train stations, inside of my eyelids, and postcards. Spitting Man gargoyle's my fave. He's not a fan of progress. Spits at Eiffel Tower. Let's go together. We'll see them up close and personal. No time to explore this trip. Love, Jake

Dear Jake,

Writing postcard style. Fits mood. Finally found worthy work. Have fallen in love with a Cajun who fills up day, but still too much time to think. Latest negative brain drain: married to man who lied. Lied again. Truth finally spurted from his lips like blood from severed artery. Had plan; plan fell through; planned some more. Signed papers; lost financial security. Moved to country, found peace. Then, you. Friendship. Flirtation. Love letters. No peace. Missing you. What next? Do you know truth? Truth's beautifully unique, but ugly's same everywhere. Damn you better know truth.

Signed, Saint Maniac, Patron of all Gargoyles

ps – high tension in small-minded US of A. I walk familiar streets and am carrier of contagious disease, something worse than leprosy. Nobody looks me in the eye. They whisper in grocery stores. Having a good time? Good. Good for you. Have a good day. Good bye. Yeah, love. Mimi

pps – Cajun is a horse.

ppps – you will never see this postcard.

Jake and Lucinda make eye contact as they leave the train, speaking volumes without saying a word. Lucinda smugly throws her duffle over her shoulder while Jake and the band distribute multiple bags between them, organizing keys and drums and balancing the load between five people before hopping aboard their reserved mini-bus to Hotel La Terassa. Lucinda beats Jake to the hotel by thirty minutes, but Odessa has the fast track to check-in and Jake is ensconced in his room before Lucinda signs her name on the dotted line. Bye-bye, nubile one, Jake thinks as he returns the smugness to its slightly humbled and envious owner. Age has its benefits, don't you know? No, you don't know. Score one for the old guy.

Jake unpacks, quickly cleans up and considers making a donation in the shower drain, but withholds the deposit because he spies a better bank down the road; he walks into the lobby on the stroke of eleven. Lucinda looks absolutely grand in her clothes. Hip to the ninth of Siberia, this girl, this sexy intelligent girl, this young woman who holds Jake's spirit captive behind the lens of her ice blue eyes. No anima rising in Jake now; no feminine spirit. Only a surge of testosterone that makes Jake feel six feet tall in his socks. His sex drive is at half-mast, a perpetual reminder of his staying power; Jake runs that flag up the pole. He is not thinking about Mimi, no, not at all. Home is where the heart is, but Jake's heart is on vacation.

. . .

Ah, Barcelona! From Frommer's: "If you took the all-out party power of Parliament's George Clinton and mixed in equal parts of the more refined tastes of Sting, then shook them up and poured them over ice, you'd get pretty close to the trippy, wild, and refined flavors that make Barcelona such a delicious drink." B-town is designed for musicians. Forget the bars; forget the museums and the architecture and the food and the beach. It's the vibe, man. It's the 1,500 years of tourist and travel industry experience. It's the international spirit and the language of Catalan and the regional pride and the whole unique gig played out every day on every street.

Barcelona is one hip flip city. And Lucinda has her finger on the city's pulse. Jake is forty-seven years old, but ageless. His body doesn't hurt much today; he can go all night. Dance? No, Jake doesn't like to dance, but he will subtly grind you against the wall with the best of the droopy eye-lidded older, but wiser players. Watch him later on; you'll get the picture. You've seen it before if a subtle level of eroticism moves you. The scene is obvious to those who fly beneath the radar, to those who pace themselves with Jake, to those who breathe like turtles. Lucinda will reintroduce Jake to an old companion, the afternoon fast-paced heat race, and Jake will, in turn, introduce Lucinda to the more sensual side of sex, to late night restraint, to the reserve tank. Lucinda understands the concept although she has never fully experienced that brand of erotic pleasure. But, that is before Jake. She's about to learn what making love looks like, and it will terrify her.

Lucinda and Jake go on a walking cruise through Barcelona, spend hours in the Ciutat Vella, traverse El Raval and Barri Gotic, and gawk at the best of modern art in the Museu d'Art Contemporani de Barcelona. They spend a few short minutes in the Centre de Cultura for history, then grab a quick lunch and an even quicker photo op at Catedral de Barcelona by mid-afternoon; finally, a postcard purchasing frenzy at Museu Picasso before they trace each other's scent back to Hotel Terrassa, before culminating the adventure with intense sexual gratification, quick release, and a long nap. Jake's hand intertwines in Lucinda's long hair; her head is on his belly, hair stuck to his juice. But, that was playtime, daytime, familiar territory to Lucinda. Her education begins at midnight. Lucinda has never known a man to look her in the eye while climaxing, but Jake does. Jake growls while he looks her in the eye, while he peaks front and center, withholding nothing. Jake is present; Lucinda is afraid at first, then accepts Jake's primal twist and shout as an anthropological phenomenon, as part of her artistic research, accepting the research component without fully acknowledging the intensity of Jake's hunger. She is embarrassed by his psychic nakedness. At this very moment, Lucinda experiences – but does not understand – the difference between fucking a boy and making love with a man. It is one of the most valuable lessons of her life, a lesson that doesn't require a Master's degree, but instead requires recognition and release, raw release. She recognizes passion, but Jake's style is unrelated to her definition of it. Lucinda is overwhelmed and confuses, from this moment on and for the rest of her life, good sex and true love, never trusting her instincts in combining the two Universal elements. She is always surprised, always off her game, afraid of the slow pitch.

Jake, of course, recognizes nothing and attributes Lucinda's high-strung nerves to her bush league status. Lucinda blames her lack of sexual release on absinthe, too much absinthe, she says, and the late hour, too late for a catch and release. There's always an excuse for Lucinda's lack of power hitting.

Lovemaking women all over the world may lament Lucinda's lack of sexual fulfillment, but the wiser members of the Divine Feminine recognize and love Jake for looking a woman in the eye, for truly seeing them, for giving the snapshot meaning. He feeds the spirit back into the soul and stokes the home fire. No, it isn't Lucinda who's chosen to represent all women on the planet; rather, she vainly attempts ignition of a vacation spark robbed of oxygen after the first and only deeply satisfying breath. Too bad for Lucinda.

Jake rolls out of bed and into the shared living space to find Peter staring at him, grinning. "Your company gone, man?"

"Yeah, thank God."

"Really? Send her my way; she's my kind of groupie."

Jake shakes his head. "Hands off, man, she's not a groupie. She's a student." Jake walks to the kitchen and makes a cup of Earl Gray with a splash of cream. "What time is it?"

"Almost ten-thirty. And for the record, new guy, all students are groupies." Jake ignores Peter's attempt at banter. "I'm supposed to meet her in the lobby at eleven. She's taking me to some church somewhere; something I have to see, she says."

"La Sagrada Familia?"

"Yeah, that's it." Jake takes a sip of his delicious elixir and pauses. "I think I might blow her off."

"No, man. You will flip out! It's the coolest thing ever. The architecture will blow your mind, dude. It's Gaudi's finest work, although he died before it was completed. The structure looks like molten lava, like something out of Doctor Seuss's The Grinch, maybe where The Grinch would live, only hipper. I've always wanted to play there. That's all I can say; you have to see it to believe it. Get a move on, man; you don't want to miss it."

Dear Mimi,

Visited museums yesterday. Picasso museum the best. Met interesting people, including art student who gives good tours. Went to La Sagrada Familia this morning and picked up this postcard. Check out the towers. From down looking up it's like being in the desert surrounded by world's tallest palm trees. Gaudi's finest work.

First gig tonight at Jamboree. Home soon. Hope you are well. Give my love to Molly. xo Jake

Dear Jake,
Visited the downtown art galleries last night. Stepped purposely on the cracks in the sidewalk to cut myself some slack, not to break my mother's back. Changing the rhyme from guilt-ridden to guilt-free. You're not a southern girl, so you may not dig. Hope you are well, too. World's Largest Sand Castle? Will visit in my dreams and sing inside the cavern. In my dream, the ocean meets its threshold. I melt at the point of contact and disappear into the steps of the tower, becoming part of Gaudi's eternal vision. Molly is doing just fine without your love. She has Ben.
Go XO yourself. Mimi

Mimi feels the heat from Jake's latest postcard, feels the heat that radiates from another woman's fingerprints. She traces Lucinda's invisible touch with the accuracy of a blind woman reading Braille. It takes Mimi less than a minute to apply emotional SPF Thirty and block out what could be, if she isn't careful, severe heartburn. Jake owes me nothing, Mimi says out loud. Mimi sits in her hammock, avoids the sun, and waits patiently for a cooling cloud cover to protect her from bursting into hot tears. Jake owes Mimi nothing.

. . .

The Jamboree is a small, smart venue with a cave-like atmosphere and a history of hosting some of the world's top performers. The vibe of earlier musical top cats dangles invisibly from ancient interior cobwebs. Of all the clubs to date, the Jamboree quenches Jake's thirst for identity; sacred tonic takes a swan dive and lands in his heart's deepest pool. He stands perfectly still for several minutes, silently acknowledging the players who have performed here before him. This is the spirit of a good musician, always mindful of the great ones who opened the door before he was out of diapers.

Odessa and the band set up one time in Barcelona, one time for a week's gig at Jamboree Jazz Club, the A-ticket for a musician hauling heavy equipment. The Jamboree pays good money and is Mecca for most musicians. Jake is thankful from the moment his perfect hands touch the keys on the first night until after the final song is played at the end of the week-long gig.

Lucinda? Lucinda who? "Hey, Jake."

"How's it going, Lucinda?" Jake can't help but notice her beauty, but her power is gone. "We have to change hotels," she says. "We're moving to the Pension Vitorio tomorrow morning."

"Yeah?" Jake concentrates on the spiraling cable in his hand, making seven perfect and equal loops before packing it in the bottom of a well-worn black canvas bag.

"Yeah, bummer, but I was thinking I could stay with you until you leave."

"That's not a good idea, Lucinda."

"Why not?"

"Because Peter and I share a room."

Lucinda shrugs. "Oh, well, just a thought. It's okay. I'll still be close enough to you. I really enjoyed your show last night."

"Thanks." Wrap it up, Jake thinks.

"Where did you go after? I waited around thinking we would get together," says Lucinda, flashing high beams beneath a thin lace blouse.

Jake politely looks at Lucinda, but shows more interest in his gear than hers. A savvier woman would have walked away after thanks. "The band went to the London Bar for a drink, grabbed some food, and headed back to the hotel."

"Why didn't you ask me to join you?"

Jake sighs and turns to Lucinda; he sees a little girl. "Look, Lucinda, I'm really tired. These gigs are kicking my ass. We have rehearsal this afternoon with Odessa, new songs to learn for tonight. I'm really busy."

"Can I come to rehearsal with you? Then maybe we can get something to eat later, or get together, you know, if you want to."

Jake kindly looks at her. "I don't think so, Lucinda. Look, you're a baby doll, but I'm really busy. I'm sorry, but I need to be done with this."

Lucinda's true naiveté is hard to watch; Jake manages one more sympathetic smile before turning his attention back to his tear-down. "Yeah, thanks old man," she says. "Go home to your boring life and rock on your boring porch or whatever you bumpkins do in Virginia. I like guys who can dance anyway. What the hell. You aren't contagious, are you?"

Jake wrinkles his nose. "That's distasteful, Lucinda."

"Look, Jake, we slept together twice. We had unprotected sex, and I'm never going to see you again in about two minutes. Do you know what I mean?"

"No gifts that keep on giving, Lucinda."

"Good. Me either, just so you know. You got lucky, Jake. You're old enough to know better; be more careful next time."

"There won't be a next time, Lucinda." Jake picks up his bag and nods goodbye.

Lucinda bitterly laughs. "Sure there will be, Jake. There's always a next time for men like you. Wait a minute, I'm not through." Jake has a momentary flashback, and subconsciously looks for a nurse's station. "I am, Lucinda," he says. "Be careful out there; you're a very special young woman."

"And you're just another musician, Jake, special in your own mind. You don't even know my last name."

"No, I don't. But let's leave it like that. Take care."

Lucinda has one more request. "Hey, your roommate Peter…he's the drummer, right? Will you introduce me?"

"Goodbye, Lucinda."

And it's over. The tour is over. Jake wins. Jake wins. Jake wins. The big bird brings the brother home.

. . .

Dear Mimi,

I will be at your house before you get this postcard. I am happy and tired and full of great stories, all of which I will gladly share with you. Know this: your doorstep is my destination. Seeking a compassionate and understanding welcome home. I will look into your soulful eyes and find comfort in your open heart.

Love, Jake

TOLERANCE

Recognize the divinity in others even when it's hidden behind the walls of apparent ignorance and stupidity, or residing in the bowels of lust, greed, and power. Remember, politicians and pontificators are people, too.

Sam Killian flies on a pink cloud fueled by high-octane notoriety. His bravado, triglycerides, and vodka infusions are also peaking, pegging, diming. Soon enough there will be no room at the top for Sam, but for the moment, the only thing low about Sam is his tolerance for his housekeeper, a fellow Friend of Bill, for waking him up. "Damn it, Margaret, you're not supposed to be here! What the hell day is this? It's not Wednesday, it's Monday, for fuck's sake!"

Margaret is a chubby, sweet ex-lush who used to like bowling, but preferred to participate drunk and naked. Now that she's four years, three months, and six days sober, her extracurricular activities lean toward your garden variety entertainment – WWF wrestling and tractor pulls, you know, family sports. She powers her way past a tile floor's grungiest grout better than Mr. Clean. "Don't you remember we agreed last week to change your day and time? I'm going to the beach tomorrow."

"Nope," Sam says. "I wouldn't have agreed to that."

Margaret used to be a pushover; not anymore. "Well, you did, and we're here." She takes a look around and is disgusted. Sam's bedroom looks and smells like a bus terminal bathroom after twenty-four hour's hard use by drunks and junkies who can't shoot straight. "You might want to put that bag of pot away; it's sitting on the table by the back door for the whole world to see. My God, this place is a wreck." She turns to Sam and studies him before continuing. "Have you been sick?"

"Yeah, sick with the flu." Sam drops his head and looks away; Margaret looks right through him, and it's embarrassing. "Yeah, right," she whispers. "Sweetie, you're back on the bottle hard, aren't you? Look, get dressed, and you and I'll go to a meeting right now. Nancy can start cleaning while we're gone. Then, I'll come back and help her while you have lunch or something." Margaret takes another look around and quickly assesses Sam's environmental wasteland. "It'll take us at least four hours to deal with this mess."

Sam quickly recovers his misplaced pride. "Fuck, no! I'm not going anywhere. And speaking of pot, a bag was stolen the last time you were here. I'm missing some other things, too. Like money."

Margaret is used to Sam's paranoia; she gives him the same old song and dance each week. "Sam, we're bonded; we're not stealing from you."

"Get out of my house and take that skinny-assed skank Nancy with you. I don't want you back in here, you bunch of drug addicts. Give me back my key." Margaret moves in to touch Sam carefully on the arm. "Sam, wait," she gently cajoles. "I know you, remember? Come on, let's go to a meeting. Let me help, or let me call your sponsor."

Sam pulls away as if her touch burns. "I fired my sponsor, and I'm firing you, too! Go run your scam on somebody else. Now get the fuck out of my house!" Venomous white spittle forms at the corners of Sam's mouth, and, for the first time, Margaret is afraid of him; his actions are far heavier than her experience. Hell, she was always a nice drunk; slutty, but sweet. She quickly walks out of Sam's bedroom and into the kitchen, where Nancy's busy eating leftover chicken she lifted out of the refrigerator. "Lord, Nancy, stop eating the poor man's food. Let's get out of here."

"Did that asshole call me a skank?" Nancy throws a leg bone in the kitchen sink. Her world is simple: she believes in the Bible, but only in the "call to action" verses; she likes the eye for an eye-type verses best.

"Forget it, Nancy, the man is sick. Let's go, we can't be around him right now." Margaret turns around and yells. "Good luck, Sam, you're gonna need it. Call me when you're ready, and I'll help you anyway I can. We're leaving now."

"Here, smell this." Nancy's face is buried in Sam's bag of pot. "Now, that's some serious skank," she says as she tucks it into her bra and walks out the door. "Much better than the last batch."

Sam moves into the large, sunny, and well-appointed den because his bedroom, smelling like four Boer goats in rut, is trashed. He sleeps on the overstuffed, newly stained cream tapestry Victorian sofa, Mimi's old reading spot – good call there, Mimi, Sam thinks – rather than in his king-sized bed; the bed is only for company, only for those weekly Saturday night special performances, compliments of Jesse. The sheets need to be washed, but Margaret hasn't been around for, I don't know, Sam thinks. Where's my housekeeper, Sam wonders? I'm gonna have to fire her ass.

Within a week Sam's new room is one big garbage dump filled with vodka bottles, used tissues, dead flowers rotting in murky green water, hard porn movies, soft porn magazines, and, as of last night, a puddle of urine in the threshold between the den and the kitchen; Sam forgets the bathroom is to the right. As Sam steps into his own void, he looks to the ceiling in search of a leak.

But, the kitchen is clean; the kitchen is a shrine, a grapefruit-scented paradise, and as Sam makes his Vitamin V breakfast on Sunday morning, the phone rings. "Speak," Sam barks. Hello is too genteel a word for Sam.

"Sam Killian, please."

"You got him."

"Mr. Killian, this is Vanguard Security; the alarm just sounded at 462 South Hamilton. Is that your business address?"

"Stupid question, of course it is."

"The police have been dispatched, sir."

"Damn it, on my way," Sam retorts, and hangs up abruptly. Just another Sunday morning aggravation, Sam thinks. Everything aggravates Sam. It takes him two minutes to drink breakfast, brush his teeth, gargle with cool mint Listerine, don a clean but permanently stained tee-shirt, and shove a Firefly baseball cap over his crusty head. Ten minutes after receiving the call, he arrives downtown just in time to watch the Fire Department soaking down his lobby; someone has thrown a Molotov cocktail through The Firefly's front window and his restaurant is on fire. Sam bypasses two policemen standing on the corner watching the action and heads straight for the smoldering front door. "You, stop! You can't go in there!"

Sam doesn't break stride as an officer bears down on him. "I own this place; get the hell out of my way!"

"I don't care who you are, mister, you're not going in!"

Sam whimpers under the weight of a large cop's body slam. "Shit, get off of me! Okay, okay, I won't go in. Let me up."

"What's your name, sir?"

"Sam Killian." Sam checks himself for cuts and bruises

as he awkwardly picks his body out of the street gutter. He finds one bloody scraped elbow and a severely bruised ego; could have been worse, he thinks, shifting his eyes toward his aggressor. This cop isn't playing. "You know I could arrest you for endangering the life of an officer, don't you?"

"Look, I'm sorry, uh, Officer Dunwoody. It's just that I have a payroll deposit in there, and I have to get it. It looks like our hardworking civil servants have the fire under control." Sam makes another move toward the door.

"Stand down, sir!" Dunwoody breathes heavily with anticipation; physical exertion is his aphrodisiac.

"Look, man, the fire's about out!" Sam whines, but backs away, taking a closer look at Dunwoody's three-story body; getting whipped by a uniformed man half my age and double my weight, Sam determines, is not in my best interest – a sobering and accurate judgment for a man on the brink of disaster. He stands down as Officer Dunwoody's partner steps in; Officer Smith is half his partner's size, twice his age, and prefers playing the role of nice cop. "You can't just walk into a crime scene, Mr. Killian; somebody deliberately tried to burn your restaurant down."

Sam looks hard at the older man and grimaces. "Well, that doesn't surprise me, Officer Smith. Make note of that – I'm not surprised. Now, if you'll excuse me, I'll just go through the back door and get out of your way."

"Go ahead, but only if you want Junior over there to throw you in the street again before I arrest you. Do you want that?" Smith smiles coldly, and Sam knows he's bested. "Because if that's the route you want to go, I can make that happen for you, and you can spend the day in jail." Dunwoody closes in again. "I advise you to stay right here, Mr. Killian."

Sam quickly apologizes for his bad temper. "I'm sorry, Officers; I'm a little stressed right now."

Officer Smith motions Dunwoody to back off. He lowers his voice. "I know you're upset, but you need to pay attention to me now; I need to ask you some questions." Smith holds a cheap pen and an official-looking clipboard.

Sam's wary of anything official, especially when it holds a triplicate form. Salesmen carry something similar, he thinks, and all they ever want is money. "What kind of questions?"

"Well, let's start with the obvious. Who might want to burn down your restaurant?" Sam doesn't hesitate. "My ex-wife Mimi," Sam snarls.

"Why?" Officer Smith looks up from his notes.

"Because she's a crazy bitch."

Smith hesitantly writes this down, and much to Sam's entertainment, demands that he watch his language. "Has she threatened you in any manner?"

Sam sighs. "No, forget it; it's probably not her."

"Okay, who else?"

"Do you watch the news? Read the paper, or maybe Playboy Magazine?"

Smith's mouth widens with recognition, forming a smirk rather than a smile. "Oh, yeah, now I know where I've seen you; you're the Vodka guy, right?"

"Right. That's me." Sam preens briefly, but catches himself; he needs another breakfast cocktail before he can become truly obnoxious.

"Well, Mister Killian, you have a lot of enemies." Smith isn't impressed by Sam's notoriety.

"Most of them Baptist, I think. The Moral Majority crawls up my ass all the time. Oh, I'm sorry Officer, did I offend you?"

A red-faced Smith turns back to his notebook and takes a deep breath. "I doubt anyone truly affiliated with the Lord would do such a thing; in my church, we pray for you." Smith silently prays for strength to refrain from cold-cocking this arrogant sum-bitch as Sam turns up the volume on his rant. "Not a day goes by without a dozen people waving Bibles in my face and yelling at my customers. 'Burn in Hell,' they scream, over and over, like it's a fucking, uh, freaking football game and they're the cheerleaders. You'd think they'd be over it by now; I've even heard a few obscenities fly from their side, but that's usually after I offer them discount shots."

Smith, controlled but seething, looks up from his clipboard. "Anyone else you can think of?"

"No, but on second thought, question Mimi; she probably hired someone to do it."

"Do you know how to get in touch with her?"

"Yeah, and if you let me in, I'll get her number and address for you. We can go through the back entrance and not disturb a thing." Smith observes Sam cautiously before acquiescing. "Dunwoody, come over here; escort Mr. Killian inside through the back, and make it quick. Mr. Killian, it looks like you'll have to close for a couple of months or so, but your insurance will cover the damage. You'll be back in the headlines before you know it."

Sam smirks. "There'll be some happy Christians celebrating my misfortune; what does Jesus think of that? Think he's kicked back with a glass of red wine about right now, high-fiving the Father and the Holy Ghost? Think I should blame this fire on Jesus?"

Officer Smith's jaw and fists clench and release. "Mr. Killian, you really shouldn't talk about Jesus that way; it's sacrilegious."

"Jesus Set Me on Fire – my new theme song." Sam laughs maniacally. "Maybe I'll put that slogan on a tee-shirt and sell them. Or, how about this one: Jesus Burnt My Bar Down – Holy Smoke!" Dunwoody steps in between the two men, saving his boss's job and Sam from unconsciousness.

. . .

Julie purchases a condominium in a large singles complex, home to three thousand residents and The Pelican, a local "member's only" shag club. Finally, she thinks; music I can move to. Finally, people who appreciate the beach scene. Late at night, when Julie sends her latest Mr. Right Now home, she paces and smokes, smokes restlessly, lighting one from the end of the other. The hole in her heart is so profoundly and invisibly deep that even sixty-minute men are incapable of finding and filling it, regardless of the size and shape and precision of their smoothest moves.

Julie works, but not with passion. She makes no friends at the hospital and is unattached from eight until five. But, on five of seven nights, Julie drinks, smokes, and dances to a one-and-two, three-and-four, five-six beat; and on weekends, she soaks up multiple Nutty Monkey banana drinks and chases them with a Midnight breakfast buffet of eggs, bacon, hash browns, and the Pelican's artery-shocking chipped beef gravy on biscuits. Julie gains twenty-two pounds in three months. Unable to wear her designer clothes, Julie shops off the rack at a local department store, but as long as the lipstick matches her nails and the shoes remain polished and the men continue to move the right foot at the right time, she is satisfied. Julie's hairstyle doesn't change, but many of its strands go AWOL and make a run for the shower drain.

ENTHUSIASM

Expression is great, but those who use enthusiasm for destructive purposes create a whirlwind of devastation. Try explaining this one to your dog.

Mimi finishes her barn detail, takes a drink of water from the pump and, cooing sweetly, quietly walks to Cajun's stall. Cajun lifts his noble head from his sweet timothy and spins to turn his good eye toward Mimi, then stretches like a cat and meets her at the wide stall door. Mimi reaches in her pocket for a mint, and her best friend nuzzles her hand, accepting the treat with soft, velveteen rabbit lips. Then he snorts, and shies violently; something disturbs him. Mimi freezes as someone behind her shouts, "Boo!" She quickly turns around, barely able to control her anger. She softens slightly when she sees Warren, but immediately lets him know she's displeased. "Warren, what are you thinking? That wasn't cool."

"Well, damn, it's good to see you, too, Mimi." Warren's talk has a swagger, but his body language doesn't; he's uncomfortable in his skin. As Mimi calms Cajun, Warren lights a cigarette, chalking up another wrong move. "Good Lord, man, where's your brain? Take that outside, you can't smoke in a barn. If David catches you, it'll be both our asses!"

"Is David your new boyfriend?"

"No, Warren, David owns this barn; he's my boss. Go on now, and pick up your butt, too; stick it in your pocket." Mimi shifts her attention back to her scattered horse. "Easy, Cajun. It's okay, babe." After a few more seconds, Cajun eases to the stall door and loudly sighs. "When you come back in the barn, Warren, start talking to me, okay? It'll help him settle if he hears you; he's blind in one eye and a little freakish because of it."

"Maybe I should just stay here instead, then." Warren's feeling freakish, too.

"Nope, come on in; just be smart this time. The more Cajun's exposed to new things, the more desensitized he becomes; he'll calm down. See? He already has. Here, give him this." Mimi hands Warren a peppermint.

"No way am I putting my hand in there. Horses and I don't get along that well."

Mimi grins at Warren, cuffs him on the shoulder, and pulls him in for a hug. "That's because you smell funny. How did you find me?"

"I called Dee last week, and she told me you were mucking stalls for a living somewhere near your house, so I drove around until I saw this barn." Warren's voice changes to a lower register, and his face loses its boyish vulnerability. "Listen, Mimi, something's happened."

"What? Are you all right?" Mimi turns her attention away from Cajun, who is calmly munching hay. She and Warren walk out of the barn and onto the wide gravel driveway. They lean against the aged fence amidst a thick border of pink cosmos; the old farm, functional and worn, wears its new party clothes to lovely effect. "Yeah, yeah," Warren answers, but nervously shifts his weight from left to right, never meeting Mimi's gaze. "It's just that I think I made a big mistake and I need to tell you about it." He stops, takes a breath, and looks at the ground before continuing. "Do you know Sam's restaurant caught fire this morning?"

Mimi is stunned. "No, but now you're scaring me. Does this have anything to do with your mistake?" Mimi sniffs Warren's shirt. "Or the fact that you smell like gasoline?" Warren shuffles, but he tells the truth; lying has never been his strong suit, and he looks up to meet her stare. "Mimi, you know I used to love Sam to death; he was like a father to me. But he really embarrassed me that night I tried to talk to him about drinking."

"Yeah," Mimi says, "I know he did. But you helped me figure some things out, and something good came out of it; you need to know that." Warren shakes his head, unwilling to accept Mimi's affirmation. "I saw Sam the other day, and he did it again, Mimi. I was just walking by the restaurant and Jesse was outside sweeping the front entrance, so I stopped to say hello."

"What made you go down there, Warren? You shouldn't have done that." Unable to tap into goodness anywhere, the young man droops like a wilting wildflower dying from domesticity. "I know, but I walk by there all the time."

"You can go another way, Warren." Mimi is gentle with the broken child; he has a lot of heart and the passion of a warrior, but his brain doesn't connect the dots when it comes to learning self-preservation survival skills. She watches Warren's face contort as he fails to dam a river of hot tears. "Sam made fun of me in front of Jesse. He thinks he's Jesus Christ Superstar now that he's been in Playboy Magazine; he made me mad, and I couldn't help myself."

Mimi's heart sinks with the weight of her next question; she already knows the answer. "Did you start the fire?" Warren kicks at the dirt and reaches in his pocket for another cigarette. "I filled up a bottle with gasoline, stuffed a rag in it, lit it, and slammed it through the front window. It felt good for a minute, but now I'm afraid I'll get caught. I need you to help me." Mimi knocks the cigarette from Warren's hand before the match reaches its intended target. "You ought to be afraid! That was a really dumb thing to do. Dangerous. You've committed a felony, Warren. Damn it, why did you tell me this?"

"I don't know, I needed to tell somebody and you were the first person I thought of. You can keep a secret," he says, begging for understanding. "You know how Sam is, he treated you like shit!"

"Yeah, I do know how Sam is; he's a sick man. But that doesn't mean I want to torch his restaurant! You shouldn't have told me." Mimi shakes her head, trying to dislodge the unwelcome information Warren shares. It sticks, though; she can't move it.

"Why not?" Warren gapes; he's surprised by Mimi's reaction.

"Who do you think the police will call first, Warren? Probably me. And if they don't call me first, they'll call me second, or third, and they'll question me, and they'll ask me if I did it, and I'll say no, and then they'll ask me if I know who did."

"And what will you say?"

Mimi looks at Warren hard. "Well, I'm not going to lie about it; I'm not a good liar, and even if I did lie, and they found out I lied, I'd be sitting in the cell right next to you! I'd be an accomplice; do you get that?"

"No, Mimi, you can't rat me out. Please don't do that." Dust devils filled with Warren's agitation swirl around them. He paces away from Mimi and reaches for a cigarette. This time Mimi lets him light it, grabs the pack from him, and lights one herself. "I need a place to stay, Mimi, will you let me stay with you? You can't tell anyone. Oh, shit, I shouldn't have come here. You don't understand."

Mimi takes a deep draw, and then another before answering. "Oh, I understand, Warren; you're in a boatload of trouble. Best thing you can do is turn yourself in. God, how did I ever smoke these things?" She tears the cigarette apart in frustration – frustration for smoking, frustration for playing a part in Warren's drama.

"Turn yourself in for what?" Mimi jumps at the sound of her boss's gruff voice. "What's going on here? Who is this?"

"David, damn it! What's with all you people creeping around scaring me? Am I deaf?" David's weathered face turns rock-hard. Without taking an eye off Warren, he demands Mimi's attention. "Mimi, answer me! What's going on?"

"David, this is Warren; he used to work for me. And he's in some serious trouble."

"Trouble's the last thing we need around here, son. Keep moving."

Warren snuffs out his cigarette, and remembering Mimi's earlier request, picks up the butt, puts it in his pocket, and looks at Mimi. "Sounds like a good idea to me," he says. "Thanks for nothing, Mimi." He walks a few yards down the driveway, then turns right and jumps the pasture fence.

"David, you don't know what's going on." Mimi looks from one to the other so fast her head hurts. "Wait a minute, everybody, just hang on." Warren looks dejectedly at Mimi. "I can't believe this, Mimi. You're going to rat me out." He continues walking through the pasture toward the woods.

"Warren! Come back here! David, the kid just set Sam's restaurant on fire – threw a gas bomb or something through the window; we can't let him go!" David's response surprises her. "Yes we can; he'll get caught." David looks at Mimi, shrugs his shoulders, and walks toward the barn; Mimi intercepts him.

"Of course he'll get caught; he just told me about it, and I can't lie for him. But that's not the point right now." David's male perspective brings out Mimi's indignant mother gene – all women have it, regardless of the number of children they choose not to bear. "I can't let him go like this, he's a basket case. Oh, no, what was that?" Mimi looks hard at David. "What was that noise, David?"

"Stay here," says David, as he breaks into a poor imitation of a fast run – best he can do with a bum knee and a bad back. "Call 911!" Mimi wastes no time ignoring David's first order and fulfilling his second as she runs like a track star to the barn's dusty black wall phone. She dials, and breathes for the first time in what seems like hours, only she's on the verge of hyperventilation.

"911, what's your emergency?"

"I think someone just shot himself."

"What's your location, ma'am?"

"900 Double Tree Lane, Double Tree Farm, off Jenkin's Bottom Road. Please hurry!"

"An ambulance is on its way now; stay calm, stay with me. What's your name?"

"Please send a police officer, too; the young man's in trouble."

"Ma'am, don't hang up; stay with me." Mimi hangs up the phone, collapses by Cajun's stall, and begins to softly keen until she sees David dragging Warren back to the barn by his arm and yelling like he's in a hollering contest.

"What were you going to do with this gun, punk? Hold Mimi hostage? Kill yourself?" David looks at Mimi and shakes his head. "This idiot can't even kill himself. You damn dumbass," he shouts at Warren. "Stop being a baby."

"But it hurts!" Warren is crying hard. "Oh, damn, my

ear, my ear."

"It should hurt, dummy; you ought to be dead right now, and you would be if Mimi wasn't here. I'd kill you just for the fun of it." Mimi moves in for a closer look, and is relieved to see only a profuse amount of blood, but no brain matter, dripping from Warren's head. "God, what happened, David?"

"Dumb kid says he shot the no trespassing sign and the bullet ricocheted and hit him in the head. Just grazed his ear by my measure. How close were you standing to the sign, you stupid piece of shit? I ought to shoot you myself for scaring the horses. I think I will. Stand back, Mimi, I'm gonna shoot this kid between the eyes and put him out of my misery."

"David! Leave him alone. Warren, sit down; the ambulance is on its way. David, can you get a clean towel or something? He's bleeding all over himself."

"Aw, Mimi, go back to the barn, please. I'm not gonna shoot this coward, the cops will do that! Stop crying, you big sissy. Look at you; you're a fucking mess, bleeding all over my gravel. Now every raccoon on this property will be coming around looking for a snack. I ought to tie you to the tree and leave you for 'coon bait."

"Warren, sit still," Mimi instructs. "I'll be right back; David's not going to hurt you. Just breathe, baby. Help is on the way."

"He can't hear you," David says, sitting on the ground and tenderly cradling Warren's head in his lap. "He just passed out, but he'll be all right." And he is, although he will never again hear out of his deformed right ear. But he makes the paper, his picture beside Sam's on the front page above the fold. Mimi, refusing all interviews as advised by attorney Jim Morris, is exonerated, but not before viewing Sam's besotted underbelly one more time.

IDENTIFICATION

One has a tendency to move toward that which one identifies, regardless of the positive or negative nature. Sometimes it's better to sit still.

Jake's plane arrives late, but nobody is expecting him. He takes the shuttle to a downtown hotel and checks in for the night, first floor room, no stairs, and no elevator. A hot shower first, then room service, then, considering his next move – it's late, but what the hell – he calls Mimi and gets her answering machine. "Hello, my favorite farm girl. Sure would like to hear your real voice; you walking the dogs, or sleeping?"

Mimi isn't inclined to welcome another surprise today, regardless of the magnificent award hidden behind Door Number One. But Jake's voice is soothing balm to her raw nerves; she picks up the receiver in mid-message. "Jake! Where are you?" Jake relaxes into the familiar voice, but intuits an edge. "Marriott, downtown."

Mimi gapes and runs her hand through her already tousled hair, forcing it to stand on end. "What town? This town?"

"Yep," says Jake. "I'm home. Well, actually, I'm homeless, remember?" Mimi pauses, and grins. "Oh, yeah, that's right; dogless, too. I'm sorry to break it to you over the phone," she states, "but Molly and Ben are married; she's part of the family now."

Jake loves the easy banter and smiles into the phone. His light shines through the wire and infuses Mimi's weary spirit. "Didn't she miss me at all?"

"Nope."

"What about the old adage, absence makes the heart

grow fonder?"

"Absence makes the heart forget, Jake." Mimi sighs into the phone.

"Did you forget about me too, Mimi?"

"Yep, as soon as the chocolates were gone."

"What if I told you there's a box of Zen orange peels in my suitcase?"

"I'd think you were bribing me to come downtown and pick you up."

"Are you extending an invitation?"

"Are you looking for one?" They pause, and consider their options. Jake speaks first. "I have a better idea. Why don't you pack a little bag and come spend the night with me?" Well, it's out there, Jake thinks. "But, only if you want to."

Mimi and Jake stop breathing at the same time. After some quick pondering, Mimi hurries to the bathroom and throws toiletries into an overnight bag. "Oh, I want to; you have Zen treats."

"How long will it take you to get here?" Mimi shifts the phone to her shoulder, freeing both hands to struggle with the bag's stuck zipper. "Give me forty-five minutes, unless you don't mind me strolling through the lobby in my pajamas."

Jake laughs. "I'm sure you can pull that off."

"Listen, Jake, I'm wound a little tight right now. Have you been home long enough to see the news? Probably not." Mimi's used to answering her own questions. "I'll explain when I see you. Can we go for a little walk downtown tonight? There's something we might want to check out." Ooh, that was selfish, Mimi thinks, and quickly adds a disclaimer. "We can wait until tomorrow if you're too tired."

"A walk would be great," responds Jake. "The spring

in my back needs to be sprung. I'll throw on some shoes and meet you in the bar. Just come on, woman; you're wasting time."

Mimi secures the dogs, and closes and locks the gate at the end of the driveway, something she's never felt the need to do before tonight.

. . .

Like old friends, Mimi and Jake hug, then carry the play to first base. Hold the kiss, release the kiss, laugh, and then kiss again and again until the bartender laughs, too. He picks up Jake's room key and dangles it in front of his face as the octogenarian couple in the corner bursts into applause. Now it's Mimi's turn to blush.

It's a short walk, only four blocks, from the Marriott to The Firefly. Vans bearing the call letters from every local and regional television station, a posse of talking heads jockeying for position, and Sam Killian, his red nose shining brightly for the cameras, overtake the street as policemen direct slow-moving gawkers away from the blackened building. Jake is stunned. "Damn, when did this happen? What the heck?"

Mimi takes Jake's hand and abruptly turns around. "Let's not get any closer; I don't want to be seen here." She spins like a gazelle avoiding a pride of hungry lions. Jake matches her stride. "I have an idea," he says. "Where's your car?"

"In the deck across the street from the hotel. Yeah, yeah," she says, reading Jake's mind in mid-thought. "The top of the parking deck! Bet the view's spectacular from there; I even have binoculars!" Mimi and Jake stand at the precipice and watch the loud, miasmic catastrophe unfold below them; it looks like a scene straight out of El

Bosco's Hell.

"What's with the cross? Look, there's a group carrying Bibles. There's the John 3:16 guy! This is big-time, Mimi; apparently I've missed something almost as mind-blowing as Sam's ego."

As they view the scene from the safety of a four story buffer, Mimi tells Jake the story; rife with tension, flush with humor, she speaks for a solid hour, leaving nothing out, and Jake is riveted until she is empty of words. They silently walk back to the hotel where a hot, steamy shower relaxes the tension from two tightly wound bodies. And after that, Mimi and Jake gently coax each other into oblivion, eyes locked.

The drama on the street, however, boils in a pressure cooker, in scalding steam, in hellfire and brimstone. Sam, dressed in chef pants and a stained Firefly tee-shirt, smiles for the cameras as six microphones are shoved toward his calm, vodka-sodden lips. "Sam, Sam! Do you know the young man who did this?" Sam shrugs nonchalantly for the crowd. "Yeah, I know him. His name's Warren Hanover, and he used to work for me."

"What was his motive? Will you press charges?"

Sam looks directly at the camera and winks. "That's between me and Warren. I'm not sure he acted alone. At this point, he's under heavy sedation at the hospital because of a gunshot wound to the head. I haven't had a chance to talk to the young man."

Reporters jockey for position. "Any idea who else may have been involved?" Sam puffs up and, serious about his air time, turns in profile. "Yeah, I have ideas, but my attorney has advised me not to discuss that publically at this time. However, I will say that my ex-wife was with Warren right before he was shot." More jockeying – a bit of shoving – it's a rather big story, and competition is stiff. "Do you think she shot him, Sam?"

"All will be known in due time, folks. She's a loose cannon, so it's not out of the question." Sam practically bows as he bids his farewell. "If you'll excuse me, it's been a long day."

"Just one more question, Sam, please. When do you expect to reopen The Firefly? You have quite a following here."

"The damage was mostly in the front lobby, bar, and dining areas. We'll take stock of that damage tomorrow and keep you apprised of the situation. Now, goodnight, and thank you."

"A tough situation for the happy hour crowd," reports the young lady with the microphone. "Now, let's go back to the studio where Angie will give us an update on tomorrow's weather." Cut.

. . .

After an unusually pickup-free weekend watching younger, thinner women dance with her regular partners, after smoking the better part of two packs of cigarettes while standing at the bar with Betsy for four hours, after drinking six very rich and creamy Nutty Monkeys, and after eating two heaping platefuls of gravy, biscuits, bacon and eggs, Julie's heart skips one too many beats. Betsy rides in the ambulance as Julie is transported from the Pelican to the emergency department of Sisters of Mercy Hospital, where Julie is not recognized as an employee. "Are you a relative of the patient?"

"No, I'm her best friend."

"Do you know how to reach her next of kin?"

Betsy is alarmed. "Is she out of the woods?"

The busy ED nurse shakes her head sympathetically at

Betsy. "If she has any living relatives, they should be notified immediately."

"Let me see what I can do," Betsy says. "In the meantime, I'm right here; I'm not leaving her side, so consider me her next of kin, all right?"

. . .

Mimi, an early riser, retrieves a complimentary local paper from under the hotel room door. She stares at the headline in disbelief.

Local Restaurant Burns; Who's to Blame?
Former Employee Faces Charges,
Estranged Spouse Involved

The Firefly Restaurant, located at 462 South Hamilton Boulevard, was deliberately set on fire early yesterday morning, authorities determined. Jimmy Smith, Criminal Investigator for the Manassas County Fire Department, stated that a homemade weapon of destruction known as a Molotov cocktail was thrown through the front window of the Firefly, spreading flaming gasoline throughout the lobby and bar area.

Sam Killian, owner, believes he is the victim of a conspiracy involving a former disgruntled employee, Warren Hanover, and his ex-wife, Mimi Lewis Killian. "The details are shaky at this point," Killian admitted. "The authorities say they got a confession from Warren. I know for a fact that Mimi and Warren were in close proximity yesterday shortly after the fire. I haven't spoken with either of them personally. Warren was shot and my ex-wife was there and was questioned by the police."

Local 911 received a distress call at 9:07am yesterday morning from a woman later identified as Mimi Killian who said that someone had just been shot at Double Tree Farm located off of Jenkins Bottom Road, where Ms. Killian is currently employed. The police report states that Hanover, scared and confused, accidentally shot himself in the ear after confessing his act of arson to Ms. Killian. A source close to Ms. Killian said that Hanover was distraught when Ms. Killian refused to cover up his criminal act.

"Remember, Warren was unconscious and on his way to the hospital while the police interviewed Mimi," cautioned Sam Killian. "I want to hear his side of the story before I jump to any conclusions."

Killian gained national notoriety after being touted in major publications such as Playboy, Esquire, and Rolling Stone magazines as "The Vodka King." His daily happy hours featuring discount vodka shots for alcoholics and his unique marketing techniques have drawn the wrath of the Moral Majority, as well as other religious groups. Killian's first instinct was to place blame on a "Bible-waving fanatic who needed a drink." However, no evidence has been found to support that theory.

Jim Morris, Ms. Killian's attorney, issued this short statement: "Ms. Killian will be exonerated in short order of all suspicion regarding this matter. She was simply an innocent bystander who helped break the case. Sam Killian owes her a public apology, at the very least, and believe me, he may owe her more."

Ms. Killian was unavailable for comment.

. . .

Mimi gently awakens Jake with a kiss on the nose and a gentle head massage. He stirs, sits up, and yawns, then pulls her on top of him. She playfully tweaks his nose and shoves the newspaper in his face. "Look at this, Jake. Look at this, can you believe it?"

"Wait a minute, let me wake up," Jake says as he rolls Mimi to the floor. "Call room service and let's get some coffee up here."

"It's on the way. Read!" Mimi drops the paper on Jake's chest and begins pacing. "Unreal!" Mimi is unplugged and borderline manic. "I owe Jim Morris a call; he just saved me a heap of trouble." Jake stretches, picks up the paper, and looks at Mimi quizzically. "Who's Jim Morris again?"

"My divorce attorney, remember? I thought he was a schmuck. Read the article while I get the door; coffee's here."

"My God! This headline! Shit, Mimi." Jake jumps out of bed, pulls on his boxers, and heads to the bathroom. "Get on the phone with Jim now; we need to figure this out. I mean, do you need to go to the police station? Are people looking for you?"

"I don't know, but I guess Jim saw the news last night, to my benefit. He may have tried to call me at home; I better check my messages. We need to get back to the farm soon anyway and take care of the dogs." Jake throws water on his face and starts dressing in last night's clothes. "Okay, let's do this," he commands as Mimi hands him a cup of coffee with heavy cream. "I'll check out while you bring the car around, then we'll go to the farm and regroup." Mimi shakes her head. "I don't want you involved in this."

Jake won't hear of it. "I'll fly under the radar; you need me because I have friends at the hospital, and you'll need access to Warren." Jake plays an ace.

"I really do want to check on him," says Mimi, pulling on a black tee-shirt over her braless torso. She ties her hair into a knot and pushes it through the back of a well-worn baseball cap, and grabs her overnight bag.

"You'll need a wingman for a few days; do you mind a houseguest?"

"Jake, of course not; please stay with me." Mimi drops her bag and closes her eyes in thought. "Oh, shoot; I need to call David. What's today? Monday? Yeah, it's Monday." She doesn't need an answer from Jake which is good because he's jet-lagging; she sorts out her thoughts without help. "I don't work on Mondays." She picks up her rough brown suede bag and swings it over her shoulder. "But I need to talk to David as soon as possible. Do you mind going to the barn with me today? You can meet my pal Cajun."

"The four-legged man in your life?" David is important, Jake is more important, but Cajun is Mimi's soul shine; Jake is smart enough to understand her passion. "Hey, he needs me," says Mimi, smiling for the first time all morning. Her demeanor changes at the thought of Cajun; the stress leaves her face, and Jake sees a different level of beauty in her soft composure. He can't help but tease her. "And I don't?"

Mimi tilts her head and looks Jake up and down. "You do for a minute; otherwise you'd be out on the streets playing a cheesy little keyboard for chump change." They gulp the last ounce of lukewarm coffee and head for the lobby.

"There's an idea," Jake says. "I'll set up in front of The Firefly; it'll be my last gig there. All my songs will have fire themes. I'll open with *You Light Up My Life*."

Mimi spins in the hall and grins. "Yeah, come on baby *Light My Fire*."

"*Serpentine Fire*." Jake and Mimi dance down around the corner into the lobby.

"*Ring of Fire.*" The laughter propels Mimi to the front door as Jake lobs another fast one in her direction. "*Great Balls of Fire!*" Mimi is laughing so hard she can barely see. "You're funny, Jake."

"Not as funny as you, Mimi." Hotel employees and patrons miss the meaning of the inside joke, but catch the joyful spirit of the exchange. The early morning lobbyists look up and smile. "It's a beautiful day," Jake says as he joins the crowd at check-out.

. . .

A large sign is posted on the locked gate: Mimi Killian Press Conference, 10a.m., Double Tree Farm. Mimi recognizes the scribbled handwriting. "David's been here," says Mimi. They unlock and enter the farm road without notice.

A ninety pound, four-legged redhead sprints to Jake as soon as she hears his deep, smoky voice. Molly's massive black bodyguard barks once and joins in the high-spirited love fest after a moment of hesitation. "Ah, Molly, I didn't desert you, girl," Jake says as he scratches behind her ears. "Mimi says you didn't miss me, but you missed me, didn't you girl? I missed you. You sure you like that black boogeyman better than me? I think Mimi lies." Jake's eyes fill with shameless, joyful tears and Molly and Ben take turns licking the salty treat from Jake's happy face; it is in Jake's nature to cry.

The phone is ringing incessantly; Mimi hears its infernally loud screech as she leaves the car, and two more calls come in before she enters the back door to the kitchen and picks up the receiver. It's Jim Morris, Attorney. "Jim! I'm so glad it's you! Thanks so much for watching my back. Whatever I owe you, I'm good for it. Just tell me how much."

"Mimi, you owe me nothing. It's gratis up to this point; that's the least I can do for you. Sam spoke out of turn last night against his attorney's advice, and I think you have a good case against him now." Mimi's brow furrows. "What kind of case, Jim?"

Jim takes a bite of a sausage biscuit and groans as mustard drips onto his pressed oxford shirt. He pours a diet Cheerwine on the stain, blots it with a paper napkin, and watches it miraculously disappear. "We can start with slander and harassment and move on to emotional distress. Any judge will rule in your favor. How does $250,000 sound to you? I'll take forty percent of that as my fee and you'll get your nest egg back. We win, Sam loses."

Mimi listens. "Well, it's worth considering. That's a huge wad of cash, and I could sure use it."

"Why don't you take a day to think about it? In the meantime, Mimi, don't pick up the phone again, unless you have caller ID. Just let it ring, okay? Every reporter in the state is looking for an exclusive with you, and so is USA Today. Remember, you are not a suspect in this case, and as far as you're concerned, it's over until we take Sam to court. Really, the best thing you can do is make yourself unavailable. Go out of town for a few days."

"I can't do that, Jim. I have responsibilities; a job for one. Animals. A houseguest. Not an option. But, I'll lay low."

Jim takes a sip of sugar. His morning breakfast causes his gut to rumble. He puts his hand over the receiver and belches with the force of a geyser. "Mimi, listen. Reporters are going to swarm your house; I'm surprised they haven't yet. If you can stand the hassle, stay home; if it gets to be too much, go on vacation, or hire a security guard to turn them away. Just let me know what you decide and I'll get the ball rolling on your case."

"I want to go to the hospital and see Warren, is that okay?"

Jim narrows his eyes and lowers his voice. "Mimi, I advise against it. The press will be all over the place. And don't call him, either. Look, just stay out of sight; that's all you have to do right now besides promise to call me tomorrow morning."

Mimi is quiet for a moment as she ponders Jim's advice before relenting. "What you're saying makes sense," she finally responds. Jim is relieved; this case is cake if Mimi follows his advice to the letter. "Promise you'll call tomorrow?"

"Yes, I promise."

. . .

Mimi listens to twenty-eight messages, five of which are from Sam:

10:45 p.m., Sunday: *Mimi, if you had anything to do with this fire I swear I'll have you thrown in jail quicker than you can find a hiding place. I know where you live, remember? You better stay in town because you're in deep shit.*

11:48 p.m., Sunday: *Mimi, I hope you watched the news tonight because I mentioned your name. Best of luck, bitch. You're going down.*

2:17 a.m., Monday: *Mimi? I'm shorry, I din'un mean taa, aaaah upshet ya.*

2:18 a.m., Monday: *Mimi, aaah, pig up the phone. I godda talk to ya now. Mimi? Oh well, this ish Sam.*

9:23 a.m., Monday: *Mimi, my attorney says I screwed up last night, and I want to apologize to you. I'll make it right, just please understand how upset I am. I think I've finally reached bottom, and am heading to a meeting right now. Please, if you can, forgive me. I know how hard that might be. I know you didn't have anything to do with the fire, and I know you didn't shoot Warren. I'm just sorry you chose to have an affair instead of working things out with me, but that's the way it goes sometimes. Say a prayer for me. I'll be in touch, although Drew says for me not to contact you at all. If you can find it in your heart, please call me.*

Three from David:

11:02 p.m., Sunday: *Mimi, are you watching the news? I'll call back.*

11:12 p.m., Sunday: *Mimi, are you there? I'm calling the paper right now. Your ex-husband is in serious trouble. But don't worry because you aren't.*

7:03 a.m., Monday: *For the love of God, don't come to the barn today. Your place was swarming with idiots when I woke up this morning. I threatened to have them all arrested for trespassing, but now they're filming trees and horse shit over here and waiting for your press conference. Just stay home, and don't worry about Cajun. I'll take good care of him. Call when you can.*

Six messages from Jim Morris, fourteen from various reporters and producers representing news stations, one from Playboy Magazine, one from Jerry Springer, and one from a woman who says she is Warren Hanover's mother, please call, he's awake and asking to speak with Mimi. He's in room 1412, Eastern General Hospital. Mimi picks up the phone, but Jake takes the receiver from Mimi's hand, hangs it up, and puts his hand on her heart, a sweet move that stops her from getting mad, an old doctor trick that works every time. "Mimi, listen to Jim," implores Jake. "He's right; you can't go to the hospital, but I can. Let me check on Warren for you. And unless Sam's there, I doubt anyone will recognize me, except maybe Warren. I'm simply a doctor who needs to check on a patient. It'll work; I know the nurses on his floor. They'll be happy to grant me access to his chart and run interference so I can talk with him alone."

Makes sense, Mimi thinks. "All right, yeah, that works for me."

"In the meantime, stay in the house. Let the dogs out, but you stay put, you hear?"

Mimi taps her foot and adopts a slouchy posture. "Yes, Paw Paw, I'll stay put. I'll peel us some taters for supper and scrub some floors until you git back. Jess leave the shotgun loaded." Her minor irritation at Jake's edict passes in a blink. Jake makes the most of the fast-moving tension. "Bake me a cake while you're at it, Mee Maw. I gotta button missin' on my work britches, too, that needs sewin'."

Mimi laughs and relaxes. "That's not the only thing that'll be missing if you keep talking like that." Jake kisses Mimi lightly on the lips, and touches her face. "I'll be back in a couple of hours, and I'll call you from Warren's room if he's in any shape to talk to you. Don't hold your breath, though; I'm not overly optimistic."

Mimi hears a ruckus outside, peers out the window, and runs for the kitchen. "Jake, somebody's on the porch!" Ben and Molly race out the door, barking ferociously. At Jake's command, the hi-fi barking stops and changes to a lo-fi threatening growl. Four brown eyes watch every move as a frenzied reporter and cameraman freeze in mid-stride. Jake moves outside and shuts the door behind him. "They bite, be very still," he says. "Bet you're looking for Mimi Killian. Too bad you missed her; she left last night for Italy. I took her to the airport late yesterday afternoon, but she'll be back in three weeks. I'm her house sitter. She planned this trip many weeks ago. I don't know what she's doing in Italy, working a wine apprenticeship or something like that, I think. As you read in the paper this morning, Ms. Killian's attorney Jim Morris issued a statement on her behalf. That's all I know. Ah, sorry about your pants, man. Luckily, dog urine doesn't leave much of a stain."

The two trespassers back away toward the parked TV van, carefully, quietly, slowly, as Ben's yellow stream squishes a rhythmic escort in time with the cameraman's alternate footfall.

Thirty minutes later, the former Doctor Jake Reston walks confidently into Eastern General's Employee entrance, purposefully avoiding extended conversation with ex-coworkers until he reaches the Recovery Unit of ICU. "Hey, my favorite Nurse Ratchet. Give me a hug, you gorgeous broad! How are you, Cathy?"

"Better now that I've seen you, Dr. Reston. But, are you okay? I was so sorry to hear about Julie. How's she doing? I hope she'll be okay." Jake freezes. "What about Julie?"

"Uh-oh, you don't know?" Nurse Cathy grimaces at her mistake.

"I just got back in town last night. I've been in Europe for over three months; I don't even know where Julie is."

"Yeah, I heard you guys separated. She's living near the coast somewhere, and had a heart attack a few days ago. They about lost her on the table."

Jake is stunned. "You gotta be kidding me."

"A friend is with her, somebody named Betsy, maybe? I think she called here looking for you. But, that's all I know. No, wait a minute. Julie works at Sisters of Mercy; I bet we can find the number."

"Track it down for me, will you? Do you mind? I have to see a patient, Warren Hanover in Room 1412."

Cathy shakes her head. "That's one lucky son of a gun, no pun intended; another skinny millimeter, and he would have checked out before he checked in."

Jake can't help but worry about Julie. "Cathy, will you look up Mercy's number right now? I'll feel better when it's in my hand."

"Sure, hang on; I'm really sorry to spring this on you. I didn't know you two hadn't been in touch."

"It's all right, Cathy, you're a baby doll." Jake pauses to appraise Cathy's new curves. "How much weight have you lost since I've been gone?"

"Eighteen pounds, Doc!" Chubby Nurse Cathy strikes a model's pose and grins. Losing weight and gaining it back keeps Cathy busy in her spare time.

"I leave and you go on a starvation diet," Jake says as he pats her ample waistline. "You really look great. Good for you!"

"We stopped bringing homemade cookies to work when you left. The other doctors can eat the store-bought stuff, but you, Doctor Reston, well, you know we're all in love with you. We bummed out when you resigned from this hellhole and deserted us; we've been too depressed to eat."

"Cathy, you're such a good bullshitter; no wonder the patients ask for you."

"Learned it from the master," says Cathy with a wink.

"Yeah, who might that be?"

"I'm looking at him." Cathy hands Jake a slip of paper. "Here's Betsy's cell number. Let me know what else I can do to help."

"You can keep a close eye on the kid, Cathy; he needs some of your TLC." Jake nods to the guard posted outside room 1412. Warren, tanked on morphine, talks a delusional string of incoherent garble while Jake takes a look at his chart, and then turns his attention to the young patient. Warren looks small – Jake doesn't remember him being so small. "Young brother, you are one lucky bastard, you know that?"

. . .

Melvin revs up Jake's car and drops it at Mimi's house, and within an hour after speaking with Betsy, Jake heads east northeast toward Mercy. Nothing surprises Mimi anymore; the man in the moon could ride a cow through Mimi's front yard in broad daylight and she would process the vision as just another day in the life.

This day turns short for Julie Reston, however. Fifteen minutes before Jake pulls into Sisters of Mercy Hospital, Julie wills her heart to shut down for business without giving final notice – but not before borrowing Betsy's lipstick. It's important for Julie to always look her best, and although the odds of losing twenty pounds in fifteen minutes are against her, you can bet by God that her face will be somewhat on. And while the surgical team cannot save her, they are amazed by the miniscule size of her heart, by the heaviness of something so small, by the lack of room in its tiny caverns. Julie's heart is made of black ice and only death has the power to melt it. "Hey, check this out! Have you ever seen such a hypoplastic heart in an adult? And it's black, like a piece of coal. But feel this thing; it has some heft to it. Oh shit, it's melting! It's going Wizard of Oz on me. Grab a camera, quick! Did you get it? Nobody's gonna believe this. Hearts don't really melt, do they? Astounding!"

Julie's body is cremated, and Betsy, her only friend, her truest friend, and Jake, her estranged husband and unaccepted truest love, deliver her ashes – seven pounds of cold, chunky, heartless dust – to Julie's grieving and confused parents, Mildred and Frank Masencup. Mildred wipes her red and swollen eyes with her cheery gingham apron. "What should we do with her ashes, Frank?"

"I don't know, Mildred." Frank wears the pants, but he doesn't make decisions. Stoically, he pats his wife on the back – the only comfort he can offer – and turns to Jake for advice. "Son, what do you think?"

"Frank, really, Julie would have preferred for me not to be involved in this decision; I'm so sorry. She was a wonderful wife and partner for many years." Jake firmly grasps Frank's shoulder. His patented hand on the heart move is reserved for ladies only. "I'll miss her."

Mildred turns to Betsy, who fumbles through her tote bag for a tissue. "Betsy, what do you think?"

"Dang, Mildred." Betsy blows her nose. "I think they could have put her in a better looking box." Mildred nods her head in agreement. "I'll find something pretty to put her in. Let's just store her in the desk drawer for now." Mildred turns her attention to Jake and kindly extends her former son-in-law a final courtesy. "Jake, thank you so much for being here; it means the world to Frank and me. Can you stay for dinner?"

"Thank you Mildred, but I better go. I'll call you soon though, okay?"

"Okay, dear, we understand." Mildred dismisses Jake with a distant hug. "You take good care now; Betsy, did you happen to bring home any of Julie's things? I know she loved that mirror we gave her, and I'd like to have it back." Betsy crosses her fingers to ward off the lie she's about to tell. "I couldn't fit the mirror into the car, so we donated it to the plastic surgery wing at Mercy Hospital in Julie's honor."

Mildred nods. "That's okay, then; Julie would have liked that."

Julie rests in a nondescript box tucked inside a desk, a lovely solid walnut antique simply appointed with a telephone and fresh flowers. The drawer is dark, and remains closed; but sometimes an aroma of bananas and cigarettes emanates from that drawer when it mysteriously opens just a crack, mystifying Frank and Mildred. This juju aroma ends on the day when Julie's mother mixes her daughter's ashes with rich soil – the humus mixing with the ashes in the Spring – and plants a Bleeding Heart which grows slowly and rarely blooms. That is, until the day Betsy introduces the Bleeding Heart to Greek Valerian, also known as Jacob's Ladder, and both species recognize they are meant to share the same soil. They grow like teenage wrestlers on steroids, take deep root, and create a most stunning visual backdrop for caterwauling cats mating wildly in the otherwise quiet, cool heat of the night.

SILENCE

Create space, peace, and time to rest and recuperate from the noises and chattering outside (and inside your head).

Sam Killian enjoys the hard work of staying sober for the second extended time in his long career as a professional sot. Thirty days at a gentrified treatment center and he's ready to change careers; he daydreams of becoming a lay preacher to the sick and weak, although he doesn't hold The Gospel or The King James Version in high esteem. His Bible is The Blue Book, and Sam is a disciple. He also digs The Oxford Dictionary and Thesaurus, American Edition. His goal: memorize three new words each day. Crapulent, pixilated, and dipsomaniac are among the new words he passionately chooses to describe the old Sam, the Sam who looked alive on the outside, but was dead on the inside. The newly aware Sam burns with the fire of a resurrected alcoholic, but he knows the territory, knows the danger of viewing clouds behind rose-tinted glasses. Dark smoke covers pink clouds, as paper covers rock.

Playboy Magazine and the Moral Majority move on to hotter topics, but at least Sam receives a mention in Esquire's Dubious Achievement Awards. Insurance covers the cost of reconstructing the beloved Firefly Restaurant, but Sam has no interest in maintaining ownership. Professionally speaking, Sam knows a downtown restaurant owned by a chef of his caliber can't survive without holding a liquor license, but he refuses to allow the demon lying dormant inside him to play in the Devil's arena. The refurbished Firefly goes on the block. After much consideration and thoughtful meditation, Sam picks up the phone. "Mimi, hi this is Sam; how are you?"

Mimi considers hanging up, but curiosity gets the better of her. "Why are you calling?" Her tone is flat, her clear head suddenly full of static. Sam knows he can't waste any time, and quickly breaks it down. "Mimi, I'm sober; I've been sober for one hundred forty-seven days."

Mimi smiles, and Sam feels it through the phone. "Ah, Sam, that's the best news I've heard lately. Congratulations!"

"Do you have time to meet me at the restaurant for a cup of coffee? I have a topic to discuss that may be of interest to you." Mimi pauses. "Sam, I don't think my attorney would consider that a smart move."

"I understand, but I have a compromise that may put this entire lawsuit behind us; at least that's my intention." Fool me once, Mimi thinks. "Can you just tell me over the phone?"

"I'd rather see you in person; I owe you a lot, and I want to look at you when I tell you what I'm thinking. Please, I won't keep you long." Sam pauses long enough to give Mimi time to sort through her emotions, and hears her sigh before answering. "Will you make me a pot of decaf, and breakfast? Shrimp and grits?"

"Sure," Sam says, laughing. "Some things never change, do they, old partner? Can you come now?" Mimi hears a renewed sense of purpose in Sam's voice, and it enthralls her. "I'll be there in thirty minutes, how's that?"

"Perfect. I'll be in the kitchen, so come to the front door."

. . .

The Firefly and The Phoenix have sold for $465,000, including the entire inventory except the road weary, battery-powered Velvet Elvis clock that has traveled with

Sam from town to town, restaurant to restaurant, for fourteen years; the deal seals an hour before Sam calls Mimi. After cleaning up borrower's debt and turning over a liability-free operation to the new owners, effective one week from today, Sam's take is a guaranteed $378,000 and change. And he wants to share. "Mimi, I know your half from me won't amount to $250,000, but if you continue with this lawsuit you won't get that anyway because your attorney gets, what, half of that or more?"

Mimi cautiously protects her hand. "It may be close enough if we can work this out," she says.

"I'm willing to do whatever it takes to make it fair for you. If I could buy Planet Earth and serve it up to you on a silver platter, woman, I'd do it; you deserve the best for putting up with all the shit I dished out." Mimi looks around at her memories – pictures of past employees hanging on the wall near the kitchen, the unique hand-painted wine cabinets, art framed by her own hand. The place looks clean and cozy, and filled with old, bittersweet love. She is overwhelmed and can't speak.

"It's true, Mimi," Sam says quietly from across the table. "I apologize, but that's not enough. What I'd like to do is give you half of the revenue from the sale of The Firefly, free and clear. Now, I know your attorney will expect something. I talked to Drew this morning and he thinks I'm crazy, but I want to pay your attorney fee. Drew will call Jim Morris as soon as I have your blessing, and I'll cut Jim a check next week."

Mimi raises her coffee cup halfway to her lips, but her trembling hand doesn't make a connection; she slowly puts it down and looks at Sam's smiling face. Mimi is confused, and not for the first time; repetitive experience with confusion does not an expert make. Mimi doesn't smile back. "I don't know what to say, Sam. I'm flabbergasted."

"How does $189,000 sound to you? Can you live with that?"

"Is this a joke? If this is a joke, Sam, it's a really bad one."

"This is the truest thing I've said to you since the first day I told you I love you. That, by the way, hasn't changed," Sam says to a still-doubting Mimi. "I wouldn't dream of asking you to take me back; I know you've moved on. But, this is the one way I can show you what you mean to me." Sam leans back in his chair and studies the ceiling before beginning again. "I want to make it right between us, to do something I'm proud of, for you. I know you don't trust Drew, but he'll draw up an agreement and all you have to do is sign it. And he'll make sure that Jim Morris signs it, too. Then, the money's yours, without any holds or stipulations. Will you agree to that?"

"Oh, Sam. Sam Sam Sam Sam." Mimi's head bobs and shakes − first no, then yes. But there is only one right answer. She looks straight into Sam's clear eyes, and sees his heart expanding. "Yes, yes, Sam, I'll agree to that."

Sam grins and pounds his fist on the table. "Well, good; I was beginning to worry about you. Eat your breakfast now before it gets cold. I'll call Drew and we'll get the ball rolling." Sam takes Mimi's free hand and kisses it. "See, Mimi, sometimes even a crapulent drunkard is lucky enough to have an angel with a sober head for business sitting on his shoulder."

At Mimi's direction, Jim Morris begrudgingly drops the lawsuit against Sam Killian and accepts a $25,000 payout, but rewrites his future contracts to state that, if a case of this nature is dropped, regardless of circumstance, the disappointing client with whom he wasted so much precious time must pay him a minimum of one half the original agreed upon value of the suit. Crap shooting is not Jim's idea of a good investment, but presenting $10,000 to his wife on her fiftieth birthday buys Jim three weeks of uninterrupted playtime with his new thirty-year old secretary while his lovely, but somewhat chubby and clueless missus enjoys an extended-stay, all-inclusive trip to an Arizona health spa. Jim, a moderate conservative, always chooses the sure bet.

The media stalkers quickly tire of all things Sam and Mimi; there's no story left. It's just another partnership gone wrong, and there are plenty of other couples with more dysfunctional profundities to follow. Old news, Mimi and Sam. Only the former employees of The Firefly speak of them with occasional sentimentality, and Melvin writes a blues tune in Sam's honor that receives a few weeks of local airplay before falling into obscurity; he calls it *Fire Starter Blues.*

My woman was a hot firestorm
Yeah, my woman was a hot firestorm
My world caught fire when she was born
Lightning is her middle name
Oh, lightning is her middle name
When she strikes, the sky won't rain
Buried deep down in my soul
Yeah, buried deep down in my soul
My burned out heart is black as coal
Whiskey, knock me down today
Whiskey, knock me down today
Lightning done killed me anyway

Jake plays his last local gig at The Phoenix during a driving rainstorm; Odessa is the featured vocalist, and just before midnight she announces to the standing-room-only crowd that she and Jake leave in two weeks for a second European tour together. "Wish us luck," she says, "we'll be recording live shows from Amsterdam to the Black Sea Jazz Festival. But, we'll be back in six months and believe me, we'll make The Phoenix our first stop – this place is home base. Hit it, guys!" Odessa shouts, and the crowd goes wild as the band kicks into *Watermelon Man*.

But the fourth set bookmarks the last time Jake ever plays The Phoenix. New owners believe a karaoke machine is a less expensive investment than a live quartet, and a DJ spinning beach music on weekends draws a mighty thirsty and hungry crowd. Thank you, goodnight, and God bless.

Mimi's bank account gestates a big wad of cash, money round and pregnant with opportunity. Soon, she buys the little cottage with the deep front porch at the end of Jenkins Bottom Road and twenty adjoining acres, including a small, old growth apple orchard and a six acre pasture bordered by a meandering stream. Big hardwood trees and clean forest surround her cozy hideaway on all sides, and in the early evening, in the pink light of the setting sun, whitetail deer nimble their way through the orchard and stop to drink peacefully, watchfully, before bedding down in the lush safety of tall grass. Every night before bedtime, Ben, dog of Buddha nature, barks to the east of him, to the north of him, to the west of him, and to the south of him, offering up a late night lunar salutation and prayer for Mimi's protection, for the continued companionship of his beautiful redheaded girlfriend, and for the safety of the deer. Ben is otherworldly; even the shy deer recognize him as a totem guide and have no fear as he patrols the perimeter.

Mimi and Jake spend hours walking the farm, naming the trees, talking. Not always though, sometimes eavesdropping instead on the conversations of wind and hawks, of flowing streams and shifting creek sand. On this particular day, Mimi and Jake remember the past and envision the future, with feet firmly grounded in the present. They sit in the orchard under a favorite tree, shoulder to shoulder, and Jake feels Mimi's vibration. He must speak these words to her out loud before the moment passes. "Mimi, I love you; there is no other person in my life who has ever given me so much of themselves. You are one hundred percent love and truth – sometimes so much it scares me. I can never match you, nobody can."

Mimi turns to Jake with questions in her eyes; she is on point. "Where is this going, Jake? You're scaring me." She turns her head to the ground and traces a tree root with her leather boots, then lifts a little wood spider from her pants and places it in the grass beside her.

Jake smiles; that simple gesture explains so much about Mimi. With his gentle hand, he palms her chin and turns her face to his. "No, listen to me. You were born special and the rest of us pale in your light. I think that's why Sam tried so hard to take you down. You intimidated him without even knowing it, just like you intimidate me sometimes." Mimi takes a deep breath and centers herself; she waits for something, but she doesn't know what it is. She remains quiet for once while Jake gathers his strength to continue. "Stick with me here," he says. "I'm not suggesting you change one silly millimeter of yourself. It's just, well; all that honesty is very hard to match regardless of how hard the rest of us try." Jake pauses before making his next statement. He looks away, sighs, and turns back to meet Mimi's liquid hazel eyes.

"You know, I never told you about the woman I slept with in Barcelona."

"You didn't have to, Jake." Mimi stands up, stretches, and extends both hands to Jake. Sitting down through this conversation begins to feel way too heavy; he grabs them and she leans back, using his rising weight as ballast. They are a balancing act now, walking an emotional tightrope with the deftness and grace of the Flying Wallendas. "But you knew, didn't you?" Jake asks, knowing the answer.

"Sure I knew," Mimi says. Jake shakes his head. "See, how in the hell do you do that? How do women know these things?"

"We're born with built-in shit detectors." Mimi laughs and releases Jake's hands. They turn toward the mossy path and slowly head toward home. "Sometimes I wish I didn't know these things, and many times I've ignored the obvious, especially with Sam. I've had many opportunities to really open my eyes and view the truth up close, but sometimes I choose to shut them. With you, it's different."

Mimi stills her mind and lifts her eyes to the blue sky. She searches for the right words in the white mottled clouds overhead; clouds sometimes hold messages for her. Retaining a childlike fascination for messages in clouds has always helped soften Mimi's hard-edged words. She speaks slowly, with kindness. "I see you clearly, and what I see is a man who loves me, but loves his music more. My eyes are open this time." She takes Jake's hand as they negotiate the flat creek rocks. Safely on the other side, she urges him to be patient while she gathers her thoughts. "Your music is the most precious thing about you. You are music; without it, you'd be dead. I'll never be a jealous mistress to your muse. But, I'm also familiar with the lifestyle of single, handsome and sexy piano players. I watched you for five years, watched you interact with hundreds of women who would gladly have given up a body part just to have you fondle them one time."

"Maybe so, but I had my eyes on you, dear." Jake's dimples are deep enough to swim in; Mimi takes a dive. "The heck you say! You hid it very well."

"Sam's bigger than me, Mimi; he would have crushed me like a bug. You know, Julie had it figured out long before I did. She used to throw your name around every single time we had a fight."

"I'm so sorry about that; I had no idea." Jake extends his hand and helps Mimi climb over the split rail fence separating the deer pasture from the cottage. They are silent in their approach to the front porch, allowing space for Jake's next thought to form. "Julie and I had a great run, or so I thought, for about four years. Double those years, you'll have the sum total of the time we were a miserable duo. She was jealous, and couldn't stand that music came first for me. She loved the doctor and hated the musician. That was my fault; I'll never be a good husband to any woman."

"I don't want to marry you." Mimi says this in the sweetest of ways; her words taste of freedom and commitment, all baked into one beautiful tart. Jake throws back his head and guffaws as he opens the front door. "Whew, glad that's out of the way. You sure about that?"

"I'm sure. Sitting around wondering who you're wrapping your legs around in Barcelona is not my idea of a healthy way to live."

"You can always go with me," Jake says, opening the refrigerator and pulling out a pitcher of hummingbird tea.

Mimi grabs two glasses from her cabinet, fills them with crushed ice, and Jake pours the bright red liquid. "What do you think of that?"

Mimi smiles at Jake's question; he already knows her answer. "My focus is building a nice little barn and round pen so I can bring Cajun here and find a buddy for him. I'm happy staying on the farm with Ben and Molly. But maybe when you and Odessa pick up a few days rest, I'll meet you at the big sand castle, or maybe Amsterdam." Thinking of Jake's travels reminds her of a certain gift he mailed. "Hey, what about that toothpaste? Should we brush our teeth with your special anti-cavity solution? No, wait. We can't do that; it's two o'clock in the afternoon. Can we?"

Jake grins and heads to the sock drawer to retrieve his illicit goods. "It's dark somewhere, and believe me, it doesn't have to be dark in Amsterdam for the coffeehouses to be filled with smokers. Let's do it!" Tube in hand, Jake digs in his shaving kit for a scalpel, then deftly performs delicate surgery as Mimi stands by, engrossed in the operation. She's not quite sure what Jake's holding, but it looks like a straw. "How'd that get in the toothpaste?"

"My friend Peter taught me a trick," Jake says as he wipes the cylinder clean and carefully opens one end. "That's some gooey toothpaste you have there, Doctor," Mimi says, eyeing the black magic inside the plastic straw. "Is it hash?"

"Yep," says Jake. "And this, my dear, is a hash pipe. Got a light?"

Mimi takes a small and gentle toke, holding it for a split second before releasing. She coughs a little, and her head immediately begins to buzz in a most delightful way. "Well, Jake, this is a fine treat," she says, and moving to her CD collection, chooses Mozart.

"It came from the Bluebird," Jake says, "my favorite of all coffeehouses. I'll bring home a menu next trip; you won't believe it. Plus, they serve the best apple pie and ice cream I've ever tasted." Jake fills his lungs with a generous hit of the sweet-smelling smoke, and hands the pipe back to Mimi, who studies it before carefully drawing once more. "Jake, guess what?"

"What?" Jake takes one more rolling hit before placing the pipe back in its hidey hole, along with the illicit black tar. Mimi giggles. "I'm really high; wait a minute. What did I just say?"

"I'm guessing something." Jake closes his eyes and grooves on his altered brainwaves. "What were we talking about?" The Dance of the Mad Hatter begins in earnest.

"Apple pie and ice cream," answers Mimi. "Oh yeah, I made a treat for us, but you'll have to wait a minute because my brain tickles and it feels so good." She floats to the kitchen, laughing so hard she has to stop at the kitchen's threshold and find her breath.

Jake's brain is dinging with happiness. "Mimi, you're spizak to the mizzu. Dang, woman, you're a cheap date." Jake laughs deeply and his brain hums like a banjo frog.

"Apple pie and ice cream would be good, but we don't have any." Mimi makes her way to the oven, and as she opens it, the aroma of late summer wafts across the room. Jake's prone on the heart pine floor, watching the ceiling fan circling, circling, circling; his stomach does a back flip as the scent of blackberry cobbler sneaks through the doorway. Mimi finds two spoons, secures a carton of French vanilla ice cream from the freezer, and slides to the kitchen floor with a pan of warm cobbler cradled on her lap. "If you want some of this, you'll have to crawl on over here; I'm not moving."

Time stands still and time marches on, but Jake and Mimi are lost in the moment. The cobbler is warm and the ice cream melts, and then the cobbler is gone, all gone, even the crust around the edges is gone.

Molly and Ben share the vanilla puddle and lick the last of the goo from the sticky faces of their giggling, satisfied masters. Jake and Mimi eventually make their way to the bathroom, wash up while kneeling by the tub because it just makes sense, then fall into a down-covered bed and dream in color until the deer bed down and Ben salutes the moon.

. . .

While music is not his passion, Sam, ever the savvy businessman, buys an established family restaurant down a dusty dirt road, a great-grandfathered farmhouse offering one unisex bathroom on the porch, a small but acoustically sound opera room, and two rusted out 1941 Chevy trucks in the front yard. Petunias grow in whitewashed tractor tires, and a granny butt directs traffic to the graveled parking lot near a well-stocked fishing pond. Thursday through Saturday, the Red Clay Ramblers play bluegrass as throngs emerge from a fifty mile radius to eat catfish, barbeque chicken and tender ribs accompanied by plenty of red cabbage slaw, cornbread, biscuits and ice tea thick with sugar, served family style for eight dollars a person, children under five free. The experience isn't complete for the wait staff unless a city customer hears the call of nature, and asks, somewhat hurriedly, the following question: "Ma'am, where's the bathroom?"

"Honey, go down this hallway here, turn right at the side door, and follow the porch to the end. Just hold the handle down for a count of three when you flush; our water pressure's a bit low during the summer. That old hound dog down there? He don't bite. Here," she says, reaching into her apron pouch, "take him a piece a' this here meat. His name's Johnny; that's because he showed up one day thinkin' we needed a guard at the bathroom, and he never left. Just make sure the door closes behind you when you leave because Johnny likes to drink from the bowl."

In the kitchen, working and sweating at Sam's side are two apt cooks: a boyish-looking man with a deformed ear, and a hippie who speaks in two-word sentences. Watching over the three amigos is the one and only Velvet Elvis wearing a smile of understanding, a look of holy redemption, quietly ticking away the hours, then the minutes, until closing. After the band breaks down at ten p.m. on Saturday night, after all sated guests have flat-footed to the car and followed the gnomes to the main road, Johnny leaves his perch by the bathroom and escorts Sam, Warren and the Hippie to the fishing pond, anxiously awaiting his treat of two fried bologna sandwiches thick with greasy mayonnaise. Even Johnny knows that pond fish sometimes strike best when offered slick bait in the silence of a still, moonlit night.

A short hour's drive away in an apple orchard off Jenkins Bottom Road, Jake and Mimi view the same full moon. "I'm missing you already, Jake. Tomorrow comes too soon, doesn't it?"

"Tomorrow is today, Mimi; can you believe it? I'll miss you, dear woman; you are my heart." Mimi settles into the crook of Jake's neck. "What are you going to miss the most?"

"Oh, that's easy," Jake says. "Everything. The way you spread mayonnaise on a tomato sandwich, with wild abandon, all the way to the corners. Or maybe the way you brush your teeth and dance at the same time. No, I'll miss you in the mornings the most, that time before you're completely awake, when you tell me your dreams. You have the most vivid dreams of anyone I know." Jake hugs Mimi closer. "Look up; look at the stars. Now is the time we write a song from a star chart. How does the sky sound to you tonight? Do you see a pattern of notes?" Mimi gazes for a moment, then hums a few bars. "*A Mighty Fortress Is Our God.* That's what it looks like to me."

"That's because you were raised Baptist."

She laughs softly and kisses Jake's forehead before moving gracefully to her knees.

"Sing me a song, Jake. Vocalize the sky for me."

Pure love pours from the fourth dimension into Jake's heart, and he is flush with music, not created by the dust from the stars, but by their essence. The stars are white, then red, then moving, dancing, singing. Mimi's arms are open. She is an open vessel receiving all the star-song she can capture and release.

Bathing in star essence, she listens, listens.

Fireflies signal across the dark meadow, beckoning Mimi home.

EPILOGUE

You're probably wondering what happens next. But Mimi charts her own course, remember? She is the girl who, after our first visit, would fearlessly stare a preacher down for making false statements about the afterlife, and now she's the woman who chooses to run to the edge of an abyss and leap without a safety net. Many of her actions aren't registered in the Original Plan.

It takes big wings, solid experience, and a bit of moxie to be considered for guardian angelship of someone like Mimi. We earn feathers, you earn gold stars. As feathers and stars go, you win some, you lose some. Bald spots come with the territory.

Her grandmother once said, "I wouldn't take a million dollars for her or pay a nickel for another one like her. All heartbreak and headache," she said. Wistful words from a wishful mouth, I say.

So what?

So what if Mimi stands a little too close to the fire? Her life, after all, is a natural phenomenon, like lightning.

ABOUT THE AUTHOR

PL Byrd, master riding instructor, seasoned restaurateur, author of two previous books and countless short stories, alternivore, good food farmer, community health educator and sometimes reluctant saint, arrived on earth in Oceanside California as the daughter of a strapping gypsy Marine and his bony, elegant orphan wife. At the age of three, she had her first out of body experience while witnessing from her Christian grandmother's mill house window a harmonic convergence of dirt road, crystalline purple light, and heavenly spaceship. Before disappearing into the thick, predawn humidity of a southern August morning, the concurrent whirl of the Universal wheel, the perfect-pitch original musical score, and the personal adieu of its Mothership pilot left young Miss Byrd awash in the knowledge that death is nothing to fear, or to seek. Even though her first published work, a poem, appeared when she was just six, Ms. Byrd has managed to remain award-free, but she claims to be in possession of the big prize. The older and somewhat wiser Ms. Byrd stays busy watching the sky.

A Note from the Author

Dear Kind Reader,

Thank you for reading my first novel. The years spent writing this work of fiction were deliciously edifying, meaning I had a few big epiphanies about the ups and downs of trying to create something worthwhile – a book much bigger than my own goofy little life.

More rejection letters than I can count passed through my hands. I kept them in a blood red file for a long time, but all eventually were put to good use: burnt in bonfires, pasted on bathroom walls and used to line the cat litter box.

Characters dropped in to audition and didn't make the cut (at least for this book), the ending changed fourteen times and, although I wanted to kill them all, only one character died, but then who's really ever seen a heart melt?

See, when you grow up watching Disney animation and Buster Keaton shorts, you know anything can happen. Hear, hear, then: a toast to the beauty of wild, unfettered imagination!

If you liked this book, please help me get discovered by other readers like yourself. Write and post a review on Amazon and/or Goodreads. Talk it up to your book club. If you're so inclined, invite me over to hang out with you and your horse. I'm a highly competent barn rat.

Your support is deeply appreciated. Thank you, again and again, for your encouragement.

Love and light, PL Byrd